Back in the Water

Tina Stevens

Back in the Water

Olympia Publishers
London

www.olympiapublishers.com
OLYMPIA PAPERBACK EDITION

A CIP catalogue record for this title is
available from the British Library.

ISBN: 978-1-80074-660-2

First Published in 2023

Olympia Publishers
Tallis House
2 Tallis Street
London
EC4Y 0AB

Printed in Great Britain

Dedication

To my family. Thank you. Also, to my grandparents, Jean and Frederick.
Love, always.

Acknowledgements

Thanks to my family who have supported me through this and have encouraged me.

BACK IN THE WATER

I was working the evening shift with my sister, Lydia. She came up to me and said, "You've got to see this. They've brought the man of your dreams in. He's a sort."

"Don't let Joel hear you say that!" I told her. I pulled the curtain back. Lydia looked at me and smiled. He was at that.

He looked at me. "It's not that bad. Just a graze. I'm Mack."

"I will be the judge of that. I'm Michael," I told him. I patched him up. I felt this strange pull towards him. I think he noticed.

"Thanks," Mack said. Then out of the blue, he continued, "Can I buy you a drink? Next Friday. Seven? The Fox and Hound?"

"Yes, OK. Seven," I replied. He left with what looked like either a mate or a colleague.

Lydia looked at me and smiled. "That's a turn up for the books. Thought you gave up on dating after you know who."

"It's a drink. Besides, I felt something," I said.

"I bet you did." Lydia laughed.

I looked at her. "You dirty bitch. Come on home. Joel would probably be a kip on the couch."

"Don't remind me. Lazy sod. He's not really. He does work hard, for an idiot. Fancy a takeaway? Can't be arsed to cook," Lydia said.

When we got home, Joel was happy to get a Chinese. Lydia told him what happened.

"Really. After you know who? What's his name? I'll check him out," he said.

"Don't be daft. I'll be fine. Besides, it'll do me good to get out there. Listen, what happened, happened."

He was waiting at the bar, with what looked like a single malt. He looked smart. He clocked me straight away. I went to the bar and got a pint. We sat in the beer garden.

We chatted for ages. "What do you do?" I asked him.

"I was in the military. Now, I run my own security firm. I run it with a couple of guys that were with me in Afghanistan. Matthew and Jacob. Matthew was with me last week. Who was that woman with you? You look alike."

"She's my sister, Lydia. Word of warning, don't mess with her," I said.

He smiled, scratching his head. We fell silent for a minute, but it felt comfortable.

"Fancy going for a walk?" Mack said. "It's a bit loud." He took his jacket off and put it over his shoulder. "Tell me about yourself."

I felt comfortable with him. After what I went through, this felt right. We walked for ages.

"You seem nervous," Mack said.

"No, not really. First date in three years." I smiled.

Mack smiled. "Fancy dinner tomorrow night? I'll cook."

I agreed. "I finish at six. So, seven thirty OK? Come to mine. I'll kick Lydia out."

We walked for a bit longer, till we got to my place. "See you tomorrow,"

We saw Lydia looking through the window. "Not very subtle, is Lydia," I pointed out.

"You, young lady, are terrible. I'm old enough," I said, walking through the door.

"I know. But after what happened with him, Michael, I'm worried." Lydia truly was worried. I hugged her.

"This feels different. Don't you think I don't worry about that? I think it about every day. I can't put my life on hold any more. Mack's coming here tomorrow night. He's cooking me dinner. So can you and Joel give us some space?" I asked. She nodded.

"I'll never stop worrying about you. You're my brother."

I couldn't wait for my shift to end. I felt different. When I got home, I could smell something good. Joel looked smug. "He got here early. He's nice."

"Hi. You're early." I smiled.

"Hope you don't mind. I want to make a start. It takes ages. Here, have a beer." He handed me a drink and all I could do was smile.

"I'm going to take a shower and get changed." I took my beer.

"What's for dinner? It smells good," I said, being nosey.

"Beef bourguignon. Lydia not keen on me, is she?" he asked, drinking his scotch.

"It's not that. It's just that I—we went through crap, a few years back, with my ex. She doesn't want round two." I was leaning against the door frame.

"Want to tell me about it?" He flung the tea towel over his shoulder.

"Don't want to put you off, truth be told," I told him honestly.

"Listen, I can handle it. Talk to me. I'm not going anywhere," he told me. So, I told him everything. That my ex had flipped out. He and Lydia didn't get on. They had a blazing row over the fact that he stole eight grand from me. I demanded the money back, got the police involved. He then stabbed me, then Lydia. He's getting out in two years. He got in only for five years. "Not long enough. I'm just worried."

"Worried about what?" Mack asked, stirring the sauce.

"Worried that he might come back, do the same. Muck up…" I stopped myself. He smiled.

"You mean muck up something that is happening here? I can handle myself. Listen, one day at a time. Can't live in the past. Live for now. Whatever happens, I'm here. Here, try this." He made me try the dinner.

"Bloody hell, that's good. Where did you learn to cook like that?" I was amazed.

"Well, had to. Army and been on my own. Plus, I enjoy cooking. Listen, I'm here if you need me. Right, get the plates. Dinner's ready. Get the wine?" Mack smiled.

"You always this pushy and bossy?" I smiled back.

Dinner was brilliant. "My God, that was brilliant! That was the nicest meal. Thank you." I got up and took his plate.

Lydia and Joel came home. "I'd better go," Mack said.

"Stay," Joel said. "You two look like you're comfortable. Lydia, stop with the dagger eyes. What's wrong with you? Jesus. The woman is bat shit crazy. Swear to God," he said to no one in particular. "Listen, Mack. Whatever is starting to happen with you two, it's good to see Michael smile. Lydia, stop. I'm sorry. Should have left her in that mental hospital." He left to get a drink.

"I better go." He grabbed his coat. "Thanks. Every Friday, I want to see you again."

"I like that. Fox and Hound. Seven." I saw him out.

"Lydia Green!" I told her. "Don't be rude. I know you're worried. I'm know what I'm doing. I promise. Trust me."

"Jesus, this is damn good." We looked at Joel, he was eating the leftovers from dinner. We smiled.

"OK, Michael, I'll give him a go."

The next few weeks went by quickly. Mack and I were getting closer. We met for dinner on the Saturday night and went for a walk after.

"You're quiet. What's wrong?"

I told him that I found out that William, my ex, was being released early on 'good behaviour'. I had to laugh.

"Does Lydia know?" he asked.

"Yes, she's not good. Joel's a mess," I told him.

"What about you?" He looked at me. "No lies. Truth."

"Not good. Worried. But at least he can't come near us," I said.

"Whatever happens, I've got your back. Now, let's talk about something cheery," he said, smiling.

We walked and talked for a while. "Listen up, I need to take your mind off things. How about a night at the pictures?"

"You don't take no for answer, do you? Bloody hell." I laughed.

"Nope." He smiled.

We went to the pictures. I felt comfortable around him.

Later, we were at my place, having dinner with Lydia and Joel. There was a knock at the door. It turned out to be William. When he realised who it was at the door, Mack came and stood near me.

"What do you want?" I asked William. "You know you're not allowed here."

"I was hoping to make amends," he said.

Lydia stormed to him and punched him. Mack pulled her away. "Come on, in now."

"Who's he?" William asked me. I looked at Mack.

"None of your business," I told Willian. "Leave, now. Leave. Don't come back." I slammed the door. Mack stood there in front of me. "Don't say a word."

"Not going to. I'll put the kettle on." He left and went to the kitchen.

Lydia was standing there. "Sorry," she said.

"It's OK," he said, putting the teabag in a cup.

"How long have you been in love with him?" she asked Mack.

He was gobsmacked at that. When he didn't answer, she said, "Not wrong, am I?"

"How long have you known?" Mack asked.

"A while now," Lydia said. "It's OK. Does he know?"

He shook his head no. Lydia patted Mack on the shoulder. "It's gonna be OK, you know. You never know, he may like you too. Give it time, love. Give it time."

Mack smiled, not convinced. He looked at her walking towards Joel. He watched them as they hugged each other for dear life, feeling jealous, but happy. He came back to his senses when I came up right behind Mack and scared the life out of him.

"We need to talk," I said. "Mack, I have known how you feel about me for a while now." I paused. "Mack, I feel the same as you," I then said.

"Mike, I don't know what you're talking about," Mack said quietly. He would not look at me and moved away from the table.

"Mack, Look at me. Tell me I'm wrong."

Mack paused, for what seemed like forever. "No, you're not," he replied, grabbing my hand.

I turned to Mack, looked at him and said, "One thing I do know is that I don't want to lose you."

He stood up and took my hand and said, "You're not going to lose me, ever. I won't let that happen."

"For God's sake, about time," Lydia said.

"How long have you been there?" Mack said, looking over my shoulder.

"Long enough to know that you two idiots belong together," she said bluntly. We just smiled.

"Stay," I said. We looked at each other. "For good," I told him.

"Are you sure?" He was surprised.

I kissed him and nodded. "Always." I then turned to my sister. "Yes, Lydia, he's staying. For good."

That was it, Mack went into work, looking smug. Matthew passed him a cuppa. "What's the matter? You're smiling," he asked.

15

Mack told him what happened. "Wow. I knew it! I knew it. Good. It's that bloke from the hospital? What's his name?"

"Michael. Why didn't you say anything?" Mack asked him.

"Simple. It had to come from you. Listen, I'm proud of you. You seem different. Relaxed. You told Jacob?" Matthew asked.

"Listening in. I agree with Matthew. Good for you. I want to meet him," Jacob said. "I always knew."

"Saturday night. That restaurant round the corner. The Oval," Mack said. "He's the one. I know it. As soon as I saw him. That was it, guys. Thanks."

We met at the restaurant and really enjoyed ourselves. "We have a surprise, Mack," Matthew said, grinning.

"Miss me?" the guy said loudly, laughing. He hugged Matthew hard. He looked at each of them and then looked at Mack. "Hello, old friend," he said and hugged him hard. "Who is he?"

There was a pause.

"In all the years I've known you, I never said anything. How did you know?" Mack asked.

"I just knew. Well, where is he?"

Mack pointed to me. "Mike, this is Malek. A top guy. Malek, this is Michael." We shook hands.

"Very glad to meet you, my friend," Malek said.

"Likewise." I liked this guy.

"Mack, how are you? Been a long time," Malek asked.

"I'm surprised. It's been good." Mack took my hand.

Malek looked at me. "My dear friend, he's a good, loyal man. He'll be with you for good."

"You make me sound like a Golden Retriever. Want a drink?" said Mack, smiling.

When we got home, Mack looked at me. "You sure?"

"Yes. Knowing Lydia, she's rearranged stuff and our bedroom," I told him. Mack had a bag with him. "Don't worry, I've got more stuff."

True to word, she had done just that.

"He's been back. I've called the police. Got a restraining order on him." I looked at her. "I'm OK. Are you?" she said.

16

I looked at Mack and smiled. "I am now. I'll put the kettle on."

Mack beat me too it. He looked at me and said, "I'm glad I'm here."

"So am I. Where did you get that holey t-shirt," I asked.

"It's my lucky t-shirt. I was about to throw it. Then we met. So now, I'm not going to. Just like me," he told me.

The phone kept ringing. It was always William. He kept coming round and round to my house. Eventually, he was rearrested and sent back to prison.

"We can breathe now," I said. "Joel, you OK?"

He was silent. "Joel, what's wrong?" Mack asked him.

"Yes, I'm good. Just worried about Lydia. She's not herself," he said.

Mack and I looked at each other. "Take her out for the night. You two haven't had a night out for a long time." I told him.

Mack was on the phone. "Right. You've got a reservation at seven at 'The Oval'. Tomorrow night," he told him.

"Thanks. What are you two going to do?" Joel asked. We smiled at each other. The penny dropped. "Oh man. Dirty bastards. That's why. You know, I'm glad you two found each other. Long time, Michael. Long time."

We spent the rest of the evening talking and spent Saturday night out. We came home and Mack locked himself in the bathroom for ages.

"Mack, Mack. What's wrong?" I asked through the door.

He looked really nervous as he opened the door and looked at me. "I'm scared."

"About?" I asked. Then I realised what he was talking about. "I'm scared too," I told him.

We spent the night together.

"Told you it would be good," I told him.

The following week, the four of us went out for a meal. We didn't hear the noise at the bar. I didn't realise until it was too late. I'd been stabbed and I collapsed on the floor.

I was rushed to the hospital. It wasn't bad, but it wasn't good either. I was in and out for days. I finally came round a week later.

"Where am I?"

"Hey, hey. Calm down," Mack said.

The doctors came in. "Welcome back, Michael. Take it easy. You've been through a lot. Good job your partner's here. Rest. I'll check on you later."

I looked at Mack and touched his face. He kissed my hand.

"You look like shit," I told him.

He smiled. He had tears in his eyes. "I'm phoning Lydia. I love you, always."

"I love you too." I fell back to sleep. Two days later, I was wide awake. Lydia was crying, Joel was in bits. Mack, by the looks of it, hadn't left my side.

"How long have I been here?" I asked.

"Two weeks," the doctor said. "You were stabbed, but you were very lucky. We had to do surgery. Let me take a look. OK, good. There is progress."

The dressing was changed. "What happened?" I asked. Mack looked at me. "Tell me the truth. We promised, no lies."

He told me that William was let out and that he was high on something and drunk. He had found out where we were. He stabbed two people while trying to get to me. One of them died. He then found us and shouted a load of stuff, then stabbed me. Then he shot himself in the restaurant. He died at the scene.

I looked at Lydia. "I'm going to be OK".

Two weeks later, I was home. I couldn't take all in. Mack, Lydia and Joel looked after me. I felt like a burden.

"Let me help," I said to Mack, who was making tea.

"Sit down," he told me.

"I've had enough of sitting down. I want to help." I was annoyed. "I've been out for a week. I want to do something. Jesus, Mack."

"Hey, I know what it's like OK? So don't start, he yelled.

"Really? You weren't stabbed, again, by your mad ex, and nearly died. I was scared that I was going to die. This is my fault," I shouted.

"How the hell is it your fault? Tell me," he yelled. "It's not your fault. You hear me? Not your fault. Jesus! When you were there, all I kept thinking was that I was going to lose the one person that I love. Losing you…" he couldn't finish.

I couldn't argue with that. "Mack, you know I hate being called Mike by anyone expect you. It feels right. I'm sorry," I told him.

"It's OK." He hugged me. "I'm never letting go. I love you."

"What's all the yelling?" Lydia asked.

I told her we had just had our first row.

"Plenty more where that came from," Mack said. "I'm glad you're here, Lydia. Mike, sit down. We need to talk."

I looked worried. He smiled to reassure me. "Don't worry. When you were in there, all I could think of was you and being with you."

Lydia cottoned on and smiled. Mack carried on. He took my hand and asked, "Will you marry me?"

I laughed. "Thank God. Yes. Yes, I will. I was going to ask you," I told him and kissed him. Lydia was crying again.

"What's going on?" Joel asked.

We told him. "Man, that's good. Real good. Finally, a time to celebrate."

"I'll call Matthew and Jacob," Mack said. "Don't move. I'm cooking," he told me.

I was amazed and happy. I began to cry. "I've waited my whole life for him. I thought…" I couldn't finish.

Mack came back in. He sat next to me and took my hand. "When you're better, we'll have that party."

Lydia came in. "I've called Dad, he'll be here in a couple of days." I looked at her.

He always makes a fuss, he'll love Mack, I thought.

"Don't look at me like that," she said.

Mack still looked worried. "I'm OK. I'm going to bed. I'm knackered," I said to him. He followed me in.

"Spill," I said, getting changed.

"I didn't think you would say yes," he told me.

I smiled. "Idiot. It was an easy yes."

Dad turned up two days later. Lydia greeted him. "Dad, he's OK, but sore. Mack's a godsend."

We saw my dad.

"Michael, you gave me a scare!" he exclaimed as he walked in my room. "You must be Mack. Heard a lot about you. Put the kettle on, old boy."

Mack did that and they spoke for ages. "You know, Mack, he phoned me and told me about you. We spoke for three hours. I've never heard him speak about anyone like that. He said you are the one. I can see why. Welcome to the family."

Mack was stunned. He looked at me and I nodded. Dad was confused.

"What?" I asked.

"Did you have a conversation, silently?" We said yes.

We had the party the following weekend. I was ready. Everyone came. It was amazing. We noticed Lydia was quite emotional.

"Spill," we said.

"I don't want to spoil your day," she said.

"Lydia!" Joel said.

There was a pause. "I'm pregnant."

"Don't fuck with me, woman!" Joel said.

"Truth. I'm not kidding." She was smiling. Joel went and hugged her.

"A double celebration!" Mack exclaimed.

We arranged to get married as soon as possible; we couldn't wait.

Two months later, we were married. Ironically, it turned out to be a one-year anniversary of being together.

Soon after, Lydia was starting to show.

"I'm getting fat," she said one day.

"You're pregnant. You're supposed to get big," Joel told her, smiling at her.

"What are you smiling at?" she asked him.

"The fact that you're beautiful and you have made me the one thing I've always wanted to be. A dad. Thank you." He took her hand. She smiled through the tears.

Mack and I smiled as well while watching them. Mack went to the kitchen and put the kettle on.

"You ever thought about it? Having kids?" Mack asked me.

"Yes. I know you have." We both smiled. "Something to talk about."

"My old man was an arsehole. I want to do things different," Mack said, passing me a cuppa. "You think we'll make good dads?" he asked.

"Damn right you will," Lydia said, standing behind us and eating a banana. "If you really want to do it, go for it. Life's too sodding short. Look at how quick you got yourself sorted. It's like you've always been together. Shut up and do it." Lydia threw the peel away.

Mack leaned against the counter. "That told us."

The next few months went by quickly. Then it happened. All of a sudden, we heard a scream. It was Lydia. "My water broke."

Joel panicked.

"What's going on?" Mack asked.

"Lydia is having the baby," I said. He smiled.

Twelve hours later, Joel called to tell us that Mum and baby were doing well. It was a girl. Maggie Ann Green. Eight pound nine. A new addition to the family. We built the cot from a Moses basket and sorted everything else out. The next day, they came home. She was gorgeous.

As Lydia went and rested, we had a drink with Joel. "Can't believe I'm a father. Two women in my life. Looking at Maggie, she's another Lydia. God help me." We smiled. On cue, Maggie started crying. Joel went to her.

He came down later, smiling. "She's beautiful. Noisy, like her mother. I'll have to live with that." We smiled at him.

With that, Lydia was there with little Maggie. "Woman, what are you doing out of bed?"

"I need to get around. Besides, this one hasn't met her godfathers yet. Where's Mack?" she asked.

We sat at the table and Lydia gave me little Maggie. Mack sat next to me, stroking her tiny head. He kissed her gently on the head. We smiled at each other.

"Hey, kiddo," I said. "I'm your uncle Michael, and this is your uncle Mack. We love you, kiddo. Always." Lydia and Joel were crying.

Mack was in his element.

"Look at you. Broody bugger," my dad said. I walked in and saw Mack with Maggie who was having her bottle.

"What are you looking at?" Mack asked me.

"You two, that's the best thing I've ever seen. Let's do it. Let's look into it. I'm serious," I told him.

"You serious?" He was amazed.

I nodded. "Let's get Maggie sorted. Wait till she's a little older. Then yes, let's do it."

Joel took Maggie. He smiled. Mack kissed me and I noticed the tears in his eyes.

"Can't wait," he said.

Two years later, Maggie was getting big. Work and home life was as good as ever.

Then one day, Lydia had a face of awe. "What's wrong?" I asked. She sat down next to Joel.

"Twins! I'm having twins!" She was so happy. I looked at Joel, who was smiling.

"How are you doing?" I asked him. His mouth was moving, but no words came out.

"He's fine. Give him a Jack Daniels," she spoke for him.

"You're joking, right?" he eventually said.

"No. Doctor confirmed it."

"We have news as well. We made a call to an adoption agency. The ball's rolling for us as well," Mack announced.

Later, we were woken up by little Maggie jumping on our bed, saying, "Up, Uncle Mack; up, Uncle Mikey. Big day. Get up, breakfast. Don't go back to sleep." She sounded like Lydia.

We did as we were told. We had had brekkie while Maggie was singing nursery rhymes. As we were leaving, all we could hear was Maggie shouting, "Bye Mummy, Daddy, Uncle Mack and Mikey. Be good. Love you all. I've finished brekkie, I want 'Peppa Pig'."

I turned to Lydia and said, "My God, she is a mini-you. Bossy."

She smiled. "Good. I want to stand on her own two feet. Isn't that right, dear?" she said looking at Joel.

He just smiled and nodded. He mouthed at us, "I'm doomed!"

Mack and I were at home when the phone rang. It was the adoption agency. They told us their agent was coming today. In an hour.

"Seriously? Bloody hell." I was so annoyed. We ran around to tidy up the house.

The doorbell rang. A lady called Carole Middleton from the agency turned up. We were so nervous.

In she walked and introduced herself.

"Hi, Carole. I'm Michael. This is my husband, Mack," I said. "Tea or coffee?" I asked.

"Coffee, milk, no sugar," Carole replied. "Tell me about yourselves."

We told her everything. How we met, everything.

"I like it. It's going to be a long process though," Carole said.

"Not a problem," I said. "All we want is to be a family."

To prove that point, little Maggie came bouncing in. "Hello, lady. Uncle Mack, I'm hungry." She was crawling all over him.

"Maggie, sit still. What's that smell?" he said.

"I blow off," Maggie said. "Can I have pizza?"

Lydia came in. "Sorry. Maggie, come on. They are busy."

"But, I want to be here. Can I, Uncle Mack?" she said.

"Do as your mum says, please. Go on," he told her.

"OK. Bye, lady. Uncle Mikey and Mack, see you later." With that, she bounced off with Lydia.

"That's our family," I said to Carole, smiling.

"She's a character," Carole said. "Nice to meet you both."

We showed her out. "I hope so," Mack replied.

He was very quiet for a while. "What's wrong?" I asked him.

"I'm just worried that it won't happen," he said. "I just want to be a dad to my kids. I just want to be better than my old man."

"It will happen. Be patient. I know that's hard for you. But, just remember, you're not your dad," I told him.

Lydia found us. "Sorry about Maggie. Did it go all right?"

"Seemed to," Mack said. "Look, I've got work to do."

"What's wrong with Mack?" she asked, looking concerned.

"He's worried it won't happen. He just wants the chance to be a better dad than his," I told her.

"It will happen. Maggie loves you two. He's so sensitive," Lydia said.

"That's one reason why I fell for him," I said. I started yawning.

Then I went to find Mack at his workplace, but he wasn't there. He said he was going to be there. I went home. Still no Mack. He had left a note that said, *"I need some space to clear my head."*

For three days, he was gone. I was starting to get mad.

"Where have you been?" I asked once he finally came back.

"I got scared about stuff, had to clear my head."

"Did you? Clear your head?" I asked.

He looked at me. "Yes, yes. I think I have. You still mad?"

"A bit. I could have been there with you," I told him.

"This was something I had to do alone. I think the idea of becoming a dad frightened me in a good way. I just want the best." Mack scratched his head.

"I can live with that. You're going to be brilliant as a dad. I mean, look at Maggie. She dotes on you," I told him.

It was getting late. We heard the door open and Lydia stood there. "You two are unbelievable. What did I tell you the last time this happened?" She was about to say something more when she had to sit down.

"Right, Mrs Green. You, for once in your damn life, are going to do as you're told," Joel said. He knelt down, looking at Lydia. "I am going to look after you, Maggie and my two babies. So, you are going to sit on your English arse and let me do my job. No arguing. Mack, if she so much as farts, without permission, slap her."

Lydia just looked at him. "OK, I'll do it. I love you."

"It worked." Joel was stunned. Maggie came in. "Mummy, are you OK? Are the babies OK?"

"Yes, we are, my darling. Now we have to do as Daddy says, OK?

"OK. You're still the boss, right?" she said. Lydia winked at her. We laughed. "Daddy, can I have a drink, please?"

"What's wrong?" I asked, sitting down.

"Yes, I know. I knew the first time I saw him; he was the one. Can't explain it," I said.

"We love you too," Mack said.

"Come on, Maggie. Let them be." Joel said. She waved goodnight.

"Get some rest, Mike. I'll see you in a while." He went to walk out the door.

"Mack?"

He turned round. "You've got to rest. Doctor's orders." I told Lydia. "Leave the worrying to us."

She kissed the top of my head.

I lay on the bed. Next thing I knew, Mack woke me up getting into bed.

"I know you're worried. But don't kick my shins."

"I won't kick your shins, when you get rid of that bloody holey t-shirt," I told him.

"Sit down. I'll do it. What do you want?" Mack said.

"I can do it, thank you. I'm not an invalid.," I was arguing with Mack. "I want a divorce!" I told him.

"Never gonna happen. Get used to it," he yelled back.

My dad looked at me. "What?" I asked.

"You two are like a couple of old women. You two are worse than me and your mother when we had a row. He's quite something, isn't he?"

"Yes. When we met, I just knew, straight away." I smiled.

"Malek! Oh my God." Dad exclaimed.

Mack and I looked at each other. "Can someone tell me what's going on?" I said, holding my empty plate.

"We met a long time ago, what a coincidence. I'm always that saying your dad said."

"Who is strong of heart, will weather the storm," my dad said.

"You remember? After all these years. Come, let's talk. I have that drink you liked. Saved it for an occasion like this. Come, let's talk." Malek said. My dad followed.

Malek and I sat there, gobsmacked. "What the hell!" Mack said.

"I think my dad's got a date!" I said.

He left and called them.

"Good boy," Mack said sarcastically. "You love me really." He was laughing.

"Right now, that's debatable." I got up. "Besides, you are coming too." That wiped the smile off his face.

"Do I have to wear a suit?" he asked. I nodded. "Shit. I hate suits."

Now it as my turn to smile. "That grey suit, I like it. I'll get cleaned up if I were you."

I walked past the living room, and heard my dad and Malek talking and laughing. I smiled and left them to it.

There was a knock at the door. It was Carole Middleton. "Shit! Sorry, we weren't expecting you. Come in."

Right on cue, Mack walked down the corridor, putting a shirt on, cigar in mouth. "What do you think? Shit, Carole. Hi."

She smiled. "Nice to see you again. Your beard's grown. I like it."

We sat in the kitchen and Mack made us the drinks. "Look, I'll cut to the chase. I put your paperwork through. Congratulations. We have a few formalities. But you're going to be parents."

My dad came in just then. "What's going on?"

"Dad, this is Carole. She from the agency," I said.

"Bloody well done. Good job, son. I'm proud of you. Both of you." He had tears in his eyes.

"Dad, you OK?" I called after him.

"I'll be fine," he said.

"I'll be in touch. Soon. Nice to meet you both again," said Carole before leaving.

Mack was really quiet.

"Are you OK?" I asked him. I went to stand in front of him and he hugged me tight.

"We did it! We're going to be parents."

"I'm happy for you. And you were smoking a cigar?" Malek pointed at Mack.

Later, my dad came in too. "Sorry. It was good to catch up. Have all of you eaten?"

"No," we said.

"Good, I'll start dinner."

"You want my help?" I asked him.

Mack and dad shot me a look. "You and I both know you can't cook!" my dad said, smiling.

"Yes. I tried it once. I was tempted to ask for a divorce. It was horrible," Mack said.

"You wanker. You said you liked it," I said.

"Watch your language, Michael," my dad said while peeling the potatoes. Mack was laughing. Malek came in. "Ah, Simon. I will help with dinner. Michael's not helping?" My dad said no.

"Good," Malek replied. That was it. Mack was in fits of laughter.

I got up. "I hate you all," I said, leaving the room.

"We love you," Dad shouted back.

How embarrassing! I went and saw Lydia.

"How you doing, Lyddie?" I asked.

"Feeling fat!" she said, eating a cake. "Put that down. Dad and Malek are cooking," I told her.

"Git," she said.

Maggie came in. "Uncle Mikey. You OK?

"Yes, I am, sweetie. You been good for Mummy?"

"I think so. Have I?" She looked at Lydia.

"Yes, you have." She smiled.

"Where's Uncle Mack?" Maggie asked.

"In the kitchen with Dad," I told her. She ran off to see him.

"Sit down," Lydia said. I did as I was told.

"You know, I'm glad what Joel and I said about you looking after Maggie if something happens to us. I know she will be safe. So will the twins!" I looked at her. "Joel and I decided that yesterday. We know you two are going to be parents. The paperwork is being drawn up."

"Lydia, don't talk like that!" I was annoyed.

"Give over. I'm gonna live forever. You know that. But if something happens to us, you and Mack are going to be legal guardians of the kids. No arguing. Understand?" she said to me. She put my hand on her stomach. They were kicking like mad

Mack came in. Lydia told him what she told me.

"Lydia." He scratched his head. "You sure?"

"I don't want my kids with anyone else." That was an order.

Maggie ran in from the kitchen. "I'm hungry."

"You're always hungry. You're like your Uncle Mack. Can't stop eating. He's a pig."

"He's not a pig! Silly. But not a pig," I was told.

"Finished," she said. "Can I have pudding please, grandad?"

"I'll get it," I told her. She was running round my feet.

"Uncle Mike. Come on." She was smiling.

"You're a pest." I was smiling too. She stuck her tongue out. Mack came and got her, putting her over his shoulder.

"Kitchen's that way," she said.

Mack said, "Maggie, go and get Uncle Mike."

I came and found them in the living room. We shook hands.

"I had wanted to thank you for what you did for us. Much appreciated."

"You sure you want to do this son?" he asked, sipping his coffee.

"Yes, I do," was all I could say, sitting in the chair.

"I'm proud of you, son. Always have, always will be. What you've got here, most people don't have. I'm a lucky man to have a son like you. If you don't mind," he told me.

"Got no problem with that. Glad you're home." I was happy.

"You OK, son?" Dad asked me. "Let me look at you."

"Dad, I'm fine. Stop fussing." I was getting annoyed.

"Oh shit!" Lydia cried.

"What's the matter?" Matthew shouted upstairs.

"My water's broke," said Lydia. Joel was panicking.

Lydia came down. Joel was scared. "It's going to be fine," I said. Matthew drove them to the hospital.

Maggie came down, half-asleep. "Where's Mummy and Daddy?"

"Gone to hospital. She's having the babies," I told her. "She's going to be fine."

"Hope so. I want a brother and a sister." She rested her head on my shoulder. "Are we a family?"

"Yes. Why?" I was confused.

"Just asking. I love my family," she said, yawning.

I smiled. "Come on, miss. Back to bed." I put her back. She was asleep as soon as her head hit the pillow.

Mack stood next to me. "Can't wait for this. Kids."

As we left the room, I said, "Sorry about earlier. I had to get it off my chest."

"It's OK, you know. It's been tough, hasn't it?" he told me.

"Just a bit. Don't ever think it will change us, it won't," I replied.

Dad was snoring in the living room. Malek was on the couch, mumbling in his sleep. I laughed.

At around three in the morning, Joel phoned. "It's twins!"

"OK, good. What you got?" Mack was smiling, shaking his head.

"Boy and a girl. Doing well. Alice and Alfie," Joel replied.

"Who was that?" Dad asked.

"Joel. Boy and a girl. Alice and Alfie. Go back to sleep," I told him.

Finally, we went back to bed, around four. I actually felt OK, for the first time in a long time. Mack as usual was snoring.

"Turn on your side," I told him, yawning, which he did.

I got woken up by the smell of bacon and laughter. Mack wasn't in bed. My dad came in with a coffee. "Thanks. What's the time?"

"Eight. How you feeling?" Dad asked.

"OK. Not bad. Smells good. I'm hungry," I said.

"You better get in quick, before Mack and Maggie eat everything. I've never known a kid eat so much," Dad said.

"What about Maggie?" I smiled.

There was a plate waiting for me, at the table.

"Morning, everyone," I said.

"Uncle Mike?" Maggie asked, dancing away.

"Yes?" I asked, eating bacon at the table.

"When's Mummy and Daddy coming home with Alice and Alfie?" she asked.

"Today or tomorrow. You're a big sister now," I told her.

"I know. When are you and Uncle Mack gonna have babies?" she asked, still dancing.

I was gobsmacked. "Soon," was all I could say.

She was smart as a whip. There was a knock at the door.

That evening, Lydia, Joel and the babies came home. It was lovely. Maggie was all over them. She loved them. Once the kids were in bed, we all talked about what had happened. We all agreed that we needed to get away. Soon. We had to let Lydia rest for a few days.

I sat at the kitchen table. I couldn't sleep, my brain was going nine to the dozen. Mack came down, rubbing his eyes.

"I'll stick the kettle on," he said, patting my shoulder.

"You all right?" he asked.

"Couldn't sleep. At least I won't kick your shins. Why you up?" I asked.

"You know I can't sleep if you're not there. Why you up? What else is bothering you?" He was so direct.

"Nothing, I'm just wired. Too much has gone on. I wish I could fall asleep anywhere like you." I smiled at him. "I realised that what I've got here is good enough," I said.

"You're confusing me," he said, yawning.

"Come on. I'm not making any sense." Even I started yawning. "Can we please get rid of that t-shirt?"

"No, we can't. It's never leaving. Like me. Can we please get some sleep?" he said, crawling into bed.

As I lay there, I looked at him, snoring his head off. I smiled.

Lydia woke us up. "You two, get up. That woman is here. You two, up. Now!"

We went downstairs. "What is the matter?" Mack was half-asleep. "The kids OK?"

"We're fine, Uncle Mack," Maggie said, eating grapes and watching Peppa Pig. He looked at the TV. I was right behind him.

"Good morning." It was Carole. She was smiling.

"Morning," we said in unison, not sure what was going on. My Dad was smiling.

"What can we do for you?" I asked.

"Good news. We have a child ready for adoption. A little girl. She is six weeks old and she's yours."

"Seriously!" Mack said. He looked at me. "Really!" He started crying and hugged the life out of me. "We're parents."

"When can we have her?" I asked.

"A bit of paperwork for now. In a few days," Carole said.

Mack and I sat on the sofa in silence. Stunned. Lydia was crying, Joel was stunned too. My dad was smiling.

For once, Mack was lost for words. "We need a bigger house!" he said.

"No shit, Sherlock." Maggie said, still eating grapes and watching 'Peppa Pig'.

"Maggie Anne Green! You're three," Lydia said. "Don't use that language again."

"I won't," she said. Mack smiled and gave her a high five.

I gave Mack his coffee. "What are we going to call her?" I asked.

"Seriously. Can I let it sink in first?" he said.

The twins started crying. "This is a mad house," Joel said.

I started laughing hard. I couldn't stop. Maggie looked at me. "You're weird, Uncle Mike."

Mack looked at me, laughing away to myself. "Let's leave Uncle Mike to go insane," he said to Maggie.

We went shopping for everything you would need. We got some funny looks when we were looking for cots while holding hands.

"Can I help you?" the lady in the shop said.

"We're looking for a cot," I said.

"As a present?" she asked.

"No, for us," Mack said. "Our daughter is coming in a few days. I like these sheets."

She was confused and intrigued. She looked at us and smiled. "You two make an interesting couple."

"That's what everyone says," I told her. I was dressed smart casual. Mack was slightly the opposite.

"Olivia," Mack said. "That's what we'll call her. Olivia. Is that OK?"

"Yes, it is. Olivia Anna Denton. It's got a nice ring to it," I told him, smiling. Mack smiled as well.

Olivia turned up a few days later. She was sleeping. She was everything. Mack doted on her. I couldn't get a look in.

"Come on," I told him. "Let's go for a walk. We need the fresh air. Dad, you coming?" I asked him.

"Thought you would never ask." Dad got Olivia ready.

It was nice with all of us out.

"I just realised something," I said.

"What's that?" he asked.

"I think this is what it's all about. Being happy," I told him.

My dad was getting a lot of attention from ladies at the park with Olivia. "Where are the parents?" one of them asked.

"Over there." My dad pointed to us. The lady looked horrified and walked away.

"Can't please everyone," my dad said. Then he saw someone looking suspicious. He nodded to Mack. "Two o' clock." Dad said, looking round. "Am I wrong?"

"What was that?" I asked Mack and my dad.

I didn't say anything, only looked at Olivia. "I thought this shit was behind us. We've got a family now, Mack. I've had enough of this shit. Come on, I want to go." I took Olivia and went to the car. Mack and Dad followed behind me.

I sat in the back with Olivia. Mack looked at me through the rear-view mirror. "You OK? I know you're scared."

"I will be," was all I said. When we got home, my dad put Olivia down for a nap. Mack got ready to go out. I watched him getting ready. He was at home in what he did. I walked over to him and stood in front of him. I felt like I wanted to say something.

"Maybe you should set up your own business," I said.

"Not a bad idea. Something to think about," he replied.

"Good. I'll get dinner ready," I said.

"No, you bloody are not. Your cooking is shit. You know that," Mack half shouted.

"What's going on out there?" Lydia said.

"Mike wants to cook!" Mack told her.

"Over my dead body you're doing that. Malek and Dad are doing it."

31

Lydia went to the twins.

I heard Olivia crying, I went and got her. "Hello, sweetheart. How are you?"

She smiled at me. "Come on, let's change you." As soon as we went down, she was gurgling away. She went all silly when she saw my dad.

He put the tea towel down. "How's my darling granddaughter? You are so cute. Yes, you are."

"I'll leave you to it then," I told my dad, laughing. I sat in the chair. This house was starting to get a bit small for us now. I mean, there were six adults and four kids.

"Right, here you go," my dad said handing me Olivia. "Dinner won't cook itself."

"Simon, water's boiling. Put peas on," shouted Malek.

"You want to tell me something!" I asked him, smiling.

"What you talking about?" he asked.

"Simon!" Malek shouted.

"You two…" I trailed off. feeding Olivia.

Maggie walked in. "Olivia is cute. Not as cute as Alfie and Alice. But she's lovely." She gave her a kiss on the head. "I'll look after her. I'll be her big sister, I'll protect her. Love you, Livvy locks."

Lydia started crying, which set Mack off. I didn't know who was more hormonal, Lydia or Mack.

"Bed time for you, Olivia. Daddy's gone a bit hormonal and girly," I told her.

The next few weeks went by quickly. We got a bigger house, and Mack got an office space for his work with Matthew and the guys. It was taking off. He even got a PA. I was feeling a bit lost in the chaos.

"Dad, you mind looking after Olivia for a bit? I want to go for a walk."

"You OK, son?" He was worried.

"Just need some air. You seen Mack?" I asked.

"No. You miss him, while he's been busy," he said.

It was a nice afternoon. I was just having a stroll, thinking. I felt out of sorts. I picked up a paper and before I knew it, I had been gone nearly two hours.

"Dad, I'm back! Dad."

It was quiet. Something smelt good. Really good. "Hello!"

I walked in the living room; the table was all set up nice. Mack came in. "Hey. "

"Hi. Where's Dad and Olivia.?" I asked.

We had dinner and talked.

"Listen, I've got a meeting with a client on Saturday night. You're coming with me."

"Do I have a choice?" I asked, knowing what the answer would be.

"No. I'm not looking forward to wearing a black suit," he said.

"Why do you hate suits for?" I asked, wondering why.

"Makes me uncomfortable.," he replied, yawning.

"Just like when you wear that bloody t-shirt at night," I said. He just looked at me. I smiled at him. "I love you."

"Love me. Love the t-shirt," he said.

"I just realised how quiet it is in here," I said.

"Good as gold. You ready for bed?" he said. Mack and I looked at each other and smiled.

"Well, that's something to talk about," I said.

Saturday night came round quick enough. Please replace with Mack asked me to go with him to the meeting with him, to the Local restaurant. It was something that was in a magazine. Not for the likes of us.

"Hey, you OK?" Mack asked.

"I feel out of place," I said. "What's the person's name you're meeting?" I asked.

"Miranda Wentworth. She should be here in a minute," Mack said.

We were chatting at the table, when a woman came to the table. "Which one of you is Mackenzie?" she asked.

Mack got up and shook her hand. "This is Michael, my husband."

"Well, I'm going to be honest. You two are not what I expected. I would not put you two together," Miranda said.

"We get that a lot," I said.

"Do you have children?" she asked, sipping her cocktail.

"We have a daughter. She'll be one next month," Mack said.

"Are you planning on having any more?" she asked.

We looked at each other and smiled. "Yes. We are."

He told her everything. I mean he didn't hold back. I sat and listened. I was stunned by his honesty, but honoured. I was proud of him.

"I like your honesty. I have an event coming up. High profile. Lots of important individuals will be attending. I need security. If it works out, more work. Can you handle it?" Miranda had the nerves of steel.

"Yes, we can," Mack said.

"Good. We have a deal. I'll send over the details, as soon I've finalised my end." She stood up and left.

"I need to change my underwear," I said to Mack. "Did you mean what you said, about me and Livvy?"

"Yes. And yes, I do want more kids with you." We got up and he took my hand. "Come on, let's go home. I'm knackered."

When we got home, we heard Olivia crying. Mack took her off my dad. She stopped. "Hey, *shh*, it's OK. Daddy's here. She been OK?"

"Yes. Just wanted her dads," Dad said, smiling. "I'll put her down. Then we'll tell him," Mack said. "Don't say a word till I come down."

Dad was confused. I just smiled. He came down and we told him that we were planning to adopt again. He was pleased as anything. "Wow. You two don't hang about."

"That's what we want," I told him.

"Good," Dad said. "How was the meeting?"

"Interesting. Sharp as a whip," Mack said. "We got the job. So good news. Coffee?"

We both nodded. My dad said, "When is he gonna get rid of that holey t-shirt?

"Don't. Been there, done that. He said it's his good-luck charm. He was going to throw it away, then we met. Can't sleep if he hasn't got that, or if I'm not there."

"OK. Fair enough," he said. "See you in the morning."

"Night, Dad. Thanks for looking after Olivia," I said.

"My pleasure, son. Night." Off he went.

Mack sat down, yawning. "What time is it?"

"Not even ten," I said. I rubbed my nose.

Mack looked at me. "What's the problem?" he asked.

"Just worried about the job you've got on. That woman, Miranda. I know you can handle yourself."

"I didn't know that you still worry about that!" he said.

"Every day of the week, and twice on Sundays," I smiled sadly. "I don't want you getting hurt."

"Tough as old boots, me. I'm a tough guy," he said, lightening the mood.

"You! Tough. You watched 'Frozen' with Maggie and cried when Eliza sang 'Let it Go'. I swear sometimes you're in a big girl's blouse," I told him. He didn't have an answer for that.

He smiled. "Good film. I want to watch the second one." He laughed.

"You sad bastard. Who have I married?" I laughed.

Olivia said, "Dadda, food."

I looked at him and laughed. "Come on. Let's go and eat. She takes after you. Always hungry."

"I love you, but you sound like a nagging wife right now," he said, smiling at me. I couldn't help but smile.

We walked in, and we were greeted by Lydia, Joel and the kids.

"Uncle Mack and Mike!" Maggie yelled. "Did you miss me? Alice threw up in the car. It smelt like her poo. Alfie was asleep as usual. Boys. Can I watch 'Frozen'? Don't let Uncle Mack watch it. He cries when Eliza sings 'Let it Go'."

We burst out laughing. It was good to have them home. Dad came in. "Michael, Carole is on the phone."

I spoke to her. "Hang on, I'll get him. Mack, Mack, come here."

"What's the matter?" he sounded scared.

"She wants to know if we want to adopt again. They have a boy. Six weeks old."

"Tell her, yes!" he half-yelled.

"OK." I told her. "When? Monday. OK." I was gobsmacked.

"What's going on?" Lydia asked.

"As of Monday, there will be a new addition to the family. A little boy. Six weeks old," I said.

"Good. Why?" Mack and I got the news that our son was coming home. Lydia asked us if we had thought of any names.

"I like Oliver. Don't know why," I replied.

"Oliver it is, then," Mack said passing me and Lydia a glass.

"You sure?" I was surprised. "Yes. I chose Olivia's name," Mack said, going back to the computer. He was scratching his head when something was bothering him.

"Something's bothering him," Lydia said.

Mack made a call. I knew he was pissed off now. He was scratching the top of his right eyebrow.

"What's wrong?" I asked him.

"Nothing," he was not happy. He got up and got a cigar and went in the garden. He didn't like talking when he was pissed off, so I left him.

I left him to it. I checked on Olivia. She was sleeping like an angel. Mack stood at the door. "How's our girl doing?"

"Sleeping like an angel. What's wrong?" I asked, walking away, so as not to wake Olivia. "It's that woman, isn't it? Don't lie to me. I know when you are lying."

"Yes, it has something to do with her. It got me thinking about what you said. Matthew is checking out the place with Jacob. My gut feeling is normally good. Check out who I'm working for," Just as we were going down, Olivia started crying. "I'll go," Mack said. I watched him with Olivia, it was sweet.

Adam came in, not bothering to be quiet. "Well, you're not gonna believe what I found out. Where do you keep the scotch?"

"Will you be quiet, Adam? Four kids are sleeping upstairs. You wake them up, I'll cut your Scottish bullocks off. Now are you going to turn it down a notch?" Lydia said with a knife in her hand.

Adam looked at me, Joel and Mack.

Joel said, "For the love of God, agree. She'll do it. She'll make it look like an accident."

"Sorry, Lydia. I'll be quiet." Adam was stunned.

Mack started laughing. "She told you off. I told you what she's like."

"What am I like, exactly?" Lydia stood behind him. That shut him up.

"Love you, Lydia," he said, trying to worm his way out of it. She clipped Mack round the back of the head. "Arsehole. Just for that, you're helping me with our dinner."

"So, what do you want to tell us?" Mack said, leaning on the door with a tea towel on his shoulder. "Mack, peel the carrots," Lydia said.

"Turns out, that Miranda is the CEO of the Tech and occasionally surveillance firm, Globe Tech. She and the company both are worth billions. She is hosting an event for more wealthy clients, who, in my opinion, are borderline paranoid. She knows how to play them. She's very smart. Three degrees. One at Oxford, Cambridge and Harvard. Top of the class. Why she wants us there, not sure. Maybe she's paranoid herself."

36

"Why? Because she's a smart-arse woman who is the boss of a firm that generates billions every year. She wants security to protect what may or may not happen. For a bunch of smart-arse blokes, you are such dumb arses," Lydia said.

None of us blokes could say anything. "Just do it. Every time something like this happens, you get scared. Mack, do you want Olivia and Oliver to grow up believing their dads had guys to stand up for what they believed in, or run away when things get scary?" Lydia spoke the truth pointing to Mack and me.

"She got stick the other day, at her induction at school, because her two uncles are gay and have a daughter. She punched the kid who said it in the nuts, saying they were idiots. And to leave her cousin alone. She told the teacher there was nothing wrong with it."

Mack and I smiled at each other. "Now, Mackenzie Foley, you're doing this. Or I swear to God, I'll poison you and I'll make it look like an accident.

"She frightens me," Adam said. Lydia just looked at him. "Michael, Adam, get plates and knives and forks."

We did as we were told. Maggie came down, "Dad, I need a poo."

"Why don't you go then?" he said. We laughed. "I thought you'd like to know. Hi, Adam. You're noisy, she said and went to the loo.

"She's a character, certainly holds her own, that one. How old was the boy she punched?"

"Eleven," Lydia said. "She's four."

Adam smiled. "She should work for you, Mack!" he said, laughing.

After dinner, there was a knock at the door. It was Carole, with Oliver.

"I know it's not Monday, can you have him now?" she asked.

"Yes," Mack said, smiling. "Come here, son."

"I know. I just thought why wait." She smiled.

"Come in, Carole," I told her.

"Here's his things and a few bits. What a lovely home."

My dad walked in. "Hi, Carole."

"Hi, Simon. Nice to see you." She smiled.

"Would you like a coffee?" he asked.

What was happening?

"Sorry, I'm in a bit of a rush. Maybe another time," she replied, walking to the door.

"I like that. Maybe Saturday afternoon. Costa." Dad seemed confident.

Mack was with me. He couldn't stop smiling. He looked at Olivier. "I think your grandad has pulled."

She left and Dad turned, smiling. "Don't look at me like that. I like her."

"We know you like her." I told him. "Be back by dinner, young man." I laughed. "Go and say hello to your grandson. Oliver."

Mack was laughing. "You dirty old git. Pulling."

Next morning, I was up with the lark. I came down to find a sight. Mack had Olivia in the high chair, Oliver in his arms, with a bottle. This was strange. I was used to seeing him with a protective vest and a gun. Tattoos. Not with two kids. Lydia was there too.

"If you two weren't married and gay, I'd have him."

"Tough shit. Can't have him." I was smiling. "Morning, Mack."

He looked up and gave us a kiss.

"You're up early," I said.

"Thought I'd give you a lie-in," he said. He gave Olivia more toast. "She's a little piggy. Always eating!"

"Just like her dad," I said, getting a cup of coffee. There as a knock at the door. "I'll get it."

It was Matthew. "He's in the kitchen. Just beware what you're about to see. Just look," I told him.

Matthew stood at the door to the kitchen, gobsmacked.

Mack looked up, Ollie in one arm, Olivia in highchair. "What?" Mack said, eating toast.

"Who the hell are you? What have you done with Mackenzie Foley?" Matthew said. "I never thought I would see this day. I can't believe it."

"A man can change, can't he? Good God, Oliver, what have you done in that nappy? Jesus, that stinks. Give me a minute, I'll change him and I'll be with you. Make yourself a drink. Come on, son," he left, leaving Matthew stunned.

"What have you done to him? I never thought he would get this domesticated. Wonders will never cease."

I laughed at him. I picked Olivia up. She was smiling away, then said, "Dada," putting her chubby hand on my nose. She then saw Mack and said,. "Dada."

Mack came over with Oliver and gave her a kiss on her head.

Matthew couldn't believe it, but smiled. "Sorry to break this up, but we need to talk."

"Give Ollie here, I'll take them for a walk. Dad, you coming for a walk?" I shouted.

"Thought you'd never ask," he said.

Matthew gave Mack a folder. "What's this?" Mack asked, sipping his coffee.

"I did some digging on Miranda. She's not as well off as she makes out. The company is not doing as well as she lets on. This thing next Saturday is to get the rich in. I mean really rich. I think we are the hired guns. I'm not happy about it. I know that companies have tough times, I get that, but this seems different. She's moving money around just to keep afloat. I'll be surprised if we get paid for this," Matthew told him.

Mack checked the computer for the bank transfer.

"Well, we have been paid, all of us, and a bit extra, by the looks of it." Mack showed him the computer with everyone's names, details. "That surprised him.

"I've got Jack looking at the place now to see what's what. Adam's looking in some of business dealings."

"You got it all figured out. Soon, you won't need me," said Mack.

"Hey, we will always need you, domesticated or not." Matthew paused.

"Spill. You got something to say, say it," Mack said, eating more toast.

Matthew smiled. "Ever since Olivia and Oliver have been here, you've chilled out a lot more. Kids suit you. Yes, you're still a stubborn prick, who's loyal to a fault. Don't change that. As I said, I never thought I would see it. But it's good. Something tells me, you are going to be the world's most protective father ever. Especially with Olivia."

Mack smiled at that. "I still have to pinch myself every day at how lucky I am to have what I have."

He didn't hear me and Dad walk in the door.

"I'll tell you one thing while Mike's not here. Without him, I'm nothing. He's the best thing that's happened to me. Same as the kids. They've made me a better man. I'm lucky." Just then, Ollie started crying.

I came into the living room with Ollie.

"How much did you hear?" Mack went red in the face.

"All of it. I'm lost without you too. You know that." Ollie settled.

"You two are lucky. Not a lot of people have what you have." Matthew nodded. "I'll see you in the week, as we need to go to the place and check out the plan."

"OK. See you kids," Matthew said. Olivia smiled at him. Oliver was crying for a feed.

"That's my cue to go," he said and left. I went and got a bottle for Oliver. "OK, young man. Give us a sec. You're like your dad and Olivia. Always hungry. It's not even dinner time."

I went in the living room. "You want me to take him?" Mack said, putting the computer down.

"Nah, I'm fine. What did Matthew want?" I said, feeding Oliver.

He told me what had happened. "Told you something about her wasn't right."

Mack looked at me scratching his head. "You are a smart arse."

Olivia crawled up to Mack, he picked her up.

Jacob walked in and saw us sitting there with the kids. He had the same expression as Matthew. "Where is Mackenzie? I've walked into the Twilight Zone."

"Shut up, and go and make yourself a drink," Mack said. "What do you want?"

He came in with a cuppa and sat in the chair. "Make yourself at home, why don't you?" Mack told him in a sarcastic tone.

"Don't worry, I will. We need to talk about Jack," Jacob said.

"Why not go to Matthew? He's his brother-in-law," said Mack as he was putting Olivia in the day cot.

Jacob couldn't help but shake his head. It was like having Matthew here. "He's fine. Just needed his arse changing. He'll want a feed soon. I'll keep an eye out."

"You are a pain in the arse, you know that," Mack told him. "You're not don't Saturday night, or any other night. You need to be with your family. I'm gonna make sure you're looked after."

Saturday finally arrived. Everyone arrived at ours around four. It was like when we first got together, before we moved here. I went and got Mack who just got out of the shower.

"They're all here," I told him.

He smiled back.

"What's the matter?"

"I struggled my whole life. When I met you, that stopped. I know you're worried, Mike. I am too. Do I have to wear this bleeding tie?"

I smiled. "Give it here. I'm sorry. Didn't mean it."

"Look at me," he told me and smiled. "Not my fault you fell for the sexiest bloke going."

He put his jacket on and looked back at me. "I've been thinking for a while now. I'm taking your surname. Mackenzie Denton. Got a nice ring to it."

"You soppy sod. You're not as tough as you look," I told him.

"When it comes to you and our kids, I'll always be the tough guy. How do I look?" he said.

"Hot. But then I am on medication. So, you can tell," I said.

They left and got themselves sorted out. Mack felt good to be back. It kicked off as expected. Rich arseholes. Paranoid arseholes, willing to part with loads of money. Our of the corner of Jacob's eye, he caught someone he recognised. He spoke into his hand.

"No. Watch him for now. Jacob, eyes on him. Don't make—"

"Don't make it obvious. Eyes on him. Keep your distance without being noticed," Jacob said.

"Smart arse," Mack said.

"Learned from the best," Jacob told him.

Matthew and the rest laughed at that. They waited for everyone to leave. Jacob came back to ours, and everyone else went home.

I was asleep on the couch, waiting for Mack, like an old woman. Mack heard Olivia crying.

"I'll stick the kettle on," Jacob said.

Mack went and got her. "Hey, beautiful. Ugh. Your bum stinks." He changed her and brought her down for a feed. She was nearly a year.

"Say hi to Jacob," Mack said.

"Hi," she said, waving.

"I still can't get over how domesticated you are."

I could hear them talking. I checked on Oliver; he was fast asleep. Mack wasn't far behind me.

"You didn't have to wait for me, you know," he told me.

"I know. Can't help it," I said, cleaning my teeth.

The next morning, Olivia woke us up, standing in her crib. Then Oliver.

"Shit, what time is it?" Mack said.

"Half six," I said. "What's that smell, you farted?" I said to Mack.

"Sod off. That's Oliver. Come on, son, let's change your arse."

I got Olivia and went downstairs. Maggie followed. "Hey, kiddo. What's up?"

"Mum and Dad were fighting last night. Mum was crying." She looked sad.

"Don't worry. Parents always argue. It'll be fine," I told her.

"Do you and Uncle Mack argue?" she asked.

"Yes, we have done. Probably have a few more. But I love him very much. Always will. Just like your mum and dad they love each other. OK?"

She nodded.

"What do you want for brekkie?" I said, putting Olivia in her high chair.

"Scrambled egg and toast please," she said, cheering up.

Mack came in with Oliver. "Morning, kiddo."

"Morning, Uncle Mack. Hello, Ollie," she said. "Can we go out for the day? I need variety."

Mack and I looked at each other. "Won't hurt to get out for the day. We'll ask your mum when she gets up," Mack said, drinking his coffee and eating his toast.

Ten minutes later, Lydia got up with the twins.

"Morning, everyone," she said.

"Morning," we all said in unison.

"Mum, can Uncle Mack and Mikey take me out for the day? I need variety," Maggie asked as she was eating her scrambled eggs. "Please!"

"OK. That OK with you two?" she asked.

"That's cool," Mack said. "Lydia, you OK?"

"Just tired," she said.

Lydia went back to bed. "Maggie, come on, love, get your shoes on," Mack said.

"OK, Uncle Mack," she shouted. "Ready. Where we going?"

"The zoo," I said. Maggie jumped up and was happy.

"Maggie, you want an ice cream?" I asked.

"Yes, please."

We were speechless. A four-year-old, saying something like a grown up and lovely as that.

"You're a good girl, sweetheart," I said.

"I know. Oh, look, a rockhopper penguin."

On the way home, all three were fast asleep. I think they had a good day. I know we did. Joel came out smiling. He saw Maggie asleep. "What the hell. What did you do? You know how long it takes to get her to sleep? Thank You. How was it?" he asked, getting Maggie out of the car seat.

We put the kids to bed. They looked so peaceful and content. I was knackered, so I took a shower. I could hear whispering from the bedroom after I came out. "Will you be quiet? He'll bloody hear us. It looks lovely, Mack."

As I came downstairs, I asked, "What's going on? What is it so quiet?"

Lydia pointed towards the living room. I was confused.

"Happy Birthday!" Mack said. He looked sheepish.

There was a picture of us on the coffee table. "Where did you get this? I thought I lost it."

"I found it after we moved in here." He gave me a brochure.

"What's this?" I asked.

He scratched his head. "Ten days in Rome. Next month. Your dad is going to have the kids. Lydia and Joel are going to help," Mack said.

"You may act like a tough guy, but you are soppy as shit. Thank you, I can't wait." I leaned back on the sofa and took his hand. "We're lucky, you know. Not a lot of people have what we have."

"I know. I'm a lucky man. Come a long way," he started then smiled. "You're getting old. I married an old man."

"Shut your face you. I always wanted a toyboy."

He winked at me. Just then, Ollie started crying.

"I'll go," I said, getting up. "Make us a coffee, please?" I asked. Ollie was fine.

Mack was asleep on the couch when I came down. I put a blanket on him and went to bed.

Just as I was dozing off, Mack came to bed. "Why didn't you wake me up?"

"You looked comfortable," I told him. "What's wrong?" I sat up.

"Nothing," he told me.

"Bullocks. Don't hide the truth." I was getting annoyed.

He sat up and looked at me. I looked at him. "Just a long day, that's all. You're like a nagging wife. We're the gay version of Lydia and Joel." He laughed.

Mack was up with the larks. Wonders will never be.

"What time is it?" I asked, half-asleep.

"Six thirty. Joel and I are going out to do work. Simon's up with the kids. So, you have time on your hands." He smiled, putting his jacket on.

I looked at him. Highly organised. I just smiled. "What you smiling at?" he asked.

"Just remembering what we did. You were so cocksure of yourself."

"Still am. Something smells good," Mack said.

Dad was in the kitchen as we came downstairs.

"Don't be mad at him. It was my idea. I just want to do things without you getting worried, or hurt. He's worried about basically everything. You, the kids. You're lucky, really lucky. Get over it. He's miserable. He may be a tough guy, but he is so in love with you." He patted my shoulder.

That got me thinking, But Mack broke my train of thought. "You still pissed at me?" \

"Just a bit," I said.

He smirked. "Stubborn bastard. You know." He stopped and sat next to me. "Don't be mad. I hate it when you're mad. You just have to be patient. Something you're not," he said.

"And you are?" I told him. I got up and walked to the kettle.

He stood there, leaning against the counter, hands in his pockets. "I'm sorry."

I just smiled. "You're an arse."

"So, what do we do now?"

Dad told Mack and I to go about as normal.

We had Olivia's first birthday on Sunday. Maggie was excited. "Cake, and lots of it. I've made Olivia a present. I'm not telling what it is. It a surprise. When Ollie is one, I'll make him one. Mummy?"

"Yes, Angel girl?" Lydia said, peeling potatoes. Maggie hugged Lydia. "What was that for, sweetheart?" she asked her with tears in her eyes.

"Because I have the best mummy, and daddy. I have the best family ever. I love you, silly Mummy. Can I watch 'Frozen'?"

"You are a beautiful girl." Lydia was crying.

Joel heard every word. "See, you crazy woman? You are an amazing mother. This is what we wanted to raise our kids to be; amazing human beings. That little girl is proof of that. I love you more than life itself." He hugged her.

Then there was crying from the living room. Maggie went to Joel. "Dad, for God's sake, get Uncle Mack away from 'Frozen'. He's only crying at bloody 'Let it go'. I wish he would let it go. Uncle Mack, you're a baby. What's wrong with you? You getting broody again?" she really told him.

"Lydia!" Joel said. "She's a mini you. I feel sorry for the guy that would marry her. He won't stand a chance. But he will be the luckiest SOB ever."

"What the bloody hell is going on in here?" my dad asked.

Maggie looked at him. "Grandad, don't go there."

I walked into a mad house. "Uncle Mike. Uncle Mack was crying at 'Frozen'. I think he's getting broody. You sure he's not a girl? He's acting like one."

Olivia was walking about. She saw me. "Daddy." Ollie was in his high chair.

"How was your day?" Dad asked.

"OK," I said. "Where's Lydia?"

"Kitchen," Dad told me.

"Lydia. This may interest you. There was a notice at the retraining centre. They are looking for nurses. Here's the number if you're interested." I gave her the number. "Ring the number, Lydia. I'm not asking." I told her, picking up Olivier. "You mucky boy. Look at you. Bath time."

Dad stood at the door. "You ready for tomorrow?"

"Yes. Just nervous." I told him, putting Oliver and Olivia into bed.

We went to Rome. We had the best time. It was the first time we were alone together. It was a well-deserved break. We were together, but we hardly had the time to be really together.

When we were there, Mack asked me, "Do you want more kids?"

"I wouldn't mind. How big do you want our family to get?" I was smiling.

"I wouldn't mind another two." He was sipping his coffee. He sat back in his chair, put his sun glasses on his head and scratched his beard. It had grown in. It looked good.

"You're very quiet. What's wrong with you?" I asked him. I felt a bit nervous.

"Honestly, nothing. I just realised how happy and complete I am. These last five years have been the best. I'm so lucky," he told me.

"You really are the toughest, sweetest man I have ever met. There is one thing I want you to do. Stop watching bloody 'Frozen'. Crying at 'Let It Go' is not a good sign. For anyone." He laughed his head off.

We flew home. We had had the best time.

"Daddy!" Olivia smiled and shouted. She ran and hugged us. Oliver kicked his legs and came to us via Joel.

"Welcome home. You two look happy. Really happy. Oh, give Carole a ring. FYI, Michael, I think your dad and Carol like each other. So Lydia says."

Mack called Carole. He had a smile that was bigger than the sun.

"What is it?" I asked.

"Carole said there are two babies that need a home after their parents gave them up. One has Down's. I said yes. A boy and a girl. That OK?" he asked.

We got everything sorted. They arrived the following week. We named them Thaddeus and Francesca.

"Mack, did you give Lydia and Joel that present from us?" I asked.

"Shit, no, hang on," he said and went to get it. Olivia started copying him.

"Shit, shit."

"Olivia, stop," I said.

She started crying. Mack came down with an envelope. "Joel, Lydia, can you come here please?" he said. They came in. Lydia had Alice.

"Here. A present from Mike and me," he said.

Joel opened it and showed to Lydia. They couldn't believe it. It was a two-week holiday to Rome, where we went.

"You can't be serious?" Lydia said. "This is too much!"

"Listen," I said to them both, "you two have done so much for us over the years. We would not be here if it weren't for you two. Mack and I are very grateful."

Joel hugged us both. He had tears in his eyes. Lydia stood in silence. She looked at us. "You two have the kindest souls."

That felt good. Dad looked at us both. "That was a wonderful thing you two did for those two."

"They deserve it. Call it a thank you," Mack said, feeding Thaddeus. I had Francesca. Olivia and Oliver were sleeping.

Mack got a call the next morning from Miranda. She had some more work coming his way. A lot more money for what they did the last time. He happily agreed. So did the guys.

Mack had his own office now. He looked like the bee's knees. The girls kept going silly when he was around. That stopped when I turned up one day after work. I only went a couple of days because of the kids.

"Hey. You must be Rachel?" I asked. "I'm here to see Mack."

Mack saw me and came out of the office.

"Rachel, this is Michael, my husband. How was work? The kids OK?"

"I think Thadd is coming down with something."

Rachel was gobsmacked. "I never knew. Wouldn't put you two together. I'll put the kettle on."

"Don't worry. We're going home, aren't we?" I said to Mack.

"Give us one minute." He went back to the office.

"How long have you two been together?" Rachel asked me.

"Married seven years," I told her.

"You're married. How many kids?" she asked. She was interested.

"Four. Two girls, two boys," I said, smiling.

"Ready?" Mack said. "See you Monday, Rachel."

She watched as we walked out hand in hand, and Mack giving me a kiss.

"Don't worry. Plenty more fish in the sea," Adam told her. "Go home, Rachel. It's getting late."

I checked Thadd when I got home. "I think he might have a cold. I'll take him to the doctor's on Monday. All he does is smile and chuckle."

We sat on the sofa that evening, like a couple of old women, yawning and saying how knackered we were.

"Can you hear that?" Mack said.

"Hear what?" I asked.

"Exactly. Nothing," was the reply.

"Mack, your feet stink. That t-shirt's getting worse," I said.

He just looked at me. "I'm having a shower when I go to bed. I was going to ask you to join me. After that girly outburst, you can sod off. As for the t-shirt, I think you're probably right," he said.

Dad walked in, looking happy with himself.

"You look like the cat that got the cream. Out with Carole, were we?" Mack said, smiling.

"How did you know that?" he asked. No one knew that.

"Jacob was keeping an eye out. After everything Carole has done for us, we just wanted to keep an eye out," he told my dad. "Family sticks together. I'll always have your back. Oh, good, 'Gogglebox'." Mack was engrossed.

Dad and I smiled and shook our heads.

"God, I'm hungry," Mack said, during the break. He got up and went to the fridge.

"You sure you're not pregnant? You're eating like anything," I said, looking at my paperwork.

"Nah, I like what I do. Has its off days, has its good days. Never thought I would go back though."

"Why?" he sat up and faced me, resting his head on his hands.

"Still can't believe I've got what I have. I get worried sometimes." I stopped to pause.

"What worries you?" He was concerned.

"That it will go wrong. I'll wake up all this is a dream." I sighed.

He pinched me.

"What did you do that for?"

"It's not a dream. All real."

I looked at his arms. "When did you get them?" I asked, pointing to the new tattoos of Thaddeus and Francesca.

"Last week. You like?" He was smiling, but I was quiet for a second. "What's up?" he asked.

"Just remembering what you said in Rome. About being happy and content. Do you think we would have met if all this hadn't happened?" I asked, not sure of the reply.

"Yes, I do." He got up and checked on the kids.

"We got any Calpol? Thaddeus' got a fever." Mack looked worried.

"Let's have a look at him," I said. "He doesn't look well. Let's get him checked out at the hospital to be sure. Dad, can you look after the others, we're taking Thaddeus to hospital," I said.

We got there and went to the front desk, thankful that Emily was there. She was good. "Michael, everything OK? Who's this?"

I told her everything. "Hang on." She went and came back. The wait wasn't long. We saw Dr Shaw.

"Right, Michael. Nothing to worry about. He's just got a really bad cold. I know your cautious as he has Down's. Just give him Calpol and fluids. He'll be fine." He looked at Mack who was scared shitless.

"Michael, who's this?" Dr Shaw asked. "Is he your body guard?"

I smiled. "No. Sorry. Hang on. Mack, come here."

Mack came over with Thaddeus.

"Mack, this is Dr Shaw. Dr Shaw, this is Mack, my husband."

"Really. Wow. You two? I suppose you two get that a lot?"

We nodded. "How many kids do you two have?" He was interested to know.

"Four. Two girls, two boys," Mack said, smiling. "Come on, let's get home to bed. Thanks. Come on, little man. You scared your dad and me."

Dr Shaw looked at us, "Good for you."

We got home and put Thaddeus to bed. Later, we told Dad what happened and went to bed.

"That scared the crap out of me," Mack said, keeping an ear out for the monitor.

"Me too. The main thing is he's OK. Our little man's OK," I told him.

"If you weren't there, I know I would be a mess. How do you keep your cool?" he asked.

"You have to. If they see you panic, they panic. You'll end up making mistakes. It's stressful. But sometimes, the rewards are good." I looked over at him. Bloody snoring.

That morning, we over-slept. Lucky Mack and I didn't have work that day. We went downstairs to the smell of food. Dad, Lydia and Joel were there with the kids.

"Why didn't you wake us up?" Mack said, yawning and rubbing his eyes.

"Seriously?" Dad said. "We're here to help. Thaddeus is OK."

Olivia said, "Daddies. Love you." Oliver copied.

"Daddy. Love you. Football. Grandad, football please," Olivier said. Francesca smiled and waved her chubby hand at us and blew us a kiss. Thaddeus smiled, then sneezed. Mack left the room.

Olivia walked in and went to Mack. She sat in his lap and wiped his tears away. "Don't cry, Daddy."

Mack smiled. "I'm OK, Olivia. Wow," he said, wiping his eyes. "Sorry, Mike." He took my hand. He had tears in his eyes again. Olivia looked worried.

"Daddy's OK, sweetheart. Park. Swings," Mack told her.

"Yer, swings. Please. Slide. Ollie, park." She got off his lap.

Oliver went, "Park. Football. Grandad, football."

"OK, kiddo. I'll get the football. Looks like I'm going to the park with you. Maggie, come on. You're coming too," Dad said.

"Yer. Can we have a McDonald's after?" Maggie asked.

"If Mum and Dad say so," Dad told her.

They nodded. Mack and I sat there, smiling. I patted Mack's knee. He grabbed my hand, stood up and kissed me. "Thank you, for our life."

We had a great time at the park. My dad looked knackered by the time we got to McDonald's. "You OK, Dad?"

"Yes. Just feeling my age," he said, smiling.

"Granddad, chip please?" Olivia asked.

When got home, Dad fell asleep on the sofa. The kids were having their afternoon nap.

Lydia saw us in the kitchen. "You two are the soppiest idiots I have ever met. You, Mack, were a tough guy. Now you're a tart with a beard. Looks good. Go and have a kip, the pair of you. No arguing." We did as we were told. Well, we didn't do much sleeping.

When we got up, we just couldn't stop smiling. Lydia later on gave us the number for the nursery that Maggie went to. Olivia and Oliver were ready for playgroup. I was ready, Mack, well, he was a bit more protective.

"I'm not sure," he said.

"Give over. They need to go, numbnuts. It will do them and us good. We'll check it out on Monday. I'm not working."

I called the nursery and we went that afternoon. The lady was rude to us.

"Are you always so rude?" I asked her.

"Well, we have never had this situation before." She was very high and mighty.

"What situation is that?" Mack asked, sitting across from her.

"Having children in our nursery whose parents, well…" she trailed off.

"You mean gay parents," Mack said. I let him do the talking. He could be direct. "Well, sorry to disappoint you. We can't all be straight. Answer me this, if you saw us walking down the street, would you say we were gay?"

Good point. Very good point. "Well, no. That's not the point."

"What is then?" he looked smug. "My kids deserve the same as every other kid. Don't judge a book by a cover. Stop being so anal. When can they start?"

She was gobsmacked. "Fine, I will enrol them. Monday, Wednesday and Fridays. Starting next week."

We left her in the chair. I smiled when we left. "You're not the most subtle man in the world as Jacob said."

He opened the car door. "When it comes to those I care and love, no. I never had that before all of you."

I just looked at him. "What?" he asked.

"Nothing," I told him.

When we got home, Dad was out with Carole, again. Joel was giving Alice and Alfie a bath. Lydia was with our kids. "Lydia, go and put your feet up. Bottle of wine in the fridge. Where's Maggie?" Mack asked her.

"Sleepover at Lucy's," she said, putting her feet on the table, with a glass of wine.

We took the kids to bed. "Say night, Olivia."

"Night, Aunt Lid-lid," she said, rubbing her eyes.

When I came down, Lydia said, "Have you told him yet?"

"No, it's a surprise. He's done so much for me, plus, it's his birthday. I know he'll cry his eyes out," I said.

"Who'll cry his eyes out?" Mack asked, eating as usual.

"I'm surprised you haven't exploded, with all that food you eat, said Lydia. sipping on her Blossom Hill.

'Don't make any plans for Friday," I told Mack.

"Why?" he asked, eating a bag of crisps.

"Just don't," I told him. "Be here for seven. And look nice."

51

"All right. What you up to?" he was getting worried.

"All will be revealed." I raised my eyebrows.

Mack looked at Lydia. He was looking round the house for clues. I just laughed. "Just wait till tomorrow night, you impatient prick."

I had spent the day getting everything ready. I was nervous. Mack came in. "Mike, Mike?"

"Shit," I cursed. "I'm in the living room," I said out loud.

When he walked in, the surprise was obvious. Candles everywhere.

"Happy birthday, Mack. Thanks for the last five and a half years. Thanks for the kids. Thanks."

He stood there, gobsmacked.

"Say something," I said.

He came up to me and hugged me. "Thought you forgot."

That was it. He was crying like a baby.

"Sit down. Here." I gave him his present. He opened it. They were photos. One of when we got together. The other, now, of our family. I got tears in my eyes too. He started again.

He looked at me. "I love you. Can we eat?"

I laughed. "I swear you're pregnant." I held his face in my hands. "You are my life."

"I thought I was the sensitive one." He laughed, wiping his eyes. He looked at me.

"Yes, it's ready. Get the plates. Got your favourite desert after."

"What, you?" He winked.

"That's later. Look." I opened the fridge. "Carrot cake."

"You brilliant man. Where did you get it?" he asked.

"That shop you love. I told them that you love the cake. They made this for you." I felt so smug.

"You're trying to fatten me up. You've married a fat old man." He was being sarcastic.

The evening went well. It was like when we first met. Not to say what we had now wasn't great, but we needed this; just being ourselves. We didn't get to the cake. Lucky enough, I put a lid on the cake as I knew Maggie would get her hands on it.

I woke up to find Mack not there. He was in the living room, eating his cake.

"It's two in the bloody morning."

"I couldn't help it," he said. "God, it's good. Not as good as you."

"Really! I've lost my husband to carrot cake." I took it from him. "Bed, now! You'll get cramps and start farting. Then you're going to sleep on the sofa," I told him.

"OK. One condition. Can we have round two?" he asked, laughing.

I left him asleep, snoring. He was smiling.

"Well?" Lydia asked me, drinking her coffee.

"I think you know how it went," I told her.

"I heard you. Twice. Dirty buggers." She laughed.

Maggie came back from her mates. She was upset about something.

"What's the matter, sweetheart?" Lydia asked.

She didn't answer. "Maggie?" Lydia asked again. "What's wrong?"

She started crying. Mack heard her and came downstairs. "Maggs, what's wrong?" he asked.

"Lucy's dad asked me about my family. When I told him that I had two uncles that were married to each other, he was horrible. What's a dirty poof and a bender? I know that they're not nice words. He was not nice. I heard him when I went to bed." She looked at Mack and me. "I think you are the best uncles I've got. I don't like nasty people. I like Lucy. But her dad was real mean to you two. Why can't he be nice?" She started crying again. "It's not fair. I don't like that."

We sat there in silence. That poor girl. Mack was spitting mad. Maggie saw that. She went and hugged him. "Sorry, Uncle Mack; sorry, Uncle Mike. I'm a lucky girl. I love you two very much. Can I have burger and chips for tea, please?"

"What do we do?" Lydia said later.

"I know what I want to do!" Mack said. He was fuming.

"What will that achieve?" I asked.

"It will make me feel better." He sat down. "What does he do for a job?"

"He is the bank manager up town. Why?" Lydia didn't like the sound of it.

"Don't even think about it?" I said.

"Why? I'm just going to talk to him. That's it." He looked at me dead in the eyes. He meant it.

"I'm coming with you. We'll sort this out together," I said.

"You are aware I'm Maggie's mum. I'm coming too."

We made the appointment for the next day at twelve.

"Keep your cool," I told Mack. He just looked at me.

"Mrs Green. Good to see you. How are you?" he asked.

"Good. Thanks. How are you?" She was ready to bite, so was Mack. He looked at us two. "I don't think I've had the pleasure. Who are you both?" He was polite.

"I'm sorry. This is Mack and Michael. Maggie's uncles."

His face dropped. "My daughter came home from Lucy's in tears. She heard you calling them homophobic slurs. What gives you the right? We have brought up our kids to treat people with respect."

"What did Mack and I do to you?" I asked.

"Listen. I have the right to my opinion," he said.

"But to make a six-year-old cry because her uncles were being mistreated? She was so upset. She doesn't understand why people like you are horrible."

There was a pause. Then Mack said, "Why do we offend you? We're the same. We got kids at home. I would never be like that. Why?"

"I don't think it's normal. I'm sorry I made your daughter cry and upset her. I can't change my opinion."

"Well, I will be taking my business elsewhere. Mack, Michael, get in the car. We're done. Move."

We left like naughty school boys.

"I hardly said anything," Mack said.

I stopped outside the bike shop. Maggie had her eye on the pink bike.

"Hang on, you two," I shouted, going in the shop. I came out with the bike she wanted.

"Michael. That's too much!" She was shocked.

"This is nothing for our Maggie. She's one hell of a kid, Lydia. I'm proud of her, sticking up for us two, and her family. She's a smart girl. This is a thank you."

When we got home, Maggie went mental when she saw the bike. "This is just what I wanted. Why!"

"Because you are our niece whom we love very much. Never change who you are," I told her. She hugged us.

"I'm lucky, you know. I have one hell of a family. I'm very lucky. Mum, can I ride my bike in the garden, before dinner?"

"Go on, baby girl." She was happy. She watched her ride her bike with pride and cried. Her Maggie. She tapped me on my arm and gave me a kiss. "You are a wonderful brother, my darling Michael."

Olivia came walking in. "Daddy, I'm hungry and Ollie did a poo. It smells. Like when Dad farts, it's horrible. I love you, Daddy." Olivia hugged me.

"I love you too, kiddo. Where's Thaddeus and Francesca?" I asked.

"With Grandad. Shall we get them? Give Granddad a break?" she asked, scratching her head. Just like Mack.

"Dad! Dad. You OK?" I asked, going in the living room. When Olivia saw him, she ran to him and hugged him.

Thaddeus smiled. Francesca crawled over to me and pulled herself by my leg. "Dad. Go and have a break. You do way too much to us. You've been a godsend.'

"Daddy, I want a poo. Where's my football?" Oliver said.

"Come on, son, we'll sort you out." Mack picked him up and put him over his shoulder. "I think we've a footballer in the family. Maybe he'll play for Chelsea."

"Not Chelsea. Arsenal. Chelsea are rubbish. Sorry, Dad, just, farted," he told him.

"You really need the loo, son. Go, I'll find your football."

Lydia was exhausted.

"Go take a bath. We'll look after the kids. I'll get dinner for you," Mack said.

"Saturday night, you, me and Mike are going out. No arguing."

"I'm not arguing. You sure you're…" she trailed off.

"Just go." Mack waved her away. She watched us, smiled and went for her bath.

When she came down, it was quiet. "What did you do? It's quiet. Did you drug the kids?"

"No. The kids are all in bed. Asleep. Dinner's in the living room. I'll get the wine," Mack told her. She looked at me.

"Is he OK? He's in a good mood. You must have shagged him hard. Twice," Lydia said.

"Lydia, I did. That's not the point," I told her, smiling.

"He's changed, you know," she said, eating her dinner. "In a good way. Being a dad suits him. The pair of you."

"So, what we doing by Saturday night?" Mack said, eating.

"Are you pregnant? You eat so much," Lydia told him. "You're getting fat," Lydia said to him while eating her cake. "How about that restaurant, what's it called? Shit, um…"

"The River?" I asked.

"Sounds good. It's supposed to be nice in there," Lydia said yawning. Next thing, she was asleep, her glass of wine nearly spilling.

Mack put her to bed. She was out like a light.

"So, you think I'm fat?" he asked me while getting into bed.

I looked at him. "No. I'm changing your name to Maureen. You're fine. I think you should take a pregnancy test. I think I got you pregnant. What's up with you lately? You worried about something?"

"Not really," he said, putting his arm behind his head.

"I know there's something wrong. You haven't got your t-shirt on. Strange." I was worried for him.

"It's not you or anything you did. You know the house I bought for us?" he said.

"Yes. What about it?" I was getting nervous.

"I was thinking about moving us in there soon. Let Lydia and Joel have this place. Your dad will come with us. I mean, the kids are growing. We'll only be up the road. I mean, we've never lived alone, together. What do you think?" he asked.

I smiled. "I wish we'd done it sooner. It is getting cramped in here. It's going to be strange though."

"You mean, being by ourselves? he quietly said.

"Yes. In a good way. I'm nervous thinking about it," I said, wondering.

I looked at him. "Don't bother putting that on," I told him. "It's coming off as soon as you get into bed. Come here."

He winked at me and got into bed. Just as he got into bed, Thaddeus started crying like he was in pain. We ran to him and I picked him up. "Hey, hey, little man. What's up? God, you're hot. Mack, get the Calpol," which he did.

"Is he OK?" Mack asked, looking at him.

"He's hot. Not sure." I was worried.

Lydia came in. "Let's have a look at you, you gorgeous boy." She took him off me.

He smiled and then out of nowhere, said, "Lid-lid."

That's what Olivia called her. He was almost a year and a half. He had never spoken till now. I was gobsmacked. Mack, as usual, had tears in his eyes.

"Wow. That's brilliant. Thaddeus. Yes, I am Aunt Lid-lid."

"I think he may have an infection. Go and see the doctor. Just to be on the safe side. Go now. I'll keep an eye on the others."

We took him to see Dr Shaw. He checked him over.

"Yes, he has a mild chest infection. He also has slight asthma, but he's going to be fine. Here's a prescription for the meds. How are you both?" he asked, looking at Mack and I.

"Good. Tired," Mack said holding Thaddeus and smiling at him. Thaddeus rested his head on his chest.

He looked confused. "After his Aunt Lydia."

Dr Shaw looked at me. "You don't mean Lydia Green, do you?"

"Yes, why?" Mack said.

"She's one hell of a nurse. And a woman you don't piss off. How is she? After everything that's gone on, we need her back."

We told him everything that Lydia had been up to.

"Wow. Well, tell her, William said hi. I want her working for me." He wrote down a number and gave it to me. "Tell her to call."

When we got home, we put Thadd to bed.

"How is he?" Lydia asked. "Chest infection and Asthma. By the way, William Shaw says hello, and wants you back working for him," Mack said, giving her his number. "He spoke fondly of you." She smiled at that.

An hour later, Matthew and Adam were at the door. They were clearly upset.

"It's Jack, isn't it?" Mack said.

We were all there, Matthew sat down with tears in his eyes.

"Mack, he passed away last night. My brother. Gone." He started crying. That was it. We all were in tears. Our beloved Jack. No longer with us. Mack was devastated. He and Matthew hugged, crying. Lydia was beside herself, so was Joel

When we got home, Mack wanted to be alone. We let him be. We carried on that day. Mack said he was going for a walk. Three days later, he came home. I stood at the door, in tears, looking at him.

"I'm sorry, Mike."

"You're sorry. That all you got? Three days. I've phoned every hospital, police station, to find you. I haven't slept, eaten. The kids have missed their dad like crazy. I thought the worst. Do you have any idea of what you put me through by walking out? But right now, I'm mad as fuck with you. Not a word."

Mack came to me. I burst out into tears.

Joel and Dad stood there, watching him on the sofa.

Dad staid, "Let me talk to my son." He meant Mack.

Joel and I left them. They talked for hours. I've heard Mack cry. But really cry. Never. He was sobbing. That hurt me, because he was hurting. Francesca came in with Maggie. She heard Mack and went running to him, saying, "Daddy. Daddy. Missed you. Naughty, Daddy. No running away. How rude!"

"He will be fine, Francesca. Go and see Daddy. Be there soon."

She did as she was told. She hugged me and Lydia. "Aunt Lydia, can I have a drink and biscuit, please?" She was polite.

"Yes, you can, sweetheart."

She took her to get a drink. I went in the garden as I needed some air. I was hurt. I thought I had lost him. I didn't want to think about it. Losing Mack would be like losing a limb. I was in tears again.

"I'm so sorry, Mike." Mack was crying again.

I can't lose you too, Mack, I thought. *I couldn't function. I hadn't slept in our bed. I've slept on the sofa. I can't function without you. If you were dead, that would have been the end of me.*

I turned to him. "I'm sorry, Jack dying hit you hard. I really am. He was a part of your life for years. We can't replace him. And I can't replace you. Ever. So, please don't leave again. I love you more than anything."

We stood there. "You need a bath. You smell like a dog shat on you."

He looked at me. "That will never happen again." He was telling the truth.

He went and had a bath. Maggie saw him after school. "Uncle Mack. I'm glad you're home. Don't do that again. Wait here." She ran off to get something. "Here, for you." She put a home-made band on his arm. "This is to remind you where home is," she said and left.

"She's way too smart for her age," Mack said to Lydia.

"I know. She speaks the truth. Like this family does." Lydia hugged him. "I'm glad you're home. Get some rest."

That night, we slept together. It was beautiful. He was back to his old self.

Back to work. Matthew was getting there too. Adam was kind of running things now. He was enjoying it. He and Rachel were getting close too.

"Nice to see you back," she told Mack, giving him his tea.

"Thanks, Rachel. Good to be back. Where are those files for Miranda Wentworth?" he asked.

"I'll go and get them," she said.

I walked in after work. "Hello, Michael. How are you? He's in his office," she said.

"Hey. How's your day?" I asked, sitting down.

"Good," he said, smiling. "I won't be long. Then we're going out."

"Where we going?" I asked.

"What and see!" he said, with a smirk on his face.

"Here are those files, Mack?" Rachel handed them to him.

"Nothing to worry about, just keeping up-to-date with the paperwork. Right, come on. Let's go," he said.

"Bye, Adam, Rachel. Go home," Mack told them.

"OK,. you're the boss," Adam said.

"Ta da." he said, standing outside 'The River' restaurant.

Everyone was so relaxed. Laughing and enjoying themselves. Joel got up and made a toast. "You are the most strong-willed pain in my arse. But, I love you. You…" He paused; you could see the tears in his eyes. "You have given me three beautiful kids. So" — he pulled out a box from his pocket and got on one knee — "Lydia, will you marry me again?"

"Joel, if I have to. Yes. I love you too." She was so happy. Everyone in the restaurant stood up and clapped.

"Did you know?" Lydia asked Mack. He winked at her.

"You sneaky bugger!" she said. Joel and Mack smiled at each other.

"I'm never getting married," Maggie said.

Joel was happy. "Why!" Lydia asked her.

"To much hassle," she said, nicking a chip from my plate.

Then the music started playing. I smiled when I heard the song. Mack had tears in his eyes.

"You two OK?" Maggie asked.

"Yes, we are," Mack said. He took my hand and kissed me. Then Francesca said out loud, "Thaddeus, you stink. I think he's done a poo or a fart." She continued eating her desert.

Mack got up. He went to get Thaddeus and collapsed.

We got him to the hospital. The doctors told us he was suffering from exhaustion. He was hooked up to monitors and drips.

"I want to go home," he whined. He sounded like a baby.

"No way," I said. "We'll go when the doctor says so."

The doctor came back. "Well. You can go home. You need to rest and take a chill pill. How old are you?"

"I'm forty-two," was the reply.

"Easy steps. Cut back on the work load. Where's the wife?"

"My husband is right here." He pointed to me.

"I'm sorry. No offence." He looked at me. "Makes sure he rests. He's not to overdo it. I want to see you in a fortnight."

We went home. Mack sat on the couch and fell asleep. I covered him up. Then I sat in the kitchen and cried. My dad came in.

"Dad, I can't lose him," I spoke, wiping my eyes. "Dad, I'm scared. That man lying on that sofa is my life. Seeing him like that, it worried me. I love him."

"I love you too. Idiot. I'm going to be fine. I have been overdoing it." He sat in the kitchen chair in his holey t-shirt. "Simon, thank you."

"For what?" Dad said.

"Giving me Mike. I'm going be fine. Just need to chill out. Adam's fine at work. He can run the place with his eyes closed. Matthew's gonna help. So, I'm going to do what I do best."

"Eating," I said. "You're one carrot cake away from being fat."

My dad laughed. We had had the shock of our lives.

"Daddies. Grandad. I did a poo. It smells."

We all thought he wouldn't talk. Not because he had Down's. Just because we thought he might take longer. Francesca was protective over him. "Come, Thaddeus, I will help you."

"OK." He took her hand and off they went.

"You two are raising four amazing children." Dad tapped my hand with tears in his eyes.

I looked at him. "Yes, I will take it easy. OK. Bloody hell, you going to nag me the rest of my life?" he said, getting up.

"Yes, I am, numb-nuts. Till I'm old and grey. Always."

"Always. Fancy taking the little ones to the park, then get Olivia and Oliver from playgroup?" he said.

"Yes. We could do with some fresh air. Francesca, Thaddeus, get your shoes, we're going to the park," I said.

"Yes!" they both went.

We watched as they tried to get their shoes on. I smiled at Francesca. "Thank you for helping your brother."

"Always, Daddy." I looked up at Mack and smiled.

They had fun running around. Mack looked chilled out. Some of the mums were eyeing him up. They got the hump when he took my hand. One said, "That's not fair."

We went and got Olivia and Oliver. They were so happy.

"Daddy. You came. This is my friend, Libby."

We said hi. "Right, come on, let's get you lot home," Mack said.

"How are you, Daddy?" Olivia asked Mack.

"I'm all right, darling. Getting better," he replied.

"Good. Can I go to Libby's party on Saturday afternoon?" she asked.

"Yes. We'll take you," Mack said. "Who wants Chinese?"

"Can I have Indian instead?" Oliver said.

"I'm popping into work tomorrow," Mack said while putting the washing up away.

"No, you're not," I told him, clearing the table. "If you go in, you will stay the whole day. Come home stressed. I'm not having it."

"I know you're worried," Mack said, putting the tea towel on his shoulder. "It's been a week and a half." I didn't look at him.

"Hey, why don't you come with me. You're on holiday," he said, helping me.

"OK. Two hours. Then home," I told him.

We put the kids to bed. All happy, clean and fast asleep. Dad was out with Carole. Lydia was out with friends and Joel was on babysitting duty.

"Drink?" he asked us.

"God, yes," I said. Sitting on the couch, feet on the table.

"How's it going? You OK, Mack?" Joel passed us a drink each.

"I'm OK. Better. Just itching to get back to work," he said, avoiding my gaze.

"Why aren't you happy about it?" Joel asked me.

"Because, he'll overdo it. Then boom, square one. You've been stressed for months. I'm not losing you. All you do is worry about everyone else. Let me worry about you for a change. You are the most stubborn prick I've ever met, you know that, right! When are you going to slow down? Jesus, Mack," I was half-yelling.

Joel looked at Mack. "What do you say to that?"

"I'm stubborn? Look at you. Trying to keep things close to your chest. Sometimes, it drives me crazy. Yes, I've overdone it. I don't want to lose what I've got," he said.

"Jesus, Mack, I know. My mum wasn't much older than you when she died. I don't want the kids to grow up without you. If that's what you want." I got up and walked away. He followed.

"You know that's not what I want," he said.

Maggie walked in and folded her arms. "For the love of God. Shut up. You two go round in bloody circles. Grow up. Look at what you've got. Right now, you two are hormonal, menopausal and girly. You two need a shag, now!" This came from a six-year-old. She walked off.

Joel looked at us and smiled. "I agree. She's a small Lydia. That's my girl." Like a proud father.

That put an end to that. "Coffee?" I said to Mack.

"Yes, please. She's right, you know." Mack sighed.

"Can't believe I'm agreeing with a six-year-old." I laughed. Everything was back to normal.

We took Olivia to her friend's party. All the mums were gushing over her.

"Olivia, where are your parents?" asked one of them.

"My dads are over there." She pointed to us.

They looked at us and eyed us up. "I think we better go." Mack laughed. "Livvy, have a good time."

She waved and said, "Bye, Dads. Love you both. Don't forget Ollie's football." She was having fun.

We walked round the town, getting a few things before getting Olivia. We sat and had a coffee. Mack was scratching his beard. "Think I'll shave it."

"Don't. I like it. You look better with it. Keep it," I told him.

"When did our kids become such smart arses?" he asked.

"They take after you. We're doing a good job with them." I paused. "Mack, I want another one. A kid, I mean."

He smiled. Really smiled. "Seriously? I'm glad you said that. I was going to ask you the same thing. We're going to have to find a bigger place, you know?"

I nodded. "There's something else."

"What?" He was confused.

"It's our anniversary next month." He nodded. "I want to renew our vows." I took his hand. Some woman walked past and gave us a dirty look.

"Really?" he said. "You're getting as soppy as me."

"Will you marry me again?" I said out loud to him. He laughed.

"Damn right, I will," he told me. we went and picked up Olivia.

"Did you get Ollie's football?" Mack showed her.

Libby's mum came up to us. "Hi. How are you both? I'm Lizzie. That's my husband Harry." He waved at us.

"Hi. I'm Mack, this is my husband Mike. Nice to meet you," said Mack. "You been good?" he asked Ollie.

"'Course I have. What's for dinner?" she asked.

"Just like her dad. Always hungry," I said to Lizzie. "Thanks for having her. Come on, you. Let's get you home," I said, picking her up.

When we got home, Alice and Alfie were at the table, drawing.

"Hey kids," Mack said.

"Hey, Uncle Mack, Uncle Mikey," Alice said. "When can we have a family day out?"

"Dunno. Be good to have one," I said. "I'll ask your mum. You kids hungry?"

"Yes," Alfie said. "What's for dinner? Malek called for you, Uncle Mack." Just then, the doorbell rang. It was Malek.

"Hello, my dear Mack. I trust Allah has kept you well."

"We're good. Want to stay for dinner?" he asked.

"Yes. Hungry. Michael, my friend. How are you?" he asked.

"Good. Mack and I want to ask you something," I told him.

"Anything." He smiled.

"We are having the kids baptised. We would love it if you would be their godfather. You're a good man," I asked him, sitting at the table.

"Mack, Michael. I would be delighted. This is a great honour for me. Thankyou. Allah has given me a good family," he said.

"Who's Allah?" Alice asked him, still drawing.

Malek smiled. "As a Muslim. Allah is our God."

"Cool. He sounds like a cool dude," She told us.

We smiled. "Yes, he is," Malek said.

Lydia and Joel came in. "Malek," Joel said. "Good to see you."

Lydia hugged the life out of him. "Miss Lydia, you get more beautiful every time I see you."

"Thank you. We've missed you. You staying for dinner?"

Mack and I smiled at each other. Lydia asked. "Right, what is it? Spill."

"We, like you and Joel, are renewing our vows next month. We're going to have another baby, too," Mack told them.

"Brilliant. Just had an idea. Why don't we do our vows the same time as you? Have a bloody big party," she said.

Mack and I looked at each other. "We like it," I said.

"Do I get a say?" Joel asked.

"What do you think?" Lydia asked.

"Why can't I win with you, woman.?" he said.

"Dad, you've got more chance of scoring in the cup final than winning with mum," Maggie said.

"Ain that the truth," he said.

We laughed. Dad came in. "Malek, good to see you. Fancy a drink?" "Thought you would never ask," he replied.

Dad and Malek started chatting. I stood at the door, smiling away.

"What you smiling at?" Mack asked, passing me a beer.

"Nothing," I told him.

Mack kissed me. "You're weird."

Lydia pulled Dad to one side. "Dad, walk me down the aisle?"

"I'd be delighted. He turned to Mack. "Now, Mack, so you want Malek to walk you down the aisle.?"

I burst out laughing. "You silly sod," he said, drinking his beer.

Malek said his prayers before the family dinner.

"Alice was asking about a family day out," I said to Lydia.

Olivia said, out of nowhere, "Did you know that the black mamba is the second deadliest snake. It lives in Africa. Its mouth is black. It can grow to about eight feet." She carried on eating her chicken curry. Mack and I looked at each other.

"Where did you learn that?" Mack asked.

"Off the telly. It was interesting. I liked the one about the black funnel Spider, from Australia," she said.

"I think she's a genius," Mack said. "She takes after me."

I just looked at him. "I think you've had too many beers."

He smiled at me, finishing his beer. Dad and Malek washed and wiped up. The kids were getting ready for bed. Thaddeus walked up to Joel. "Uncle Joel, read a book please."

He read him the book, during which, Thaddeus fell asleep. "I'll take him up," Joel said.

Francesca followed, rubbing her eyes.

"Oliver, Olivia, bed," Mack said. "Come on. "

"OK, Dad," Olivia said. "Did you know that Turkey is the only country to be half in Europe and half in Asia?"

We sat down with our drinks. Mack came in and gave me a present. "What is it?" I asked.

"It's something I wanted to give to you for a long time."

I opened it to find this amazing box of things he collected over the years of me and him.

"This is amazing. Why?" I looked at him.

"Just because being with you is easy." He had tears in his eyes.

Lydia started crying. "Lydia!" Joel said.

"I'm OK," she said, wiping her eyes. "One piece. Seven kids between us. We've survived a lot. Our vows are in three weeks. Joel, I'm only going to say this once, 'cause I've had a drink. You are the best thing that has ever happened to me. Thank you for putting up with my shit and our kids. God, I'm a lucky woman. I love you, Joel Green. Never forget that, arsehole."

"There it is. Normal," Joel said. "I love you too, Lydia."

Mack's stomach started rumbling. We started laughing.

Lydia turned to him. "Are you sure Michael didn't get you pregnant? I can get a test done."

"Why does everyone think that?" He sounded surprised.

"Because you are a pig," I told him. "Don't worry, you're still hot."

That cheered him up. He smiled his head off. I smiled back and winked. We talked for a while. Then bed.

Mack went to put his t-shirt on. "Don't bother putting that on," I said to him.

"Why?" He was confused. I stood in front of him and kissed him.

The next morning, we got ready for Whipsnade Zoo. Mack and I were whistling in the kitchen, smiling.

"Why are you two so happy this morning?" Joel said, yawning.

"No reason," I said, drinking my coffee.

"Give over," Lydia said. "You two are noisy when you do it. You woke me up twice. You're like rabbits. No wonder Mack's always hungry."

"Almost," I said munching on toast. Mack looked at me and smiled. "I know what you're thinking!" Lydia said raising her eyebrows. He went red.

The day was brilliant. The kids loved it. Us adults were knackered. Olivia came out with all these facts.

"Look Fiordland penguins. They eat squid."

"How does she know so much? She's so smart!" I asked Mack.

"She's smart like me!" he said, laughing. "She's smart. You're a smart arse. There's a difference," I told him. He laughed.

"Grandad?" Francesca asked him.

"Yes, love?" he said.

"I love you. You're the best. Can I have an ice cream?" She was scratching her head, like Mack. My dad smiled.

When we were going home, the kids fell asleep. What a day!

Lydia was looking at dresses for the day. "Found it!" She said out loud, making Mack spill his beer.

"Bloody hell, woman. Nearly had a heart attack," he said.

"Give over. What suit are you wearing? Don't say t-shirt and jeans," she told him.

"Actually, I've got that sorted. Picking them up tomorrow." He was pretty smug.

Lydia was surprised. She looked around. "You got that thing for Michael you were talking about for the day?"

"Yes. I'm such a romantic." He was smiling.

She put her magazine down. "I knew then that you loved him. You were this tough guy that wanted to impress him. When you two got together, you mellowed out. A lot. Your love for him is undeniable. You love him hard. Am I wrong? I've never met two people who, even after all these years, still love each other. I see how you two fall in love with each other every day. The way you both look at each other. Wow. That's love. Real love. The kids came along. You two became your best. You adore Michael, don't you?" She was kind when she said it.

"Like you wouldn't believe. Even after all these years, Lydia. My love for that man... I will never fall out of love with him. I'm the lucky man who found him. You know, I still get nervous when I'm round him. That went when I met him. Every time we're together, it's like the first time," Mack said.

"My God. Your every straight woman's dream guy. Shit! I should have married you. Bullocks. Now I'm in love with you."

Mack burst out laughing. "Sorry, Lydia. I've married the man of my dreams. Want a glass of wine?" He got up.

"Just give me the damn bottle and a straw," she told Mack.

"Come on. Let's watch 'Beaches'." She smiled.

"Lydia. I may be gay, but I'm not that gay," he said, having another beer.

The day of our wedding vows renewal arrived. Everyone was busy getting everything ready. I was so nervous. Nine years. Best nine years. He came out the shower and I couldn't keep my eyes off him.

"Oh, for God's sake!" Lydia said, smiling. "Like rabbits."

"I'll be down in a minute," Mack told me, buttoning his shirt.

I was ready and nervous. A few finishing touches. Then done. The garden was done up beautifully.

"Mike."

I turned round to find Mack in the most handsome suit. "Wow," I said. Mack smiled at me and kissed me. He handed me an envelope.

"What's this?" I asked him looking confused.

"Open it," he said.

I opened it. "Do you remember, when I said I was going to change my surname?" I nodded. "It's official. I'm now Mackenzie Denton. I know it's taken nine years."

"Don't think I can handle any more." I was gob smacked.

There was another envelope. I opened it. It was the deeds to the house next door. "For us and the kids. We're still going to keep the house I bought for your dad, but this is for us."

I had to sit down. I was amazed, lost for words. Mack sat opposite from me, smiling. "Thank you," was all I could say. I started crying. He put his hand on my neck.

"Don't cry."

I looked at him. "I will never stop loving you."

Dad went to get Lydia. "Oh my. Lydia. You're stunning," my dad said.

"Thank you. I'm ready. Nervous. But ready. Let's go." She took Dad's arm.

We were ready. Lydia came down. She truly was stunning. Joel's mouth dropped open. "Close your mouth. You're catching flies," I told him, smiling, standing next to Mack who took my hand.

Jacob stood there. He went on with the ceremony. Each of us had written our vows.

Joel's were short and sweet. "Lydia, I will never stop loving you. All these years, you have made the happiest. Thank you."

"Joel, my life with you has been the best. You've changed my life. Thank you for making me a mother, a wife. I promise to never stop being a pain in your arse." We all laughed.

Now it was our turn. I was so scared and nervous. I had tears in my eyes. I looked at him. "Mack, you are without a doubt the best thing that has happened to me. Without you, I'm nothing. You're my life, the only one that makes sense. I will never stop loving you. You're my soul mate."

That was it. Mack was in tears. "Mike. You are my everything. You saved my life. You are my home, my life, my love. I can't be without you. I love you forever."

My dad started crying, loudly. "Dad, that's Mack's job." He looked at me. Lydia, Joel, Mack and I stood there.

"Brilliant. Bloody brilliant. What a wonderful day," Lydia said. "Joel, I never say it enough. I love you. Thanks for putting up with my shit."

"Love you too. I don't have a choice. I like my balls where they are," Joel told her.

"Good lad," she said. "I need a drink."

Joel and Mack went and got the drinks. Lydia took my hand. "What!" I asked quietly.

"We found our soulmates," she told me.

"Yes, we did. I will never tire of him." I looked at Mack.

"You're oh so beautiful, Lydia." I kissed the top of her head.

"Thanks, love. You're not so bad either. Joel, where's my drink?" she said.

My dad shook my hand. "That was beautiful. Proud of you both. Very proud." I waved Mack over. He gave me a drink.

"Here's a late gift from me," said Dad.

Mack opened it, then spat his drink. "Simon, this is too much."

I looked at it. It was a cheque for five grand. "Dad. We don't need your money. This is too much."

"Not taking no for an answer. Put it to some use. Lydia has one too."

"Thank you. Well, in the spirit of giving. Here. From Mike and me." Mack pulled out an envelope and gave it to him.

"You serious?" he asked.

"Yes, we are. You've done so much and more for us. Consider it a thank-you. It's half hour away," Mack said. I agreed.

"I'm supposed to look after my kids." Dad started crying.

"Dad, we love you." I hugged Dad tight.

"Everyone. I want to make a toast," I said. "Thank you for being here. We are so blessed for what we have here. And to those we have lost. Jack, you may not be here. But you are always in our thoughts and prayers." Matthew nodded. "To our family. May we always be together, as a family forever. Salut!"

There was a knock at the door. It was Carole, with my dad, carrying a little one. Mack and I walked in the kitchen. "Hey, Carole."

"Sorry to intrude on this lovely day. I have another addition to your growing family. Can you take her?"

"Hell yer," I said, taking her. She was fast asleep. "Hey, beautiful. Welcome home, sweetheart."

"Rae Morgan Denton," my dad said.

"Rather fitting, don't you think?" I said to Mack. At that moment, Lydia and Joel came in. Lydia gasped. I got up. "Rae, this is your Aunt Lydia and Uncle Joel."

The kids came in and saw us. "Is this our new sister?" Francesca asked.

"Yes, it is, sweetheart. Her name's Rae."

"We'll get her cot and bits ready," Lydia said. "Joel, Matthew, give us a hand."

Matthew looked at me. "We've come a long way, haven't we?"

"Damn right we have. Thank you for everything you've done. Thank you for being my friend." I shook his hand.

"No, Thank you. Jack would love this. I wish he were here." He had tears in his eyes.

"He is. He's always here. He never left," I told him.

Mack came in. "Mike, let's put our little angel to bed." He gave Carole a kiss. "You're our guardian angel. Welcome to the family. Come on, Mike. Let's get her into bed. Kids, bed." They followed.

Matthew gave Mack a scotch. They talked in the garden. "I have to tell you, Mack, you are a lot stronger than what you were. I saw you with Rae. Man, you are one hell of a father. All your kids around you. My God. I never thought you would have five kids. Five," he said, sipping his scotch.

Mack smiled. "Mike made me who I am. You know what I was like."

"Don't under estimate yourself. You've come a long way. You're the toughest gay man with tattoos I've ever met," he said.

Mack laughed. "Remember when we were in Afghanistan. How I was? Now look at me. Five kids, taken Olivia to get first party and cooked shepherd's pie on a Tuesday night. I was asleep by nine thirty."

Matthew was in hysterical with laughter. That started Mack off laughing.

When everyone left, the four of us sat in the living room. "What a lovely day," Lydia said, yawning. "Still can't get over the fact that we have a new addition to our family. She's gorgeous. Come on. Bed. All of us. Busy day tomorrow."

We checked on the kids, sleeping like babies. Little Rae, the newest Denton.

Rae woke us up early. Smiling. We took her downstairs. She was nervous and grabbed onto me. She soon came round. Eating toast like it was no one's business.

Thaddeus walked up to Rae and kissed her. "I like my new sister." And walked off.

"I enjoy being at home with the kids. I know Olivia and Oliver are at nursery. Francesca and Thaddeus are going soon."

"You thought about doing something different?" he asked, packing some of our boxes.

"Hadn't thought about it." I thought about it.

"Come on. Don't worry about it now. Let's move to our new place. Can't wait." He winked at me.

"Dirty bugger." I laughed.

Everyone came and helped out. We were only moving in next door. But it felt like we were moving mountains. Mack was planned on where everything went. Organised to a tee. Thankful the kids were in nursery. Dad had Rae for the day. By evening, everything was in its place. The kids loved it. It was like we were there for ages. Lydia was crying.

"Give over, Lydia. We're next door. You silly cow," Mack told her. "Anyone think we've moved to bloody France."

Joel laughed his head off. Lydia gave him the look.

That evening, we put the kids to bed. Then it was us. Just us. The first time in years. Apart from Rome, and the odd day. I felt like when we first met. Mack could sense that. He took my hand. "I know how you feel."

Then he dozed off. *Nine o'clock. I married an old man.* I nudged him. "Come on. Bed."

Rae stood up in her cot, rubbing her eyes. She smiled and said, "Dada." I started crying.

Mack smiled. "It's OK. It's OK." Rae fell back to sleep.

I woke up to the kids running around. I came down, smiling.

"Dad?" Olivia asked me. "Can I have a dog called Baxter? Dad said no. So, I'm asking you. Can I?" I laughed.

"No. I'm with your dad on this," I told her. Mack and I smiled at each other. He handed me a coffee.

"OK, now?"

"Yes. Any toast?" He handed me some. Rae was happy. "Right, kids, come on. Nursery. Get your shoes."

Lydia came in her dressing gown. "Where's the bloody milk?"

"Come on in. Help yourself," Mack told her sarcastically.

"Dad, come on. We're going to be late," Oliver said.

Mack met Joel outside and took the kids to school and nursery.

"So, how was your first night?" Lydia asked, raising her eyebrows. I looked at her.

"We were in bed by nine," I said, munching on toast.

"You sad bastards. I thought you two would have christened every room in the house." She was serious.

"We're not dogs you know!" I said, shocked at that.

"No. You're like rabbits. Where you two get your energy from, I don't know." She sipped on her coffee.

Mack came home. "Mike."

"Kitchen," I called back.

"Right, I'm off," Lydia said. I just smiled.

"Hey, I've got an hour before I go to the office." He winked.

"An hour. Make it two," I told him. He smiled his head off.

Mack went to the office, whistling. I went with Lydia to pick the kids up. She looked at me. "Dirty buggers."

"Not my fault I'm all that!" I told her smugly.

She shook her head. We took the kids for lunch. Noisy buggers. Mack and Dad met up with us. It was a nice afternoon.

"Got some news for you," Mack told me. "Adam and Matthew are going to run the business. I'm still going in every day. Or every other day. What do you think?" he asked.

"How's your new place, Dad?" I asked him over coffee.

"Really nice. It's a nice thing that you did for me," he said.

"Least we could do, after what you have done for us. How's Carole?"

"Where's Mack?" he asked.

"I'm in the loo. Be out in a sec!" he said. "Right, I'm here."

"You're so not subtle," I said. He chuckled.

"I've asked Carole to move in with me," he said.

"Good for you," I said.

"I agree." Mack raised his coffee cup.

"Doesn't bother you?" he asked.

"No, why should it? You've got to be happy," Mack told him.

"It's not going to be weird? I'm seeing the woman that gave you the kids." He actually sounded happy.

"Listen, Dad. We're not the most conventional of families. Look at me and Mack. Lydia came in this morning, nicking milk in her dressing gown. The kids didn't batter an eyelid. Olivia wants a dog. Ollie won't get out of his Arsenal shirt. Fran wants a fish called Einstein. Thaddeus wants Thomas the tank. The only one that's OK is Rae and she can't talk yet." I told him.

"Point taken," Dad said, sipping his tea.

Mack was laughing his head off. So, my dad and Carole. Good for him.

I got Mack a Harley Davidson bike for Christmas. I'd seen him eyeing the same one for months. So, I got it. I hid it at Dad's till Monday. Christmas came. Everyone came to us.

"Mack," I called.

"Yes?"

"Close your eyes and take my hand," I told him.

"What?" he looked confused.

"Just do it."

He did as he was told. We went outside. He face was a picture when he saw the bike.

"Merry Christmas, Mack," I said, smiling.

"How did you know?" He was dumbstruck.

"I saw you looking at it for months. Here's your jacket." I gave it to him.

"Thank you. Did I ever tell you I love you?" He kissed me.

"Every day of the week, and twice on Sundays," I told him. He was chuffed to bits.

He gave me my present. It was a break back to Rome, where we went before.

After Christmas, we took a ride on his bike. Dad and Carole kept an eye on the kids.

We drove to the coast and stopped for lunch. People had done a double take at us, sitting at the table, holding hands. We were completely different. Then walked along the beach, hand in hand.

Mack was working on his computer, on the dining room table. "What you doing?" I asked, passing him a coffee.

He grinned. "You'll have to wait and see."

My phone rang. It was Olivia's school.

"Hello, this is Michael Denton." I waved at Mack. "Is Olivia OK? We'll be right there."

"What's that all about?" Mack said putting his jacket on.

"There's been an incident at her school. She's not hurt." We were worried.

When we got there, Olivia was sat outside the head's office. She had been crying. Mack sat next to her. She hugged him tight. She was shaking. "God, Olivia, honey, what's wrong?"

He looked at me. "Livvy. What's wrong?" I asked. She hugged me tight.

We went to the desk. "Hi. We're Olivia's parents. Mike and Mack."

"I'll let her know you're here," the secretary said kindly.

The head came out. "Hi, I'm Ms Devon. I take it you're Olivia's parents. Come in."

"What the hell is going on? Our daughter is shaking," Mack said.

"She was being bullied by some of the kids 'cause they found out her parents are gay. Don't worry. The kids have been pulled out of school. The kids' parents are being dealt with. I don't and will not tolerate this behaviour. I brought her here to calm her down. Your son Oliver is here too, correct? I'll call for him too. Take them home. Give them a couple of days. I'll have someone come talk to her. I'm sorry."

"You OK, Olivia?" I asked her.

"They were being mean about you both. That made me upset." She was crying.

Oliver came in and saw Olivia crying. "Olivia. What's wrong?"

"Some kids were being mean," I told him.

"Because you're gay?" Oliver said. I nodded. "Olivia, take no notice. Just remember, we have the best parents ever. Do you know how lucky we are? I don't care that they're gay. I love them. They are jealous of us. We are happy. They're not. Dads? I'm glad you two are my dads. I'm lucky and I love you. Come on, Olivia. I love you too and Fran, Thaddeus and Rae. Can we have pizza please?"

We had tears in our eyes. "Yes, son, you can. Come on," Mack said. "I'm proud of you, son!"

"Same to you with knobs on. The pair of you," he said. "Just remember, Olivia, they're arseholes."

"Language, Ollie," I told him.

"Sorry, Dad. Can we still have pizza?" he said.

"Yes," Mack said. "Come on."

We took them to Pizza Hut. "How you doing, Olivia?" we asked her. "Be honest." I asked her gently.

"I'm OK now, Daddy. They were mean and horrible. It frightened me a lot. At least, I have Libby. I don't care what you are. You know that. Oliver's right. Most of the kids at school have one parent. We're lucky we have two. Sorry, I scared you. I love you. I need a wee," she said.

We took them home. Lydia had Francesca, Thaddeus and Rae.

"Thanks for that," I told her.

"How is she? Poor girl," Lydia said.

"Hi, Auntie Lydia," Olivia said.

"How are you!" She smiled at her.

"I'm OK. I was scared. But not any more. Night, Auntie Lydia." Mack took them to bed.

"You OK, Michael?" Lydia asked me.

I sat at the table. "I will never understand it, Lydia. Shit, Lydia. Our girl was scared." I was hurt. Mack put out his hand on my shoulder. I held it tight. "Our little girl was terrified. She was shaking." I leant forward.

"She's going to be fine. Oliver said the truth," Mack said, running his hand on my back. "Olivia said, most kids have one parent. She was lucky she had two."

Lydia smiled. "Wise words from a six-year-old. You two are good parents. Never forget that. I'll leave you two to it," she said.

"Thanks, Lydia," Mack said.

"That's what's family does," she said and left. Mack and I were quiet for a minute.

"Lydia's right," Mack told me.

"I know. Just hurts that our little girl went through that." I looked at him.

"I'm not little. I'm six. Other people are idiots. They need a kick in the nuts. Can I have a drink, please?" Olivia said.

We laughed. "Come on, you. Drink, then bed," I told her. I looked at Mack who smiled back.

Joel came round the next day. "Hey, can you do me a favour?" he asked

Mack and I.

"What is it?" I asked, putting the paper down.

"I have no idea what to get Lydia for her birthday. I've been leaving hints. What do you get a woman who doesn't ask for anything? I want to do something special for her. Out of the ordinary. She's done so much for me and the kids. She never asks for anything. In all the years I've been with her." He was welling up. Mack and I looked at each other.

"We have a few ideas," Mack said. "I know of the right place. I'll make a call tomorrow."

Mack put a call in to an old mate, who now ran a venue business. He had a place just for the occasion. "All sorted," he said, getting off the phone.

"That was quick," Joel said, surprised.

"I'm a man of many talents," he said, smiling.

I turned to Joel. "Don't let him take over," I whispered and smiled. "He'll make it all girly."

"I heard that," he told me, smiling. "I did a good job organising our wedding vows day."

"Can't argue with that," Joel said. "You two did look good. I could use the help."

That made Mack smile. "You've done it now."

Everything went according to plan. Joel and Mack worked together. A lot of people thought they were together. Mack thought that was funny.

"Lydia. You ready? The car will be here in a minute," Joel said.

"Ready. Where are you taking me?" she asked him. She hates not knowing.

"Wait and see," he replied with a smug look on his face.

"Close your eyes," he said, getting out of the car. She shot him a look. "Lydia Denton." He only said her maiden name when she annoyed him.

"Come on," he said. She opened her eyes. "Happy birthday!"

For once, she said was speechless. "How did you pull this off?" she said.

"I had some help," he said.

She looked our way. "Thank you," she said. I pointed to Mack. "That doesn't surprise me." She hugged us.

She turned to Joel. "You wonderful man. I thought you forgot."

"You never would let me forget. You do so many wonderful things for us. I wanted to do something special for you," he told her.

Oliver had his football. He was about to bounce it.

"Don't even think about it," I told him. His face was a sight. He wanted to play football.

Mack was quiet. "What's up? You did a good job," I told him.

He looked at Joel and Lydia. I looked at them. I read his mind. "You are the biggest idiot. Yes, we are going to be like that. We are now."

He looked at me and smiled. "Always."

The evening went better than expected. Everyone was happy.

"We should do this more often," Mack said.

"Well, Easter's coming up the week after next. Get everyone for a family dinner. I'm not working. I know family's a big deal to you. It is to me too. You know that. Don't tell Lydia. You are the glue to this family as well. We'll never lose what we got, Mack. It's too important."

He just looked at me.

Francesca said, "Dad, you're a softie, right?"

Mack nodded.

"Can I have that apple pie and custard?" she asked.

"No, Fran. It's bed time," I told her.

"Those kids have got you wrapped around their fingers," I told Mack.

"Can't help it." He was smiling. "And on that note, kids, bed, come on. Say good night to Granddad and Carole."

Mack came down. "Finally, peace and quiet. What time's 'Gogglebox' on?"

"I'm recording it," I told him.

Carole started laughing. "You two are funny. I'm glad I made you parents. How long have you been married?"

"Almost eleven years. Best eleven years," Mack said.

"It's been interesting." I looked at him.

"Did you know straight away that Mack was the one?" she asked.

"Yes. In an instant," I told her.

"Same as. We knew there and then, didn't we?" he said.

"I fell in love with him as soon as I saw him," I told her.

"I'm the romantic type," Mack said, winking at me. I just shook my head.

"Stay the night. It's been a long day. The spare room's free," Mack told them. I started yawning.

I got called in the office at work. "Michael, come in. Don't worry. Nothing to worry about," my boss Beverley said. "How's it going for you?"

"Really enjoying it. Where's this going?" I was confused.

"Glad you asked. Congrats. You've been promoted to charge nurse. I'm aware of the kids. Same hours. It'll start when you come back after Easter."

When I got home, I couldn't talk. Mack was cooking dinner. I sat at the table. He had a sip of beer and looked at me.

"What's wrong?"

"Give me a beer. I've been promoted," I said

"That's good news. Is it?" Mack passed my beer. He threw the tea towel over his shoulder.

"Yes. It is." I took a sip of beer.

"So, what's the problem? I can't see one." He smiled.

Olivia walked in. "Hey, Dad. I want to be an entomologist when I grow up. We did science today, and I knew all the names of the bugs. Ryan Jenkins called me a know-it-all. I called him an idiot. I think bugs are interesting. Can I have drink please?" Olivia took her drink. "When's dinner ready? I'm hungry."

Mack and I smiled at each other. "Where does she know all this science stuff from?" Mack said.

I shook my head. "I have no idea."

"Kids, dinner!" Mack yelled.

I got Rae. She smiled her face off when she saw me.

"Daddy. Missed you."

"Missed you too, kiddo." I told her.

We spoke about what they wanted to be when they were older. We knew what Olivia and Oliver wanted to be. "Fran, what about you? What do you want to do?"

"I want to be an architect," she told us while eating her peas.

We got smart kids. "Thaddeus, what about you?" I asked, sipping my beer.

"I want to be a doctor, and help people."

"Oliver, what do you think Rae will be when she grows up?" Mack asked.

"She looks like a lawyer," he said. As usual, he was the first one to finish his dinner.

When we cleared up, the kids were watching TV. Olivia and Oliver were arguing over the remote. "I want my Blue Planet on. It's got bugs on. It's about the poisonous frogs. Their poison can attack your nervous system in seconds," she said.

"I want the football on," he said.

"Right. No telly. Find a book," I said.

"Really? A book!" Olivia said.

"Yes. Go," I said.

Mack was laughing.

"You're no help," I told him. "You're supposed to help me."

Thaddeus came up to Mack with a book. "Please read me *Thomas* before bed."

"Come on, son." They went and sat in the living room. Mack had started wearing glasses.

"We've got smart kids," Mack said, clearing up the toys. "They take after you."

"Come off it, Oliver takes after you. Give yourself some credit," I told him. "They look up to you. They love the outdoors. You're always there when Ollie plays footie. You're always in their corner."

"True. Can't imagine my life without them." Mack sat in his chair. I gave him a coffee.

"I was thinking of us taking the kids out for the day. What do you think?" I sat opposite him. He smiled.

"What's so funny?" I said, sipping my drink.

"Just remembering a conversation I had with Matthew. How it changed from being in Afghanistan to now having kids and being knackered by nine thirty. I wouldn't change it for the world. I love it. How about the Natural History Museum?" he told me.

I nodded. Mack got up to get another drink, he heard our song and held his hand out. "Fancy a dance, Mr Denton?"

"Thought you'd never ask," I said.

We took the kids to the museum. Olivia came out will these facts no one knew. Halfway through, my phone rang. It was Carole. It was about Dad. He was in hospital.

We rushed down there. "Where is my dad? What happened?"

She smiled. "You need to ask him!"

"Dad, what the bloody hell happened?" Mack was standing behind me.

"Well, um. I pulled something while we were doing something." He was embarrassed.

Mack got it and burst out laughing. "Your dirty, randy old bugger. This is brilliant."

"Really, Michael, could you roll your eyes any louder?" Dad said.

"Bloody hell. I thought there was something wrong. I don't want to know about your bedroom activities."

"Come on, let's go. I'm so embarrassed," I said. Mack was still laughing. "Mack!" I said.

We went home. "At least he's happy," Mack said over a scotch. "Do you think Simon wants to hear about our sex life?"

"True. It's my dad. It's weird," I smiled. "God, I hope we're not like that when we're old."

"I do." Mack put his drink down. He looked at me. "I'm looking forward to the day when we're his age, when we'll still be together like that. I know we are close, but that closeness is important to me." Mack was serious. He never told me that.

"I feel the same as well." I smiled. Mack smiled too.

"Fancy an early night?"

"Come on. We'll have to be quiet," I told him.

I phoned Dad the next morning. "How you doing?"

"I'm OK. Embarrassed," he said.

"You, embarrassed? What if it were me in there with an injury?" I said.

"Point taken. Anyway, we still on for Easter Weekend, like we used to do when you were a boy?" Dad said.

"Yes. The kids are going love it. Can't wait to see their faces. What time you coming round?"

"Eight in the morning," Dad said. "See you then?"

I hung up and put the kettle on. Mack came down in the famous holey t-shirt, scratching his head.

"Who was that?" he asked, making toast.

"Dad. He's coming here at eight tomorrow morning." I gave him his coffee. "To do the stuff the kids love, the clues, everything." He smiled. "They love it. Here, got something for you. "I gave him a present.

He sat at the table and opened it. He smiled at me with tears in his eyes. It was a photo of us and the kids. My dad took it. Mack loved photos of the family.

"I love it. Thank you."

We heard the kids come down. Francesca piped her head around the door. "You two, stay there for a minute."

"What you lot up to?" Mack asked her.

"Wait and find out!" She smiled and left. The present was a DVD.

"Play it," Oliver told us.

"Who helped you do this?" I asked, putting it in.

"Grandad and Auntie Lydia," Francesca said.

We watched the DVD. It was a compilation of when we got the kids and of Mack and I being happy. At the end, the kids waving saying "We love you."

Mack and I were shocked. Then we started crying. It was amazing.

"Why?" Mack said through the tears.

"Because we are lucky." Olivia stood in front of us. "We have the best dads in the world. We love our funny family. You two are awesome. Most of my friends have one parent, but we have two."

Mack and I started crying again. Thaddeus came up to us and placed his hands on our faces.

"Don't cry, kind Daddies. Where's Thomas?" he walked off.

We didn't see Lydia standing there. "See, God blessed you two with a wonderful family. I'm nicking some milk; we ran out again."

"Why don't you go to the shop?" Mack said.

"Can't be arsed," she replied in her dressing gown. "What time are we coming round tomorrow?"

"Ten," I said. "Bring some milk."

"Cheeky bastard. Don't forget, dinner at ours tonight. Takeaway," she said.

The kids went "Yeah!"

Rae walked up to me. "Daddy?"

"Yes, darling?" I picked her up.

"I want be a nurse like you. Can I have a cat?"

I laughed.

Mack laughed too. "At this rate, we're going to have a zoo in here. A dog, fish, cats."

"Don't forget the bugs!" Olivia shouted.

"Bugs! Who wants lunch?" Mack shouted.

We put our hands up. I went and helped him. He stood there and shook his head.

"Come here," I told him.

Francesca came in. "Get a room! Can I have some Doritos, please?"

"They take after you. Their smart arses," I told him, getting the Doritos. He laughed.

While we were at Lydia's, out of nowhere, Olivia said, "Did you know that there are over three thousand species of Stick insects. They're mainly in the tropics. The male can live up to a month and the female a year. Pass the curry, Uncle Joel."

Joel passed her the curry. He looked at Mack and me. "What the hell? Where did she learn this stuff?"

"Have no idea," I told him. "She's a walking encyclopaedia. She's seven and really smart. They all are. Fran wants to be an architect. Rae wants be a nurse. Ollie wants to play for Arsenal. Thaddeus wants be a doctor."

"Why bugs though?" Joel asked Olivia.

"Because they're different. It's interesting, Uncle Joel. Just like us," Olivia told him.

"So, we're bugs now!" he replied back.

"No, Uncle Joel. I mean, we're different. Our family is different. Can I have saag aloo, please?" she asked.

We all looked at each other and smiled. She hit the nail on the head.

"You're a smart girl," Lydia said.

"I know, Auntie Lydia. Sometimes, it hurts," she told her.

"I need a beer. Who wants one?" Joel asked us.

We put our hands up. We were at the table talking, while the kids were watching TV.

"We've come a long way, haven't we," Lydia said.

"Yes, we have," Joel replied. "None of us are the same as before, especially you, Mack."

"What do you mean?" he said, sipping his beer.

"You were this confident guy. You still are. But you were scared to admit how you truly felt. You were scared. Then you and Michael got together. That changed. You looked lost and afraid," Lydia told him.

"I know. I think we all were. We were running from everything. That was then. This is now." He took my hand. "I am at peace, now. At long last, I have a family I can count on."

"Good. You're making coffee," Lydia told him. "What is all that noise in there?"

We went to see what was going on. The kids were singing and dancing to Pharrell Williams' 'Happy'. They didn't see us, it was funny How they were doing their own moves, singing away.

"The next generation," I said. Lydia and Mack stood taking photos. The kids noticed us standing there.

"Hey, not fair," Alice said.

Mack said, "Come on, kids, bed. Busy day tomorrow."

"Do we have to?" Francesca asked.

"Yes. It's the treasure hunt tomorrow, for all of you."

We got home. "I had fun today, Dad," Olivier said getting into bed. "Can't wait for tomorrow. Love you. Night."

"Night, son," Mack said, smiling.

"Dad?" Oliver said.

"Yes, son?" Mack said.

"When I grow up, I want to be just like you."

Oliver fell asleep. That made Mack's day.

"I heard that," I told Mack while getting the food ready for tomorrow. "You should be proud."

"I am. Really proud. I never thought I would hear those words. Wow." He was helping with the vegetables. "Where's the lamb and chicken?"

"Fridge.," I said. He went to the fridge and saw the cold bottle of his favourite beer in there. "Wow. Last time I had this was just after we got married. The first time. I've been looking forever. Mike, you are a genius."

"I got a whole case, out back." I stood at the counter.

"You never cease to amaze me. After all these years…" he said.

"Because I like to keep you on your toes. Now where's the chicken and lamb?" I smiled.

"Shit. I'm cooking tomorrow. You know I like cooking," he said.

"I'm not going to argue. Mack?" I asked him.

"Yer?" he said, sipping his beer.

"Fancy a weekend away?" I asked.

He grinned and winked. "I like the sound of that."

"Good. I booked a holiday apartment by the coast next month. Take the bike. Four days, you and me." I was glad he said that.

"I will never understand why you love me so much, after all these years," Mack told me.

"Because you are the most honest, decent human being I've ever met. Now can I have a beer?" I said.

"You can have a beer. Then bed." He winked.

The next morning, the kids were up early. They came in and jumped on our bed. "Treasure hunt! Treasure hunt!"

"Breakfast, the works," Thaddeus said.

"Then what?" I asked them.

"Family walk, to the park," Rae said. "Then treasure hunt."

Dad came at eight with Carole.

"Your first Denton tradition," Olivia told her. "Carole, thank you for making Grandad happy. He's a good guy." She finished eating her bacon.

When we came back, they went crazy for the treasure hunt. "This is brilliant," Thaddeus said. They got small little pressies.

Lydia came to us at twelve. "Maggie, Alice and Alfie, look in the living room. There's something in there for you all." They went in and saw their pressies. Alice got her paint and Easley. Alfie got his book and Maggie got her stereo.

"You two spoil our kids like mad," Joel said.

"Hey, they're our only nieces and nephews Mike and I are going to have, let us do it every now and then," Mack told him. "Hey, help me with dinner." Joel followed

"Saskia's parents think it's strange we say prayers before dinner," Francesca said.

"What did you say?" Joel said.

"I told them that we do it because we are thankful for what we have. And we are lucky to have what we've got," Francesca replied, eating her peas.

"Uncle Joel?" Francesca asked him.

"Yes, baby girl?"

"For an uncle, you're pretty cool," she told him.

Joel had look on his face. "Hey, Lydia, you hear that? I'm cool."

Lydia just shook her head. "You'll have to watch your head on the way out. It may not fit through the door."

"Maggie. What film shall we watch?" Mack asked.

"Definitely not 'Frozen'. You cry like a girl. How about 'Avengers End Game'?" she asked.

We all agreed. "Looking forward to this," Lydia said.

"Why?" Joel said.

"Jeremy Renner," was all she said, smiling.

"Dirty moo," I said, giving her a glass of wine.

After Easter, everything went back to normal. I started my new role as charge nurse. Mack got more work. Then we started planning Dad's engagement party.

"Dad, have the party here," I told him. "Be easier."

"Thanks, son," he replied.

"What's wrong?" I asked him.

"Just nervous, that's all. Been a long time," he smiled.

"Give over. I like Carole. She's done so much for Mack and me. She's a breath of fresh air." I sat next to him.

"Do you miss your mum?" he asked, taking his tea.

"'Course, I do. You know that. But you've got to move on. You have to be happy. Mum would be happy." I patted his arm.

"When did you get so wise?" he told me.

"Learned from the best, old man." I smiled at him.

"Cheeky sod. What time you and Mack leaving" he asked.

"In an hour," Mack said, patting my dad's shoulder. "You going to be OK with the kids?"

"Yes. Lydia coming round with her lot in a bit. So, no worries."

"We'll be back Sunday," I said, getting up.

"What you got planned?" Dad asked us.

Mack grinned.

"Wish I never asked," Dad replied.

"Not just that," I said, smiling. "Haven't been to the coast for ages. Not since Christmas. Want to see the ocean."

We left when Lydia came round. Mack was in his element on his bike.

"Wow. You've got taste. Well, you married me twice. This place is amazing," he told me. "It's massive in here."

"Well, the truth is, it's ours," I told him, smiling.

"Fuck off. You're kidding, right?" he said, dropping his bag on the sofa.

"No, I'm not. You're not mad?" I asked.

"No way. The kids are going to love it. Especially in the summer." He just looked at me.

"Well, I like to keep it interesting." I took his hand.

"No kidding. I'm hungry," he said. "Let's go get dinner, before we do anything else," I told him.

We had a nice meal. People didn't bat an eye when they saw us walk in, holding hands. They were surprised when we ordered a couple of beers.

We walked along the beach. "I can get used to this," Mack said.

"Used to what?" I asked..

"All of this. Getting away from it all. I can see why you love it." He looked at me.

"That's why I did it. It's important to me that we do things like this. The kids need it too. You know. They need to have change as well. Get them out and about. Being here will do us a world of good," I said.

"You sound like your dad. Come on, don't know about you, I'm feeling a bit tired." He winked at me.

Sunday came round to fast. We couldn't wait to see the kids. When they saw, they came running out to see us.

"We should go away more often," Mack said, laughing.

Olivia said in a matter-of-fact tone, "Dad, I've decided I want to learn a new language."

"Really?" Mack said, smiling.

"Yes, sweetheart. Come on. All of us need to talk," we told them.

They looked worried. Francesca looked scared.

"Hey, hey. Listen," Mack said. We could see they were scared. "We love each other, like you wouldn't believe," Mack told them.

We said together, "We brought a family home, by the sea."

"For us. So, when summer comes around, we can go there. That's what we wanted to tell you," I told them.

"Cool! I can play football on the beach," Oliver said.

"I can find bugs!" Olivia said.

Francesca was quiet. She got up and walked in the garden.

We went after her. "Francesca. Talk to us. What's wrong?" Mack asked her. She started crying.

"What's going on?" I asked, hugging her. "Fran?"

"Promise you won't divorce." She wiped her eyes.

"Promise. Where's this coming from?" Mack asked, wiping her hair from her face.

"Three of my friends' parents are getting one. They hate each other. I couldn't bear it if I lost you and you hated each other." She was scared.

"Let me tell you something," Mack told her. "When I first met your dad, I knew he was the one, just like that. I loved him then. I love him now. After all these years. Your dad is my life. I can't be without him."

She looked at me. "Same as. I love your dad very much. I can't be without him either. We will never leave each other. We can't bear to be apart," I told her. "You OK now, Fran?"

We hugged her tight. She nodded. She had her favourite toy with her. Her dog called Digby. She had it whenever she was worried.

"Wow," I said. "Our kids thought we were divorcing."

"It's sad that's what they were thinking." Mack was speechless.

We looked at Francesca. She was cuddling Digby.

"Mack, let's take her out. Ease her mind a bit more," I started.

"Go on, take her out. I'll be fine. Kids are watching TV. Go," Dad told us when we asked him.

"Francesca. Get your shoes and coat. We're going out. Bring Digby," Mack told her.

We took her to see the horses. Her face lit up like Christmas morning. She was in her element. Afterwards, we took her to get ice cream. Then the park.

"Thanks, Dads. I'm sorry."

"Don't be. We told you, it's not going to happen to us," I said.

"You sure?" Fran said.

"Yes," Mack said. "Your dad and I are soul mates."

"What's that?" She was confused.

"When two people are meant to be together, for the rest of our lives. We are stronger as a unit rather than on our own. I can't live without your dad," Mack told her.

"Really!" She was smiling.

"Yes, really. I can't be without your dad, too." I told her.

"I feel better now," Francesca said. "Can I go on the slide before we go home?"

"How did it go?" Dad said.

"Good. Really good," I said, smiling. "Dad, thank you. Thanks for everything you do for us and the kids." I hugged him tight.

"Son, I wouldn't have it any other way. See you later," Dad told me.

While I was at work. I got my next patient. It was Matthew. "Oh shit," he said.

"Hello to you too!" I told him.

Lucinda looked confused. "You two know each other?"

"Ah, yes," I said. "This is Mack's best friend and he is my kid's godfather. So, what's up?"

"My ankle. I think I've broken it," he said.

"What did you do?" I asked, looking at it.

"Football. I went in for a dive. Shit, that hurt. You this tough at home? Don't answer that."

"Right, going to send for an X-ray. Your knee looks swollen too. Let's have a look. Lucinda, take him, please. Matthew, I'm going to call your wife, OK? And Mack," I told him.

His wife Anna turned up. "Michael, is he OK?"

"Yes. Looks like he broke his ankle and bruised his knee. We'll know more when the X-ray comes back.

Mack came in. He had been in a meeting and had his best suit on. Lucinda was dribbling. "Who's that?" she said to me.

"Lucinda," I said. "That is Mack, my husband."

"You lucky prick." She was envious. She watched as I went up to him, hugged and kiss him. Sarah came over and stood next to Lucinda.

"Who's that handsome devil in the suit?"

"Michael's husband!" she said.

"So unfair. Does he have a brother?" she asked.

"Excuse me. Can you take me to X-ray?" Matthew said.

"Shit. Sorry. Come on then," Lucinda said.

He came back. He had broken his ankle and his knee was just swollen. "Right, plaster on that ankle. Six to eight weeks in cast. Rest," I told him.

"I'll make sure he rests," Anna said.

"So will I," Mack said. He looked at me. "What time do you finish?"

"Ten minutes. We have to pick Ollie up on the way home," I told him.

"OK. I'll meet you out there. Ladies," Mack said, smiling.

"You two are terrible," I said.

"Dad, you two coming to my game Sunday morning?" Oliver said, getting in the car.

"Yes, why?" I asked. "We always do."

"Ryan's back on the team. His dad's a twat," Oliver said.

"Ollie, language," Mack said, driving.

"Well, he is. Ryan's dad called you a couple of queers, whatever that means, and said that you shouldn't have kids because of that. I don't understand," Oliver said.

"Does he know what your dad and I look like?" Mack said.

"No. Why?" Oliver said.

"No reason," Mack said.

"What are you planning?" I asked, getting out of the car at home.

"Don't worry, I'm not going to do anything stupid," Mack said, getting Oliver's bag.

"That's what I'm worried about," I said. Mack smiled and hugged me round the shoulder.

Sunday came round. "Dad?" Olivier said to Mack.

"Yes, son?" he said, putting his football bag in the car.

"Don't do anything stupid. But I'm OK if you punch him," Oliver said, getting in the back. Mack laughed.

I said, "Olivier!"

"What? You and Dad have always said to us to speak the truth and to be honest, within reason," Olivier said, putting his seat belt on.

"He's got you there," Mack told me.

I couldn't argue with that.

"That's Ryan's dad." Oliver nodded to the guy in the black jacket. Mack nodded.

The match went well. Oliver's team won. Two—one. Mack clocked Ryan's dad. "Give us a sec," Mack told us.

"Hi. You're Ryan's dad?" Mack asked him.

"Yes. Your boy on the team?" he asked.

"Yes. Yes, he is." Mack smiled. "I'm Oliver's dad. There is his other dad," he said, pointing to me.

The penny dropped. Before Ryan's dad could say anything, Mack said, "Listen to me. My boy came home upset after he heard you talking shit about me. Now, whilst I don't like people like you, I can live with that. You homophobic prick. My boy, however, is a different story. If I hear from him that you've been talking shit about me and my husband, and Ollie gets upset, and I mean, upset, this is going to be a whole different conversation. I won't be so polite. Now, do you understand me?" Mack said.

Ryan's dad nodded. "Good," Mack said. "Glad we understand each other. Enjoy the rest of the day."

"Right, come on, Ollie. Mike, let's go," Mack said, scooping Ollie over his shoulder and holding my hand. Ollie laughed.

"What's for dinner, Dad?" he asked Mack.

"Beef and all the trimmings," Mack said.

"Why didn't you punch him?" Oliver asked.

Mack looked at him in the mirror. "Listen, Ollie. Violence does not solve anything. That conversation worked. What would punching him solve? Nothing. It wouldn't achieve anything. Talking is the best way. That's what your dad and I do. Talk about everything. What do we say?" he said.

"Truth and honesty is key. No lies," Oliver said.

"That's right, son," Mack told him.

"But why do people dislike those who are different?" Oliver always asked good questions.

"Don't know, son. The way of the world. But be true to yourself and others. Now, let's get you home and cleaned up." Mack was good with his kids. I just smiled.

"Dads?" Oliver said to Mack and me.

"Yes, son?" Mack replied.

"I love you both," Oliver said looking out the window.

"We love you too," I told him.

On the way home, it was quiet. Not in a bad way. Just thinking.

"Ollie, go take a shower before lunch, please," I told him. "How the hell did we get deep-thinking kids like ours? They are so caring, thoughtful and wonderful. Not caring about what others think," I said, getting the potatoes out of the cupboard.

"Because that's how we wanted to raise them," Mack said, putting the oven on. "Being independent thinkers, speaking their minds."

Rae came in, holding her toy dog Jonas

"Hey, Angel girl. What's up?" I asked her.

"When can I get that cat? I'd like a tortoise shell one called Olaf." She was in a matter-of-fact tone. "I am nearly four."

"Soon. Rae. OK? Family film night. Your turn, Rae. What shall we watch?" Mack asked her, putting the beef in.

"Despicable Me Two," she said. "I like the song 'Happy'."

"That's what we are watching." I smiled at her.

She smiled and hugged me. "Can I do drawing, please?"

"OK. For a while," Mack said. She was happy.

The doorbell rang. "I'll get it," I told Mack. It was my dad. He seemed upset.

"Dad. What's wrong?" I asked, going to the kitchen.

"Rae, be a love and go in the living room. Your dad and I need to talk to Granddad," I told her. Off she went.

"Carole left on Friday. She's not coming back," he said.

Mack gave him a beer. "What happened?" Mack asked, sitting on the chair.

"She went back to her husband. End off." Dad was upset.

"Wow. That's cold," I said. "Sorry." I looked at Mack, who read my mind.

"Simon. Stay here for a while. Not asking. You need family round you. OK?" Mack said. "Shit, potatoes are boiling."

"All clean," Oliver said. "Granddad. Are you OK?"

"I will be. How was football?" he asked. "We won. Dad had a word with Ryan's dad. He was being an arsehole," Olivier said.

"Language, Oliver," Mack said.

"You've said worse," Oliver said. Dad laughed. "When's dinner ready? I'm starving."

"Soon," Mack said. "Go and watch TV for a bit."

"Smart kid," Dad said. "Smart arse mouth, like you, Mack."

Mack went into work the next day to find Matthew working. "What the hell!" Mack said. "Three weeks. What's wrong with you?"

"I'm bored. Needed to do something," he replied.

"If Mike saw you, he'll go mad," Mack said, getting a coffee.

"Don't tell him then," Matthew said, going through the paperwork. "I'm going in an hour, anyway. What's this?" He found something on Miranda. "Looks like she's gone out of business. Shame." "What are you doing for Michael's birthday on Saturday?" Matthew asked, tiding up.

"Have no idea," Mack said.

"That's not like you," was the reply. "You two OK?"

"Yes, we are. I want to do something special, different."

Matthew grinned. "I got an idea. He's working Saturday morning, right, for a couple of hours?"

"Yes, why?" Mack asked. "For God's sake. Surprise him at work," he said.

The penny dropped. He was thinking about how to do it. "Got it."

"Finally." Matthew was relieved. "Come on. Take me home, before Anna kills me."

After he took Matthew home, Mack went to see Lucinda and Sarah. He told them about his plan. They promised to be part of the plan, and keep quiet.

Saturday came around. I got ready for work. I was sure Mack had forgotten about today. "I finish at twelve."

"OK. See you later," Mack said. "Kids, get ready, we're going shopping."

Off I went. Not in a good mood.

"Hey. What's up?" Sarah asked.

"Mack forgot my birthday. After all these years," I said.

"Don't be daft. He's potty over you," she told me.

An hour before my shift ended, Lucinda came in. "Michael, come with me. You need to deal with this. Now!"

I ran to the entrance. "Stop," she said. "Close your eyes."

"Lucinda, I haven't got time for this." I was impatient.

I heard the music. It was our song. "Open your eyes," she said.

Mack was standing there, in his best suit, smiling. Everyone was there watching.

"Happy Birthday, Mike." He took my hand. Everyone clapped. Even the patients. Lucinda and Sarah were crying.

"Come on," Mack said. "The kids have surprises."

I got my coat and looked at the girls. "You two are terrible."

They just smiled.

Mack had brought the bike. The kids were singing 'Happy birthday' when I got in at home.

I had to get up and leave the room.

"What's wrong?" Mack asked.

"You've given me so much. What can I ever give you in return?" I asked.

"Just you. Always. I thought I was the hormonal one," Mack told me. He hugged and kissed me. Fran saw us.

"Not again. Do you two never stop kissing?" she asked.

"No. We'll never stop kissing," I told her.

"Your too old for that!" she said and walked off.

"Are we old?" I asked Mack. "Never. Not for anything," he told me. "Come on. We haven't had your favourite cake," he said.

"Dads?" Olivia said.

"Yes?" we said, eating cake.

"On Friday, can you come to school as we have a day where our parents tell everyone what they do?" Olivia asked.

"Yes. We can," Mack said. "Right, bed. Come on, you lot. Past your bed time."

She started laughing. "Stop tickling me."

They followed him. I sat back down with my beer.

"He loves being a dad, doesn't he?" Joel said, smiling.

"More than you know. He's a good dad." I was smiling.

At that second, Francesca ran in with Digby the rabbit, jumped on me and hugged me. "I love you, Daddy. Happy birthday."

The next few days were busy at work. It was mayhem. Mack was busy too at work. He picked me up Thursday after work.

"You look familiar. Do I know you?" I said to Mack, laughing.

"God, I feel the same. Hey, Sarah. How are you?"

"Good. Thanks," she said. "Right, let's get you home. We've got an early start tomorrow. Olivia's school," Mack said.

"Shit. Forgot," I said.

The day at Olivia's school went well. Just as we got out, we got a call from the hospital. It was my dad. He had had a heart attack.

"Where is he?" I was in bits. "He's in recovery. He was lucky. The doctors are keeping him for a while," she said.

He was asleep. I came out and cried, then I went back in and sat with him.

"Hey, Dad. How are you?" I sat next to him.

"Well, I've had better days. I'm going to be fine."

The doctor came back to see Dad. "Hey, Michael. I didn't realise that he was your father. Mr Denton, this heart attack was a warning. You are going to take it easy. You'll have to take medication, change your diet."

"Dad, I'll let you rest. See you later," "I told him.

I got home and sat on the sofa. Mack came in. "How is he?"

"Not good. But alive. I'm scared. That man has been through so much. Done so much." I held my head in my hands.

"We're going to look at after him," Mack told me. "He's the closest person I've got to a father."

"How did the kids take it?" I asked him, yawning.

"Not well. They cried. It affected Francesca hard. She hasn't let that dog go." Mack was sad. He had tears in his eyes.

Just at that moment, the kids came in.

"Is Grandad going to be OK?" Thaddeus asked me.

"Yes. He's gonna be fine. With a lot of rest and help from us all," I told them. Francesca didn't look convinced.

"Right, all of you up here," I told them. "Fran, come here."

They all sat on the sofa with us. Fran sat in my lap. "Granddad hurt his heart. But, it is going to be OK. Fran, Grandad is going to be fine. I'm just sad that he's in hospital. So, we are going to help him get better."

"Will he be home soon?" Rae asked.

"When the doctor says so. He has to do as he's told. He's never liked that. Fran, he's going to be fine." I was crying.

"Daddy," Fran said. "Here. You need him more than me at the moment." She gave me Digby. "Can I have some breakfast?"

"Come on. Let's get you fed. Get some sleep, Mike. I've got this," Mack told me.

Malek came in. "My dearest Michael and Lydia. I am here to help. Simon's a good man. He who is strong of heart, will weather the storm. I saw Simon.

I told him I shall stay at his. With our help, his strength will rise. I know it's hard now, but Allah has plans for him. It is not his time. Allah says so."

Oliver walked up to Malek. "When you next pray to Allah, will you thank him from me for looking after Granddad for me? It means a lot that Allah is helping him. He's nice."

"Oliver, I will. Allah hears all our prayers. He has heard you, my child," Malek told him.

"Cool. Stay for breakfast. Dad has put the kettle on. You can tell me more about Allah," he said.

"Michael and Mack. Your children are full of wonder and heart. You are good parents. You are raising them well. Your children will always be in Allah's heart", he told Mack and I.

"Your tea's getting cold," Oliver shouted.

Malek smiled. "I have been summoned by a seven-year-old."

"See," Mack said, smiling. "Dad's going to be looked after. He ain't got a choice, with Malek moving in."

Dad came home three days later. We were all there.

"Anyone would think this was the Spanish inquisition, with you lot here," he told us. "Ah, shut up, and do as you're told," I told him.

"You tell him, Dad." Thaddeus said, giving me a high five.

Malek turned to us. "I'm taking him for a walk now."

"Do I get a say?" Dad asked. We just looked at him.

"Take that as a no." They left.

"Malek's good for your dad," Mack told me. "Maybe they'll get married." He was laughing.

"Wouldn't be surprised. I was with them in Tesco's yesterday. They were arguing over what to have for dinner. You should have seen the look some of the people gave them. It was funny. I heard one say a white guy and a Muslim man as a couple," I told him, smiling.

Mack was working when Matthew came in. "Cast off, I see," Mack said, peering over his glasses.

"Thank god. It was driving me mad. How's Simon?"

"Good. Malek's been a godsend. I swear they're like an old married couple. Olivia accidently called him grandad at the park yesterday. It was funny. People looked and stared."

Matthew smiled. "How's Adam?"

I'm fine. Busy. I have news for the both of you. Rachel, they're both here." Rachel came out smiling.

"We're getting married, and we're having a baby."

"Congratulations!" Mack said. He was getting emotional.

"Not again. God help us," Matthew said.

Rachel looked confused. "What do you mean?"

"Mack may look as hard as nuts. But in reality, he's in a big girl's blouse. When he and Michael got married, he cried for two hours." Matthew grinned.

"You embarrassing git," Mack told him.

"You're welcome," he said.

Rachel laughed. Mack told her and Adam, "I'll talk to Mike, see if you want your engagement party at ours."

"Thank you," Rachel said. "Want a coffee, you two?"

"No, thanks, Rachel. I'm taking him home." Mack pointed to Matthew, "Then I have to pick up Rae from a friend's party."

Adam chuckled.

"What's so funny?" Mack said, putting his coat on.

"You. You're not the same. You've changed. In a good way," he said.

"Why does everyone say that?" Mack said.

"Because it's true," Matthew said. "Come on, let's get Rae before she tells you off."

When she saw Matthew, she smiled. "Uncle Matthew. How's your ankle?" she said, holding Digby.

"Daddy, I'm hungry. What's for dinner?" she hugged Mack.

"Fish and chips OK?" Mack told her.

She was happy.

When they got home, there was fighting and arguing. "What the hell is going on in here?" Mack shouted.

That shut them up. They were arguing over the remote. "Give it to me. Now! Get a book. Not a peep," he said.

I walked in. "What's up? Lydia, Mack."

"Sorry about that," Lydia said.

"You OK?" Mack said.

"I'm OK. Just really tired," she said.

"Lydia. No lies. Come on," I told her.

"I think I may be pregnant again," she said.

96

"That's good news?" Mack looked confused.

"It is. But what if Joel doesn't want another child? I'm getting old. Really old. Look at me." She was really crying. "I was going to do a test but the kids started mucking about."

"Do you have the test on you now?" I asked. She nodded.

"Go and take it. Go on," I said. "Go and get Joel."

"Is Lydia OK? Kids, go in the living room," Joel told them.

Lydia came down, crying. "Shit, Lydia."

"I'm pregnant, Joel." She buried her head in his shoulder.

"Lydia Green. I couldn't be happier. It's going to be OK."

"You sure?" she asked. He nodded yes.

"It's like the mating season round here," Mack said. "Adam and Rachel are having a baby and getting married," he said.

"Double celebration," Joel said. "Maggie, Alice and Alfie, come here. Mum's having a baby."

"Please, be a boy, please be a boy," Alfie said.

Maggie wasn't happy. "Maggie Anne Green. What wrong?" Lydia said. She was crying. "When the baby comes, you won't love me any more."

"Hey, you listen to me, baby girl," Joel said. He was getting upset. "You are the most amazing girl ever, like Alice. I remember when you were born. You had these big brown eyes. I held you and you just looked at me. You stole my breath. When the twins came along, you helped your mum and I. Man, you're just like your mum. I'm proud you're my little girl. We love you more than life itself."

Maggie flung her arms around him. "Love you, Daddy."

"Love you, too."

Maggie went to Lydia.

"Love you, Maggie," Lydia told her. Maggie hugged her. She then kissed Lydia's stomach. "Hey, little one. I'm Maggie, your big sister. You're going to have a good life."

That was it. We were all in tears. "Wow," I said. We wiped our eyes and had a beer. Except Lydia.

Mack had an important job on. He had his vest on. He could tell I wasn't happy. "I'll be OK," he said.

"Last time you had one of them on, you got shot, remember? Hate those bloody things." I left the bedroom.

"Mike. I know you hate them. But sometimes, I have to. It's not all the time." He tried to convince me. "You're such a worrier."

He proved me right, when I got a call from the hospital. Mack had an accident. Lydia kept an eye on the kids.

"I'm OK. I'm OK," he said, sitting up.

"You're an arsehole. What happened? You don't tell me, I'll find out. Talk," I said.

"A guy had too much to drink at this swanky party. Went to stop him, he stabbed me. It's not that bad." He winced.

Flinn, the nurse I worked once or twice, came in "Hey, Michael. How do you know," he looked at the chart, "Mackenzie Denton?" he asked.

"He's my husband. How bad is it?" I was mad.

"Not that bad. Just needs cleaning and twelve stitches," Flinn said.

"Told you. You never listen," Mack said. "The kids OK? Shit, they must be worried."

"They don't know. They were in bed when I got the call. Lydia is with them." I sat down. Mack looked at me.

"Sorry, Mike. Didn't mean to frighten you." He saw how worried I was. I looked at him.

"It's OK." I tried to smile.

I got Mack home. He was a bit sore.

"Bloody hell, Mack," Lydia said. "You had us worried."

He sat at the kitchen table. "I'm OK, Lydia. It's not as bad as it looks."

"But next time?" She handed him a coffee.

The kids came down and saw Mack. "Daddy," Olivia said. "Are you OK? You poor thing."

The others said the same thing, except Oliver. He was quiet, which was not like him.

"Oliver. Talk to me," Mack told him.

"Don't you leave me, Dad." He was upset.

"Come here, son," he told Oliver. "Look at me."

Oliver did as he was told. "I'll never leave. This was an accident. Yes, I had stitches and was in hospital. But I will always come home to you."

"Why do you do your job?" he asked, wiping his eyes.

"Because I like it. Sometimes, things go wrong. But I'm careful. You ask Matthew and Jacob." Mack looked at him with a smile.

"I want to be like you when I grow up. But I don't want to lose my dad. Please be careful." Oliver hugged him.

"I will. Kids, listen. Me and your dad will always be here for you. You guys are everything to us. You're not going to lose us. Ever. Understand?" he said, with Oliver in his lap.

Before they said anything, Lydia burst out crying. "That's lovely."

Fran looked at me. "Is she crazy?"

"No. She's having a baby." I smiled at her.

She asked Lydia. "How do you do it?"

"I just do. It's hard work. But I love my kids." She rubbed her stomach.

"I'm nervous. I'm having just one," she told Lydia.

"It's natural. I'm nervous. I've got four. But it's so worth it." Lydia smiled at her.

Lydia laughed when she saw all the kids dancing. "Look, Rachel. This is why it's worthwhile."

All the kids, ours and Lydia's, were singing and dancing to their song; 'Happy' by Pharrell Williams. It was funny to see them dancing away and singing loudly.

"Look, Mum," Alfie said. "This is fun."

"See, Rachel?" Lydia laughed. "Worth it."

"Good. Here are the scans. It's a boy!" she told him, smiling.

"Yes, a brother!" Alfie said.

Mack smiled. "Thought of any names?"

Lydia nodded. "Yes. Joel and I have decided on Jack."

"That's grand." Mack was happy. "I better go before Mike thinks I'm having an affair."

"You won't do that. You love him too much," she told him, smiling.

"Yer, I do, I always will. Kids, don't forget, we're leaving early in the morning. Be ready," Mack said.

"Yes, Uncle Mack," the kids said together.

When Mack got in, he saw me in the kitchen, making a drink.

"Dad, can I take my football tomorrow? Can we have fish and chips for tea?" asked Oliver, bouncing his footie.

"Yes on both."

Mack smiled at that. Joel, Lydia and the kids turned up with none other than fish and chips.

"Aunt Lydia. You're a mind reader! That's what I asked Dad for tea.

She's good," Oliver said.

The kids loved the house.

"Dad. Can we live here and rent the other place?" Francesca asked, holding Digby.

"That's an interesting question. Why do you ask that?" I said, putting her into bed.

"It's not that I don't love where I am. I love the beach, Dad. I'm calm here. I love it here," Francesca told me.

"I know what you mean, kiddo." I smiled at her. "Hey, shall we get a dog?"

"Really! Olivia would love that. So would I!" Francesca said.

"I'll talk to your dad, OK?" I told her.

"OK. Dad?" she looked at me. "Is it OK to be different?"

"Yes, it is." I was confused by the question. "Why do you ask?"

"Some of the kids think it's strange that I want to be an architect, and I love drawing. They think the music I like is weird. I'm only eight. Did you know what you wanted to be when you were my age?" She was interested to know.

"Yes, I did. I always wanted to help people, make them better. Never be afraid to be different." I smiled at her.

"I know. That's what I told Hannah. Night, Dad. Love you." She got into bed.

"Fran OK?" Lydia said.

"Yes, she's fine. She's a deep thinker, that one," I said, taking my beer from Joel.

"Takes after you," Joel said.

"Well, that's different and out of the blue. She also wants to live here and rent out our place," I told him.

"You agree with her?" Mack asked.

"Kinda." I went quiet. I just looked at him.

"Let's go for a walk. You OK for a bit with the kids?" Mack asked.

"Yes, go. Lydia's asleep anyway. I need the quiet." Joel smiled.

We grabbed our jackets and went out.

"How long has it been since it felt like this?" Mack asked, holding my hand.

"Only since we came up for your birthday. I love it up here." I was deep in thought.

"It was an idea. Something to think about. I'm serious though, Mack."
I got up. "All I was thinking of was giving us, the kids, a break from the
norm. Nothing would change except this."

"Are we getting old?" he asked.

"No. Just changing, Mack. We've been chasing our tails for years. I
want the kids to have a different way of life. Is that so hard?" I started
yawning. "Just think about it."

Mack sat next to me on the sofa. "I'm sorry. I'm an arsehole."

"I know. But I still love you. I can't be arsed to go to bed. Stay here,"
I told him. He didn't argue. "Want to make up?" I asked.

"Thought you'd never ask." Mack said smiling.

"OK. Christ," I said.

"That's Blasphemy!" Maggie said.

"Where did you learn that word?" Mack said.

"Mrs Henderson told Laurel off for saying 'Gone With the Wind' was
a stupid old film. She said that was blasphemous."

We laughed.

"Bacon and eggs and sausage OK?" Mack said.

The kids all cheered. Lydia came down. "Sorry, I over slept." Her
stomach was getting big.

"Lydia, you rest today with Joel, we're look after the kids.

"You sure?" she said, making a coffee.

"How does a day at the beach sound?" Mack said.

"Cool. I'm taking the football," Oliver said.

Oh," Lydia said.

Joel sat up. "Lydia, you OK?"

"Jack's kicking like mad in here. Bloody hell." She finished her coffee.
We all looked at her.

"Oh, piss off. I'm not due for another six weeks. Any food left?"

"Come on, kids, let's go. Rest, woman," I told her. She just looked at
me. An hour after, we went out.

Joel called. "Hospital, now. Lydia."

We rushed down there. Little Jack was born six pound nine. He had a
good set of lungs on him.

We took the kids home. Lydia stayed the night at the hospital.

"I can't believe I have a brother. I'm a big brother. That's cool," Alfie said, "Night, Uncle Mike and Mack."

When we got home, everything went along as normal. Dad was a lot better. Malek had decided to stay with him, to help out, which as a godsend.

I was busier than normal at work. Jack was doing really well.

Mack came home from work looking tired and annoyed. He did his usual; scotch, cigar, garden.

"Are we leaving?" he asked. Francesca was behind him.

"We're trying something different. You're not leaving school," I told them.

"Are we going to the house by the sea?" Francesca asked.

"We're thinking about it," Mack said.

"Good. You two, listen to me," Francesca said. "You work this out. You hear me? Sort yourselves out. You," she pointed at Mack, "stop being grumpy, pull your finger out, think about what you've got. Put that cigar out. It's bad for you. And you," she pointed at me, "don't let him get grumpy again. It's annoying. Now, I want some lunch, I'm hungry. You hungry, Thadd?" Thaddeus nodded.

She told us. We never saw her like that. It was good. We had to smile. When we didn't move, she said, "Get up, you two. Don't make me ask you again."

We did as we were told. I looked at Mack. "Remind me not to get on her bad side again."

Dad and Malek came round for dinner.

"How you doing, Dad?" I asked, putting plates on the table.

"Yeah, not too bad. I'm doing OK. With Malek on my case, don't have a choice."

"This is true," Malek told us. "We have daily walks. Sometimes, people confuse us for a married couple, which is odd. We seem to get funny looks when in Tesco's."

"Only when you told me what we were having for dinner. I told you that's what we had Monday," Dad told him.

Mack started laughing. "This is great. Why weren't we invited to the wedding?"

Dad just looked at him. "You stupid sod."

During dinner, Oliver was very quiet. "You're quiet, what's wrong?" Mack asked him.

Oliver ignored him. "Oliver, Dad's talking to you," I told him. "What's bugging you?"

"Oliver, talk," Dad told him. "Whatever you say, you're not in trouble."

"Ryan's being saying stuff about Dad," he said, looking at Mack.

"Shouldn't listen to him," Mack said.

"His dad says you're cheating on dad. Is it true?" he said bluntly.

"Look at me," Mack told him. "His dad is a lying shit bag. I will not, nor have I ever, cheated on your Dad. I would never do that. I love him a lot. I'm going to smack that shitbag." Mack was fuming. He got up and walked away.

Oliver looked sad. "He's not mad at you, Oliver. He's mad at Ryan's dad. Dad has never cheated on me. I know that man inside out. He's never liked to me. What Ryan's dad said was wicked and nasty." I told him.

Mack came back in. "Ollie, come here." He hugged him.

"I'm not angry at you. That man is a nasty human being. I'll deal with him. Don't you worry. I'll take Matthew with me. OK. I love you, Dad."

"I'm sorry your feelings were hurt. That's not fair," Mack said hugging him.

Mack called Matthew and explained what had happened. "Let's get that son of a bitch." They went to the local pub, where Ryan's dad was. He didn't notice them. They caught up with him by his car.

"Hey. Remember me?" Mack told him.

"Yes. What do you want?" he said, trying to find his car keys.

Mack just chuckled. "You want to go there? OK? My boy was upset again, by a comment. You saying I've been cheating on my husband. My son wouldn't talk or look at me."

He thought it was funny. "It's just a joke."

Mack punched him in the stomach. "What is your problem?" Matthew asked him.

He didn't answer. "You are a sad little man. I don't care about me," Mack said. "My son is a whole different kettle of fish. My son's feeling and well-being is everything. You fucked with the wrong guy," Mack told him. "Don't you care?"

"He's a kid. He'll get over it," Ryan's dad said.

Mack punched him in the face. "He won't. If I said shit about you and your son heard, what would you do?"

He didn't have an answer. "Stay away. Keep your mouth shut," Mack said.

"Who the hell do you think you are?" he said, wiping his nose.

"People that give a shit," Matthew said.

In the car, Matthew drove. "You OK?" he asked.

Mack nodded. "Oliver. The look he gave me. I never want to see that again. The disappointment." He wiped his eyes. "What hurts the most, how hurt he was. Thanks," Mack told him.

When he came in. Oliver was waiting for him. "Sorry, Dad."

"Come here," Mack said, giving him a hug.

"I hurt your feelings." Oliver was crying.

Mack smiled. "I've sorted him."

"You punched him?" Oliver asked.

"Yes. Twice. Stomach and face," Mack said, still hugging him.

"Good. He's an idiot. Did you make his nose bleed?" He seemed happier. Mack smiled. "I want to be like you when I grow up. Can I watch TV before dinner?"

Mack nodded. Oliver got up. He turned round. "You know what, Dad?"

"What's that?" Mack scratched his head. "You and Dad are good parents. I don't care about anything else." He gave Mack the tightest hug ever and gave a kiss.

I was leaning against the door. "You shouldn't have hit him, but I see why you did it." I went to the fridge and got a couple of beers. I sat at the table with him.

"They are our kids, Mike. I will go hell and high water for them and you. I don't regret hitting him. Not one bit. To think it's OK to say and do that. Sick. Not on my watch." He took a sip of beer.

I smiled at him. "You are the toughest, sweetest man."

Just then, we heard screaming, and Olivia saying, "That's cool!"

"What's going on up there?" I said.

"Rae saw a spider and screamed. I think it's cool," Olivia said, looking at the spider. "Can we keep him?"

"No," I said. "Put him in the garden. Ugh!"

"Don't you like spiders?" Olivia said, chasing me round with the spider. Mack was laughing.

"Olivia! Spider. Garden, now. Mack, stop laughing." I got out of their room. *Spiders, disgusting.*

"Dad, you're such a girl. Grow up, it's a spider," Olivia said, putting it in the garden. "Night, Dads."

Rachel and Adam's wedding day came. Mack and Lydia were organising everything. Kids playing about and Lydia shouting, "Don't get bloody dirty!" I was wandering like a lost soul. Dad saw this. "Go and get the drink table sorted."

Mack saw me and came over. "You OK?"

"Yes. Strange not being us. It's weird," I told him, giving him a drink.

"Well, we have done it three times. Can't be greedy." He laughed. "Right, come on, let's get changed."

"OK. Promise me one thing," I asked him while getting ready.

"What's that?" was the reply.

"Don't cry," I said, laughing.

"Sorry, can't promise that," he told me.

"Wow! Look at you two," Lydia said to us. "You look good."

"So do you," I told her, kissing her head.

Rachel looked beautiful. Matthew walked her down the aisle. Then Mack started crying. I just shook my head.

"Really, Dad. So embarrassing," Thaddeus said. I laughed.

The party was at ours. It was like Deja vu.

"Care to dance, Mr Denton?" Mack held out his hand.

"Thought you'd never ask." I smiled, taking his hand.

"This brings back a lot of memories," I told Mack.

"Yes. It feels different, not being us. Can you believe it's been twelve years? Where's it gone, Mike?"

Mack looked at me. "Gone too quick. Look at the kids. How quickly they're growing up." We looked at them.

Rae was screeching. We looked at Olivia. "Olivia. Stop chasing your sister with a worm. Put it down. Wash your hands. Please," Mack told her.

She was disappointed and we laughed. He leaned into me. "I'm would marry you again in a heartbeat."

With Adam on honeymoon, Mack was working in his place. He had loads to do, which was keeping him late at work. Finally, he got in help.

"Hi. I'm home," Mack said. Quiet. "Where is everyone?"

I had left a note. *"At Lydia's."* He ran round thinking there was a problem. "Everything OK?" He was out of breath.

"Yes. Just keeping an eye on Jack while Lydia has a bath. Joel's gone out with a mate," I said, holding Jack.

Mack smiled. "Forgotten what that was like."

"You're not getting broody again?" I asked him.

"God, no. Five's enough," Mack said, taking Jack from me.

"Why don't we take Lydia for a night out next week?" Mack said, giving him his bottle. Lydia came down.

"Thanks for that," she said. "Don't you look cute," she said to Mack.

"We're taking you out next Friday for dinner," I told her.

"That will be nice. What about the kids?" she asked.

"Leave it to us," Mack said. "We won't be too late. I'm going to be working from home. Matthew is going in for us.

"OK, if that's what you want," she said.

"Give Jack here. I'll change him." Mack gave him to me.

"You are aware Jack is my son?" Lydia was sarcastic.

"You need to rest. Let me deal with him. The kids are having sleepovers. So, I'll put him to bed. Then we'll go," I told her.

"Pushy bastard. Telling me what to do." She sat down.

When we got home, Dad and Malek were happy to keep an eye on the kids for two hours. "By the way, Fran wants a horse called Jonas after her rabbit. Olivia wants a tarantula named Beatrice. So good luck with that." Dad laughed.

"Let's do it!" Mack said.

"Now?" I asked.

"Not that!" Mack said. "No, let's seriously think about moving."

"You're sure?" I asked. "It's a lot."

"Thought of nothing else since the summer," Mack said.

"Wow." I was gobsmacked. "Didn't think you would think about it."

"Yes, well, I'm thinking of semi-retiring anyway," Mack was telling me this now.

"Come on, Rae. Bed. Don't worry, you're never leaving. Shall I tell her?" I asked Mack. He nodded yes.

"Your wish is coming true," I told her. Her eyes lit up.

"What wish?" Rae was excited.

"The one where we live by the sea." When I said that, her face lit up.

"Daddy, really?" She was really happy. She hugged us both. Daddies?" she asked.

"Yes?" we said together.

"Can I have another brother or sister, please?" She was so innocent when she did that.

"Something to think about. Now bed, young lady." I told her. I picked her up. She rested her head on my shoulder.

"Love you, Daddy," she told me.

"Love you too, Rae. Always." I told her.

When I came down, Mack was still at the table.

"You're thinking about it. What Rae said?" I asked him.

"Yes." He smiled. "I know. I'm worse than a woman."

I laughed. "I want to think about that. Well, sort of. It's a lot to think about. OK. Let's do it."

"Seriously. Bloody hell. Six kids. Mike." He held my hand.

I looked at him. "I know." I smiled.

"It's a lot of changes." he told me.

"I know. We had to put up with worse in the past," I told him.

So that's what we did. The kids were on board, so was everyone else. We moved, got the kids into new schools and rented our place. Then our new arrival came. His name was Callum. Family complete. I got a job at the local surgery as a nurse. I really loved it. Normal hours. Mack was in his element.

"I had no idea," Laura, the HCA said. "I think it's lovely. Six kids. Bloody hell. They're characters, aren't they?"

"You have no idea," I told her.

"How long have you two been together?" she asked.

"Twelve years, next weekend. Been through some real tough times," I said, looking at Mack with Callum in his arms. I smiled.

"I know. I remember those days. It's better now," Laura said.

"Thanks," I said. Olivia came up to me. "Dad, I can't find Beatrice and Loki." She was looking around.

"You're kidding?" I was getting jumpy.

"Who are Beatrice and Loki?" Laura asked.

"Her tarantulas," I said.

Then Fran screeched. "Olivia, your spiders."

"Good," she said, getting the box to put them in.

Laura laughed. I said, "Not funny. Fran wants a horse." That did it.

Laura was in fits of laughter.

Mack got us a beer. "Good idea of yours to do this. What do you want to do next weekend?" he asked me.

"I have no idea. I was thinking of a quiet night in. Just us. Dinner. Movie," I told him.

"Like the sound of that, a lot." We hadn't done that in for ever. Mack looked at me. "Looking forward to it."

We then heard a breaking of a window. We looked at Oliver.

"Sorry! My foot slipped on the football and that's what happened. Oops! Sorry," Olivier said.

We had a laugh. Lucky enough, it wasn't major. I kept thinking of what I could get Mack for our anniversary. *What do I get a man who has everything he could want?*

Our anniversary came. I got him a second bike. He loved it. "This is way too much," he said.

"OK, I'll take it back," I told him. I laughed. He handed an envelope. It was a trip back to Rome. "Seriously!"

"This is our time. We fought for this. I love you, always. You're kinda sexy when you're quiet. He laughed. So, did I.

"So, what film do you want to watch?" Mack asked me.

"Do we have to watch a film? We've had dinner. Fancy desert?" I winked.

He smiled. "Was hoping you'd say that."

The next morning, we woke up to the smell of burning. We ran downstairs. The kids tried to make breakfast. Thankfully, it as just toast. They looked sheepish.

"It's OK," Mack said. "Bloody hell."

"We wanted to help," Thaddeus said.

"Come on, kids. We'll do brekkie," Mack said. "Then we'll go to the beach for the day."

We had a good day. The kids loved it. We had lunch our as well. The kids ate like anything. Callum was getting big. He was nearly one. The kids loved him and they helped. Rae was protective over him. He loved her.

"That was a lovely weekend. We need to do that all the time. They are more chilled out," I said to Mack after we had dinner.

"Yes. I think we should get a dog," Mack told me.

"Anything's better than those bloody spiders," I said.

The next day after school, we went to pick them up "Right, kids. When we get home, We've got a surprise at home," Mack said, putting Callum in his seat.

"What is it?" Thaddeus asked.

"Wait and see, young man," I told him.

When they saw her, they loved her. Thaddeus called her Holly. She's a Jack Russell. Our family was happy.

I caught Mack wiping his eyes. "I know," I told him.

Lydia, Joel and the kids came up the following weekend. It was the bank holiday. Maggie and the kids loved Holly.

"What are your new neighbours like?" I asked Joel over breakfast.

"Don't ask. I said good morning to them. They ignore us. Lydia says they got sticks up their arse. They hate the noise. Lydia has already had a row with the woman over how noisy the kids are. She misses having you there. She loves the time we have together. So do I. We miss you, a lot." Joel said.

"Hey, we miss you too. I've got an idea," I told Joel. "Lydia, Mack, come here." I told them my plan to annoy Lydia's neighbours. And for us to come up next weekend to annoy them. "Michael Denton. That's not nice," Lydia said. "Let's bloody do it. Can't wait to see that bitch's face when you lot turn up with Holly. Brilliant."

"Listen, can I stay at yours on Tuesday? Got a meeting with Adam," Mack asked Lydia.

"Yes. Bring some stuff with you for the weekend while you're at it. Makes sense. Make sure Olivia doesn't bring those bloody spiders with you. Can't stand them," she told Mack.

Mack went on Tuesday and took some stuff with him. He met the neighbours who did not realise they were renting his house.

"Ah, Francis. This is my brother-in-law, Mack. Mack, this is Francis." She was trying to be polite.

"Nice to meet you." She saw my wedding band. "Nice to see a young man married. How long, if you don't mind me asking?"

"Twelve years, just gone," I replied.

"Children?" she asked. Lydia and I looked at each other and smiled. "Yes, I have. I have six kids. And a dog called Holly. FYI, I'm married to a man, *this* man." I pointed at Mack." Have a good day."

Her face was a picture. She looked like she wanted to move. She couldn't; she had signed a two-year lease.

"She's a delight," I said to Mack as I closed the door. "Poor Lydia and Joel." It quieted down after the kids had eaten and they were watching a film or two.

"So, how's life by the coast?" Lydia asked us.

"Love it," Mack said, sipping his beer. "Glad Mike suggested it."

Lydia looked sad. "What's up?" I asked her.

"It's strange not having my family next door," she told us. "The kids miss their cousins around. "Mack and I looked at each other. "There's a place near us, up for sale. Big house," Mack said.

Lydia and Joel looked at each other. "Something to think about," Joel said.

"Seriously?" Lydia said.

Mack had another meeting. I got a call later from Matthew. "Michael, don't panic or worry. Mack's in hospital."

"What the hell happened? Is he OK" I was worried.

"Yes. He had a panic attack," he told me.

"I'm on my way." I hung up. Lucky for me, Dad and Malék were there.

"I told you not to worry," Matthew said when I got there.

"Seriously, Matthew. Where is he?" I asked them.

"Through there." Matthew pointed to the single room.

I walked in. "Mike. I'm OK." I didn't look convinced. "I don't know what happened."

"Bloody hell, Mack. I am so worried. After your collapse at the restaurant…" I put my head in my hands.

"Mike." I looked at him. "They've done tests. I'm fine!"

"That's it. You're taking it really easy. No arguing. I'm not going to lose you, not until we're really old." I started crying. "Mack, you're the love of my life. For once in your life, you are going to do as you're told. By me. End of discussion."

Mack was silent. "OK. Come here."

I went to him and hugged him tight. "Please, Mack. I need you. The kids need you. It's Callum's second birthday next week. We can't lose you. Ever."

That was it. I was really crying. Matthew drove us home. The kids came running out. Oliver waited with Dad.

"Ollie, come here," Mack said. "I'm going to be fine. Dad told me I have to take it really easy. Otherwise, I'm in trouble. Sorry, I scared you."

Oliver hugged him. "Please don't leave us. I got scared. You better do as you're told. Otherwise, we are all in for it."

Mack smiled. "I promise, I won't. I'm taking it easy."

Oliver came up to me. "Are you mad at Dad?"

"Come here." I sat him down. "No. I'm not mad at him. He got me worried, that's all. I love Dad very much. He scared me too. A lot. Dad and I are good. Promise."

Oliver hugged me. "Love you, Dad. Very much."

"I love you, son. Always," I said, wiping my eyes.

"It's OK. I'll help tell him off if he pisses you off," Oliver said.

I laughed. "Language, Ollie."

Mack did as he was told and Callum enjoyed his birthday.

"Daddies. Cake. Please. Chocolate," he said.

"In a second," Mack said.

Callum started to throw a tantrum. Rae told him off. "No, Callum. Daddy said in a second. Wait."

"OK, Rae-Rae. Sorry, Daddy."

"How does she do it?" I asked Mack. He shrugged.

"How you doing?" I asked him, whilst sitting in the garden.

"I'm OK," Mack said, looking at me. "Really. I'm good. I'm sorry I scared you."

"I know you are," I was quiet. "I am lost without you. My life without you is nothing."

"Soppy sod." Mack was trying to make light of it. I got up and walked inside the house. I was getting upset. I didn't want to get that way in front of the kids.

"Mike?" Mack said, calling after me. "I really scared you, didn't I?"

"Just slightly," I said

"I get it. Hey, I promised to slow down and I will." He stood in front of me.

I looked at him and slightly smiled. He smiled back and kissed and hugged me. "Right, if you two have stopped snogging," Lydia said, "Callum wants his cake. Any wine left?"

We laughed. "Come on," Mack said.

Lydia said to us, "I've never known two people to be so horny all the time."

"Well, if you've got it," Mack replied. "Smug twat," Lydia said, getting the wine. True to his word, he chilled out a lot more and went on his bike. Then we went back to Rome.

"Right, get your suit on," Mack said.

"Where we going?" I said, getting ready.

"Wait and see," he told me. It was an open-air opera. It was brilliant. I started crying, which made Mack laugh.

We got home, relaxed and very happy. The kids missed us, like mad.

Callum jumped up and down. "They home. Daddies are home. I've been good. Haven't I, Rae?"

"Yes, you have," Rae said.

"Really good. Better than last time," I said.

Dad and Malek came up to see us on the Friday.

"Hey, what you doing here?" I asked, letting them in.

"Thought we'd surprise you. Plus, I miss my grandkids," he said, smiling. "How's you, Malek?"

"I'm good. Glad to be alive. Where's Mack? I've been worried about him."

"I'm fine, Malek," Mack said, coming through the back door with Callum. "Go wash your hands, son."

"Hi, Granddad. Hi, Grandpa," Callum said washing his hands.

Malek hugged Mack. "I've been worried. So worried."

"Honestly, I'm doing fine. Seeing the doctor on Monday for a check-up and a chat. Sorry for worrying you. Drink anyone?" he said, going to the kitchen.

Malek followed him. "Are you sure? You gave us a fright!"

"Sure. Really," Mack told him.

"I'm cooking dinner tonight," Malek said.

"So, Dad. You and Malek? When's the wedding?" I said, smiling.

"Cheeky sod," Dad told me. "You want a hand, Malek?"

"I'm fine, thank you," he replied. I looked at Dad. "Really?"

"Piss off," Dad said.

"Stop swearing, granddad," Thaddeus said.

We then heard a thud. Mack had had another panic attack and collapsed. I sat with him, in our room.

"I'm calling the doctor."

The doctor came and looked at him. "He's fine. What's bothering you?" I doctor asked.

"Nothing. I've cut down on my work load. Getting more exercise. Doing more. I'm seeing the doctor on Monday."

Mack saw the doctor on Monday. They did blood tests, ECGs. Nothing. He suggested talking to a counsellor. Mack agreed.

I phoned Dad. "What am I going to do? Jesus."

"All you can do is be there for him. Support him," he told me.

Mack was sitting on the couch, beer in hand.

"Talk to me?" I said to him. He took my hand. "No lies, please."

He was quiet for a moment. "I started having flashbacks about my childhood. I don't know why. Really. I thought it might have been about my time in Afghanistan. But no. It's weird. I can't explain it."

I listened. He looked at me. "Hey, it's not you or the kids. That I'm sure off. I'm really happy. You know it. The counsellor is helping me. Why don't you come?"

"OK. I'll come. I'm here for you. Always. I just hate seeing you like this. You don't need it." I smiled sadly.

"I hate seeing you sad when I have one. The kids get me." Holly jumped up and sat next to me and fell asleep.

"Don't worry about me," I said. "Stressing doesn't help."

Mack rubbed his hand through his hair and scratched his head.

"I don't want to be a burden to you," Mack said. I got annoyed.

"Right, you listen to me. You have never been or will you be burden to me. We are in this together. I'm sticking with you. God, you are the most stubborn prick I've ever met. Have you had these before?" I asked him.

"Once," he said. He then smiled.

"What's funny? When did you have one?" I was trying to keep it together. "It's kinda embarrassing," he said scratching his head.

"I'm waiting," I said. "Spill."

"OK. You ready? You remember when we got married? He looked at me. I nodded. "This is embarrassing. When we were on our own, before we were really together that night, I was in the bathroom having a panic attack. I thought I wouldn't be good enough for you." He was blushing.

I laughed. "That's why you were in there so long. Shit. Really, Mack. Bloody hell. Well, that night was rather good. We didn't sleep much. I'm not going anywhere. I'm with you all the way."

"What would I do without you?" Mack sighed.

"Well, I am the best thing that's happened to you. Coffee?" I said, getting up. Mack smiled. Olivia came down.

"Why you out of bed, miss?" I asked her, giving Mack his coffee. "Loki's gone walkies again." She wiped her eyes.

I was jumpy. I hate spiders. "Found him," Mack said.

"Come on, back to bed, Olivia," I said. I tucked her in. "Dad?"

"Yes, Livvy?" I said, tucking her in.

"You and Dad are the best. Some of my friends don't have a dad. I'm lucky I have two. I think it's sad they don't have a dad. But they can't have you. I love you."

"We're not going anywhere. Not ever. Night, Livvy," I told her.

"Night, Daddy." She was asleep.

"She OK?" Mack asked.

"Yes," I told him what she said. "See. You're not a burden to them, either. Go for a run in the morning. Would do you good."

So that's what he did. I joined him as well. I enjoyed it. "Good idea. That helped," Mack said, using a towel.

"Going for a shower. You joining me?" He smiled.

In the coming weeks, everything was good. Mack didn't have a panic attack. He went to counselling. So did I. It helped a lot. Mack worked from home on his computer.

As I was picking the kids up from school and nursery, Mack called me. "Don't come home just yet."

"Why?" I asked.

"Wait and see. One hour." He hung up.

"What's he up to?" Thaddeus asked.

"No idea, Thadd. No idea," I told him.

We got home. The house was done up really nice.

"What's all this?" I asked. The kids and I were stunned.

"This," Mack told us, "is a thank you for sticking by me. All of you."

"Mack, I'll always be here," I told him. The place looked good.

Callum got out his pushchair. "Is there cake, Dad?" he asked.

He smiled. "Yes, son." Callum was happy.

Lydia called that evening to talk to Mack. "How are you?"

"Doing good. How are you?" He was putting the washing up away.

"Good. That silly bitch is still annoying. Good news. We put an offer on that house near you yesterday," she said.

"Brilliant," I said as I heard her on the speaker, getting a couple of beers out the fridge. "Let's hope so." Jack started crying.

"Bloody hell. It's a mad house in here. See you later. Love you," she said.

"Love you too," we said and hung up.

A few days later, Mack was at the table, looking at the computer. He was mulling something over.

"What's up? And don't say nothing. I can read you like a book," I said.

He smiled. He ran his hands through his dark hair and took off his glasses.

"You need to slow down. We've been saying it for... how long?" I said.

"Really. OK. I'll do it. What's for dinner?" he asked.

"Really. It's eleven in the morning. Oliver's just like you. Always hungry." I laughed and got up to put the kettle on. I put my hand on his shoulder. "Make the call."

Mack did just that. "Done." He sighed. He looked relived. "Looks like I'm going to be at home a lot more than usual." He stood next to me, smiling.

"You should have done it a long time ago." I hugged him.

"Come on, we have to go and pick Callum up from Nursery. He's going to go nuts when he sees us both."

True to word, he went nuts when he saw both of us. "Park. Can we go to the park? Please? Then get Rae from school."

We took him to the park. He was happy. It was good to see him smile. He saw his friend Declan and they played together for a while. His mum saw us.

"Hi, I'm Mandy. Declan's mum. You must be Callum's parents."

"Hi. I'm Michael. This is Mack. That's our Callum," I said.

"He's a spirited good boy," she said that as a compliment.

"He is," Mack said. "Mind you, he has two older brothers and three older sisters."

She was amazed. "Six kids. Blimey! I can just cope with three."

Callum came to us. "Dads, I need a wee. And I'm hungry."

We smiled. "Come on, young man. Nice to meet you, Mandy."

"What do you want for lunch, Callum?" I asked.

"Fish fingers, beans and chips," he said.

"What do you want to be when you're older, Callum?" Mack asked, giving him his lunch.

"Kind," Callum said, eating his fish fingers. Mack put his hand on his heart and smiled. "Can I have a cat?"

"We'll think about it. We're gonna have a zoo at this rate," I said. Mack laughed.

Lydia phoned that night. "Good news. The house is ours. The kids are so happy. Lucky, it's coming up to summer. They're in their school for September. So that's sorted. At least, it's ten minutes from you lot. So how is everything?"

"Good," I told her. Told her about Mack.

"Good. How long you been telling him. How is he?" she said.

"He's OK. He seems more relaxed. I'll always worry about him," I told her, putting the washing on.

"Yer, well, you two are made for each other. Always at it. Like rabbits." Lydia rolled her eyes over the phone.

"We haven't lately. I miss it." I sounded sad and she noticed. "Don't worry, it'll happen. Listen, I got to go. Packing to do. Tell the kids I love them. Auntie Lydia and Uncle Joel will be there soon."

We hung up. I got a shock when I realised Mack was behind me.

"Shit, Mack, you scared me," I told him.

"Sorry. I'm sorry we haven't been close lately. That's my fault," he told me, looking sad.

"It's not your fault. You've been through a lot." I smiled at him. He had that bloody t-shirt on.

"I want to change all that. Every time I think about it, I get nervous, like when we met." Mack looked at the floor.

"Let's change that now," I told him. "The kids are sleeping. I want to be with you. Now."

That was it. We took our time. We were both nervous. It was like our first time. We slept in each other's arms.

We got woken by a load of noise. "What the hell!" we said. We ran downstairs. Lydia was there with Joel and the kids.

"What are you doing here?" Mack asked.

Joel gave him and me a coffee. "Moving day. Surprise!" he said.

"We got in early. Thought we'd pop over for a while. Busy last night." Lydia smirked. We smiled.

"Auntie Lydia?" Thaddeus asked.

"Yes, my darling boy?" she said, taking his plate.

"Can I help you unpack? I want to help," he asked.

The others asked to help as well. "Let's all help," I said.

We went and helped. Mack was whistling away. I was singing away. We kept looking at each other like we were dating. By the end of the day, we had done a lot. Joel ordered pizza.

"Thanks for that," Joel said, handing out the beers.

"Stay the night, you lot. It's late. We got beds for everyone. We'll make do. The kids are asleep upstairs anyway. I'm not asking," Lydia told us.

Mack had to go and get his t-shirt.

"Really. That thing has seen better days."

"You know the score," he told me, smiling.

"But twelve years. Hate it. I'm going to throw it away."

"I'll divorce you," he said.

The next day, Lydia pulled us to one side. "There's something up with Rae. She's had Jonas up to her ear. She won't eat her breakfast. She always eats her breakfast. She's not talking either."

"Rae, come here," I told her. "Dad and I want to talk to you."

"What's wrong, sweetheart?" I asked her.

"Bad dreams, Daddy," she said. She had Jonas to her ear.

"What was the dream about?" Mack asked.

She sat on my lap, head on my shoulder, and sighed. "The monster came back to try and take me away. Said I was a naughty girl. Am I?" She looked at me.

"No, you're not, Rae. You're a good girl. The monster won't take you away. He'll have me and Daddy to deal with."

"He frightened me. He said I never see you again or Auntie Lydia and Uncle Joel."

Lydia came in. She had tears in her eyes. "Rae. Look at ne. It was a dream. Oh, sweetheart. Daddy's right. The monster, Opie, is naughty, not you. We love you very much. Jonas too."

Rae smiled. "Promise, Daddy, Auntie Lydia?"

"Promise," we said together.

"Come, Rae. Let's get you brekkie. You and Jonas must be hungry," Lydia said, taking her.

Rae looked at us. "We'll be there in a second. Go with Auntie Lydia."

"Poor love," Mack said. I couldn't talk.

"Come on. Let's go sit with her." I said, getting up.

We sat with her and everyone. She was eating her breakfast. "What shall we do today after we've helped you?" I asked.

"Don't know," Lydia said.

Olivia spoke up, looking at Rae. She walked over to her and kissed Rae on the head. "Love you, Rae. First things first. Rae's been upset. So, we need to cheer her up." Oliver smiled. "I know. Our song. Would you like that, Rae?"

She smiled widely. "Yes, please."

The kids went in the living room. Alice put the stereo on. "Come on, Rae, let's dance."

Then they were. All of them dancing to 'Happy'. We all watched. Lydia cried. Joel was filming it on his phone.

"Dad?" Alice asked Joel.

"Yes, sweetheart?" He smiled at her.

"There's a farm round here. When we've finished here, can we go?" she asked.

"What do you reckon, everyone?" he asked, looking at everyone.

We all agreed. The house was more or less done. We went. Alice was in her element. She loved it! Fran and Rae loved the horses. Callum loved the goats.

"Can I have a horse instead of a cat?" Fran asked

When we got home and the kids were in bed, Mack wanted to talk.

"How would you feel if I went and did a job next week? It's only for a few hours."

I wasn't happy. "I'm not sure. But knowing you, you've made your mind up. Haven't you?"

When he didn't answer, I said, "OK. If you want to."

That week came. Mack did the job and came home. He looked happy. "It went well. I told Matthew it was a one-off. He agreed. Truth be told, my heart wasn't in it. Matthew saw that, said I was an old man. I told him to piss off." We didn't see Callum there.

"Naughty words, Dad. Stop it," he said, looking at his book.

"Sorry, son," Mack said, smiling.

"Yes, well. I can live with that," I told him.

"What you looking at, Callum?" I asked.

"A book with animals. Want to be an animal doctor," he said.

We smiled. "We've got smart kids." Mack said as I smiled.

"We were having a BBQ. It was gonna be noisy. My lot. Lydia's lot," I said.

"OK. Thanks," she said. "What shall I bring?"

"With our lot, paracetamol," I told her, smiling.

She laughed.

When she came, the kids were happy to see her.

"Laura!" Maggie said. "Glad you're here."

Olivia looked confused. "Laura, have you seen Beatrice and Loki? They got out again."

"Bloody hell. Those spiders are going to be the death of me," I said, not happy. Laura couldn't stop laughing.

"Here, have some wine," Lydia said, giving her a glass.

"So, how's work?" Lydia asked, taking a sip.

"It's OK. Sometimes, it's quiet. But it's good," Laura said.

"I've applied for a job there," Lydia said. "Jack, what are you doing?"

"Looking for my rugby ball," Jack said. Laura smiled.

"Kids. Drive me potty. But I love them. They grow up so fast." Lydia smiled, watching them play and read. I caught Mack looking at Laura. Joel saw it.

"Don't even think about it," he said.

I put the shopping down and looked at them. "Tell me what?"

"Laura has managed to get you an interview for the senior HCA job," he said, smiling.

"What?" I had to sit down. "Laura, you've been there longer than me. You should have it. You're good at your job," I told her.

"So are you. Listen, I don't want it. You would be good. Same hours and days. Thought the money might help," she said.

"Laura, thank you. This is embarrassing. I put your name forward too." I laughed.

"You're kidding." Laura laughed. "What a pair. Your face, though, when you walked in."

"Yes," I said. Laura got up and patted me on the shoulder.

"I'm off. You know, you two are lucky. I wish I had what you two have. Just to be nosy and curious" — Laura was nice and genuinely interested — "is what you have true love?"

Mack answered, "Yes. Yes, it is." He took my hand.

"You sneaky fucker," I told him. He laughed. "My heart sank when I came in. I didn't know what to think. Thank you."

"I know what you were thinking. I couldn't do it. Let's go and get the kids, before Lydia goes into one," Mack said.

The kids were in the garden, actually behaving. "OK. What have you done to the kids?" I asked her.

"Don't be daft. I was waiting till bed time," Lydia said. "So, did Laura get you that interview?"

"Yes. I'm not gonna ask how you know that. I got Laura the same interview," I said.

Rae saw me and smiled. "Daddy. I missed you." She hugged me. She had Jonas.

Just then, Mack came to pick me up. "Hey, ready?" he said.

"What's up?"

"Callum's just had the biggest tantrum in Sainsbury. Fran told him off. Over the bloody trolley."

"Sorry, Dad," Callum said.

Next day at work, I got called in the office. She smiled.

"Well, thanks for that. You off for two weeks?"

"With my kids. What they want. See you in a fortnight." I couldn't wait to get home. I fell asleep on the couch when I got home. Mack woke me up.

"I married an old man." He laughed.

"You're older than me by three years. So, who's old?" I told him.

"OK, rub it in," he said. "What do you want to do tomorrow, before we pick the kids up?"

"How about a ride on the bike? Haven't done that for a while. Then lunch," I said.

"Like the sound of that. Dinner's ready," he said.

After dinner, Mack had another panic attack. His first in months.

"Sorry," he said. "Don't worry. First in months. Good sign."

We went for that ride on the bike. It was good to get out. Mack was smiling.

"What you smiling at?" I said, giving him his drink.

Just enjoying the day with you. Can't a man enjoy the day with his husband?" he said.

"Well, I've always brought a smile to your face. Nice to see it," I told him.

He shook his head. "I fancy a big party at home."

"There's me thinking you fancied me?" I laughed.

"I do." Mack laughed. The lady brought our dinners and gave us a funny look. We laughed. "Sounds like a good idea. Getting everyone together. I miss that."

That lady who brought us our dinners kept giving us a dirty look. Mack looked at me. "Come here." I knew what he was going to do. He kissed me.

"Wow. That was good," I told him. "You're in a good mood."

"Just happy, let's go and get our kids," he said.

We got a call that night. It was Dad. Malek had had a fall and was in hospital. I woke Mack up.

"What! What's the matter? The kids?" Mack went back to sleep, snoring.

"Bloody useless."

Next morning, Mack came down, yawning and scratching his head. "What?" he said.

"You don't remember Dad calling to say Malek had a fall and is in hospital?" I said making toast for Oliver. "Ollie, toast. Come on."

"All right, Dad, chill out," Oliver said.

"Where did you learn that?" Mack asked.

"Charlie at school. Tells everyone to chill out," Oliver said.

"I heard the phone ring, you talking. Sleep," he said.

"Malek fell and he's ended up in hospital."

The phone rang just then; it was Dad.

"OK, I'll let them know."

"Well?" Mack said. "Olivia, Rae, brekkie.

"He's bruised his ankle. He has to rest it for a couple of weeks," I told him.

"Dad?" Callum said to me. "Can I have that goat?"

"No. You can't have a goat. What about a cat?" I asked, giving him more toast.

"Cats are boring. Goats are cool. Can I have some jam?" he asked.

We got a few things for the party. Lydia called. "Have you seen Maggie?"

"What? Isn't she at school?" I asked. "Hang on." I told Mack. He made a call to Matthew. "She went. I got a call saying she's gone."

She was crying. Matthew turned up twenty minutes later. "Well find her, Lydia," Matthew said. Just then, Maggie came in.

"Where the hell have you been? The school said you weren't there?" Lydia said.

Maggie didn't say a word. She was upset. "Maggie. Talk to us for God's sake."

She sat next to Lydia. "Mum, sorry. The girls are picking on me because I'm mixed race, and my uncles are gay. And I started my... you-know-what. I'm bloody sick of ignorance. Why are some people fucking arseholes." She got up and ran to her room, crying.

Joel came in. "What the hell happened?" Lydia told him. "Shit."

"I'll go talk to her," Lydia said.

"No. I'll do it," Joel said. He knocked on the door. "Maggie."

"Go away." Maggie was crying.

"I'm not going." He went in. "Get up."

Maggie got up and say next to him. She leaned her head on his shoulder.

"Dad, I don't understand. I'm not bad," Maggie said.

"You listen to me. You are not bad. You've got a heart of gold. There are people in this world that are like that. Why? Even I don't know why, and I'm the adult. But there is good in this world, believe me. I'm sorry it hurts. Really, I am. But you have proved the world wrong, my darling girl."

"How?" Maggie looked at him.

"Because, baby girl, you care. In here counts, he said, touching his heart. "You look at what you have achieved. Brothers and sister that look up to you. You teach them how to be, who they're supposed to be and what not to be. Keep that in mind. Those you hate will never matter. I love you, Angel girl." He looked at her with tears in his eyes.

Maggie hugged him. "I love you too, Dad. I don't know what I'd do without you. What do I do about my girl problem?"

"That's for Mum." They laughed.

When they came down, Maggie ran to Lydia. "Sorry, Mum, it won't happen again. I promise."

"I know, my darling. I love you," Lydia told her. They went to the school and sorted out the problem. Maggie wasn't in trouble for what happened. They were glad she was OK.

They came to ours for dinner. Maggie hugged me and Mack.

"Don't worry. Come on, Maggie May. Family time now." I hugged her.

Rae went up to Maggie and gave her a drawing. It was a picture of all of us. "Thank you for being my cousin, Maggie. I love you," she said and hugged her. Lydia cried. So did Mack.

"I swear I married a woman," I told Joel, drinking my beer. Joel laughed.

Dad and Malek came over; Malek with his stick. They were arguing over something.

"What's up with you two?" Mack asked, closing the door behind them.

"Malek won't take his anti-inflammatory pills," he said.

"I did. I took one before we came out," Malek said, sitting down.

Oliver was smiling his head off.

"What are you smiling at?" Dad asked him.

"You two act like an old married couple. I should start calling Malek granddad. The kids at school already think he is, when you picked us up yesterday. They think it's funny," Oliver said.

I laughed and spat my beer out. Malek laughed as well. "It's true. Besides, at least I get to see my family."

"I'm glad you're family too, Malek. It's nice that you keep Grandad in check," said Oliver and everyone laughed.

"Hey, you cheeky sod," my dad said. "You're like your dad."

"I can't believe you two are making me go to school on my birthday. Really? Come on!" Olivia said.

Mack was on the kitchen table, on the computer. He took his glasses off. "Young lady," he said, coffee in hand. "Listen, your dad and I are picking you up after school."

"So, where we going?" She was excited.

"Olivia, wait and see. Right, school. Lydia's taking you. Bye, hun. Love you."

"Love you too," she said, going to Lydia's car.

When the kids were in bed, Mack looked deep in thought. "What's going to happen when they grow up and leave us?"

"Oh my God. We're not even there yet! What's wrong with you? No more kids. Shit. You'll have me. You're an idiot. You on your period?" I said to him. He laughed.

"They're growing up fast. That's all I'm saying." He took a beer from me.

"Olivia is eleven, numb-nuts. Let's enjoy the time we have now." I just shook my head.

Early next morning, Mack got a call from Matthew. Nothing serious. Just wanted to go through some stuff. I left him to it. "Love you," I said, going to work.

"Love you too," he said, smiling.

I didn't have five minutes at work. Blood tests, checks. Staff meeting after work. Mack was waiting for me after work. When we got home, it was quiet.

"What the hell!" I said.

"They've been good as gold. Even my lot. They've been busy doing something. To be honest, they are up to something. Right, kids. My kids, let's go, bath then bed," Lydia told them.

"What shall we do for Dad's birthday?" I asked Mack, settling on the sofa. "How about a BBQ? How about sending him on a mini-break with Malek?" He told me. He looked tired.

"Good idea. You're looking tired," I told him

"Seriously, I'm OK. Really," he said, yawning.

When Dad's birthday came, it was funny. Dad and Malek were arguing.

"Grandad, Malek. Will you two shut up for five minutes and enjoy yourself? Dad, tell them," Francesca told them.

I laughed. Well, they did just that. Matthew took over from Mack at the BBQ. He came up and kissed me. "What was that for?"

"Just because. You give him his present?" Mack said.

"You're kidding. Seriously. This is too much," Dad said.

"Come on, Dad, you do a lot. You need a break," Mack said.

"So do you two. Working your arses off," Dad said. "In twelve years, you've been away twice. Twice! For God's sake. So, here."

Dad gave us an envelope. A week away to the South of France.

"Don't look at me like that. The pair of you. Malek and I are staying here. Matthew's coming up. Lydia is helping too. So, shut up," Dad told us.

So off we went. A week away. No kids, just us. It was good. Mack was happy. "This has been the best week ever. I miss the kids like mad. I've missed you," Mack said.

"Missed you too," I told him. "I've enjoyed being with you. Thank you, for everything."

The kids were so happy to see us. Rae was stuck to me for ages. "You OK, Rae-Rae?"

"I missed my daddies lots," she said.

"Rae, look in that bag," I said, smiling.

Her face was a picture. "Another bunny, like Jonas. Jules. Thank you, daddies."

"Oliver, Callum, Thaddeus, hurry up, school. The girls are ready," Mack called.

"Chill out, Dad," Olivier said.

"I'll give you chill out if you don't get a move on," Mack told him as he ate his breakfast.

"Right, come on," I said, getting my keys.

"You're not going out like that, are you?" Thaddeus asked.

"Why?" I asked him.

"You're in your pyjamas," he said. "You're like Auntie Lydia."

Mack laughed. "I'll take them. Come on. Back in a bit."

"What we going to do for Oliver's birthday? Can't believe he's going to be ten," Mack said, making us a drink.

"I know. I can't believe he's so much like you. Smart mouth." Mack smiled. "Funny enough. I spoke to someone at Arsenal. They have agreed to let us have a tour. Then a party here." I had a smug look on my face.

"How the hell did you pull that one off?" Mack was in shock.

"My good looks and Scottish charm." I was laughing.

"There's a good reason why I married you," he told me. "He's going to love that."

Oliver's birthday came. We were all ready. "Ollie, come on. We're going to be late," I told him.

"Where we going?" He stomped down the stairs.

"It's a good surprise, Ollie," Thaddeus said. "Stop being grumpy and get in the car. Do as you're told, Oliver James Denton," Thaddeus told him.

He face lit up when we got there and inside. "This is so cool. Thank you very much. Sorry for being grumpy," Oliver said.

"That's OK. Forget it," Thaddeus said. "Let's look around. I like it here. It's fun."

Off they went. Oliver got a signed shirt and a goodie bag. Then, we came home for the party. Everyone came. "This is cool. Thadd, Callum, want to play football?" he asked.

Then after we had a few drinks, we started dancing away. Lydia, Joel, Mack and I dancing to Goldfrapp and Stevie Nicks.

"This so embarrassing," Thaddeus said.

"This is so going on YouTube," Maggie said, filming us.

Lydia caught wind of it. "Maggie Anne Green, put that bloody phone away."

Maggie couldn't stop laughing. "You're all so old."

"We're not old," Mack said. "Shit, my knee."

"There, there, Dad. You want a walking stick?" Thaddeus said.

"Cheeky sod," Mack said. The rest of us laughed.

Oliver came up to us and hugged us. "Thanks for today. It was a nice day, even with Thaddeus telling me off." He started yawning.

"Come on bed. Been a long day," I said.

Callum was asleep as soon as his head hit the pillow. Rae on the other hand was wide awake.

"What's wrong, Rae?" we asked her.

"Scared of the monsters. I don't want them taking me away." She looked scared.

"We told you they won't, Rae. You're our baby girl," I told her. She smiled.

Fran came in. "I'll stay with Rae tonight. I'll look after Rae. You're my little sister, I'll protect you." She hopped into bed with Rae.

On Saturday, Dad came round with Malek. Then Lydia, Joel and the kids came too.

"What's going on?" Mack asked. We were confused.

"Right," Dad said, "you four out. Come back in an hour."

"What are you lot up to? Maggie?" Joel said.

"Hour. Go," Jack said, pointing to the front door. So, we were kicked out by our bloody kids. We're the adults. So, we went for a walk along the beach.

"Can't believe we were pushed out by a bunch of kids. What's up with that?" Lydia said, holding Joel's hand.

"Hey, don't knock it. An hour. No kids. Just grown-ups. How long since we have had that?" Joel said.

I got a call from Dad. Time to come back.

"Really? Do we have to?" Lydia said.

"You sound like Jack when it's bath time," Joel said. Lydia stuck her middle finger up.

When we got there, we were told to close our eyes, which we did. We stood in the middle of the living room. There was pictures everywhere, of us, Joel, Lydia and our kids. From babies to now. On both sides. We were in shock.

"This is beautiful," Lydia said.

"Take a seat. All of you," Alice said, smiling. We sat on the couch, looking at the telly. "This is for all of you. Watch."

A DVD was played. It showed us all over the years and ended with them saying thank you to us. That was it. We were all in tears, crying like babies.

"Told you," Alice said.

"Thank you," Lydia said through the tears. Mack and I couldn't talk. We were in tears. He held my hand. Then Callum made us laugh. "Can I have that goat now?"

I rushed to the hospital. "Mack!" I was panicked. The doctor came along. "Well, he's OK. We did a load more tests, like we did before. Nothing to worry about," he said.

"I know you are," I said to Mack. "Come on, let's take you and Dad home," I said.

When we got home, Malek was there. "Great Allah. I'm glad you're here. You must take care, my friend. Allah has given you gift of love and life."

"Thank you. Where are the kids?" I asked.

"In their rooms. Just beware, Oliver has been crying. When he heard hospital, he got scared," Malek said.

Mack went to see the kids. They were peacefully asleep.

The next morning, the kids were quiet. "You OK, Dad?" Callum asked.

"Yes, son. I am. Sorry for scaring you all," Mack said. He looked at Oliver, who didn't look back at him.

"Can we go to school now please?" Oliver said, getting up and getting his bag.

"Ollie," Mack said. Oliver ignored him. "Ollie, I'm OK."

"Whatever," he said. He went and waited outside. I looked at Mack. He was upset.

When I got home, I said to Mack, "Go and pick him up from school. Talk to him. You're both hurting."

He did just that.

Oliver looked at him. You could tell he was upset.

"Come on, son. Let's go for a walk. Give us your bag."

The silence was awkward. "Why you having these attacks? Is it us kids that are doing it?" Oliver was blunt in his questions.

"Ollie. It's to do with my childhood. Look at me," Mack told him. "You kids are not the cause. Not now, not ever. You kids are my life. I love being your dad. I'm proud of you kids."

He smiled. "Why was growing up hard for you?" Oliver asked.

"Because, my family couldn't accept me. They made it hard for me, for years," he told him.

"Why? Because you're gay, and you love Dad?" Oliver said.

"Yes, because of that. It's been hard for years. But when I met your dad, it was the best thing ever. It hurt a lot. Sometimes, it still does. Make sense?" Mack asked him.

"Sort off," Oliver said, scratching his head. "I'm sorry they were mean to you. I'm sorry as well. I wasn't very nice. Dad. You know, there's nothing wrong with you, right?" Oliver looked at him.

'I know that now. Listen, there's going to be people who don't understand, or like the way me and your dad are together. That's them. Not us. That's their problem," he told him.

"OK. Got it. Can we go now, before Dad starts cooking? You know that won't end well," Callum said.

Mack laughed. "Dad?" Callum looked at him.

"Yes?"

"Love you, Dad. Always," Callum said, hugging him.

"Love you too, son. Always." Mack hugged him back.

"How did it go?" I asked Mack later.

"Good," he said, drinking his coffee. He told me what happened.

"Glad you worked it out."

"What's a family tree, Grandad?" Thaddeus asked my dad.

"It shows your ancestors, who you're related to, going back hundreds of years ago. Why?" he asked Thaddeus.

"We have to do one at school," Thaddeus said, drinking his juice.

"What do you have to do for school?" Mack asked, looking in the fridge for dinner. "Ahh, lasagne."

Dad told him. "Sounds interesting," Mack said chopping up carrots. "Soon. Go and watch telly for a bit." Mack shook his head.

Christmas came round really quickly. The kids got all excited about it. Rae went up to Mack on the couch. "Daddy?"

"Yes, my darling Rae?" Mack asked her, putting his book down.

"Will Santa come and see me again?"

"Yes, he will. You have been a good girl. What would you like for Christmas?" Mack told her.

"A princess dress and a cat. What do you want, Daddy?" Rae asked, playing with Jonas and Jules.

"I got everything I need, Angel girl," He told her.

"But you have to have a present. That's a rule from Santa.: She was almost eight but she was sweet and innocent.

Christmas morning came around. Everyone enjoyed the day. Rae went to Mack and gave him a present.

"What's this?" Mack asked Rae.

"Open it." She looked at me and smiled.

It was the most wonderful thing ever which brought him to tears. It was a large photo frame of him, me and Rae over the years.

"That's my favourite." Rae pointed to the one when she arrived to us as a baby in the garden.

"Why this one, Rae?" Mack wiped his eyes.

"Because it was the day I came home and you and Daddy wanted me and love me." She hugged Mack tight. "Merry Christmas, my daddy." Mack and I were in tears.

"It's not even ten and I'm crying," Lydia said, wiping her eyes.

Rae went up to Lydia. "Auntie Lydia. Uncle Joel?"

"Yes, baby girl?" Joel said, picking her up.

"No more monsters. I did as you said. They've gone. Thank you." She hugged them.

"Rae," I said, "open that box. The pink one."

She went to the pink box. She opened it and her face lit up. It was a kitten. A tortoise shell. A boy.

"Thank you, Daddies. I'm going to call him George. Look, Olivia." Rae was in her element.

Olivia was happy. "You're a good girl."

Dad was in the kitchen with his hand on his heart, holding back the tears. "My God. That little girl. I swear she's an angel. She never asks for anything. None of them do. But Rae." I hugged my dad.

After dinner, we gave Lydia and Joel a present. It was a family holiday to Spain for a fortnight. The kids got presents.

"This is too much," Lydia said.

"Why?" Joel said.

"Because you deserve it. You've been and done everything for us for fourteen years. Everything. Plus, you're family."

"Uncle Mack and Mike, thanks for the presents, Alfie said.

130

"We're cool. I can live with that," I said to Mack, who smiled.

Mack gave me my present. Theatre tickets and a dinner reservation to the restaurant we wanted to go. The waiting list was way too long.

"How did you manage this?" I asked him.

"Luck of the draw," he told me.

"Here's yours." I have him an envelope. It was a weekend away to a cottage that he loved. "Wow. You know me too well. Thank you." He kissed me for the longest time.

"God, get a room. So embarrassing," Rae said. "Can I have a mince pie, please?"

"Yes, you can, my Angel girl." I laughed.

"Yes, well, can't argue with that. I'm thinking of getting you a Zimmer frame for your birthday."

"Cheeky bastard. Well, at least I'm still good at some stuff," he said, winking at me. "Listen. I've got a meeting with Matthew on Friday. He's coming here, Nothing too serious. Matthew knows what's been going on."

Mack and Matthew's meeting went well. That Miranda woman was trying to get us to work for her, for nothing. Mack told her to piss off.

"How you doing?" Matthew asked, sipping his tea.

"OK," he said. Mack gave him a really good drawing of us and Jack drawn by Maggie.

"I'm surprised you remember Jack," Matthew said.

"'Course I remember him," Maggie said. "I still got that giraffe he brought me for my birthday when I was eight. That's not going anywhere. We miss him too, you know, Uncle Matthew."

That brought a tear to his eye. "Thanks, Maggie."

"Come to ours for dinner. Lydia, Joel and the kids are coming to remember Jack. Simon and Malek will be there," I said, standing behind Mack.

"OK. I will," Matthew said.

When we picked the kids up from school, Rae asked me, "Dad, what's a moron?"

"Where did you hear that?" I asked, looking in the rear-view mirror.

"Well, Mrs Bradshaw said to Miss Henderson that her husband is a moron for forgetting the washing powder while shopping," she said, holding on to Jonas and Jules and looking out the window.

I smiled. "It means he's an idiot, for forgetting.

"You never do that. You're not an idiot. You remember things," she told me.

I laughed. "You're funny, Rae."

"I know. I'm like you, aren't I? She was smiling.

"Yes, you are, darling," I said, parking the car at home.

Rae got out of the car. "You know, Miss Henderson fancies you. I caught her looking at you. She had a funny look on her face. It changed when she saw Dad walk up and kiss you. She said, 'So not fair'. That'll teach her, won't it."

"Rae Morgan Denton, you are the sweetest, funniest girl ever. Don't ever change who you are. That's an order." I kissed her head.

"OK, I won't. Promise." She skipped inside. "Olivia, Loki is out again. Bloody spider."

I couldn't stop laughing or tell her off for swearing.

"What are you smiling at?" Mack asked as I walked indoors.

"Just Rae. She's turning into a real character," I told him.

Callum didn't look happy. Mack and I sat him down. "Callum, what's wrong, son?"

He was upset. "My friend Annabel, her mum and dad are fighting. I saw a bruise on her arm. A big one. When I asked her about it, she got upset. So, I gave her a hug. I saw another one on her neck. Is someone hurting her?"

"Did you tell your teacher?" Mack asked. He shook his head no. "Was that wrong?"

"It's OK. Don't worry. Dad and I will talk to your teacher," I told him. "You did the right thing telling us. What's her last name?"

"Barton, I think. Hope she's OK. She is a nice friend, Dad. I hate seeing her like that." Callum was a good boy.

We spoke to Callum's teacher, who promised to look into it and would keep them informed. A few weeks later, Callum's teacher asked to see us.

"All I can tell you is that Annabel is being taken into care. Callum did the right thing. He's a good boy."

Mack looked at me. I knew what he was thinking. As soon as we got home, Mack made a call to social services.

"Dad, is everything OK?" Callum asked him.

"Hope so, Callum," Mack told him.

A few days later, we got a call from social services asking if we could foster Annabel. The answer was a yes.

They dropped her off. Scared was an understatement. Mack and I went outside with Callum. Before we could say anything, Callum went to Annabel.

"It's OK, Annabel. You're safe, Nothing is going to happen to you here. I promise. Dads," he said, pointing to us, "are good parents. They're the best. They'll make sure you're safe."

Olivia came. "Annabel, welcome home." She took her hand. Rae gave her Jules.

The lady from social services had tears in her eyes. "I wish most parents raised kids like yours."

Mack put his arm around me. "This is how it should be."

We had our dinner to remember Jack. Malek said Grace.

"Who's Jack?" Annabel asked innocently.

"Family, dear child. Family. Just like you," Malek told her. That made her smile.

"Family game," Jack said. "Maggie, it's your turn."

She picked Twister. "This never gets old. Annabel, this will make you laugh when the grown-ups do it and fall over. It's hysterical," Maggie told her.

"And it goes on YouTube." Alice laughed. Bella laughed. We played and laughed for ages. Annabel came up to Mack and me in the kitchen.

"You OK, Annabel?" I asked her.

"Thank you for helping me. I like this family," she told us. Annabel turned round and went back to play. We both had tears in our eyes.

"Dad?" I said to my father. "I would like you to meet your new granddaughter, Annabel."

Dad knelt down. "Hey, kiddo. How you doing?"

She nodded. "OK."

"I'm your granddad. Is that OK?"

"Yes. I'd like that. Can I call you dad? Is that OK?" she asked me.

"Yes. I would like that," I told her.

She went to see Rae. "Here's Jules," She said, giving the rabbit back.

"Annabel, Jules is for you. She'll keep you safe. Like Jonas helps me. So, keep her." Rae hugged her tight.

Callum came up to Mack and me after dinner. "Thanks for helping Annabel and making her my sister."

"Hey, you did the right thing in telling us what was happening to her. That's a brave thing you did. We're proud of you, son," Mack told him. Callum smiled.

"So, with that," I said, smiling, "go get that envelope over there." I pointed to the microwave. He opened it.

"Oh. Really?" Callum's face lit up. "You adopted me a goat? Thank you."

"We're going to see him next weekend," Mack said. "Good lad."

As Callum walked away, he turned round, looked at us and said, "You know, I'd do it again," and walked off.

When we were getting ready for bed, Mack sat on the end of the bed. I sat next to him. "What's up?"

"Just thinking about what Callum said earlier. He's got a good head on his shoulders for a six-year-old," he said.

"Well, they all have. I mean, look, we taught them well. You're the one that guides them that way," I told him. "Come to bed. Been a long day." I smiled at him.

"That's not what I was thinking, actually," I told him.

"Thank God. It's been a while. I've missed it," he said.

We took Callum to see his new adopted goat. He called her Annabel.

"I don't look like a goat," Annabel said.

We laughed. They loved the donkeys. "I like these ones. They're funny," Thaddeus said.

"No more pets," I said. "Seven kids, two spiders, a dog, a cat and now a goat. We are looking like a zoo," I told him.

The following Tuesday, Lydia got a call from Maggie's school.

"What's wrong?" I asked when she was getting her coat on.

Lydia was upset. "Maggie got beaten up."

"I'm coming with you," I said. Joel was spitting mad. Maggie came out and was crying. We went to the head's office.

"What the hell happened to my daughter?" Joel said.

The head explained that some of the kids started it and it was the same as before. They didn't like that she was mixed race and she had two gay uncles. As Maggie defended herself, one kid punched her in the face and another pulled her hair, and brought her to the ground. Two kids went to help Maggie and called the teacher.

"We've offered Maggie counselling," the head said.

"Thank you. Maggie won't be in school for a few days. We put our kids in your care. I am pissed, beyond belief," Joel said. He got up. "We're leaving, now!" Joel said. We didn't even argue.

"Maggie, you OK, baby girl?" Joel asked her.

"No, Dad. I'm not." She hugged him tight.

"You guys go home," Joel said. "Maggie and I are gonna go for a walk."

They went to their favourite place. The lake. They sat on the bench and were quiet for a minute.

Then Joel spoke. "Look at me, Maggie," which she did.

"My courageous baby girl. You defended yourself. I'm so sorry about this. You didn't deserve this. Just remember, never let the light from your heart disappear. You are so much like your mother. That's a good thing. People like that are cruel, jealous and wicked. Just remember, always remember, there is good everywhere. Maggie Anne Green. I love you," Joel Said.

"Dad, it hurts. In here." She pointed to her heart.

"It will, for a while. But remember, you are strong, so very strong. You want ice cream?" Joel smiled.

"Yes. Chocolate chip mint and strawberry." She smiled.

"OK. Don't tell your mother. She'll kill me. It's before dinner." Joel hugged her tight.

When they got home. Lydia hugged her. "Chocolate chip mint and strawberry. Good choice." She smiled. "Dinner in ten."

"How's Maggie?" Mack asked as I walked in. "Mack, she's putting on a brave face. She's going to be fine," I said.

When I got back to work with Lydia, it was as hectic. We liked it. "Brings back memories, this," Lydia said. "I rather do this than work back at the hospital. Although, you did meet Mack there."

"Can't believe that was almost fifteen years ago. Where's that gone?" I said, on a break. "It seems like yesterday. We've been through a lot."

"Look at what we've got now. If we hadn't been through that, we wouldn't have what we have now. Shit, gotta go. Mr Campbell has a blood test, like five minutes ago."

"See you later. Right, Miss Holden's staples need removing," I said to myself.

When I got home, I was knackered. "Work OK?" Mack said, looking up from his laptop and taking his glasses off.

"Ran off my feet. Even when I went in early. Haven't had time to fart. How was your day?" I got up and put the kettle on.

We woke up to screaming. It was Annabel. She was shaking. She hung on to me, shaking.

"Hey, hey. What's wrong?" I asked.

"I had a dream that they took me away from here, back to them. They were nasty. Please don't make me go back."

"Annabel. Look at me," Mack said. "You're not going anywhere. This is home. Forever. Dad and I promise never to send you away. This is your home."

Callum came in with his pillow and duvet. "Bella, we'll never leave you."

"Nor shall we." Olivia was there with the rest of the kids. All with their pillows and duvets. Annabel stopped crying.

"The bad dreams will leave, Bella," Rae said.

We left them too it. All asleep, together. "We need to get her counselling. She needs it. It would help us as well."

We arranged for counselling. Lucky enough, they had an appointment for the following afternoon. We took it. We were all pretty nervous. Annabel looked at us. "Promise they won't take me away?"

"Promise, Bella," I told her.

She smiled.

The counsellor was shocked when all of us walked in. "Hi, lady," Thaddeus said.

"Well, this is interesting," said the counsellor. "Who's Annabel?"

"Bella. I like Bella." She said holding my hand tight.

"OK, Bella. Would you like your dads to come with you?"

She nodded. The rest played quietly. We were there for an hour. Poor Bella. She was scheduled for once a fortnight. For an hour.

"Who's up for McDonald's for dinner?" Mack said.

The kids went mad. "Only 'cause you're knackered and can't be bothered to cook," Oliver said.

"Straight to the point." Mack smiled at Oliver.

We had the party the following Saturday. We knew we were getting old. We kept yawning. "How old are we?" Lydia said.

"You're like, really old," Maggie said. We looked at her.

"How you feeling, Maggie?" I asked her.

"I'm OK. Better than I was. Those kids said I should be ashamed of having you as uncles. I'm not ashamed of you. I'm proud of you."

"I'd rather have this life now than all those years ago," Joel said.

Annabel came up to me sat on my lap and fell asleep, with Jules. I put her to bed.

When I came down, Mack had the photo albums out. The kids were looking at them. Mack and Lydia had tears in their eyes. I looked through them.

"I remember these ones like it was yesterday," I said.

They was the ones where we had the kids and the one where Mack and I got married.

"Yes." Mack couldn't talk. He was crying. "I remember when I asked you, I was afraid you would say no. I threw up for an hour, Lydia. Where did you two go on your first date?"

"Where did we go? It was that nice restaurant. The Paddock. Do you remember, Joel?" She looked at him. He was asleep. "He's an old man. Idiot too. But I love him. Arsehole." The kids laughed.

"Dad?" Fran asked Mack. "Why are these taken in the garden with and is in the garden?"

"Because I wanted you all to feel the fresh air and it was a chance to bond with all of you." He had tears in his eyes again.

"Why don't you do that with Bella?" Oliver said, with his arms round Mack's neck. "Dad, she's lost. Bella needs to know she's loved. You did it with us." Oliver kissed his cheek.

"Are you glad you two got us?" Rae asked.

"Yes. Oh God, yes. We always wanted to be dads," I told them.

"I'm really proud to be your dad. I'm glad we got you," Mack told them. We heard Bella crying.

"I'll go," Mack said.

"Hey sweetheart. Come here. Bad dream again?" She nodded.

"Hey, bad dreams will go. Tomorrow, you and me are off to the farm you like. That OK?" I told her, hugging her.

"Can I feed the animals by myself?" She looked at me.

"Yer, you can. Bella, no one will ever hurt you again. That's a promise. We love you, Bella Denton. Always."

So off they went. It worked. They had a lovely day. Bella's face was a picture. "Did you enjoy yourself!" I asked her, giving her a drink.

"Yes. Thank you, Dads." She hugged us both tight. "I'm going to be all right, aren't I?"

"Yes, you are," I told her, still hugging her. "Always."

"Can I go play with Olivia in the garden, please?" Bella asked, giving me the cup back.

"Off you go," I told her.

She stopped, turned round. "I'm good to be happy here."

That set Mack off crying. "See, it worked. You menopausal twat." I kissed him and smiled.

"Right, I'm cooking," I said.

Olivia said, "Dad, stop crying like a girl and take over. We'll get sick if he cooks."

Mack started laughing. "I'm better than you."

"That cheered you. What's for dinner?" I asked.

"Sausage, mash, beans." Mack winked.

Later that evening, we spoke about what we wanted to do. Before we could say anything, Lydia stood at the door, in tears. Hands on her stomach. Mack and I looked at each other. "How far are you?"

"Two months! Shit. Shit. Joel passed out. Maggie laughed, said we are too randy. Alice and Alfie and Jack are like whatever. Five kids. Oh my God. Condoms. Why didn't I use them?"

We laughed. "You slut!" Mack said.

"Hark at you, Mack. You got Michael pregnant seven times. You are at more than me," Lydia said sarcastically. "You're like randy rabbits. I'm too old for this shit. Oh my God."

"Don't look at him, he didn't get you pregnant!" I told her.

"Fuck off, nob-head." She started laughing. "I'm scared. I'm not as young as I was. Maggie's nearly fifteen. The twins are twelve, Jack's ten.

Shit, Maggie's birthday is in three weeks."

"We'll help," I told her. "Listen, we have a few ideas."

Lydia got up. "I'll better go, I'll have to make sure they helped Joel off the floor. Knowing them, they've probably drawn on him. Maggie's probably drawn a dick on his head. What are you two going to do?"

"Well," Mack said sarcastically, "I'm going to make love to Mike and hopefully get him pregnant."

I winked at Lydia who just smiled. "Night, randy rabbits."

Mack shyly smiled at me.

"What?" I asked him.

"I could never get bored being with you. It's like the first time, after all these years. You know I still get nervous even now."

"I get like that all the time as well. When we're together, I don't want it to stop." I just looked at him.

He kissed me slowly, we made love right there on the sofa. He looked at me, I nodded yes, I wanted to do it again.

"I don't want to stop being with you."

Mack smiled. "Mike, we'll never stop being together."

I just smiled at him. We were together, really together. We fell asleep in each other's arms.

We woke up, Mack had tears in his eyes.

"What?" I asked while stroking his head.

"Last night was beautiful."

"It was," I said. "We better get up; the kids will be up soon and it's family day."

We went to the beach. The kids running around. Maggie was on her phone, listening to her music. It was quite good.

"What's that you're listening to? It's quite good," Mack asked.

"It's 'Haevn'. 'Where the heart is'. Logan got me into it. Good, innt, Uncle Mack?" she asked.

"Yes, sweetie," Mack said.

"Is Mum going to be OK, with the baby on the way? I'm worried about her," she told me.

Mack smiled. "She's going to be OK. Tough as nails your mum. We'll be here to help."

Maggie looked at Lydia. "I don't know what I'll do without her."

"You're just like her, you know." Mack put his arm round her shoulder.

Jack shouted. "Maggie, come and get your ice cream. Chocolate chip mint and Strawberry."

We laughed. "Come on. Better get it before Jack eats it," Mack said.

Joel was fussing over Lydia. "I'm fine. Sea air will do the baby good. Thought of any names?"

"I like Emily for a girl, or Nathaniel for a boy," Joel said.

"I like them. Sorted. They're the names," Lydia said.

Joel was confused. Alfie saw this. "Dad, just go with it. It doesn't happen very often."

"Dad, whose turn is it to choose a film?" Francesca said to me.

"It's Bella's turn to choose," I said, putting the popcorn on the table. "What do you want to watch?"

"'Up'. You know, the one with the balloons and the grumpy old man." Bella smiled.

"'Up', it is then," Mack said.

Ten minutes into the film, Mack was asleep, snoring. So Oliver put two popcorns up his nose to stop him snoring and two in his eyes. "That'll teach him for ruining film night."

Mack woke up when he couldn't breathe. He looked at Oliver.

"What?" Oliver said, smiling. "Your snoring is annoying. *Ssh*."

"Smart arse," Mack told him.

"Takes one to know one," Oliver said, eating popcorn.

"Right, kids. Film's finished. Bed. Come on," I said.

For once, they didn't argue. They were yawning. I carried Rae to bed. They were asleep in minutes.

"That was easy," Mack said.

"I like days like these. What are we getting Maggie for her birthday? She's fifteen, Mack," I said.

"I was thinking of us taking her shopping," Mack said.

"I think she'd like that. Sorted." I smiled.

Maggie's birthday came around. She was excited. We took her shopping, while Dad and Malek kept an eye on the kids. She was spoiled. Then we went out for dinner.

Maggie gave Lydia a present. "What's this?" Lydia asked.

Maggie smiled. It was a teddy bear for the baby. "Maggie, that's very kind. Why?"

"Because I want them to know that I will always be there for them. I'll help Mum." Maggie hugged her.

"You darling girl," Lydia said with a tear in her eye.

"This for you, Maggie," said Olivia, giving her a present. Maggie opened it. It was a photo of them as kids together.

Maggie smiled. "Thank you. I really love it. Thanks for today."

"One more thing," I told her. I gave her an envelope. It was tickets to see her favourite band. 'Haevn'.

"You got to be shitting me!"

"Language, Maggie," Joel said.

"Sorry." She hugged us.

"I'm taking you," Mack said, "to keep an eye on you. Matthew's coming too. It's seating down so we can see you. So no going out of eye shot. OK?"

"OK. No problem. Can I ask Logan?" she asked Lydia.

She nodded yes. "Who's Logan?" Joel asked.

"A boy in my class," Maggie told him.

"Boys, hell no," he said.

"Chill out, old man. He's a friend. That's it," Maggie said.

"Old man. I'm not old," Joel had the hump.

"Give over, Dad. It took you five minutes to get the chair at home. Then your knee and ankle clicked. I thought you were going to fall over and really hurt yourself. Then you farted. It smelt like you died." Maggie looked at him.

Mack and Matthew took Maggie and Logan to the concert. Logan looked shit scared of Mack. "Is he always like that? Giving people the death stare?"

"No, he's constipated," she said.

Matthew tried to hide the fact he was laughing. Maggie looked at him in the rear-view mirror and smiled.

"Besides, you're lucky, he didn't get the famous clipboard." Mack smiled. He knew she was winding him up. So, he played along.

"The clipboard?" Logan was scared.

"Oh, yes. Every time she meets a new friend, they have to go through me and the board. Twenty questions. If you don't get twenty right. You can't be friends."

"But Maggie should decide who are her mates," Logan said.

"You want to walk?" Matthew said.

"No, sir." He turned to Maggie. "Are they always like this? You said one is your god dad?"

"Not always. You know they were in the army. Mack's my god dad. We're also related." Maggie's good.

Logan was shitting himself. "He's my uncle. His husband and my mum are brother and sister. Family's important to us. Isn't that right, Mack?"

"That's right, Maggie. We're a close family." Mack was trying not to laugh. Logan looked at Mack. "You don't look gay. I mean you got loads of tattoos." Mack gave him a look.

"Thank God we're here," Logan said. We all started laughing.

"That's twenty quid you owe me," Maggie told Mack. "Told you he was easy to wind up."

"You're good," Logan said. "Are you really gay and Maggie's uncle?"

"Yes on both counts. But I'm serious on one thing through. Don't try anything. Matthew and I are sitting one row behind. OK?" Logan nodded. "Good lad. Come on."

Matthew said to Logan, "You're lucky. The last friend of Maggie, he didn't like. No one found him. Good luck." Maggie heard him and smiled.

They had a good time at the gig. Mack as usual fell asleep. Matthew woke him up. "Really!" he said.

"What? I've got seven kids, two spiders, a cat, dog and a goat," Mack said.

The gig ended. "Thanks, Mack." She hugged him.

The next day, Oliver came home pleased as a punch. "What's up with you?" Mack asked him, giving him a drink.

"Do you remember I had to a talk about someone who I looked up to and why in English?" Oliver said between sips.

"Yes. How did you do? What did you talk about?" Mack asked.

"I got an A. I spoke about you and Dad."

I walked and say next to him as he said that.

He looked up and said, "Because you're there every day, gave me a family, you love me for who I am. Most kids go through life not having what we have. That my parents are just the coolest. I told them, I don't care that they're gay, it means nothing. You teach us every day to be better people. Don't take nothing for granted."

That was it! Mack and I were crying at the table. Oliver just looked at us. "You two are so weird. What's for dinner? I'm hungry." Oliver got up and got another drink.

As we sat at the table, Bella spoke. "Excuse me," she said.

"What's the matter?" Mack asked.

"We forgot to say grace," Bella said.

Bella said grace and gave thanks for what we had, be grateful for what we got. Be kind to those who need it.

With that, my phone rang. It was Joel. The baby was on his way. I phoned Mack who got our kids. I got Lydia's.

"Is Mum going to be OK?" Jack said.

"Yes. She is. You're going to be a big brother, Jack."

Joel called. "She's here. Emily is here. Eight pound six. She's beautiful, Michael. The kids OK?"

"They're fine. We'll keep them here until you come home," I told him.

Emily was the sweetest thing ever. Mack was crying.

"No more kids for crying out loud. We've got twelve kids between us. We've got a primary school," I half shouted.

He looked at me. "OK. OK. Come here, Emily." He took her in the garden. He walked her around. I smiled. He was brilliant with her. She fell asleep. "Mum, do you want a drink?" Maggie asked.

"Tea, please," Lydia replied.

"OK. Alice, go and tidy your room; Alfie, go and tidy the living room. Jack, come and help me please. Mum, sit down with Emily. You too, Dad." Maggie told them. They did it.

"I can get used to this," Lydia said.

When we got home, Mack asked, "What was all that, earlier?"

"I could see you getting broody again. I saw it in your eyes. I'm sorry. Just really tired." I sat at the table and sighed.

Rae looked worried.

"Rae, honey, I'm fine. Come here."

I hugged her. "It's not me?" she asked.

"Darling, no, it's not. I'm just tired. She rested her head on my shoulder. "Bed, miss. Go on," I told her.

Off she went. "I'm going for a walk," I told Mack.

I walked around for ages, just thinking. I actually enjoyed the quiet. I sat on the bench where Mack and I sat and smiled. Next thing I knew, it was morning. I had loads of missed calls from Mack. He was shitting himself. I ran home.

When I walked in the door, he was on the phone to me. He turned round. "Where the hell have you been?" he yelled. "Shit. Mike. Are you OK?"

I just stood there. "Sorry. I just walked. I was thinking about everything. Then I fell asleep on our bench."

"I was thinking the worst. I thought you'd—" He sat on the sofa.

"For God's sake, no!" I raised my voice.

The kids came down. "Are you arguing?" Fran asked.

"We've stopped now," Mack said, scratching his head. Rae looked sad and went to her room crying.

"I know you are. I was getting panicky. You wouldn't answer your phone. I thought you left. He stopped, looked at me. "Did you really fell asleep on the bench?" he asked.

"Yes. Someone even put a cup with a fiver in it next to me." I smiled.

He laughed. "I married a tramp."

"At least I've still got my looks," I told him.

He shook his head. "Come on, let's get home and go out for lunch."

That evening, we talked at length about everything. I loved the way we talked, so openly and honestly. We never lied about anything. In fifteen years! We looked at old photos of when we met.

"Look at us," I said. "We haven't changed much."

Mack put the album down. I knew what he wanted. We made love right there on the sofa. It was better than ever. He smiled.

"Really!" I said. "Three times."

"Damn right," he said. We smiled. It was amazing.

"Lydia's right. We are randy rabbits," I told him.

Olivia was very quiet when she came down.

"What's up?" Mack asked, giving her breakfast. "Olivia. What's wrong?" Mack asked. She didn't answer. She was clearly upset about something.

"Olivia. Sweetheart. What's wrong?" Mack asked again.

"Leave me alone." She got up and ran to her room.

"I'll go," Mack said. He knocked on the door. "Olivia. Olivia. What's—" He saw the bed sheet on the floor. The penny dropped. "Sweetheart."

Olivia was in the corner crying. Mack sat next to her. He put his arm around her. "When did it happen?"

"During the night. I had a pad that Maggie gave just in case. Why does it happen?" She was so upset.

"It happens every month. You're growing up, It's part of becoming a grown up." Mack had a tear in his eye.

"I don't want to grow up, Dad. I want to be your little girl forever," Olivia said.

"Olivia Anna Denton, you will always be my little girl. Even when you've grown up and got your own life, you'll never stop being our little girl. If you want, I'll call Aunt Lydia and she'll go with you," Mack said.

"No. I wanna go with you and Dad. I want to spend some time with you both. I don't want to grow up." She hugged him tight.

Mack was crying. "My baby is growing up. I love you, Olivia."

"I love you too, Dad," Olivia told him.

Mack and Olivia came down. They told me what happened. I started crying. "My baby is growing up."

We took Olivia out for the day. We got her what she needed.

"Talk, Olivia. Tell us," Mack said.

"I'm scared about growing up. I don't want to leave you behind." Olivia started crying, which set Mack off.

The waitress said, "Everything OK?"

I nodded. "Olivia. You will never leave us. Growing up can be tough. But it's going to be OK. Dad and I will always be here. Always. You're our eldest," I said, getting upset. "I'm proud of you, kiddo. Even when you're married."

"Hey," Mack said, "let's not get that far. You're giving me a heart attack. I don't want my baby girl getting married. Ever. Do you hear me?"

Olivia started laughing. Then she said, "I'm so glad you're my parents. Thank you for today. I feel better. Can I have cake?"

That evening, we checked on the kids.

Olivia said to Mack, "Dad?"

"Yes, darling?" he said at the door.

"I know I'm thirteen, but can you read me a story, like you did when I was little? I miss that." She smiled.

He sat on the floor, next to her, and read her favourite story to her, *Goldilocks and the Three Bears*.

"Night, Olivia. I love you," Mack told her.

"I love you too, Dad. Always." She fell asleep. He came down crying and told me what happened.

Oliver came down and saw Mack crying.

"Why you up?" Mack asked.

"Need a drink, old man," he said.

I couldn't help but smile. They were so alike. "You coming to my game on Sunday?"

"Yer. We're gonna be there," Mack told him.

"Didn't want you forgetting. You are getting old." Oliver was sarcastic. "Do you want your Zimmer frame or your scooter?"

"Get to bed." Mack was trying not to laugh. I on the other hand burst out laughing.

"All right, old man. Keep your hearing aid in! Can you hear me!" He was laughing.

"Smart arse," Mack said, smiling.

"Learned from the best, old man," he said back. "Love you, Dad."

"Love you too, son. Bed," Mack said, smiling.

"He's just like you, got an answer for everything," I said.

We went and checked in on Lydia and Emily. "How's it been?"

"She's an angel. She sleeps during the night. I swear I got the wrong child. The kids have been brilliant, especially Maggie. Five kids. I'm pushing bloody fifty. How are you two doing?"

"We're good. Really good," I told her. "I've been thinking of cutting down at work. Thinking of going down to four days."

"Sounds good. Can you afford it?" she asked.

"Yes, we can. If Mike stays at four days. If they need him, it's overtime. I've got some work coming my way for a few weeks so money's good," Mack said.

Work was interesting. Laura had told me she was leaving. "Why? Where you going?" I asked.

"For another job. I'm not enjoying it any more. I'm working up the hospital. So, I'm moving on. End of the week," she told me.

Laura left. I took her out for a drink. "Keep in touch. Lydia's birthday is on Saturday. You can meet Emily. She's cute."

"So no more kids then!" she said, smiling.

"Sod off. My house is a zoo. Olivia is thirteen, starting to get into boys.

Oliver is Oliver. Like his dad. Fran and Thaddeus are always doing pranks. They glued Mack's arse to the toilet seat. Rae wants to be a nurse. She bandaged my finger to nose. Callum wants another goat and Bella wants to be a pilot," I told her.

She couldn't stop laughing. "I love hearing about your family. You ever watched 'Modern Family' on Sky One? It's like that. Olivia still got those spiders?"

"Oh god, yes. Do you know what she did? She put Loki on my head. Then ran off," I said.

Laura was in hysterical. She couldn't stop laughing.

When Saturday arrived, the kids loved seeing Laura. Bella took a shinning to her. Laura had brought a friend. "Who's that?"

"Hope you don't mind. His name is James. I've been seeing him a couple of weeks. I didn't say anything. I wanted to see how it was going," she said.

"It's fine," I said. "He seems nice."

James and Jack spoke for a while. I had Emily. She was getting big. She was six weeks now. I forgot what it was like when the kids were babies.

Thaddeus asked. "Were we this little?"

"Yes. You grow up so quick. What do you think?"

"She's lovely." He gave her a kiss, then went and played.

Mack saw me with Emily. "She's cute. Is she snoring?"

"Yes."

Lydia said, "Come on, miss. I'm getting you home to bed. Thanks, you two. Lovely day. See you later. Kids, come on."

Off they all went. Laura followed suit with James. "Dad, Malek, you two want to stay the night?" I said, tidying up.

"Might as well. Malek's asleep anyway." Dad helped. "How are you and Mack? I worry about you two."

I smiled. "Dad, we're fine. Really. Why do you worry?"

"I don't want anything to happen," he said.

"Simon. Honestly, we're fine. We talk. I mean really talk every week. We promised always to be honest and upfront. Never to lie," Mack said, holding my hand tight.

"OK." My dad looked at Mack. "You're a good man, Mack. I'm proud of you."

We started laughing. Malek was really snoring.

The next few days, all the kids and Lydia were acting oddly. They were all up to something.

"What are they all planning?" Joel asked. "Lydia has been quiet, so I know something is up."

"I don't like it when they're like this," Mack said. "Last time they were like this, my arse was stuck to the loo seat."

"Good. You lot are here," Francesca said. "You lot. Here. Sunday morning. Ten am," she continued, pointing to us guys.

Sunday morning came around. Ten am sharp. Then it clicked. Father's Day. Mack was crying, as usual. The kids had made Mack and I a new photo album of us and the kids. Just us.

"This is lovely, kids," I said. "How long you been doing this?"

"A while," said Callum. "It was worth it though."

Maggie and the others did the same for Joel. They got a bottle of his favourite scotch. He started crying.

"Really, Dad?" said Alfie. "You're like Mack. You are the best Dad."

Then our lot gave Dad and Malek a present. "What's this?"

"A present from us. It's father for you two, you know," Thaddeus told us. "But I'm not related to you," Malek Said.

Rae went and hugged him. "Yes, you are. you\re our other granddad. You're there every day for us. We love you very much. Allah blessed us with you."

They did them a photo album too. "Excuse me for a moment," Malek said. He left the room. He went to the kitchen. I followed him. "You OK, Malek?"

"Yes, my dear friend." He wiped his eyes. "I'm grateful for all this. What Rae said was lovely."

"Well, it's true," Rae said. "Granddad Malek. You're family. Never forget that, that you're here with us. I'm glad you're with granddad."

"So are we," said Thaddeus. They went and hugged. All seven of them. Father's Day was good.

"Granddad Malek, your turn to say grace." Olivia said.

He said grace in Arabic.

"Dad," Maggie said to Joel. "Here."

"What's this?" he asked.

"Open it." She smiled. He opened to find a photo of them, by their favourite place, the lake. He couldn't talk. He was crying. "Maggie Anne Green."

"Dad," she kissed his head, "I'll always be your baby girl."

She went and help to clear the table. Joel looked at Lydia.

"Don't look at me. That was all her. Alfie's right. You are a good, good father."

"Family film. Dad, your turn," Oliver said with his arms round Mack's shoulder. We watched 'Lord of the Rings'. The kids fell asleep. It was a good day.

Work without Laura was quiet. I was enjoying the new role. We had a new girl who was covering for Lydia, who was hard working. She didn't answer much. Good at her job, but she didn't like talking much.

"How's the new girl?" Mack asked.

"Hard working. Good. Can we go home? I've had enough. Glad to go home. How's my Rae?" I asked her.

"OK, Dad. School is boring. I like the weekends, they're fun, plus tomorrow is family day. So, something to look forward to. Must feed George when I get home. I swear he's a pig."

I laughed. "You're funny, Rae."

Mack had been quiet. "What's the matter?" I asked him.

"Nothing in particular. The guys have asked to help out next week for four days. Just nervous. That's all. Don't want to have a panic attack or anything," he said. I rolled my eyes at him. "Could you roll your eyes any louder?" he asked.

"Listen. You're going to be fine. Arsehole," I told him. "When you going?"

"Tuesday to Friday morning. So, I won't be here. I'm going to miss the lot of you like crazy, you know that," he told me.

"You know it'll be the longest we've been apart in fifteen years. So, you'll have some making up to do when you get home," I said.

The next few days went fast. Mack came home early.

"How did it go?" I asked.

"knackered. Good. Missed you lot like crazy. I'm glad we spoke every night. It drove me nuts not being here," he said.

It was awkward. "What time are the kids back?" he asked.

"Dad's taking them till five." I smiled.

He got up and just looked at me. "I've been waiting for this all week." He smiled.

The kids came home at five. "Dad, where are you?" they yelled.

We came downstairs.

"Daddy!" They hugged him like mad. "We missed you."

"How are you, old man? Did you pop a hip? Did your hearing aid fall out?" Oliver said sarcastically

"How old do you think I am?" he asked Oliver.

"Try really old." Oliver was laughing.

"You are a sod." Mack laughed. Oliver hugged him tight. "I really missed you, Dad. I know you have to work but I missed you."

"I missed you too, son. I missed you all," Mack said.

"Mike, how would you feel if I did a couple more days next week? Then that's it?" he asked while we were drying up and doing the washing.

"Yes. That's fine. Honestly. You look happier. A lot happier." He could tell I was worried.

"You know I'm not leaving, right?" he said, putting the clothes in the dryer.

"I know that, numb-nuts. I suppose I'm not used to us being apart. I hate being in an empty bed," I told him.

Mack was laughing. "Well, I can't help being a stud muffin."

"You've been in the medicine cabinet again. Weirdo," I said.

"Who's a weirdo?" Callum said.

"Your dad," I said. "Why you up?"

"Had a dream I broke my ankle kicking a pigeon, because he went for Bella. Stupid pigeon. Can I have a drink?" Callum said.

We laughed and gave him his drink. "Can we go to the farm for family day? I like the farm."

"Yes. We can. Why do you like the farm?" I asked.

"I just like the animals. I like family day." He started yawning.

"Come on you, bed," Mack said as he put Callum to bed.

"Love you, Dad. Always." He fell asleep. Mack smiled.

"Dad?" Thaddeus asked me. "Can I take this frog home?" He opened his hand and this massive frog jumped out. "Shit. No." Thaddeus laughed.

"You bugger."

"Dad, you scream worse than Dad," Fran said, eating her ice cream.

Bella was having fun. She was excited over the sheep. "They're funny. That sheep just pooped."

"What's wrong, Olivia?" I asked.

"I'm OK. My stomach hurts a bit. You know. Aunt Lydia gave me some tablets." She smiled.

"You want to sit down?" I asked her.

"I'll be OK." I put my arm round her shoulder. Then Olivia started laughing. We could hear the rest of them singing 'The Lion Sleeps Tonight' at the top of their voices, with everyone looking.

"We're a bunch of weirdos. But I love my family. Dad, I hope we're like this forever." Olivia hugged me.

"I have a feeling we will." I smiled.

"You want me to come in for three days? I don't mind. To be honest, I could do with being with grownups," Lydia asked.

"How's you and Mack?" Lydia then asked.

"We've been OK. I miss him when he's not home. I don't like it," I said.

"When was the last time you actually talked? I mean really talked?" she said, getting ready for her next patient.

"Three weeks ago," I told her.

"Not good. You talk all the time. You know, I admire you two for always talking."

When I got home, Bella came running to the door. "Close your eyes, Dad. Don't open them. Rae, help me please."

They brought me in. Something smelt good. "What's going on?"

"Open your eyes, Daddy," Rae said.

I opened them. The living room looked nice. "What's this?"

"Well, Grandad Simon and Grandad Malek helped," Olivia said

"You and Dad have been looking so sad, so this is for you," Fran said.

"Where is Dad anyway?" I was confused.

"Gone to the shop with Joel. He hasn't a clue. We're going to Aunt Lydia's when Joel comes back," Thaddeus said.

At that moment, Joel and Mack walked in. "What this?" Mack said, taking his coat off.

"Daddy and you have been sad. This is for you two," Rae said.

"Come on, kids. Let's go," Joel said. "Simon, Malek, come on. Lydia has some scotch for you two."

There was a silence between us. Then we started talking at the same time. We sat at the table, hand in hand. "Mack, I've missed you. I've missed this. Talking, everything. I hate being away from you. Are we OK? God, I'm scared. I can't—"

"Chill out. I've told you so many times, I can't live without you. When I was away, I hated being on my own. Empty bed, lonely. No kids. It was like before I met you. My life's here, with you and the kids. Matthew saw this. I was frightened to talk. I love you, dumb arse. Can we eat, I'm starving." Mack said getting up. "I missed it all," he said.

"Damn right. I've dreamed of this my whole life," Mack told me. Just then, the kids came in with Dad.

"You two are OK? You two not sad?" Rae asked, sitting in my lap.

"Thanks, kids. Just what we needed," I said.

"Now, Dad. Could you hear everything Dad was saying? We know you're a bit deaf," Oliver said to Mack.

Mack hugged him tight. "Are you OK?" Oliver looked confused.

"Yes, I'm fine. Ollie, do me a favour?" Oliver nodded.

"Don't change. None of you change," he told the kids. They all hugged him. My dad and I smiled.

"Careful, he's an old man, everything is falling apart. Soon the dementia is going to kick in," Oliver said out loud. That was it, we all laughed. We put the kids to bed.

"So?" my dad said to both of us. "Was the fight worth it?"

"Yes," I said. "Those kids are brilliant." Mack nodded.

"Thank you," Dad said. "Love you, son." he said and left.

"That was a turn up for the books," Mack said.

"Surprised is not the word. Sneaky little sods." I was smiling.

Mack started yawning. "Come on, bed. I'm tired."

"What are we going to do for Lydia's birthday?" I asked Mack. Just then, Maggie can in with a couple of bags.

"Hey, what's up?" Mack asked.

"Can I keep these here? There pressies are for Mum from us lot. You know, she can be really nosy. I want it to be a surprise from us kids," she

said.

"No problem. Maggie, you OK?" Mack asked.

"Kinda. There's this boy," she said, smiling.

"Boys. You're a bit young," Mack said, giving her a drink.

"That's what Dad said. I'm nearly sixteen," Maggie said.

"It's not Logan, is it?" Mack acted like the protective uncle.

"God, no. He's a friend. He's called Clarke." She was shy.

"I think you should talk to your dad," we said.

"OK. How do you know? I mean, how did you two know?" Maggie was curious.

"I knew when I first met him. I knew it was him," I said.

"Same as," Mack said. "As soon as I saw him. That was it. I fell in love there and then. I never felt like that."

"Wow. So romantic," Maggie said. We smiled.

"Come you, Maggie. I'll walk you home before your mum sends the sniffer dogs round," Mack said.

"Love you too, kiddo," I told her.

When Mack came back, he was smiling. "She's growing up."

"Olivia is not far behind. She is fourteen in five weeks. Boys," I said.

"No. Can't handle that. My baby girl. I don't want any of my girls dating," Mack said.

"Why can't I have a boyfriend?" Francesca asked.

"Because I'm your dad, and I said so. Plus, you're my little girl," Mack said.

"You're so weird. I'm twelve. I'm way too young to have one of them. Besides, I don't want one," she said, getting a drink.

Francesca looked at him. "Why are you scared of us growing up?"

She had him there. "Because I am. That's why," he said.

"Dad?" Thaddeus asked me.

"Yes, son?" I asked. "I need my inhaler. My asthma," he said.

"Sit down. Let's get it. You're going to be OK." I told him. I gave it to him and checked his pulse.

After fifteen minutes. "How are you now?" I asked, looking at him closely.

"I'm OK, Dad. Just worried, haven't had to use for a little while." He looked at Mack. "I'm OK, Dad. It was an asthma attack. No need to worry. I'm gonna go sit down for twenty minutes on the sofa, so Dad can keep an eye on me. Then I will take it again." He did that.

Mack hated seeing him like that. He went and sat with him. Thaddeus put his head on his shoulder. "Dad, I know you hate seeing me like this. I'm OK. Always."

"Thaddeus, I'll always worry about you. You're my son. I love you," Mack told him, smiling.

"I love you, Dad. I love you as well, Dad," he told us.

"We love you very much too," I told him.

"Can we go for a walk later, when I'm OK?" he asked.

"Yes, we can. You're a good lad, Thaddeus," I said.

"I know. You two are good dads. Don't forget that," Thaddeus said.

Mack had tears in his eyes. Thaddeus wiped his tears away.

"You're a big old softie, aren't you? Can we go for that walk now?" Thaddeus got up.

"Mack, you're quiet. What's up? Everything OK?" Lydia asked.

"Just worried about Thaddeus. He's been through a lot for a twelve-year-old." Mack smiled sadly.

"He's a spirited boy. He's fine. He's a tough cookie. He's going to be fine. Michael always makes sure he's OK. The check-ups are fine." Lydia tapped his hand.

Thaddeus saw they were talking about him. He walked up to Mack. "Daddy. I know you're worried about me. I'm OK. I will be all right. So, stop bloody worrying." Thaddeus kissed and hugged him tight.

"See, told you," Lydia said. "You're a good dad, Mack. A very good dad. I remember when you first got Olivia. You knew what to do straight away. Then the rest followed."

They both smiled. Then they started laughing. Olivia put Beatrice on my head, I went to get up, but the chair was stuck to my where Thaddeus had glued my bum. Oliver was in fits of laughter, he then tripped on his football. It was hilarious.

It was getting late. "Come on, kids. Home, dinner then bed," I said.

"OK. Can we have pizza?" Thaddeus asked. "Please!" He looked at Mack.

"What do you think?" Mack asked me.

"Why not. Just this once though," I said.

"Rae, your turn for a film," Mack said.

Rae asked me to read her a story. *The Princess and the Pea*. Her favourite. When I finished, I said to her, "Don't ever change who you are, my Rae-Rae."

She smiled and said, "I promise."

We had Olivia's party to arrange. She walked in, looking sheepish. She pulled my sleeve. "Dad, I don't want a party."

"Why? Don't you want your friends around?" I asked her.

"Dad, the truth is, no one wanted to come, expect Seth. Can Seth come over?" Olivia said. She was a bit upset.

"OK, Seth can come over. Sorry, baby."

She hugged me tight, she was crying.

Mack walked in. "Hey, what's wrong?"

"No one expect Seth is coming to her party," I told him.

"Who's Seth?" Mack said. "Do I have to get the clipboard out?" He was trying to cheer her up.

"Dad, you're so embarrassing." She started smiling. "Please, can Seth come over?"

"'Course, he can. As long as he's doesn't talk or hold your hand," Mack said, getting a drink.

Olivia looked at me. "I'm gonna hate the day when I'm older and I tell him I'm getting married." She was laughing.

"No way. No. You're not getting married. Ever. No boys, no. Not having it," Mack said. "None of you girls are getting married."

Olivia was laughing. "You are so weird, Dad. Please, I want to spend it with you. Family day. Chinese food."

"OK. If that's what you want," Mack said. "Come here." She hugged him. "Fourteen. I remember your first day at school. Your big brown eyes. So excited. Couldn't wait to go. Now you're fourteen."

She smiled. "You're so soppy. I'm going to have start calling you Mum. I'm glad I've got you lot. My birthday with my family. Better than a party. Glad I've got Seth. He's a good friend."

"I'll be the judge of that," Mack said.

Olivia smiled. "I'm never gonna to win this, am I?"

"No, you're not. You're my baby," Mack said.

"We can do what you like." Olivia just hugged us both tight. "I'm a lucky girl. You're a silly sod."

Seth came round at three. "Hi, Mr Denton." We both said hi. He looked nervous. "Happy Birthday, Olivia." He gave her a card.

"Thank you, Seth." She looked at Mack. "Dad, chill out. Don't even think about the clipboard."

"The what?" Seth looked worried.

"Don't worry," I said. "He's protective over our kids. Come on, we're going to Lydia's.

We went to Lydia's. Olivia was spoiled. Maggie saw that Mack was not keen on Seth. "Uncle Mack, he's cool. They're friends. Relax."

"Hey," Joel said. "Maggie, when you're a parent, you can't help it."

"So," Mack asked, "what do you want to do when you're older?"

"I want to be a physicist," Seth replied.

"Really." Mack was starting to ease up. He went for the clipboard.

"Dad. Put it away. Don't make me come over there!" Olivia said.

He did as he was told. "Mack!" I told him.

Seth left after dinner. "You were embarrassing, Dad," Olivia said to Mack.

"Hey, I'm looking out for you, young lady," Mack said.

We all stood there. I waved them to the conservatory.

"He's a friend, Dad, that's all. Why are you so afraid of me growing up?" she yelled.

"Because I don't want you to. I wish you could stay here," Mack yelled back.

"Dad, loosen the reins a little. When I go to uni, what are you going to do? I'll always come home. But let me grow up. You're an idiot. I'm fourteen. You can't keep us wrapped up in cotton wool. I really hate you, Dad," Olivia yelled and stormed off.

"Olivia! Olivia!" Mack called after her.

"Go away! I really hate you." She slammed her bedroom door.

"She hates me," Mack said to me as the kids went to bed.

"No, she doesn't," I said, making a coffee. "You have to accept she's growing up. I don't like it much either."

"I'm her dad, I'm supposed to protect her," Mack said.

"You are every day. She knows that," I said. I turned round to see Olivia standing there with her teddy Georgia.

"I'll leave you to it," I said.

"Daddy, I'm sorry. I didn't mean it." She hugged him. He hugged her back.

"It's OK. I'm only looking out for you. I will do that for the rest of your life. Same as your dad. I'm finding it hard that all of you are growing up," he said.

"So am I, Livvy. I'm finding it hard too. You're our first born," I told her. We sat on the sofa. "I remember when we got you, Olivia. My heart melted. Your big brown eyes, looking everywhere. Always wanting to do things quickly." I had a tear in my eye. "Olivia, you are our heart. If we had our way, you'd stay little. We're just worried that you won't need us were you're older and have your own life."

"Well, that's stupid," Olivia said. "I will always need you both. Even when I am older and a doctor in entomology. I will always need you. I'll always be here for family weekends, holidays. You're my dads. I'm sorry for being rude and nasty, Dad. I love you very much. Both of you. Night," she said.

"Told you," I said. I got up and made a drink. "You're an idiot."

Mack looked sheepish. "Well, she is my baby."

Rae came downstairs. "Dad? Have you and Olivia made up?"

"Yes, love," Mack said.

"Good. I won't leave you both," she said, holding Jonas.

"Good girl." Mack was happy.

"Someone has to look after you both when you're old and can't walk," she said.

We both looked at her.

"What?" she said.

"Don't worry, Rae, that was funny," Mack said. "Come here." He hugged her tight. "I don't want you growing up. Understood?"

She nodded and laughed. "You strange weird man. You know Olivia didn't pick a movie. Let her pick a movie tomorrow. It's only fair, please. I don't want her missing out."

Mack did his usual. He fell asleep. So, Oliver did his usual; he put popcorn up his nose and in his eyes. Then Oliver couldn't stop laughing. One of the popcorn went up Mack's nose.

"That's hilarious. Let me do it again!" Oliver said. "Don't worry, it'll come out in the morning, when you have a poo, Dad."

We were in fits of laughter. The connection they had was uncanny.

"Are you ever gonna stop annoying me?" Mack asked Oliver.

"Never, old man. Get used to it," Oliver said, laughing.

Mack got a call; it was Matthew asking if he could help out one last time.

"I thought you were done." I was getting annoyed.

"They need my help. It's just one night." Mack was upset.

"If you want to go, just go." I walked away.

He left. Our first argument in ten years. He tried calling. I didn't answer. I wanted him home.

Mack came home. I was washing up. "Hey," was all he said.

I walked away. "Mike, please." I stopped.

He walked up to me.

"Mack. I feel I'm losing you."

"Never. I want to be here. I just helped out. You're not losing me." He stood next to me.

We made up. "I like it when we make up," I said, stroking his neck.

Mack sat up. "Even when we don't make up, I love being with you."

The next day, at breakfast. "Fran, put your phone down. Ollie, stop picking your nose," I told them.

"Guess what?" Fran said.

"What? You finished with that?" Mack asked her.

We were getting ready for our walk.

"Dad?" Bella asked. "Where's Rae?"

"What do you mean? She's not in her room?" I was starting to panic. "Rae-Rae?"

"What's the matter?" Mack asked. I told him.

We were looking for her. Mack phoned Dad and Lydia.

"Dad!" Callum shouted to us.

"Rae Morgan Denton. What the hell!" I said. "You scared us. Why were you hiding?"

Dad, Malek and Lydia came round.

"I heard you and Dad arguing again. It hurts my heart when you argue," she said.

Lydia put her hand on her mouth.

"Darling, we're so sorry,: Mack said. "We didn't mean it."

"Sorry, but I didn't want to hear it. You're not going to give me away, are you?" She was frightened.

Mack and I started crying. Oliver walked up to Rae and hugged her tight. Then he said, "You listen to me, Rae, they're not going to give you away ever." He had a tear in his eye.

"But I was naughty. I did something wrong." Rae was so kind.

"Yes. You did," Oliver said. "You're my baby sister, I love you." Oliver was crying.

Mack got the photo of when she was a baby in the garden with him. "Rae. This is everything to me. When we got you, you were crying because you were scared. As soon as I took you and went to the garden, you stopped. You rested your head on my chest and fell asleep."

"OK. Sorry. Can we go for that walk now? Can I have an ice cream? Please!" she said.

We always caved in. Mack and I walked hand in hand. Holly was barking to be let off the lead. Rae was with my dad, holding his hand.

"You OK now, Rae?" Dad asked.

"Yes, Grandad. I'm OK. Promise I won't scare them again. I mean it," Rae told him.

"Good girl. Now about that ice cream. What flavour?" He smiled.

"Strawberry?" Rae smiled.

Over dinner, it was quiet. A bit too quiet. "Right, let's talk about it," I said. "What's wrong with everyone?"

"We don't want to go back to school in two weeks," Bella said. "It's so boring. Can't we stay here?"

We laughed. Dad said, "You have to go, Bella."

"But Granddad, we do so many different things. It's so more interesting than school," she told him. Dad got choked up.

"What's the matter?" I was confused.

"That's the first time Bella called me grandad." He was as soppy as Mack.

Bella smiled. "Grandad?" Bella asked him.

"Yes, Bella?" He took her plate.

"Can we spend the day together? Just you and me. The others did. I would like that a lot. Is that OK with everyone?" she asked. Everyone nodded and smiled.

"Settled then. What do you want to do?" she asked him.

"How about shopping then lunch, then ice cream?" Dad asked.

"You read my mind. Thanks, Grandad," Bella told him.

We made sure that Rae was OK.

"You OK now, Rae?" Mack asked her.

"Yes, Dad. I'm fine. I'm sorry that I did that," Rae said.

"My little girl. I can't believe you are eleven." He had a tear.

"Why the tears?" Rae said.

"Because you are growing up. You're not a little girl." He smiled.

She smiled. "I always be your little girl. Night, Dad."

"I think we should have a BBQ before summer's out," I said. "We haven't had a chance to let our hair down for a while."

"I like the sound of that," Mack said. "Be good before the kids go back to school. Plus, it's Joel's birthday."

Alice came in. "Hello. To what do we owe this pleasure?" I asked.

"Dad's home early from work. Any chance I finish making his present here? I asked Mum, she knows I'm here," she said.

"'Course, you can. Stay for dinner?" Alice nodded.

"What you making him?" I got her a drink.

She pulled out this statue that she started. It was a replica of Joel. "Bloody hell, Alice, that's brilliant." She smiled.

"You like it? I wanted to do something different for Dad. I like making things. Mum said I should apply to Art school when I leave school," she said.

"I agree. You're talented. I can't do that. I'm mean you're fourteen." I was amazed. Mack walked in. "Good god. That's brilliant, Alice. Just like your dad. You should go to Art school," he said.

"Mum said that. How's Rae, Uncle Michael? Mum said she was upset. She so sweet and kind." She was holding Joel's feet.

"She's fine, love. She gave us a fright. Can't get over how good that is." I was as baffled by how good it was. Even Mack was gobsmacked.

"Dad, close your mouth, you're dripping," said Callum.

"I can make one of you and Uncle Mack if you like?" Alice told me.

"I'd like that a lot," I told her.

"Done," she said. "Can I keep it here, till Saturday?"

"Yes. I'll put it in our room," Mack said. "You hungry, kiddo?"

"Always. Can I help, Uncle Mack?" Alice asked him.

Alice helped with dinner. "Come on, Alice, I'll walk you home," I told her.

"Thanks for letting me stay. I enjoyed it."

"Good. Oh, before I forget. Can you take this food for the BBQ to yours?"

Cuppa?" Lydia asked, boiling the kettle.

"How you been?" I asked her.

"Busy, with this one," she said, looking at Emily. "Listen, can you have the kids on Friday? Maggie be at Rose's. Jack's at Devon's. So, it'll be the other three. Want a night in with Joel."

"That's fine. We'll have till Sunday if you like. You two come for the BBQ then go home," I told her.

"Really, thanks? It's been a while since we spent time together. What time?" she asked.

"I'll get them about lunch time Friday," I told her. "You know we can have them more often if you want. You need a break."

"So do you and Mack," she said. "You know you haven't been out, just the two of you, in almost two years."

"I know. You can talk?" I said. "You and Joel hardly spend time together. So, we're in the same boat."

She just looked at me. "Smart arse. But seriously, I love my kids like you wouldn't believe. I would give my life for them. They are the best things ever. I'm so proud to be their mum."

"We love you too, Mum," Maggie said. The others were behind her. "Sit down, Mum. Now." Lydia sat down. Alfie smiled.

"Here, Mum, from all of us." They gave her a bunch of flowers and chocolates.

"What's this for?" Lydia started crying.

"Because, you do a lot for us. This is our way of saying thank you," Jack said. "Mum, you're great. What time is dinner?"

"Cheeky sod. Take out, OK. Can't be arsed to cook," she said.

They were happy. "Alfie, Alice, little Emily. You're coming to Mack and mine too Sunday. So, I'll pick you lot up around two. So be ready," I told them.

When I got home, Mack was on the phone, being coy and secretive.

161

"What you up to?" I asked him.

"Nothing." He had that look about him.

Oliver saw that. "He's up to something. He's acting weird. No more than usual."

Mack was being very secretive. So Oliver asked him out right. "Are you cheating on Dad?"

"No, I'm not. I'd never do that, ever! Where's this come from?" Mack asked him.

"Well, you've been on your phone a lot, you're not telling Dad what's going on." Oliver scratched his head.

"Sit down," Mack told him. "I'm planning a surprise for your dad. A good time, just me and him. Bloody hell. I won't do that. Not to your dad and not to you lot."

"Good. Glad to hear it. Don't screw it up, old man. Now can we go, please?" Olivier said.

Mack smiled. "Oliver, don't change. And tell the truth and be honest."

"Well, you and Dad brought us up like that. I hate lies, you know that. You're not mad, are you?" he asked.

"Not by a long shot, kiddo. Come on, let's go out," Mack said.

Joel's birthday came around. He loved the statue that Alice made for him. "That's really cool."

Joel and Lydia looked relaxed for the first time in a long time. I was kind of envious. Mack saw this.

"Here!" He gave me an envelope.

"This is what I've been planning for a while. Just us. A long weekend away. We haven't had that for over two years. Same as Lydia. We need a break. To that cottage. Three days. Simon and Malek are coming up." He scratched his head and smiled.

"We need this. Just us. Thank you." I smiled.

Oliver and the rest saw this. "Happy now?" Fran said, putting her arm around my shoulder. "We need a break from you two. You drive us crazy."

"Really. You need a break?" I said to her.

She laughed and hugged me. "I'm joking, Dad. You two have a lovely time. Dad, don't worry. Just have a good time. We'll be good for Grandad."

So off we went. Three days of just Mack and I.

"You look nervous," Mack said to me.

"It's nice just us. I missed it," I said, taking his hand. "What's for dinner?"

Mack laughed. "I was thinking of something else."

The three days went by quick. We laughed, talked and recounted. It was nice. As we pulled in the driveway, we heard shouting.

"What the hell!" I shouted.

They all started talking at once. He did this, she did that. Then out of nowhere, Rae shouted, "That's enough!"

Everyone stopped. She had never done anything like that before.

"Olivia, give me your phone. Oliver, put the footie in the garden. This is stupid. Everyone, sofa, now! Stop fighting!" "They did as they were told.

Callum was about to say something. "Not another word," she said. "There you go, Dads. They want their own way. Behave till dinner, or so help me God."

We couldn't believe it. Our little Rae. She found her voice. So quiet and innocent. We were proud of her.

"Next time we go away. Rae's in charge," Mack said.

At dinner, they all said sorry to us and Rae. "Good," she said. "Fran, you're washing up; Ollie, you're drying. Bella, you're putting away." They didn't argue.

"Rae, how do you do that?" I asked that.

"I had enough of the arguing. Poor Grandad. I thought he was going to fall over. Poor sod. He needed a hand. You're not mad, are you?" She looked at me.

"No, Rae. Thank you." I heard her humming. She was happy.

First day of school came around. Mack loved taking them to school. They hated it.

"This is so embarrassing," Olivia said. "I should be going with my friends. I'm nearly fifteen."

"Have a good day, honey," Mack shouted. Olivia was horrified.

Oliver thought it was funny. "Good job, old man. Do I have to go?"

Mack looked at him. "Go!" The others followed.

The next few weeks flew by. Every week was hectic. Olivia had a row with Mack about walking to school.

"I'm nearly fifteen. I want to walk with Seth and Laurel. It's embarrassing."

"I embarrass you? It's not safe out there," he told her.

"Oh my God. It's ten minutes. No other dads take their kids to school. I'll be glad when I leave home. It's not fair," she yelled.

"Not going to happen," he said.

"You really don't trust me, do you? *Ahh.* I hate you," she yelled back. She stormed to her room and slammed the door. Mack was really upset.

Over dinner, it was awkward.

"Olivia, talk to me," Mack said.

"Why? You clearly don't listen to me. What's the point? You hate me," she said.

"I don't hate you!" he told her. "I'm protecting you."

"From what? I wish you weren't my dad." She left the table.

Mack had a tear in his eye.

A couple of hours later, Olivia came down. She asked me, "Where's Dad?"

"In the conservatory. Go easy on him," I told her.

"Dad, can we talk, please?" she asked him.

Thaddeus left and hugged Olivia.

"Come here, Olivia," Mack told her.

She started crying. "Dad, I'm sorry. I didn't mean what I said. I'm glad you're my dad." She was really crying. "Olivia, Olivia. Sweetie. It's OK."

"I don't hate you. I'm so sorry. I hate school. I hate it." Something else was wrong.

I came in. "Olivia. What's wrong with school?"

She was quiet. "Olivia Anna Denton," I said. "Truth, no lies."

"The kids at school make fun of me, because I'm adopted. They say we're not a real family. I hate school," Olivia said. She came and sat next to me. "I don't understand."

"Sweetheart, I don't know why they're like that. But we're happy. Some don't even have two parents," I told her.

"It's so not fair. Can I stay at home?" she asked.

"Nice try," Mack said. He scratched his head. "Olivia. To us, you're our daughter. Don't be ashamed of who you are, or how we raise you."

"I', not. I don't care that I have two dads, who love each other. I love my life," she said.

"Except the kids who are horrible," I said.

"Well, yer. Dad, I'm sorry for being a cow," Olivia told Mack.

He smiled. "Livvy. We're OK. How about three times a week you walk home with Seth and Laurel?"

"Deal. Love you, Dad. Both of you. Dad. Can you read me a story?" She smiled at me.

After I read her a story I came down and saw Mack looking at the photo albums. "I told you she doesn't hate you. We have to go through this with Francesca, Rae and Bella. Why are you looking at these!" I asked him.

"Just remembering. Forget how little they were. Coffee?" he asked. I nodded.

"I wouldn't change a bloody thing on how we've done things," I told him. "We've done a good job with the kids. I remember when we had them. I would sit on the end of the bed, next to the cot, so I could hear them breath… with seven amazing souls. I'm a proud dad. Not a lot of people have the chance to do what we do. I count my blessings every day, *every day*."

"I know how lucky we are. This right here is what I've been fighting for. My life has purpose, meaning. I love the life I have. I have everything I need." He was teary-eyed as he took my hand. "Thanks for everything. I love you."

Mack met me from work with Francesca. As she saw me, she ran right up to me. "Dad, how was your day? Is Laura OK?"

"Lydia will cheer her up. She's OK. Busy day. How was school?" I asked.

"It's so boring. Dad, can I be home-schooled?" She looked at us.

We both said together, "No."

"Worth a go." Fran held our hands. "How long have you been married?"

"Almost sixteen years," Mack told her. "Why do you ask?"

"I just think it's nice that you love each other to be together that long. Will you be together forever?" The question was so sweet.

"Yes," I said. "Always. I love your dad very much. Always will."

"Same as me," Mack told her. "I love your dad very much."

"That's sweet. When I get married…" Francesca started.

"Yer, that's not happening," Mack told her.

"Shut up! Listen, you," she told him, "I'll tell you this. I'm growing

165

up. I'm going to university. I may get married. So, get used to it. For a guy who looks tough, with those tattoos, you are sweet." She looked at me. "Has he always been like this?"

"You have no idea," I told her. Fran laughed

When we got in, all we could hear was shouting.

"What the hell is going on?"

"Olivia won't get out of the bathroom," Bella said. "Ollie keeps kicking his footie on the door. Rae is reading."

"Where's Thaddeus?" Mack asked.

"Over there." Bella pointed to the sofa. Thaddeus was having an asthma attack. "Mike, Thaddeus is having an asthma attack." That shut every one up. After half an hour, he was OK.

"You scared us, son," we told him.

"Don't like worrying you both," Thaddeus told us.

"This worried us. Your health is a concern," I told him. "As for you lot. That can't happen. Phones, now! No arguing."

They looked at Mack. "Do as you're told." They handed them over. "Thaddeus, how are you?" Mack asked.

"I'm OK. Sorry," he said.

"Don't be. You hungry? Or is that a silly question?" I asked him.

"What do you think!" He smiled. "Sausage and mash and peas."

"On it," Mack said.

Rae sat next to Thaddeus, and read him a story.

"We need to get away for the day. All of us. Being indoors, it's not doing them any good. What shall we do?" I asked him.

"You know, the hills are not far from here. Near the pub," Mack said. I nodded. "Sunday, day out. Good job it's bank holiday this weekend. We're walking on each other's toes."

Over dinner, we told them what we were doing. They agreed.

"Sorry for earlier," Oliver said. Olivia agreed. We told them no mobile phones, nothing.

Sunday came around. We were all glad to get out the house. The kids loved the open space.

"I didn't know this was here," Rae said. "It's really nice. It's peaceful. We should come here more often." She took my and Mack's hand.

"You OK, Rae?" I asked her.

"Yes, I am. I'm getting hungry. Thanks for today. Promise me something, you two?"

"What's that?' I asked her. "You lot, come on. We're going to get lunch."

"We'll always be together." She looked at us.

"Always, Rae," Mack told her.

She smiled at us. "Good."

We had some looks at the pub. We didn't care. It was a good day. "Dad, when we get home, can we watch a film, please?" Bella asked us.

"What would you like to watch?" Mack asked.

"I heard Lydia talk about a film called 'The Lost Boys'. Said it was an old film," Bella said.

"It's not that old. OK. 'Lost Boys' it is then," Mack said.

While we were watching the film, Oliver was engrossed. "This is well good. Old, but good. Good choice, Bella."

"Dad, can I ask you a question?" Francesca asked.

"What is it?" I asked. The rest were picking up the rubbish.

"What does adoption mean?" she asked. Everyone stopped and listened.

"It means your birth parents gave you up for whatever reason to someone else. Whether it was that they couldn't cope or passed away. Whatever. Why do you ask? Do you want to find them?" I asked.

She shot me a look.

"No, I do not want to find them. I just wanted to know. I'm happy here. If I could tell them one thing, it would be, 'thank you'," Fran said.

"Thank you for what?" Mack was confused.

She looked at us. "I would tell them thank you for giving me you two as my dads, and giving me my family. You were there when I had chicken pox, hurt my knee when I fell off my bike. Came to my plays. I don't want to ever find them when I have you two. You two are my parents. I have brothers and sisters, who I love. I've got every I need. Don't forget that." Fran had never been that honest.

"I agree with Fran," said Olivia and the rest of them.

"I don't want to find them. Ever. This is my home and family," Thaddeus said.

"Are you guys sure?" I asked.

Oliver came up to me sat next to me. "Dad, our lives are here. This right here is it for us."

Mack and I couldn't talk. We couldn't argue with that.

"Now, it's bed time. It's late. Come on," I told them.

Oliver was yawning. He hugged me. "Thank you. Come on, bed. Everyone. Love you, Dad."

We checked on them like we always did. Fran was getting into bed.

"I meant what I said," Fran told us. "Tell me about when you got me."

"Ah Fran," I told her. "You were like Olivia. You were crying. You were so tiny. But we knew you were here to stay. You were very curious. Always into everything. When your dad took you in the garden, you fell asleep just like that. I remember when we got you colouring pencils. You stuck them up your nose." She laughed. "That's what you did. When we tried to get them out, you hid behind your granddad. Laughing, saying catch me. Your proper laugh. I wouldn't change a thing with any of you." She got out of bed and hugged me."

Fran looked at me with a tear in her eye.

"Francesca Sophia Denton. I'm glad God gave us you."

Fran smiled and wiped her tears away. "You mean that?"

"With bells on. When we got the call saying you were on your way to us, we couldn't wait to meet you, and welcome you home. Your dad was on cloud nine when he met you. He wrapped you up in your blanket. You were at peace. Don't tell your dad, but I thought it was hilarious when you glued his bum to the loo seat. I love you, darling," I told her. I looked at her. She was fast asleep in my arms. I had tears in my eyes.

"Love you." I smiled, through the tears.

We took them to their favourite place on Monday. The farm. Callum couldn't wait to see his goat Annabel. "She's lovely."

They started singing, 'The lion sleeps tonight' and doing all the actions. Mack and I were knackered. So, we ordered pizza for takeout. They were happy. Oliver was quiet on the way home. He was only quiet when something worried him.

"Ollie, sit down. Talk to us?" I asked. "Truth?"

"Dad, I don't want my birth parents taking me away from you. You're my parents." He was getting upset and hugged me.

"Ollie, that's not going to happen. You're our son. Mine and your dad's. Your life is here." I held him tight.

He looked at Mack, who was upset too. "Dad?" he said to Mack. He hugged him tight.

"Ollie. Your dad's right. You're our boy. Always."

Oliver wiped his eyes. "Really?" he said.

"Really," I told him. "Always. This is home for you."

He looked at Mack. "Dad? You OK? You're not mad?"

"I'm OK. I'm not mad at you, ever. We will never lose you. Oliver James Denton, look at me," Mack told him.

Oliver hugged him. "Dad, I feel better. I love my life here. Thank you for having me. I love you both. Can we watch a film before bed?"

"What do you want to watch?" Mack asked.

"The new 'Jurassic World' film?" he said.

He sat with us through the film. Mack got up to get a drink. I nodded to Oliver to go follow him.

"Dad, I'm sorry. I never meant to hurt you. I was scared, that's all. Does that worry you?" he asked.

"It did not worry me at all. I'm not mad at all. You spoke the truth, like we taught you. Come here." Mack hugged him.

Rae turned round. "Will you two hurry up? We've paused for ten minutes. Will you stop worrying, Dad? No one's going anywhere. Air down and shut up!"

"Bossy moo," Oliver said. "When did you get so bossy?"

"Ollie, you're an idiot. Sit down. Love you, big brother." She smiled.

Oliver smiled and hugged her.

Work was getting busy.

"How are you, Laura?" I asked her.

"I'm good. Don't forget Mrs Bradshaw at twelve. Full blood count," she said. I laughed. "How's you?"

"Usual. It's like a zoo. Olivia's getting ready for mocks, can't believe that. Can you order some more bandages today? I've put you and Lydia on a first aid course, one after the after."

"Sure. You getting used to the promo? You're good," she asked, eating a biscuit.

"You're a messy cow. Yes. It's like you've never been away. Shit, gotta go," I told her.

I ended working late every night for a month.

"Everything OK?" Mack asked.

"Just knackered. Don't have to do that again."

Olivia and Francesca were arguing over the remote. "Give it here," I yelled. "Haven't you homework to do?"

They looked me. "You've got exams, Olivia."

"If you paid attention, Dad, I've got one left. Tomorrow morning. I have been studying. Hard." She went to her room.

"Sorry, Dad," Fran said.

"So am I. Shouldn't have yelled," I told her. I went and saw Olivia. "Olivia, I'm sorry. I shouldn't have shouted."

"You been working so hard. You forgot I had all these exams. I am stressed out as well. I'm sorry as well." She put her head on my shoulder.

"That's no excuse. How do feel you now?"

"OK, I guess. The teachers think I've passed." She smiled.

"I'll be OK," Mack said. "I'm a tough nut."

"Give over," Olivia said. "You are terrible. You cry at 'Frozen'. You wanted Matthew to keep an eye on me when I went shopping with Maggie. You cried at 'Beaches'. The list is endless. You're a wimp."

"OK." He laughed. "I give up. True. I'm just protective."

"Protective my arse," Olivia told him. She hugged Mack.

We laughed. "What's for dinner?" she asked.

"Your fave. Roast Pork," Mack said. She looked at him and grinned.

Olivia passed her exams with flying colours. All A*s. Good signs for her GCSEs. We were proud as punch.

"See, I told you. Don't forget parents evening Thursday afternoon. Four o'clock," Olivia told us.

We went to parents evening. We got a few looks from others, when they saw Mack and I holding hands with Olivia in front of us. Olivia didn't care. Mack was fussing over Olivia. "Dad, stop it. Dad, tell him." She was laughing.

Her teacher was impressed with Olivia. He told us that if her results were anything to go by, her actual exams will be good. Mack was well proud.

"Right, on the way home, we're going to that cake shop you like and we're buying it."

"Really! Thanks," Olivia said.

When we got home, we got a call from Joel to say that Jack was in hospital. He had broken his arm trying to protect Alice from kids who tried to rob her.

"How are you both? You told the police?" Mack asked.

"Yes. I feel bad," Alice said. "I should be protecting Jack. I'm his big sister."

"Shut up, Alice. Family stick together," Jack said. "I'll do it again. Alice, I'm fine, OK? It's just a broken arm."

"You two OK?" I asked Lydia and Joel.

"We're OK. Jack's tough as old boots. Like his dad," Lydia said.

Joel on the other hand said, "That shit shouldn't have happened. Thank God it was just around the corner."

"Dad, chill out. They're idiots. They were caught. Main thing is we are OK," Jack told him, while he was doing his homework.

"He told you," Lydia said. "Olivia, I hear you passed all your mocks?"

"Yes. All of them. A*s. Dad got my fave cake," Olivia told her. "Don't forget Sunday family dinner, you lot!"

Dad and Malek came round to see how we were. The kids were happy to see them.

"How are you all?" Malek said. They all started talking at once. They laughed.

"Granddad, I got A*s in my exams," Olivia said.

"That's good news. Still want to be a bug doctor?" he asked.

"Too right. Better check on Beatrice and Loki." Off she went. Dad pulled me to one side and gave me an envelope.

"What's this?" I asked him.

"It's something that I put away for the kids to help with university," he told me. It was a cheque for five grand.

"Dad, I can't. It's mine and Mack's job to do this."

"You listen to me. You two can help. This is a start, so they don't have too much debt. I'm their granddad. I want to help."

Mack came over. I gave him the envelope. "Simon!"

"This is for them. Now, I want a coffee, please."

I hugged my dad. "Thank you."

That was a nice surprise.

That evening, Mack and I spoke about the cheque. "That was nice of him," Mack said.

Lydia came round for coffee.

"What do think Malek wants for his birthday?" I asked her.

She sighed. "Haven't a clue. In all the years we've known him, he's a man of mystery. I think he'll be happy with a family dinner and a scotch!"

We both laughed. "We have to do something. He's always stuck by us, thick and thin. He's a good man," I said.

"We'll come up with something," Lydia said, eating her apple.

That we did. We had a family meal that he wanted. The kids had made him, like they did with us, an album of pictures of ours and Lydia's kids together. A bottle of his fave scotch. Alice made him a drawing in a frame of all of us, with Malek in the middle. With the family motto *"Those who are strong of heart, will whether the storm."*

"Alice. This is beautiful. All of you, thank you. This means everything," Malek said. With a tear in his eye.

"Malek. You're family. Family stick together. Never forget that," Alice told him.

That was it; Malek started crying. Then Mack started.

"Bloody hell," Oliver said. "You're so hormonal, Dad. I said, you're so hormonal."

"I'm not deaf," Mack told him.

"You soon will be, old man." He turned to Malek. "Grandad, you're the best." Olivier then said in Arabic, *Those who are strong of heart will whether the storm.* Malek and everyone was surprised.

"How did you learn that, my boy?" Malek asked.

"My friend Ahmed and his dad taught me. They think it's nice that I wanted to learn that. You've taught me a lot, Grandad. Here, this is for you." Oliver gave him a copy of the Koran. Inside was an inscription that read, *Family is key to happiness.* It had all our names in it. Malek's and my dad's, were at the top.

"Oliver. This means a lot to me. Thank you. You are a good boy," Malek told him.

"Grandad. I'm fourteen. Not a boy. I'll tell you one thing. I'm glad you're here." Oliver hugged him.

When they left, Mack and I sat on the couch. "What Ollie did for Malek was sweet. What Alice did was sweet too. Ours and Lydia's kids are brilliant," I said.

"Those kids are amazing. I love being their dad too. I keep thinking of when Fran and Thaddeus glued your arse to the loo seat." I was smiling.

"That's not funny," Mack said.

"No, it was hilarious," Oliver said, laughing his head off. "Oh dear. Don't look at me like that. It was," he told him.

Mack couldn't help but laugh. "Why aren't you lot in bed?"

"It's Friday. We're allowed one hour after normal bedtime. You are losing your marbles, old man. Dad?" He looked at me. "How do put with him? You need a medal. Really, look at him. He's deaf, got a dodgy knee, has trouble getting out the chair. What?" I was laughing, so were the rest. He looked at Mack.

That evening, we spoke at length. "Ollie is so you," I said.

"Like you. Would you change things?" I asked.

"No. The way we did things then brought us here to this point. I haven't had a panic attack in almost a year. Mike, when we met at the hospital, when you patched me up, God. I knew."

"I knew too." I looked at him and smiled. I kissed him.

We were woken up by the kids arguing about what to do on family day. Olivia was on the phone, talking to whoever. Callum started swearing. He kicked his foot in the chair.

"Callum Theo Denton. Language! What the hell! It's like a football match gone wrong in here. Your hooligans! Olivia, no phones on family day. Fran, stop annoying Thaddeus. Where are Ollie, Rae and Bella?" I said.

"We're in the kitchen," Bella shouted.

We went in. They were trying to make breakfast. Mack and I smiled. "Sit down all of you. I do the cooking in this family," Mack said.

"Why doesn't Dad do it?" Bella asked.

"Because he's shit!" Oliver said. Mack laughed.

"Oliver, language," I said.

"Well, it's true. You two always said tell the truth and to be honest. Sorry for swearing. But it's true. So there!" Oliver said sticking his tongue out at me.

Lydia popped round to put the meat in the fridge for Sunday dinner. She made herself a coffee.

"Help yourself, Aunt Lydia," Oliver mocked.

"Don't worry, I will. Where we going today?" she asked.

"The hills, the park and then pub lunch," Oliver said.

Then Joel and the kids came in. "Mack, Michael, get your arse into gear!" Alice said.

"All right, Lydia, keep your hair on," I said.

"For once that weren't me." Lydia smiled.

"That would be me," Alice said, laughing.

"Come on. Olivia, put that phone down," Mack told her.

The day was brilliant. Emily loved having piggy backs with Oliver. "You're funny Ollie Wally. Mum, I need a wee. Let's go."

Off they went. Emily singing.

That was it, they all joined in. Singing their song, and doing their dances. Lydia had a tear.

"Hey, what's wrong?" Joel said.

"Joel, I'm just happy," she told him.

He put his arm around her shoulder. "Lydia, so am I. You drive me bloody crazy. There, I said an English swear word. I wouldn't change a thing."

"Dad, can we eat, I'm hungry. Like really hungry. Let's go!" Emily said. "Ollie, piggy backs, please."

Oliver happily did as he was told. "She's so bossy," Oliver told Joel.

"You have no idea, Oliver," Joel replied.

Bella took our hands. "You know before you adopted me, I was sad, very sad." the rest of them listened. She had never spoken of it before. "I felt like I didn't belong. I don't know why they didn't love me, or hurt me. Who does that? I don't care any more. I forgive them. You and Dad changed that for me. You all did. This is what I dreamt of. A family that wants me, loves me and who care about me." She wiped her tears away. "Callum, thank you for what you did for me."

"Bella, I'd do again. This is home now." He hugged her.

"Can I have my fave? Scampi and chips?" she asked.

"Bella," my dad said to her. "Telling us that was brave. We will always be here for you."

"Yes, we will," Malek told her. "Allah gave us a gift in you. Good things are coming your way, my child."

Bella had more tears, but smiled. She hugged them.

After lunch, we took the kids to the park. Maggie and Olivia said they may be too old, but it was fun.

We all spoke about Bella. "That must have been awful for her," Joel said.

"How could anyone do that?" Lydia was crying.

"All that matters now is she's home," my dad said.

"Callum saved her. That boy is a miracle," I said.

"They all are," Mack said.

We turned to see what they were doing. We burst out laughing. Jack and Thaddeus were karate chopping each other. Oliver was swinging Emily round. Alfie and the rest were playing tag, by kicking each other and who could fart the loudest.

"We've raised a bunch of weirdos," Lydia said, laughing.

Oliver heard this. "If we're weird, you're senile. Old woman."

Joel was trying not to laugh. "I'm not senile or old, young man," she told him.

"Really! You used to come to our old house to get milk in your *dressing gown*. Your hair scared off the squirrels, 'cause you were too lazy to go to the shop. Now who's weird. Scary Mary." Oliver folded his arms. Everyone was laughing their heads off.

"Right, come here, you little shit," Lydia said, running after Oliver.

He was laughing. "Try and catch me, old woman. The time I'm finished with you, Lydia, you are going to need an inhaler."

Joel nearly wet himself, laughing. The others started chasing Lydia and laughing. She sat on the swing to catch her breath.

Then Thaddeus said, "Here, Lydia, borrow this." It was his inhaler. She laughed.

"Come on. Let's go home," Lydia said. "I'm knackered."

We sat Bella down later to talk to her. "What you told us today was brave. We're glad you are OK."

"I know. I'm happy now. That's all I want. I've got what I wanted. Callum's birthday is coming up. I want to get him something special from me. Can you help me please?" She smiled.

"'Course we can!" Mack said.

The shouting started again. "Why all this fighting? Olivia, phone away. Ollie, stop with the footie, I'm losing my mind," Mack said.

"You already lost it, old man," Oliver said.

I was glad to get back to work. Mack had a meeting with Matthew and Jacob.

I walked in. "Lydia, sorry. You got Jack's school on the phone."

She rushed past me. Before she could answer, Lydia came and got her coat.

"Jack got in a fight at school. He was defending his friend, Yussef, against the kids who calling him a Paki. They punched him in the face. What's the world coming to?"

"Call me later, ok?" I said as Lydia turned to leave.

"Will do. Love you!"

The next day, they came to us. Jack was still upset. Malek sat him down to talk to him. "What you did was brave, Jack."

Jack had tears in his eyes. He hugged Malek. "Granddad, they were so cruel. He didn't deserve that. He's my friend. Why are they like that? I don't get it."

"People fear what they don't understand," Malek told him.

"Why would they fear him? He's the same as me. His parents are the same as Mum and Dad. So what if their religion is different? I care that my friend got hurt. No one should go through that," Jack said.

Before Malek could answer, there was a knock at the door. It was Yussef and his parents.

"We want to thank you for what you did for our son, Jack," Mr Hussain said.

"That's OK. Yussef is my friend." Jack then got upset. "I'm sorry those boys were mean." He started crying.

"Can we play in the garden, Mum?" Alice said.

Lydia nodded. As they left, Jack went up to Yussef's parents. "I'll always be his friend. I'll look after him. He's stuck with me." That brought a tear to Yussef's parents.

Malek had a proud look on his face. "Jack Marcus Green, you are a good, kind soul."

"You taught me to treat people how I would want to be treated," Jack said.

I came home from work one day to shouting from Mack and Olivia.

"Oh my God. It's a school trip! What's wrong with you?" Olivia shouted.

"What's going on?" I said. Rae and Callum stood behind me.

"Dad, tell him. You know, I'm going on that trip to Madam Tussauds next Wednesday?" she said. I nodded.

"He wants to send Matthew to keep an eye on me. Are you crazy? I'm with the school. I hate you. I'm not a child. Let me breathe!" she shouted at Mack. "I'm fifteen!"

"Olivia! That's the point! God, you're so stubborn," he shouted.

"Stubborn! Me! Oh my God. Who was it that wouldn't let me go to Maggie's for her party, even though you can see the house from the kitchen, unless you walked me there? You're such a dick! When I go to uni, I'm never coming back! Ever!" she screamed. "You hate me! You're a control freak."

"You listen to me," he shouted. "You are my daughter. I will always protect you. Anything could happen to you out there." Then he said something that he shouldn't have said and he regretted it. "Fine. If you get into university, don't come back then. Ever."

Olivia's face said it all. Her bottom lip quivered, then the tears. She ran to her room.

"Rae, Callum, go in the conservatory," I said. "What the hell, Mack? What are you doing? She's going with the school. She's going to be fine." I put the shopping down. "Yer, you shouldn't have. That was horrible. She's testing us. She's a lot like you. She gives as good as she gets. She, like you, can fight her corner. That's one thing we've taught her," I said. "Let her calm down. Then talk to her. Go easy."

Mack went into the garden with a scotch and a cigar. Something he hadn't done in a long time. This had really upset him. Olivia came down.

"Sit down," I told her. "Come on."

She sat down. "Olivia. Look at your dad. He hasn't done that for a long time. He only does that when something worries him," I said.

"Why is he so overprotective?" She wiped her eyes. "He really doesn't want me to come back?"

"That's so not true. You're both stubborn as each other. He's frightened that something may happen. He's a softie, really. You know that. Listen. Hang on. Mack, get in here!" He did.

"Right, you two, go for a walk, sort it out," I told them.

She took his hand. "Why are you so overprotective?"

"Do you remember me and Dad telling you what happened to us and what we went through?" he told her.

"Yes. I do. Wasn't easy," she said.

"I don't want that for you and the rest of you. Olivia, all I want is for you to be safe. I know I do things the hard way. You kids, Dad, Lydia and her lot are my everything," Mack told her.

"You can't have that pressure, Dad. When you had those panic attacks, you scared us. Listen, I know you want to protect us. Let go a little once in a while. I'm sorry." She looked at him. He smiled.

"OK. I'll try. Not going to be easy. Olivia, I never meant what I said. I do want you to come back. You know, you're just like me. Fighting your ground."

"That's what Dad said," she told him.

"Want an ice cream?" He smiled.

"Thought you would never ask! Did you always want to be a dad?" Olivia asked him.

"Oh yes. Your dad always said I was a broadly bugger." They both laughed. "I didn't have a good childhood. So, when I met and married your dad, I wanted a family. A large family. So, sorry for being slightly overprotective!"

"Slightly? Sorry about your childhood. But, what you and Dad are doing with us is pretty cool. My friends are jealous that we spend time together. You know my friend Laurel? She says I'm lucky that I have two parents. Her dad left; you won't leave us?" she asked.

"Olivia! Listen, my dad, he didn't want to know me either. I want to be different." Mack hugged Olivia. "We're busy during the week, so that's why it's important to spend time together. Right, let's get that ice cream!"

"I love you, Dad, always." She laughed.

"Happy now?" I said to them as they walked in the door. They nodded.

"Dad?" Oliver said. "Dad tried cooking. I nearly had to call an ambulance. Just not on. Dad, you can't boil a sodding egg. Dad, cook please, I'm starving."

Later that afternoon, we got a surprise visit from Adam.

"Jesus, Adam. How are you?" I said. He was smiling.

Mack and Adam greeted each other. "Miss you at work, pal!" Adam told Mack.

Adam was lost for words when he saw the kids. "Maggie, you got big. Shit. How old are you?"

"Nearly seventeen." She laughed.

"Who are you?" Olivia asked Adam.

Adam looked at me. I smiled. "I worked with your dad. Still do to a certain extent. I remember you as a toddler. What are you, twelve?"

"Fifteen." She smiled. She looked at me and asked, "Where's Dad?"

"Garden." She left to see him.

"Your lot grew up quick. Have we known each other that long?" I nodded. We looked out at the garden. Olivia and Mack were talking.

"He's a good Dad. So are you," Adam said. "How's Rachel and Daniel?" I asked.

"Both good. Daniel's eleven. Where does the time go?"

"Haven't a clue. Look, when we have the party, all three of you come up for the weekend," I told him.

Told him to man up. What's happened. Move on," she said.

Adam laughed. "What?" Mack said.

"Something you used to say. Olivia, you've got the same principles as your dad. You've done a good job, you two. Right, I'm off." Adam got up. "See you later. Call me when the party is?" He shook our hands.

Mack sat on the kitchen chair. Olivia was making us another drink. She put her arms around our necks. "It's OK, you know. The pair of you. What you did then for us and now. I'm proud of you both. I'm glad we're all here, together. We wouldn't be here if it weren't for you." She turned to Mack. "I know you and I have had our moments. But I love you and you, Dad. Always." She hugged us both tight. "I've got homework."

Mack was in tears.

"Oh, for God's sake!" Oliver said. "You on your period again? Get a pad from Olivia. You been watching 'Frozen' again. Did you hear me, old man! Get a grip. It's nearly dinner! Oliver went to the fridge.

"Get a glass!" I told him.

"How did you—" he said.

I smiled. "Fourteen years. Orange juice. Glass!"

Oliver smiled and did as he was told. Fran couldn't believe her eyes.

"My God! Ollie has a glass! Did you get hit on the head!" she said.

I laughed. Oliver looked at her. "Rotten moo!"

"Love you!" she said.

Mack and I laughed. "I love you too, Fran." He kissed her head. She smiled.

"Dinner! Come on!" Mack said. They ran like the wind.

"Fran, stop fidgeting; Olivia, no phones at the table; Thadd, finger out your nose," I said. Rae started laughing. "Why you laughing?" I asked.

"We are the biggest bunch of weirdos. But at least we are happy." She carried on eating her veg. We just looked at her. "What!" she said.

Callum and Oliver cleared the table. Bella and Fran washed and wiped up. Olivia was helping Rae and Thaddeus with their homework. So, Mack and I took advantage and sat and watched TV.

"What did you put in the dinner?" I asked.

He laughed. "Don't knock it!"

Callum brought us a cuppa each. "OK, who are you lot?" I asked. "What do you want?"

"We're a bunch of aliens that have been sent to drive you crazy, and then steal your brains for research purposes," Oliver said.

I just looked at Mack and shook my head and smiled. "That boy has an answer for everything," I said.

"Damn right, I have. Now, old man, can I have that cake Lydia made, or do I have to wait till Christmas?" he asked me.

"Go on. You got homework?" I asked.

"No. Makes a bloody change. Oh chocolate," he said. "You lot want some?" He cut everyone a slice.

Rae sat next to me with a book she liked with George next to her, purring. She smiled. "Dad, don't forget we have to take George and Holly to the vet's soon, for their check-up."

Adam and Rachel came up with Daniel over the weekend.

"I love this place," Rachel said.

"The beach is ten minutes away," I told her.

"Dad, can Daniel and I play computer till dinner, with Callum and Oliver?" Thaddeus asked.

"Fine. Living room," Mack said.

Just then, Lydia and Joel came in with the kids. The boys went and played computer.

"You've done good here," Adam said. "Nice place. You should be proud."

"Thanks," Mack said. He went to the kitchen and got some beers. "You've got good kids. So, you ever worry that that biological parents will, you know...?" Adam whispered.

"All the time," I said.

"Yes, same as me." Mack looked at the kids happily playing together. He didn't notice Callum in the corner. "Those kids are my life, Adam. I'd never thought I would have such wonderful kids." Mack had tears in his eyes. "I don't know what I'd do without them." He was quiet for a minute.

Callum came round the corner. "Hey, Callum. You OK?" Mack wiped his eyes.

"Dad, I know you're worried. But we told you before. You and Dad are our real parents. We're not leaving you. So, stop worrying." Callum hugged us. He looked at us. "We're not going anywhere." Callum looked at Adam, and out of nowhere said, "Where are you from? Your accent is weird!"

"Callum!" I said.

"What! I was only asking. You told us to speak the truth." He folded his arms. Adam laughed.

"I'm from Glasgow in Scotland," he said.

"Cool. Dad, hurry up with the food. At this rate, I might have Holly," Callum told Mack. Adam couldn't stop laughing.

On the Wednesday, with Rae, we took George and Holly to the vet's. They were fine. We went and got some cat and dog food. Next thing I knew, Rae saw some kittens. She was smiling like mad. The black one took a shinning to her. She was smiling.

"Dad, he's cute. Please! Please."

I relented. She was really happy. She called him Toby.

Mack smiled. "You cave in with her."

"I know. It makes her happy," I said.

"I know. I agree. He loves her," Mack said.

Fran saw Toby. "Hey, where did he come from?"

"Dad got him for me," Rae said. Fran smiled.

"Fran, can you help me with my maths homework. I'm not as good as you," Rae asked.

"Yes. Get you maths book. I'll help you," Fran said. It was nice to see them spending time together.

Mack had some work thrown his way he was happy about. He enjoyed it. I didn't get to see him much for a month. It was long hours.

"Glad you're home, Dad," Thaddeus said. "Dad has been sad without you. You have missed a lot of family days. That's not on. Thankfully, you haven't missed my birthday. You would have been in trouble, mister. Now, can I have a drink?"

Mack got him his fave. Orange juice. "How's your asthma been?"

"Good. Not one for a while. Can we go to the farm for my birthday, please? I like it there," he asked us.

"OK. What would you like for your birthday?" I asked him.

"More books," he said.

"OK. How's school?" Mack asked. "Boring. I do like science and English. What's for dinner?" he asked.

"Your fave. Spaghetti Bolognese and garlic bread," Mack said. "Want to help?"

His face lit up. "Thought you'd never ask. Let's go! I like helping." Mack and Thaddeus went off.

Later that evening, Dad called to say that Malek had a mild heart attack. He was in the hospital. Turns out, he had angina.

"Is Grandad Malek going by to be OK?" Thaddeus asked.

"Yes. He's going to be fine," I told him.

A few days later, we went and saw Dad and Malek. They were arguing over the medicine Malek had to take.

"That's enough!" Bella said. Everyone looked at her.

"You listen to me, young man," Bella pointed her finger at him. "You are going to take those bloody pills, look after yourself. If you don't, you'll have me to deal with. Now take your bloody tablets. Now!"

Malek's face was a picture. He did as he was told, while she was watching. "Good. Any more trouble out of you, we are going to have a problem! Understand?"

"Way to go, Bella." Oliver said.

Dad said to Bella, "Teach me that!" She smiled.

We went out for Thaddeus' birthday and watched him playing with his brothers and sisters, laughing at the sheep. He thought they were hilarious.

"Thank you for today. Thank you." He had tears in his eyes.

"Sit down," I said. "Why the tears?"

"I am happy to have this. I am a lucky boy. I like days with my family, it's important to be together. I like the sheep, they are funny. Am I a good boy?"

Mack scratched his head. "Thaddeus, you are a very good boy, who helps out and is independent, kind and funny. We are very proud of you. Now, how does a McDonald's sound?"

Thaddeus smiled. "I love you."

"We love you too! Come on," Mack said.

Later that evening, my dad came round to get Bella. "Malek isn't taking his meds. So, I need your help."

"That man will be the death of me," Bella said, getting her coat.

"What happened?" I said.

Bella shook her head. "That man is stubborn. I had to smack his hand. I made him eat his chicken and salad. I told him if he didn't do it, I will move in. He got the picture."

We laughed. "You're bossy for eleven."

"I know. Can I read a book before bed, please?" Bella asked.

"What we going to do for Lydia's anniversary?" I was scratching my head.

"You got nits?" Oliver said.

"No," I replied.

"Then why are you scratching your head like a baboon?" he said.

"Haven't you got homework?" I told him.

"Haven't you got nit cream?" Oliver said. "How about sending Lydia and Joel to that cottage you go to?"

"That's a good idea. Mack, what do you think?" I asked. He wasn't paying attention.

"Dad, what's up?" Oliver said.

"What! Oh nothing. Just thinking of our anniversary and a family holiday," he said. "Yes, send them there. They will like that." He was smiling.

"Really!" I said. "We haven't had a family holiday before."

The kids loved the idea. We sent Joel and Lydia away to that cottage for a long weekend for their anniversary. Just what they needed.

After school, Rae was doing her homework when she asked Mack a question. "Daddy, what's a miracle? Are they good?" Just as he was about to answer, I walked in from work in a bad mood.

"That bloody, stupid woman. You do your job, then she fucks up. God, why do I bother!"

"Good day?" Mack asked.

"Really! Some people are so stupid." I hadn't even noticed Rae sitting at the table with Mack. "Idiots. Some people are so ugh! That Liz is so stupid. A chimp could do her job better with bells on the silly arse cow. I need a beer!"

Rae was laughing, which started Mack off. "I'm having a bad day, and you are laughing? What's wrong with you?"

"You called her a chimp!" Rae said. She got up and hugged me. "Sorry you had a bad day. Why don't you take her to the zoo and leave her there?" That made me smile. "Would you like a cuppa instead of a beer?" she asked.

"Go on then. What were you two talking about?" I asked.

"Miracles," Rae said.

"It would be a miracle if she did her job properly," I said.

That set Rae off laughing even more. "You're so funny. Oh dear." She made us smile.

"Dad, when are we going on holiday?" Olivia asked.

"Not sure, why?" Mack answered.

"Well, I've got to know where we're going, so I can plan what I'm wearing, all those sorts of things. Isn't it obvious?" she said.

"No. No boys. Not having it. Told you before," he said. I just smiled and shook my head.

"Oh my God. You too prehistoric. Get a grip. You're an idiot!" she said, going to her room. "Love you!" she said going up.

"Love you too." Mack smiled. "I'm losing my hair and mind."

"What do mean losing!" Oliver said. "You've lost your mind, and I'm going to buy you a woolly hat for that bald head of yours."

I burst out laughing. "Oh my God, this is so funny!"

"I'm glad you find it funny," Mack said.

Oliver hugged him. "What colour do you want your woolly hat? Blue is good or pink?"

We all laughed. "Ollie, I'll have pink! We're proud of you, son," Mack

said.

"What's for tea?" he asked. "Don't forget, it's your turn to say grace, Dad?" he said to me.

I nodded. I rang Dad that evening to see how they were. "Why don't you spend the weekend? Have a rest here. I'll even get Bella to keep an eye on Malek.

"Done!"

Lydia called to say thanks for the other weekend. "I can see why you two love it there. It's beautiful. Joel loved it. What are you two doing for yours?"

"Haven't decided yet. Got Alfie's and Alice's birthday coming up. What do they what?" Mack asked.

"Haven't a clue! Can't believe they're fifteen. Bloody hell. What they like changes every time they sneeze. So, your guess is as good as mine. Surprise them," she said. "I'll pop over to bring the meat for Sunday. I made Ollie a cake as well. That will keep him quiet for ten minutes." We both laughed.

Our anniversary came round. For once, we didn't go away. We had the biggest surprise. Lydia, Joel and the kids came over. Alice had made us a sculpture of us two.

Then our lot had made us a photo album of Mack and I over the years. They also chipped in with Dad's help. A night at our fave restaurant. Mack was going to cook, but we got takeout instead. "Thank you for this," we said.

"Dad, are you two happy together?" Francesca asked us.

"Yes, we are. Why?" I asked.

"I hope when I get married, I'm as happy as you two," she said.

We smiled. "What did I say about you getting married?" Mack said.

"Over your dead body. You're an idiot." She smiled. "You know, when we do grow up, we'll always come home."

Mack had been busy with meetings with the boys. They wanted him to work. He said no. He was happy with what he was doing. My dad and Malek are good, with Bella keeping Malek in check. I think he was scared of her to be honest.

Rae had been very quiet the last couple of weeks. She hadn't been herself.

School said they hadn't had no problems.

"Rae, what's wrong, honey? Talk to us. The truth!" Mack said.

She didn't talk for a minute. "Rae!" I asked.

"I'm growing up," she whispered. We were confused.

"You know." Then the penny dropped.

"When?" we asked.

"Two weeks ago. Olivia helped me. Don't be mad. I don't want this. I don't want to grow up," Rae was crying.

"You sound like your sisters," I said. "They said the same thing. It's a part of life."

"I don't want to grow up and leave. It's stupid. I'll be alone if I leave. It's scary out there," she yelled.

"Hey, you will never be alone. No matter where you end up. Right here matters," I said.

"Yes, the world is scary. We know that," Mack told her. "Eyes on me." She looked at him. "Rae, wherever life leads you, right here matters. Yes, growing up is scary and it's hard. But we, as a family, will always be here. We stick together. You know that."

"What about you two?" Rae asked. "You will be all alone."

"Oh, Rae. We will never be alone." I was getting upset.

"Who will look after you?" Rae was worried.

"Honey. It's not your job to look after us. Don't be afraid to grow up and step in the big world. We've got you, Rae. We will be right behind you. The same as the rest of you." We turned round to see them listening in.

"Kids, listen. Whatever life throws your way," I said, "we've got you. I know it's going to tough. But we've got all of you. Remember, you kids are our pride and joy. We will always be here for you.

Rae got up and yelled, "I don't want to go and leave you. Please don't make me go!" She ran to her room.

Oliver went and spoke to her. "Rae. It's Ollie."

"Go away, Ollie.: She was crying. Mack and I stood by the door, listening.

"Rae, whatever happens in our lives, we will always be a family. We will never split us up. I'm scared too, you know. About finding my way. You know what gets me through? This, our family. Rae, come here." She sat next to him, her head on his shoulder.

"I'm worried that we will get lost along the way," she said.

186

"We won't. You know why?" He looked at her. "Because we are like magnets. You have the kindest heart. I'll never forget the day we went to the zoo. Dad got attacked by the meerkats. Out of all the animals. Bloody meerkats. You couldn't stop laughing. You fell on the floor. You called him the biggest div-head ever. Don't worry, Rae, we will always be close, we'll never be apart. I love you, Rae. Don't ever change who you are. You the sweetest, kindest sister." He wiped a tear from his eye.

"I love you too, Ollie. Thank you. You can come in now, Dads," she said.

We went in. "Can't believe you still remember the meerkats," I said.

"That was so funny," Rae said. "Can we go again? Please!"

Mack was laughing. "They're so little. They really went for you. Yes, we can."

I looked at him. "I hate you."

Rae was in her element. She hugged us both. "I love you both. This is going to be fun."

"Glad you're feeling better now!" I told her, smiling.

Lydia came in looking happy and sad at the same time. She showed us Maggie's A levels mock results. Straight A's.

"I'm so proud of her. She's worked so hard." Lydia was crying. "My little girl. All grown up. She's applying to Oxford and Cambridge. They say she'll have no problem getting into either. She wants to do physiology. What am I going to do?"

Then Joel came in. "Ahh. The results. I know how you feel, Lydia. She's my baby girl." Now he had tears. "I don't want her to go. But I know she'll be fine. I so proud."

Maggie and the kids came in and saw them crying.

"Oh my God. Are you OK?" Jack asked.

"It's my results," Maggie said.

"We're proud of you, Maggie. The thought of you going to university…" Joel was bawling his eyes out.

"I'll never be far away." Maggie had a tear in her eye. "I'm scared too, you know." She hugged them.

Then Mack started crying.

"Oh my God!" I said, putting the kettle on. Then they started laughing.

"I hate all this change. It got too much. I felt I was going to lose it. I'm sorry. I screwed up, big time," Mack told me.

"I know you are, look at me," I told him. He did. "We have to talk at all times. You know, I hate it when we don't talk. It hurts. Really hurts. I love you. I forgive you."

We were crying. Mack kept saying I'm sorry.

"Granddad, can we come down, now?" Francesca asked.

"Come on. Go and see your dad," he told them.

Francesca wiped his eyes. "What you did was stupid. You frightened all of us. You need to talk. Like you taught us. Walking away, not good. We, as a family, have to stick together. We love you, old man. You have to accept what you did. Never again, you hear me? Never again. Love you." She hugged him tight, so did everyone, expect Oliver, who hung back. Everyone saw this.

I went to him. "Ollie, sit down."

"I hate him." He was angry.

"No, you don't. Don't ever say that," I told him.

"I'm mad at him. Real mad. Anything could have happened." Oliver put his head down. "He doesn't care, he ran away and left us."

I nodded to Mack to talk to him. "Come on, kids."

"I'm sorry, son. I was way out of line. I do care. It got too much. I should have talked. Your dad's right. He always is," Mack said.

Oliver got up. "I thought you abandoned us. I thought you don't love us. I hate you! I hate you!" Oliver started hitting him. Mack took it. Mack kept repeating "I love you, I'm sorry" over and over. Oliver sat on the floor, with Mack next to him. "Dad, I thought you didn't want me."

I heard this.

Mack turned round. "Look at me. Shit, Ollie. I will always want you. I always wanted you. I'm sorry I hurt you."

Oliver looked at him and saw his lip was bleeding. "Oh God. I hurt you."

"Don't care about that. That will heal. You on the other hand… I won't do it again." He put his arm around Oliver.

"Dad, I need you and Dad in my life. I want you both together. Dad was so sad, crying. That was hard to watch; the two most important people in life hurting, without each other. You're each other's right arm. You're better together," Oliver said. "I'm so sorry I hurt you. Dad, don't do it again, please."

"You have my word," Mack told him. Mack looked tired.

The next morning, it was quiet. Rae saw this. She turned to us. My dad was making tea. "Dads, get your coats. We're going for a walk. That OK, Granddad?"

He smiled and nodded. We walked a while before she spoke. She looked at Mack. "You idiot. You tell me off for running away. You hypocrite. Talking is what we do. You should have talked to Dad. You take the weight of the world on your shoulders. Your heart is so soft. Like me." She smiled. "You have to tell Dad what's going on. You goon. Pull a stunt like that again, I'll kick you in the bullocks and wish you a Merry Christmas."

"Rae!" I said. "Where did you learn that?"

"TV. And Aunt Lydia," she said.

Mack laughed. "OK," he said. "I'm sorry. It was wrong. I'll talk more to Dad, OK?"

"Good. Come on. It's getting cold. I need a cuppa," Rae said.

When we got home, we told my dad how it went and what Rae said.

"Rae said that?" Dad was surprised.

"Oh yes!" Mack said. "What a mess I made."

"Yes, you did. Stop mucking up," my dad told him. "You've learnt your lesson. Listen, you two really need to talk. So, the kids are coming to mine tonight. So, talk. Really talk."

We went to talk.

"Ollie, it's OK, son. Eyes on me." Oliver looked at him. "It's OK."

"But," Oliver said.

Mack hugged him. "It's OK. I'll tell you what me and your dad told the others." I walked in and say next to Oliver.

"We were so thrilled to have you home. You were three weeks old. Olivia couldn't stop looking at you. She used to kiss your head and say my bee. We are lucky to have you. I'd never seen a kid eat so much." Oliver smiled. "When we gave you your bed time bottle, you had your blanket and then you held onto my ear. I remember when we took you to see the animals. You had a tantrum because you wanted to bring a donkey home. A bloody donkey." Oliver was laughing.

"The bond you two have is wonderful," I told him.

"I love you too, Dad. Always. I'm sorry," he said.

"Don't be. Your first day of school. You grabbed my hand, you looked at me and said, that made us laugh like mad, 'I'd rather shit in the woods then go in there!'"

Oliver roared with laughter. He hugged us both, then looked at Mack. "Come on, old man, I'll get your walking stick."

"There it is. Shit, my knee," he said. That did it.

We were at Lydia's having a cuppa when Maggie came in. "Hey, Michael, Mack. You OK?"

"Yes, we're OK," we said.

Lydia turned to Maggie. "There's a letter for you." She gave her the letter. Her face was a picture.

"What's the matter? Maggie!" Lydia was worried.

"It's from Oxford university. I've got a conditional place there, depending on my results. Shit, I'm off to Oxford." Maggie was stunned. For once, Lydia was lost for words.

"Let me look at that bloody letter," she said. She read it. Lydia got up and walked to Maggie. "I'm so proud of you. Maggie Anne Green. You've worked so hard for this. You…" Lydia was in tears.

Joel walked in. "Lydia!" She waved the letter at him.

"Oh Maggie." He was choked up. "My little girl. I'm the proudest father ever." She grinned.

"Mum, Dad, you helped me so much. I wouldn't be here if it weren't for you," she told them.

Lydia was really choked up. "Mum, you OK?"

She waved to Maggie to come to her. "My beautiful, beautiful girl. You have done me so proud. I still see the little girl in you. Always will. You have done so many wonderful things with your life. We need to celebrate."

"It's just conditional, Mum," Maggie said.

"Don't give a monkey's. My daughter the genius. Smart arse," Lydia said. As usual Mack was crying now. So, Maggie opened her bag and threw a tampon at him.

"For God's sake, Mack. I love you cos you're family. But you're so embarrassing."

I laughed. "Way to go, Maggie." Mack looked at me. "Well, it's true.

Big girl's blouse."

My dad was picking the kids up and came to Lydia. My dad was well chuffed. Ollie called her a smart arse. She clipped him round the ear and told him to bugger off. Then they had a cushion fight.

"I need a pissing drink now!" said Lydia.

"It's only four thirty, you old slush!" Oliver said to her.

"Who you calling old?" Lydia said to Oliver.

"You, you daft old cow!" Oliver got her with the cushion. Then Maggie did it.

"This is fun!" Maggie said.

"Help, Joel!" Lydia screamed.

He shook his head, laughing.

"I give up!" Lydia said, laughing.

Maggie hugged her. "Love you, Mum!"

"Can we go bowling, please?" Maggie asked.

"Yes. Haven't done that in a while. We'll go Friday night. That OK with you, Michael?" Joel said.

"Yes. Looking forward to it. Right, come on, kids, dinner," I told them.

"See you later." Maggie hugged us.

"Proud of you, Maggie," Mack told her.

Friday came along. We loved bowling.

"Hey, Rae. How's school?" Alice said.

"OK. Ally Cat? I need your help!" Rae said.

Alice smiled. "You haven't called me that in a long time. I missed that. What do you need?"

"Dad's birthday is coming up. Can you help me make him something special?" Rae asked nicely.

"For you, Rae, anything," Alice told her.

Mack was deep in thought. "What are you thinking?" I asked.

Mack took my hand and smiled. "I want to renew our vows again. I was thinking of your birthday". Mack smiled. "What do you think?"

I smiled back. "Yes. Let's do it. Can you believe it's been eighteen years?" We looked at each other.

"I know. Where's it gone?" Mack said.

We looked at our family. Thaddeus loved bowling. He was good at it. He was beating Oliver.

"So not fair!" Oliver smiled.

"Suck it up, big brother!" Callum said. "Hey, you two OK?" he asked Mack and I.

"Yes, Callum," I told him. "Dad, what does renewing vows mean?" Callum asked.

"It means we will say our wedding vows again. We've done it before," Mack told him, smiling.

"That's nice. Oh, my turn. Can you help me, Dad?" he asked.

"Come on." I smiled.

We told Lydia and Joel what we were planning for my birthday.

"Three times! Wow! You love getting married," Joel said. We smiled.

"Good," Lydia said. "It shows you're committed to each other. Oh, a new frock! "

So, it came around. Jacob did the ceremony.

"Thank you, old friend," I said to him.

"I'm glad. You two have had your moments. But you stayed strong. I remember when we met. I knew then."

Mack stood next to me. He was scratching his beard.

"Thanks, Jacob," Mack said.

Rae came bouncing in. "Dad, open your present from us." She grabbed my hand. They followed. Mack undid his tie. Even now he hated them.

"Close your eyes, sit down." I obeyed. "Open."

I was taken aback. It was an ornament of myself, Mack, the kids and Lydia and her lot.

"My God. It's beautiful," I said.

"It's from all of us," Rae said. "Ally Cat helped."

"That never gets old," she said.

Mack sat next to me. I took his hand.

"Happy birthday, Dad. And wedding day," Thaddeus said.

I cried. "Thank you, Mack." He kissed my head.

"I propose a toast," Jacob said. "We stand here today, with family, to celebrate love, life and family. Mack, Michael, stay strong and loyal. You need each other. Salut!"

We raised our glasses. "Alice," I said to her. "That is beautiful. Thank you."

"Don't thank me. It was all Rae. She and the rest helped. Uncle Michael, happy birthday," She said.

"Kids. Come and get your dinner," Mack shouted. "Ollie, leave some for the rest of us. Pig!"

"You're a fine one to talk! You had a dinner the size of a pyramid. Then you had half a cheesecake. Then you started farting. You smelt like you died. You're the pig! Give the fork, you deaf old git!" Oliver said. "I said, fork, not spoon. Idiot!"

Jacob couldn't stop laughing. Which set us all off.

"Those two are so alike," Jacob said. When Mack wasn't looking, Oliver put a chip on his head.

"Ollie!" Mack said. Oliver stuck his tongue out at him.

I kept looking at the ornament. Mack saw me. He stood next to me, putting his arm on me. "It's amazing," I said.

"Dad!" Bella yelled. "Can everyone stay? We're comfortable. We don't want to move. Please!" she said.

We all turned round to see the kids, ours and Lydia's kids on the sofa, with the telly on.

"Jack, what do you want to watch?" Thaddeus asked him.

They all had blankets and popcorn. "Don't forget to open your card, Dad," Francesca said.

"Put 'Bumblebee' on, that's good," Jack said.

"Do we have a choice?" Mack asked. "Go on then. I'm never going to win. Mike, you OK with that!"

I held my hands up, smiling. "Lydia, Joel. Stay, it's late, anyway. Jacob, stay, you might as well. Or are you staying at Dad's? It's like a hotel in here."

Jacob was staying at my Dad's. Lydia and Joel stayed.

Everyone was really busy before summer. Mack and I were working long hours. Olivia was done with her exams.

"I can't wait till this is over!"

We had missed family day three weekends in a row because we were so busy.

"Right! That's it. I've had enough of this! All we do of late is bloody argue and fight. I hate this!" Francesca yelled. "We pulling away from each other. It's like no one wants to be here any more." She went in tears to the garden.

We all stopped. We went and saw Francesca in the garden. She looked so sad. She had Digby. We sat on either side of her.

"Fran, we're sorry," I told her.

"So am I. I just hate this. We're all so sad. You two arguing as well. I'm surprised you haven't given me away for being horrible to Callum yesterday." She was crying.

"Right, you listen to me," Mack said. "We will never give any of you away. Why do you kids think that? Ever. Families argue. Look at me!" She did. "We've all got on each other's nerves this month. We need to do something. Anything." Francesca put her head on my shoulder.

"Dad, we need to be a family again. We need to have fun." Fran looked at me.

"Come on, let's start now. Callum, choose a film," I said. "Ollie, get the popcorn. Olivia, turn your phone off." They all smiled.

Summer came. We had to take Ollie to footie camp, girls to their activities. The night, before Olivia's results, she was so nervous. She came down.

"Daddy. Can't sleep. Nervous." She had Georgia with her.

I just saw my little girl, aged six not sixteen. "Come here. It's going to be fine. You've worked hard. You've nailed it. Don't worry, your dad and I are coming with you. Ollie has to come too, got to drop him off at footie after."

We got her results. Nailed it. A*s. On the way out, Oliver and Mack were mucking about. Oliver was Spider-Man and Dad was old man, instead of superman. Oliver was mucking about and tripped over. Olivia looked at me. "Dad, they're idiots. That's so embarrassing. What's wrong with them?"

I shook my head. Didn't have an answer.

"Olivia," Oliver said as he got out the car. "I'm glad you did really well. I'm proud of you. You worked hard. Love you."

"Love you too, Ollie bear. Always. Thanks." She was smiling.

We smiled too.

"Right, lunch. Where to?" Mack said.

"You and your stomach!" Olivia said. She looked at me. "Dad, has he always been a pig?"

"You have no idea, Olivia," I told her.

We went to her favourite place. It was an old-worldly cafe she liked.

We looked at her and smiled.

"What?" she asked.

"We're proud of you, Olivia. You've worked hard for this. Here, for you!" We passed her a present.

"Dads, you shouldn't have!" She opened it. It was a necklace she wanted. She opened the clasp. It was a photo of all three of us. She had tears in her eyes. "It's beautiful. Thank you." She hugged us tight. "Couldn't have done it without you. "

We went for a walk along the beach. She held our hands and then looked at Mack. "Can I have an ice cream? Please."

"OK! You kids have me wrapped around your fingers," he said.

"I like days like this," Olivia said to us.

"Why's that?" I asked. We sat on the bench.

"Look around us. Everyone is too busy running around, not noticing anyone. We make time. I know we've been busy. But that's why us kids love family day," she said. "No matter how we go on in life, right here is what matters. I'll always love this. Being with my family. I've got prom coming up. Will you both help find a dress, please?"

"'Course we will, Olivia," I told her.

"When we do, don't cry, Dad," she told Mack. He smiled. We left and went home. Everyone was happy that Olivia had passed her exams.

I was thankful for Friday. Holiday for me. I saved my holiday, so I could have three weeks off. I did my stupid holiday dance in the kitchen. I went for a beer.

Mack looked at me. "When did you lose your mind? You know it's only two."

"Piss off. I've been waiting a long time for this. Party time," I said. "You're not working?"

"No way. Family time. We need this. All of us. Don't forget, we've got to get Olivia a dress tomorrow."

We got her the dress she wanted. It was beautiful. We both cried our eyes out, which embarrassed her.

Lydia, Joel, Mack and I actually had a night out. Just us four.

"No kids. Thank God," Lydia said. "It's nice to put grown up clothes on." We talked for ages. Mack and I held hands. One drunk took offence and started giving us verbal abuse.

"I suggest you leave! You're making a fool of yourself," Joel said.

"Fucking queers," he kept saying. Mack and I got up and walked out, followed by Lydia and Joel. We got a cab back to ours.

"That was quick," my dad said.

We told him what had happened.

"Well, I hope he chokes on his vomit. Well, there's dinner left over. Drink?"

"You read my mind," Lydia said. Mack was quiet for the evening.

"You know he was a mindless idiot," Joel told Mack.

"I know. But it still hurts. I thought people moved on," he said.

"Some are like that still. Can't change them," Lydia said. "They're not worth worrying about."

"She's right," Dad said. "Look at what you got."

"Me. A good-looking bloke. With a sense of humour," I said.

Lydia laughed. "You are full of shit."

We laughed and had dinner. We actually talked, like we did in the old days. We all needed it. We had a few drinks, more than a few. We had hangovers in the morning.

Luckily, my Dad didn't have that much and got on with breakfast. Lydia threw up in the loo God knows how many times. Joel was semi-coherent. Mack and I had never in ten years got that drunk. He was still bummed out about that guy from the pub.

Thaddeus saw he was upset, and sat next to him on the sofa. "You know, it's OK. To be different. There is nothing wrong with us. It's other people that are stupid. I'm sorry that idiot hurt your feelings." Thaddeus showed him a picture of him and Mack and me, when Thaddeus was little. "This is special. Because I know I belong. You belong here, Daddy." Thaddeus told him. "Come on, Daddy. We all need a walk. To clear our thoughts."

"Thaddeus," Mack said to him. "You're a good lad. Thank you."

Thaddeus smiled. "You're welcome."

Then Lydia said, "Do we have to go for a walk? My head is killing me!"

"That will teach you for drinking for England. You silly moo!" Thaddeus told her. "Suck it up, old girl, and get your coat. Do your hair. It looks like a bird's nest." He looked at Joel. "Is he dead! Wake him up,

Maggie!"

Maggie laughed. She tickled his face. "What! What! My head."

Oliver was laughing. "Thadd, you sound like me! It's brilliant. Come on, it's starting to look like an old folk's home in here."

We had a good walk. Cleared the air. Mack felt better. Lydia was a sight for sore eyes.

"I'm never drinking again! This is torture."

Jack looked at her. "You daft cow! It's your fault. But I'm glad you had a good time, Mum. You deserve it. Within reason. Here!" He got her a fizzy drink and a chocolate bar. "Drink and eat, Mum."

"You're a good lad, Jack. I'm proud of you, son." She hugged him.

"Mum, I love you. Always will. I'll always look after you. Mum? You're glad we're this crazy? Our family, I mean?" he asked.

"Damn right I am, son. Life is what you make of it. You kids have changed my life. I'm so lucky to have you all."

Jack smiled. "Mum, why do you leave the porch light on?"

"That's easy. No matter where our lives take us, that light will bring you home. Look at us!" said Lydia and Jack looked at us.

"This is our wonderful life. Who cares that we're different. Just remember one thing. God, put us all together for a bloody good reason. I'm glad he did. Jack Michael Green, I'm a proud woman for having you in and your siblings in it. I love you Jack." She had tears in her eyes.

"I love you too, Mum. God, look at Dad. Idiot!" Jack said.

Joel was in the floor, with Emily jumping on him, then shouting, "Get up, fart face!" Lydia and Jack laughed like mad.

"Emily, leave your dad. Come on. Let's get lunch. I'm hungry. Emily, God's sake. Stop beating your dad up." Lydia told her. Emily didn't like that. Joel looked relieved. "Thank God."

We all went and got lunch, then home. We all got comfy on the couch. "Dad, can we have pizza hut for tea tonight?" Bella asked.

"Yes, we can! Mack?" I asked him.

"Damn right. Too knackered to cook! Callum, Rae, Thaddeus, choose a film each. We start now. Oliver, stay out of the snack til' dinner," Mack said.

Oliver's face was a picture.

"Feeling better, Dad?" Thaddeus asked Mack.

"Yes, son. A lot better," Mack told him. "Thank you, son."

Olivia asked if we could take her to prom. Seth and Laurel were going together. Three's a crowd. She had no one to go with.

"I'll go with you," Oliver said.

"Really!" Olivia said. "I don't want the kids to tease you."

"I don't care about them. I care about you. You're my big sister, I don't want you to be alone. So, Dad, can I?" he asked me. I said yes. "Good. Olivia Anna Denton. I'm taking to the prom."

"Thank you, Ollie bear." She hugged him tight.

The time came for prom. Lydia and Maggie came to help get Olivia ready. Lydia came down and gave us a box of tissues. She took one. "She's beautiful. Close your eyes."

"Open your eyes," Lydia said after a short while.

Olivia stood in front of us in her lilac and cream dress.

"Daddy!" she said to us.

"You're beautiful. Wow!" I said. Mack started crying. Then I started. "That's our baby! Mack."

"Oh my God," Olivia said. For once, Oliver was lost for words.

"I'm so glad I'm going with you. Come on," Oliver said. We took them. We hung around. My dad was with the others. We had dinner out, which was good. We got a call from Olivier. They had had enough. They wanted to come home.

"Hey, you two OK?" I asked.

"Yes," Olivia said. "Some are acting like idiots. We didn't want to be around that."

"Yes. They were being stupid. Plus, some were getting a bit drunk. We did enjoy it. Olivia, you look amazing. I'm glad I came with you," he said.

We took them home. Olivia nodded off on Oliver's shoulder. "Priceless!" I said, looking at them.

While Mack and I were making a drink and watching the news, Olivia came down with her fave book. "Daddy, thank you both for taking me with Ollie. Can you read me my fave book?"

"I'd love to. Come here," I told her. "

I'm glad I went with Ollie," she said. "I know he can be annoying. But he's lovely. Don't tell him I said that." We both laughed.

I read her the story. She fell asleep in my arms. Slightly snoring. "Come on, Olivia. Bed."

"Can't I stay here?" she said.

"Come on," I said. She gave Mack a hug. "Love you, Dad. Night. Thank you."

"Yes. I can't believe how quickly they are growing up. Soon, they won't need us," Mack said. "I worry about them every day."

"They will always need us," I told him.

The next morning, we woke up to quiet. We looked at each other. That's not right. We rushed downstairs, to find the kids had made us breakfast. All of them, smiling away. We looked at them, we were sure they had been swapped. They never did this. "What's this for?" I said. We sat down. The food looked good.

Bella said, smiling, "You do a lot for us. This is a thank-you. "

Mack was already eating. "This is good," He said with a mouthful.

I looked at him and shook my head. "I swear I married a pig."

The kids started laughing. "How do you put up with him?" Callum asked me.

"I have no idea, Callum. When we first met, my god, I thought he had seven stomachs. At one point, I thought Tescos was going to run out of food," I told them.

They were laughing. Mack looked up. "What! You want yours?" he asked me.

"Piss off. I'm hungry. See? Pig!" I said.

"Has he always been that way?" Francesca asked, smiling.

"You have no idea." I smiled.

Mack started burping and farting. "That was good."

"Right now," I said, "my decision is changing."

They laughed. "Hey, I'm in good shape. I could run a marathon," Mack said.

"Give over!" Oliver said. "You get out of breath running a bath!"

We all laughed. "You annoying sod!" Mack told Oliver.

"Come on. Let's go for a walk! Get some fresh air!" I said.

Oliver and Mack kept annoying each other. The rest of us were shaking our heads and laughing. I kept thinking what a wonderful life we all had. It brought a tear to my eye. Rae and Bella saw it.

"Dad, are you OK? Why are you crying?" Bella asked.

"I'm happy, that's all. Just thinking how lucky I am," I said.

"Are you sure?" Rae asked. "I don't like seeing you like this."

"Honesty I'm fine. This is what your Dad and I wanted. A big family," I said, looking at them.

"Yes, I am. Oh my God. Girls, look at your brother and Dad!" I said. Oliver was running around Mack, flicking him with a stick.

"What's wrong with them?" Bella asked.

"I wish I knew. They are so alike. They're weird!" I said.

"That's putting it mildly," Rae said, smiling. "I'm glad we're a bunch of weirdos. Normal is boring."

I told them to pack it in. They were as bad as each other. "When you going to grow up?" I told Mack.

"Never!" he smiled. He kissed me. I just smiled.

"Dad!" Oliver shouted. "I'm hungry!"

I shook my head. "That boy will eat us out of house and home. I wonder where he gets that from?" I said, looking at Mack, who was laughing. "You need a haircut, Oliver."

"Never! I don't want one!" he told me. "Dad, don't let him make me get a haircut." We just laughed.

"You cruel parents!" Oliver told us. "This will scar me for life. I need therapy." We laughed. "Not funny."

Oliver got his haircut. "Hate you!" he said.

"McDonald's!" I told him.

He smiled. "Come on! I need cheering up. Big Mac and fries!" Oliver grinned.

"You're a cheeky sod! Come on!" I told him. Oliver just laughed. As we were walking home, Oliver asked me, "What's it like being a parent?"

"Tough, hard work. Most of rewarding. Why?" I asked him.

"I just hope when I'm older, a lot older, when I have kids, that I'm half the dad you two are, I hope I'm a good son," he said.

"Ollie. You will be a good dad. You're a good son. You kids have done me and your dad proud. Being a parent is a journey. You don't get a manual. You learn along the way. Even now, we're learning. But no matter what, I won't change a thing. I'm proud of how you lot have turned out. " He rested his head on my shoulder. We walked home in quiet.

Lydia, Joel and the kids came round for family night. It had been a long time since we did that. It was as if should. The kids singing and dancing away. Life as it should. As soon as the food was laid, there was silence.

"Alfie, you choose family film for tonight," Bella told him. He chose 'Guardians of the Galaxy'.

I had tears in my eyes. Mack saw this. "You OK?" I nodded yes. He kissed my head and smiled. Callum looked at me.

"Are you having a mid-life crisis. You're doing a lot of crying lately." I just laughed.

The new school year came around. The kids started it. Us adults loved it. We got a call from Rae's school.

When we got there, Rae saw us. "Daddy. They were so mean. Take me home." She wrapped her arms around me. Alice told us they were picking on her because they tried to make her pick on the new girl. When Rae said no, they emptied her bag, took Jonas, ripped him up and called her names. Some she wouldn't repeat. The pushed her around the playground. They kicked her and got her. Alice stopped it. Alice had tears in her eyes.

"Uncle Michael, she's so sweet and kind. She just wants to be kind and protect everyone. They ripped Jonas up. Poor Rae." She was in tears.

Rae wouldn't let me go. Mack looked at Rae who was so scared.

"Daddy, please," she was screaming. Hitting me. "Why me! I'm not bad. I try to be good. Why do they hate me? Not fair. Don't make me go back."

We were on the floor by the sofa. So, I told her what I told the others. The day we brought her home. Mack sat on the other side of her.

I held back the tears. "I remember when they brought you to us. You were so tiny. You were wrapped in a pink blanket and the tiniest pjs. Your Dad took you 'cause you were crying. You stopped. You had your bottle, and fell asleep. As you got bigger, you had the biggest smile. As soon as saw us, you ran to us tight. You loved your angel wings so much, we had trouble taking them off you." She was calming down.

"You loved singing princess songs, and loved your rent and tea parties. We will get you another Jonas. Two. You are loved, Rae. You are loved." She was asleep in my arms. My thirteen-year-old daughter. Afraid. Mack put her on the sofa. I was in tears. Dad came in. "My God. How is she? Thank God Alice was with her."

Mack told him. I was upset. Alice came in. She wanted to be with Rae. She was upset as well.

"Granddad, I don't understand why people are so stupid. She's the kindest person. They were so horrible. I mean really horrible."

"I don't know, Alice. No one deserves that. It's cruel and unkind." Just as he was to continue, Rae woke up. "Daddy, Daddy?" We came running. She was shaking still.

"Hey, how are you?" Mack asked her. She hugged him.

"Scared, Daddy. I'm scared," she said, crying again. Alice sat next to her. Lydia and Joel listened.

"Rae. It's going to be OK. Sit next to me. Come on. I want to tell you something." She did just that. Alice paused.

"Rae, I don't know why they are like that. I don't have an answer. But I do know that there are very good people in the world. Those people are not worth it. Not by a long shot. But you have friends that will have your back. We as your family will always have your back. I helped you. So will everyone else. We love you, Rae. Never change your kind heart. I wish everyone was like you. This world will be a better place. We'll get another Jonas. Now go and have a shower, wash your hair. I'll be there soon," Alice said. Rae did as she was told.

"I love you, Ally Cat," Rae said. She went for a shower. She came down with her favourite book. Alice combed her hair, as promised. Bella gave her Jules.

"I know he's not Jonas, but he'll do, till you find another one."

Rae said, "Thank you."

"Daddy," she said to Mack, "I'm hungry. Can we have dinner? Burger and chips. Please."

"On it, sweetheart," he said.

Mack and I smiled. Lydia had tears in her eyes. "I swear that girl was sent from Heaven. She's like a fragile China glass. Rae has always looked up to Alice. Keep her off for a few days. Do her good and you two."

"Already thought of that. Stay for dinner, Alice?" I asked.

"That OK, Mum, Dad?" Alice asked. They nodded.

"I'll bring her back about eight," Mack said.

After dinner, we sat on the sofa. Mack took Alice home. Rae was sat next to me. I read her favourite book. *The Princess and the Pea.*

"I'll always love this book. I'll never get bored. Am I going to school?"

"Not for a few days. You've been through a lot," I told her.

"I'll never understand mean people," she said. "I wish they could be

202

kind."

"I wish that too, Rae. But sometimes in life, you meet people that are like that. Always remember, there is nothing wrong with kindness and being good," I told her. "Life is what you make of it."

"That's what Lydia said." Rae started yawning.

Mack walked in. He sat down next to Rae. "How are you, my angel?"

"OK." She rested her head on his shoulder and fell asleep.

When she went back to school, Callum was with her. So was Alice. There was a teacher nearby. She made friends with the new girl. Her name was Grace. Alice was happy. "Soon, you won't need me."

Rae looked at her. "I'll always need my Ally Cat." That brought a tear to Alice's eye.

Work was going well. We were putting in more overtime, just to get ahead of ourselves. Lydia did the same. "How long we going to do this?"

"Just till the end of the week. Just think, Christmas is coming. The extra will come in handy," I said.

"True. I'm looking forward to Christmas. Emily, is bouncing around like mad. She wants to meet Santa, like now. The kids were like that. Brings back a lot of memories. You coming to us for Christmas? Make a change. Simon and Malek are staying over. Right, home, come on," Lydia said.

Thaddeus and Mack were waiting for me.

"Hey, Aunt Lydia," Thaddeus said. "You OK?"

"I'm good, my darling! Looking forward to Christmas?" she asked. "You bet I am. Aunt Lydia? Can you help me choose a present for Dads, please?" Thaddeus asked her. She nodded and smiled.

Thaddeus looked at Mack and I holding hands, then looked at Lydia. "Lydia, do you think I'll be as happy as Dads when I'm older? I want to be like them!

"Yes, I do, Thaddeus. You are like them in so many ways. You're kind, helpful and a decent young man. Always remember, love trumps hate. You're a lucky lad to have parents like them. I'm lucky to have you as my nephew," Lydia told him.

"Thank you, Lid-lid. I am lucky to have you." He smiled.

"You haven't called me that for years. Miss it." She smiled.

When we got home, the kids were either doing their homework or reading. Fran and Bella were putting the clothes on the line.

"Right, where's our kids?" Mack said.

Callum said to us, "Well, we are getting older. We can help out. We want to help out."

Oliver came in from football practice. He was annoyed.

"What's the matter?" I asked.

"Don't want to talk about it," he said, walking to the garden. That didn't sound good. He takes after Mack when something worried him.

"Talk, young man, come on," I told him.

He rested his head on my shoulder. "Some of the kids are arseholes. They're not taking it seriously. They take the micky out of one of the kids. The coach don't do nothing. I tried talking to him. I think he's given up. I don't know what to do," he said. "It's not fair, Dad."

"That's a tough one. Have they tried getting a new coach? What about trying to do something new?"

"Tried all that. Tried to talk to the school. Maybe Dad should become the coach. That'll teach them. I don't understand! Dad, can I invite Devon round for tea next week?" Oliver asked.

"Yes, you can. You're a good lad. Dad's doing your favourite for dinner. Mexican and tortilla chips. Ollie, in this life, there are going to be people that are like that. If you do the right thing, it's going to be OK. Take a shower, you stink, and clean your footie boots," I told him.

He got up, hugged me. "I love you, Dad." He kissed the top of my head.

"Dad. When I'm older, I hope to be half the man you are." He went and had his shower. I put my hand on my heart and smiled. As usual, at dinner it was quiet. I watched as they ate in peace and quiet.

"Dad, can we watch a film, please!" Bella asked Mack.

"Go on. What are we watching?"

"'Avatar'," she said. "I like the blue people."

Oliver was sticking Twiglets in Mack's ears and up his nose, while he was sleeping. "For God's sake, Ollie. What's the matter with you? Dad, can we swap him?"

"This is fun. He's so old," Oliver said.

"What!" Mack woke up and sneezed out the twiglets out his nose.

Oliver burst out laughing. Mack looked at him. "It was Holly. She did it."

"Don't blame the dog! Twiglets. Why?" Mack was smiling.

"Umm, because no one likes Twiglets. You were asleep, and my arm twitched. So?" Oliver told him.

Mack laughed. "You're never going to stop, are you?"

"Never!" Oliver smiled. "It's fun." Oliver hugged Mack.

"Right, come on, kids. Bed," Mack said.

"It's Friday," Callum said. "We're allowed one hour after bedtime."

"Got you there," Thaddeus said. Mack and I laughed.

"You kids are way too smart for your own good," he said.

"We take after you two," Rae told them, smiling at them. "Dad, can we spend family day like this tomorrow? All of us playing board games and stuff. Instead of going out?"

Dad and Malek came round for family day. Dad was at the table with Callum playing Scrabble. "Grandad, what was Dad like when he was younger?"

Dad smiled. The kids listened carefully. "Your dad was kind and quiet. Never really gave us any trouble. As he got older, he enjoyed going out. The usual stuff. Now I say it. Your dad sounds quite boring." We laughed.

"Were both dads always together?" Callum asked.

"Yes," Dad said. "Your dad never had anyone serious. That all changed when they met. They haven't left each other's side in almost twenty years. Your dad is so much happier with your dad by his side. And vice versa."

They looked at me. "It's true. Granddad never lies. I'm lost without Dad."

"That's really sweet." Olivia smiled. "It'll be strange if you two weren't together. We wouldn't have what we have if it weren't for you two. I'm glad it worked out."

Mack smiled. "You know, so am I, Olivia. Your dad and I wouldn't change a thing."

"Why would you?" Bella said. "I got my happy ever after."

"I agree," Francesca said. "We all got what we wanted."

My dad was crying. "Oh God. Not you as well," Oliver said. "Big girl's blouse," Oliver said. He got up and walked up to Mack and me and put his arms around our shoulders. "I am so grateful to you for having me. I know I muck around. But I wish when I'm older that I'm half the parents you two are. I love you very much, and the rest of you." He kissed our heads. "Now let's take Holly for a walk."

Seeing our kids mucking about was hilarious. "Oh my God. Dad, tell him," Olivia said. "Oliver, you annoying shit."

"Oliver, stop annoying her!" Mack was laughing.

"It's not funny! I can see where he gets it from! Not fair." Her phone went off. "Oops! Sorry." She smiled.

"Give it here," I said. "Remember—"

"No phones on family day. Sorry, Dad." She looked at me. "Can we go along the beach. That's our favourite."

It was good to see everyone having fun. Holly chasing the seagulls. "Ice cream, Dad! Ice cream, please!" Oliver shouted.

"Oh my God. Could you be any louder!" Olivia said.

"Yes, I can! I am a cape crusader. Loud mouth!" Oliver started running around like a bat out of hell.

Olivia looked at us. "He needs medical attention."

"I don't need medical attention. I need a large ice cream. Then dinner. Come on, Dad. Let's go!"

Mack and I laughed. Olivia shook her head and laughed. Thaddeus and Francesca were running in the sea, and getting wet. Rae, Callum and Bella were running in circles, then playing rock, paper, scissors.

"Ollie. You're a pig! I've never seen anyone eat so much!" Rae said at dinner. "Slow down. Idiot!"

"I'm a growing lad," Oliver said, with a mouthful of chicken. "You're bossy!"

Rae smiled. "Whose turn is it to choose a film?"

"Mine," I said. I chose a classic. My favourite. 'Notting Hill'.

Well, the film went down well with the girls. The boys thought it was mushy. Thaddeus was snoring away. Oliver was quiet.

"Dad, can you read a story before bed?" They always liked a story. They didn't think it was silly. I read him the *Enormous Turnip*. Which he loved.

"Kids, why do you still love a bed-time story? You're getting older?" Mack asked.

"I dunno," Callum said. "It's just nice. I will always like it."

After training, Oliver was smiling. "Brilliant, Dad. You too, Uncle Matthew. Uncle Matthew? What was Dad like before us?"

Matthew smiled and told him that Mack was a good man who worked hard and treated people fairly. He was a deep thinker. "When you kids came along, your dad was at peace. I remember coming to visit when you were a baby. Olivia was in her high chair. You were in his arms. You put your hand on his face. You both smiled. I knew then that your dad was home. Really home." Matthew looked at Oliver, who had tears in his eyes. "Oliver, you're lucky that you have two wonderful men as parents. I see you, I see your dad. Both of them. Your dads are there, always. In here." He pointed to his heart.

We got out of the car. Oliver wiped his eyes. "Thanks, Uncle Matthew." He held Mack tight.

Oliver came in, saw me and hugged me tight. "You OK, Ollie?" I asked.

"Always, Dad. Always. I'm hungry," Oliver said.

"Just like your dad. Take a shower. You smell," I told him.

At dinner, Matthew joined us. He couldn't stop laughing at us.

"Thaddeus, stop nicking Rae's chips. Bella, use your fork. Olivia, phone away," I told them. "I need a gin and tonic."

"Alcoholic," Oliver said. "Can I have one?"

"No. You kids are driving me insane!" I said.

Oliver rolled his eyes at me. "We're driving you crazy? We're the ones with parents who are old and stupid and forgetful."

"I'm not forgetful," I told him. Matthew was smiling.

"You are!" Oliver said. "You took us to school in your *pyjamas*. You hadn't brushed your hair or cleaned your teeth. You looked like a tramp, who stole the family car. So don't give me that look. See what we have to put up with, Uncle Matthew. You need to get your facts right, Dad. Plus, you need to take your old-dad tablets. Both of you! Now can I have that cake Lydia made? It has my name on it. Love you!"

Matthew shook his head. "That boy is funny."

"Really!" Mack said. "He stuck Twiglets up my nose and in my ears. Then blamed Holly. I can still smell then now!"

After school one day, Olivia asked if she could go to a mate's house to study.

"Who are they?" Mack asked, getting breakfast ready.

"Rosie. It's only for an hour. Please!" she asked.

"OK. I'll take you and pick you up. No arguing," he said.

"Deal. Can't believe you agreed," Olivia said. "Thanks, Dad."

Mack took her to Rosie's. They heard shouting from inside.

"Daddy, take me home. You know I hate shouting. Please."

"OK. Come on. Phone her later. You're shaking," Mack said.

As soon they got home, Olivia ran into me, shaking. "Livvy. Livvy. What's wrong!" Mack told me what happened.

"Sweetie. It's OK. I'll phone later. Don't worry. Go and get changed. How about your fave when you come down? Milk and a Twix. Go on."

She sat with me on the sofa. "You loved this when you were little. When you got scared, this helped. You're quite soppy. You OK now?" I asked her.

"Yes. Can I have another Twix?" She smiled.

"Not before dinner," Mack said. "I phoned Rosie's parents. It was an argument. Nothing more. Rosie's fine."

She said thank you. We just sat there.

"Everything else OK, Olivia? What's up?"

"I'm fine, Dad. Just nice to have five minutes with you, that's all. Dad, there is something on my mind."

"What's up?" I asked.

"Don't be mad, both of you," she said.

"Oh my God. You have a boyfriend!" Mack said.

"Shut up! Really. If I had a boyfriend, you and Uncle Matthew would hunt him down and bury him in the garden."

That made him smile. "No. You remember when we spoke about our biological parents? I don't ever want to meet them. I would thank them."

"For what?" Mack said, sitting next to Olivia.

"For giving me you two and my family. I'm glad I'm here. Even though you are an overprotective twat, who won't let the reins go!" She looked at Mack, who laughed.

"Tell it as it is, why don't you!" I told Olivia.

"Well, you did bring us up to speak our minds, within reason. I'm grateful. Always. Is dinner ready?" Olivia smiled.

Joel walked in. "Got a beer?"

"Help yourself!" I said.

"I will. I need a favour. It's Lydia's fiftieth in a couple of weeks. Can you help with a party and something special for her? I've been racing my brain. Alice is doing something from her and the kids. I'm lost. You know

I'm useless at this!" he said.

"Get her a bottle of wine. That will shut her up for twenty minutes," Oliver said, looking in the snack drawer.

"Not before dinner," Mack said.

"How can you see from there?" Oliver said.

"Joel, take her to Rome. Like we did. You both need it. Go in style. You and Lydia deserve it."

"You know," Joel said, "Oliver, you are a genius!"

"I know. It hurts sometimes. Can we have the party here?" Oliver said.

We both agreed. I told Joel about the place we went to. "It's beautiful there this time of year. It's relaxing. Dad and I will keep an eye on the kids," I told him.

"Thanks. We need this. I miss actually spending time with her. Don't tell her I said that. Not to say the kids don't make it right. But the thought of not having that smart-arsed woman. Well—" He couldn't finish the sentence. His phone rang. It was Lydia.

"I'm at Michael's. Jesus, woman. Can't a man have a beer with family? You drive me crazy. Shit!" He hung up. "Man, That woman is mad."

"I wish I never suggested going away. You're a dead man," Oliver said, smiling. We laughed. Joel stuck his middle finger up. "Joel Green. How rude are *you*. That's swearing!" Callum said. "No beers for you."

"Boy, that's not swearing, man! I'm over eighteen. I'm an adult," Joel argued with Callum.

"Adult my arse! You were laughing at 'Scooby Doo' the other day. You act like a ten-year-old. Bella caught you watching 'Peppa Pig'. It was the only time you were quiet. You better go home, before Lydia nails you to a crucifix and slaps you stupid," Callum told him. We laughed.

"Smart arse boy. You're like your father!" Joel told Callum while leaving.

"Which one? Love you, Joel. Missing you already," Callum shouted after him. Joel was laughing.

Lydia and everybody came round for her birthday. "I can't bloody believe I'm fifty. Fifty!" she said.

"I can," said Jack. Joel started laughing. Lydia shot him a look. He stopped.

"I look all right for fifty, right!"

"Believe that. Believe anything," Alfie said. "I think you've had too much wine!"

"I haven't even started!" Lydia said. "You kids picking on me. How rude."

"Right, old girl, close your eyes!" Maggie told her.

They brought out her presents. They had handmade her presents. "Beautiful," she said.

Joel gave her the present. The holiday in Rome. She was lost for words. There was more. We got her an album of us. We love photos. To remind us of our lives together. She was crying. Bella went to her. "Auntie Lydia, look at me." She did.

"You are a wonderful person. Do you remember when I came home, I was crying so hard. You hugged me so tight and told me I would never be lonely? I would be loved. I will be grateful for ever, for that. Thank you will never be enough. Happy birthday, Aunt Lydia." Bella hugged her tight.

Lydia was bawling her eyes out. That started everyone else off.

"I need a drink! Bella. Home is here. You are in a family that will never leave you." Lydia wiped her eyes.

"Mack, get the food ready. We're hungry. Michael was going to do it. I don't fancy a trip to the hospital," Maggie said.

"I'm not that bad!" I said.

Oliver laughed. "Dad, you are. You sad, senile old man."

"You little sod!" I told him. Oliver hugged me.

"Lydia," Rae said. "Close your eyes." They brought out her birthday cake.

"Where did you get that?" Lydia asked.

"I made it. With Granddad's help. You like it?" she asked.

"Love it. Thank you, Rae. Thanks," Lydia said.

"Lydia," Joel told her. "I have one more gift." He got out a box from his pocket. "This is one thing that means everything." He opened it. It was an eternity ring.

"Joel!"

"Lydia. You are everything to me. I'm glad I got you and the kids." He put it on her finger.

Mack started crying. "Oh my God! What a day!"

"Oh my God!" Alice said. "Everyone is so girly. Mack, you sure you're not pregnant? You're a wimp! I understand Mum crying. But you! You sure you're not a woman? You act like one!"

"Thanks, Alice. No food for you!" Mack told her.

"Whatever. I'm having some anyway." Alice stuck her tongue out. "Salad. Boring! Really, boring!"

After everyone went home, everyone was in bed. It was two thirty in the morning. I heard a noise from downstairs. No good waking Mack. He could sleep through a hurricane. I grabbed the baseball bat. Then I saw Rae sitting on the couch. She yelped. "Bloody hell, Rae! It's two thirty. Why are you up?" I put the bar down.

"Couldn't sleep," she said.

"What you looking at?" I rubbed my eyes going to her.

"The photo album. We love our photos, don't we?" She smiled. "Why do people have these?" she asked.

"To remember what it was like. It's like a journal. Move over," I told her. We looked at the pictures for ages.

"I like these ones," she said, pointing to the ones where we were together.

"They were good times," I said.

Mack came down. "Thought I heard talking. What you looking at?"

I showed him.

"Ah, the album?" Mack asked.

She was yawning. "Just remembering how happy we are. That t-shirt has had it, Dad! It's knackered." She fell asleep. We smiled.

The next morning. We felt like a broken record. "Olivia, phone away. Thaddeus, finger out your nose. Fran, hurry up, come on. Going for a walk," Mack shouted.

"OK, OK, old man," Francesca said.

"Callum, t-shirt on back to front. Bella, eat your bacon. Stop playing with your food. Rae, finish your tea," I said. "Where's Ollie?"

"I'm here. Just been to the loo. That spare bacon?" Oliver said.

He was always eating. We got ready to go. Mack and I held hands. The kids were running about.

"Ollie, stop annoying. Oh my God!" Fran said. "Dad, tell him!"

"Stop it!" we both said together. An old couple gave us a dirty look.

Callum saw that. "What's up with them? They've never seen parents out with their kids before?"

"No. They are old farts!" I said. Callum laughed.

Right on cue, Oliver farted. Loudly. "Thank God. Thought I was going to explode. One of my many talents! I am the fart machine!"

"You're weird, Ollie," Bella said.

"I am not." He started running around. "What's for lunch?"

"We've just had breakfast. I swear you have seven stomachs!" Thaddeus said.

 Oliver smiled. He started walking. "I'm too old for this."

"You're fifteen!" Mack said, shaking his head.

"Dad!" Oliver said to us.

"Yes, son!" we said.

"Can it always be like this?" he asked. "I mean, us doing stuff like this. This is important."

"Son, it'll always be like this," I told him. Oliver smiled.

"Good. Now let me annoy Rae! Ta da!" he said.

"Ollie, you annoy me, I'll kick you in the nuts and wish you a Merry Christmas," Rae said, pointing her finger at him.

"You wouldn't dare, missy moo bags," Oliver said.

"Try it and find out. Plus, you won't get any lunch," Rae told him. His face was a picture. He stuck his tongue out. Rae smiled and said, "I love you, Ollie bear."

"I love you too, Rae," he said. We just laughed at him.

Then we heard a yelp. As usual, it was Oliver. "I'm OK! I'm OK! I didn't see the bin."

He was trying to play footie with a stone and kicked the bin.

"That boy is a danger to himself. Let me look?" I said. "You're a menace."

Oliver smiled. "You know I try!"

That evening, the kids were in bed.

"Can you hear that?" I said to Mack.

"What!" He was confused.

"The quiet. It's nice," I said.

"I love you, Mike. Always have." Mack kissed me.

In the morning, we couldn't stop smiling. We started singing. The radio was on. We started singing the family song, 'Happy'.

We turned round to see the kids, just standing there. Looking at us.

"What the hell is wrong with you two?" Bella asked.

"Where are our parents? It's too early for this!" Thaddeus said.

"Can't we be happy?" Mack said, laughing.

"Not this early, numb-nuts!" Francesca told us. "Jesus. Your two are weird."

"Oh bacon!" Oliver said. He started eating.

"That's all you can say. Oh bacon!" Callum said.

Olivia and Rae just shook their heads and sat down.

"Weirdos," Olivia said under her breath.

"What?" I said.

"Nothing, old man! Nothing!" Rae said.

"So, who's up for the zoo?" Mack said. "I think the aliens came last night and swapped you two. Now you're here to confuse us and drive us insane!" Oliver said, between mouthfuls.

As we got to the zoo, Bella went straight to the llamas. She started laughing. "They're funny. Look at them! *Ughh!* It spat at me! Dad, tissue. Dirty sod!"

We laughed. "So not funny! Could have germs!" Then she smiled. "I still like them."

Olivia walked with us. "You OK?" I asked.

"Yes. Getting too old to run around!" she said.

"You're sixteen, young lady!" Mack said. "You should be having fun!"

"Fun, my arse! Can't go to a party without you having an asthma attack!" She looked at Mack.

"You know it's my job to protect you," he told her.

"Yer, yer. I know, old man. You're too old! Just remember. We will always come home." She smiled. "Oh my God! What is he doing? He's an idiot!" Olivia said looking at Oliver.

Oliver was running around chasing the ducks, making noises. They were chasing him. "Look at this. It's fun! Aww! He bit me!" he said.

"Really!" Olivia said to Oliver. "Could you be any more stupid! Don't answer that. Dad, can we swap him?"

"I'm not stupid. What I do is an art form," he shouted. One duck bit his bum! "Aww. What's wrong with these ducks!"

We laughed our heads off.

"Come on, lunch!" I shouted. They ran like moths to a flame.

"Ollie needs a doctor and tablets!" Thaddeus said.

Francesca smiled, looked at me and said, "Can I wind Dad up for a minute?" She told me what she was going to do.

"Go for it!" I laughed.

"Dad," she said to Mack, "got some news for you!"

"What is it?" Mack said, finishing his mouthful.

She smiled. "I've got a boyfriend. His name's David."

That was it. "No! No bloody way. No boys. You stop that right now. You are going to give me a heart attack. No!" He pointed his finger at Francesca.

She burst out laughing. "Oh Dad. That was funny! I don't have a boyfriend. I wanted to wind you up."

Mack looked at her. "You little moo! How could you do that to me? So not funny. Did you know about this?" he asked me.

We laughed at him. "Love you, Dad!" she said.

"Don't talk to me. I want you to stay little forever!" Mack said.

"Why do you kids like winding me up?" Mack smiled.

"Because it's fun. And it brings meaning to our lives!" Thaddeus said.

Oliver laughed. "Good job!"

The following week, Alice came over. She was worried.

"What's wrong!" Mack asked.

"I think Rae's being picked on again. Her and Grace don't talk any more. Grace is with the girls that picked on her. She's been looking sad, Mack. She's so fragile, Mack. I'm worried about her." Alice had tears in her eyes.

"OK, Alice. We'll sort it. Come on, let's get you home, before your mum sends the dogs out."

I got in early from work, Mack told me what happened with Alice.

"Oh, poor Rae."

We sat her down. We sent the rest to the conservatory. "We know that you and Grace don't talk and you're being picked on again. Why didn't you tell us?" Mack asked her.

"What's the point, Dad?" she said. "No one cares any more. I try and be kind and nice. I try and help, like you taught me. I just be nice." She started crying. "It's not fair." She came to me and hugged me.

"Rae, I'm sorry. Really sorry. There's every point."

"No, there isn't. One friend. That's all I want. I don't want to be around

214

any more." She sighed.

"Don't you ever say that again!" Olivia said. "Rae Morgan Denton. We love you so much." She started crying. "I went through that. I had a birthday party. No one came. They didn't talk to me. I have now two friends. You will have a friend."

"Why do they pick on me?" Rae asked.

"I don't know. It's sad they are like that. We will look after you, never change. You are perfect just the way you are. You have the kindest heart." Olivia was crying again. "You're a good soul. Please don't say things like that. Rae, you are so kind and sweet. We need you. You're my baby sister."

Rae flung her arms around Olivia. "Thank you, Olivia." Rae then smiled. Then laughed. Oliver came out in Rae's fairy wings.

"Fran made me do it. It's degrading! Rae, you will have friends. Don't worry! It'll be OK. Can I take these off now, I look like an idiot."

We laughed. "You don't need fairy wings to look like an idiot," Callum said.

"Thanks, Callum. Nice one! What's for dinner?" he asked.

"You and your bloody stomach!" Rae said, smiling.

There it was. Back to normal, whatever that was.

"Dinner!" Mack shouted.

"Food. Yummy," Oliver said.

"Dad, can we have a film. Please!" Bella asked. "Rae, what shall we watch?"

"'Mary Poppins'. Please! Please, Daddy!" Rae looked at me with those soppy eyes. I could never say no to Rae.

"Go on, sweetheart."

"Thank you, Daddy," she said, smiling.

"She's a daddy's girl, Rae." Mack smiled. "It's sweet."

"Dad, where's the desert?" Oliver said.

"You're a pig!" Mack said. "Ice cream. Bottom drawer."

"Hark at you, numb-nuts. You had two helpings of carrot cake last night. Fat pig! I'm a growing lad!" Oliver said.

"Didn't have two helpings," Mack said.

"Oh you're a lying sod. I saw you. I'm surprised you're not diabetic." Oliver ate his ice cream. I was laughing my head off.

"What!" they said together.

"Like father, like son."

"Daddy, film. Please," Rae said sitting next to me in her pyjamas. They loved the film. Even Oliver. "I like that superwhat song. Catchy."

"Who's snoring?" Thaddeus asked. "It's loud."

It was Rae. She was tucked under my shoulder with her new Jonas and her blanket. Mack and I smiled.

Olivia smiled. "Defo a daddy's girl. So sweet."

"Rae, come on, bed," I said.

"Don't want to. Stay here. Please!" she said.

"No, come on. All of you, bed," I said.

"Story, please, Daddy," Rae said dragging her blanket behind her. I read her a story.

"Thanks, Daddy!"

"Always, Rae."

Mack had made a coffee. "Well, that was a good night," he said.

I smiled. "They certainly are characters. All of them!"

"You're telling me!" Mack said. "I wish we did it so sooner."

"Wouldn't have it any other way," I told him.

Lydia came in, sat down and was quiet for a while.

"Maggie passed her exams. Straight As. She's off to Oxford in September. My little girl. Almost eighteen. Where did time go? You know, I am proud. She still wants be in the police force. But wants an education." Lydia was crying.

I made her a coffee. "You know you did a good job, right? That girl is you. You and Joel have done a good job."

Just then, Joel and Maggie walked in. "Mum! Why you crying?" Maggie asked.

"Because you have made me the proudest mother ever! I remember when you were born. You were this small bundle of joy. So curious. Always looking around. Like a nosey neighbour. You were always asking questions. Loved annoying Michael and Mack. As you got older, you were always trying to wrong a right. Fighting for what's right. Maggie Anne Green, you have done me and your dad proud, young lady." Maggie had tears in her eyes.

Joel looked at Maggie. "You know, you're the first Green to go to university. I held that letter in my hand. Boy, I'm so proud, my baby girl. University! I am proud of you. Made me the proudest father. Never forget how talented you are."

"I love you two very much. You and Dad have done everything for us kids. I am grateful for you two. Here!" She gave them an envelope.

"Maggie!" Lydia said.

Maggie had saved her pocket money up and booked them a table at their favourite restaurant. She had also paid for their dinner.

"Please, Mum, Dad. This is a thank-you. My thank-you. Mum, Dad, I wouldn't be here if it weren't for you. I'm going to miss you."

That was it. We were all in tears. Crying like babies.

So, come September, Maggie was at Oxford. We all went to get her settled. "Maggie. From Mack and me," I told her. It was a picture of us three. Before the rest of the kids came along.

She cried her eyes out. "I'm scared. Really scared."

Malek looked at her. "Those who are strong of heart will whether the storm. Maggie, go in there and find your feet. We'll be here. Always. Christmas will be here, in a breeze. Go, my child."

That was that. Maggie was at off at university. When we got home, it was quiet. Mack went in the garden with a scotch and a cigar. Olivia watched him for a minute. She went to him. I just watched.

"Dad! You OK? You seem sad!" She took his hand.

"I'm OK, Olivia. I'm OK. You know, when you see your child growing up, you want the best for them. You never want them hurt. Always to protect them. No matter how old they get. So, when you grow up and go in the world, and we can't be there, it hurts. Here" — Mack pointed to his heart — "we know, you have to find your feet, but all we want is to keep you safe. That's why I do the things I do. Dad is the same," he said to her.

"I understand," she said. I sat next to her. "You know, you and Dad are good parents, don't you? You two have done a good job with us. I wonder about Ollie though. He's not normal."

"Hey. Yes, I am!" he said. "I'm hungry and I just farted."

"See?" she said. "But Dad, you two are good. Better than most."

"Does it bother you that two men brought you up?" I asked.

"No way!" Fran said. "Look at what you have done. Family days. You're there when we do homework. You talk to us. You're there always. Some kids don't have that! I think we are lucky."

"I don't know any different. This is normal to us!" Thaddeus said. "It is normal. It's good to be different. At least we're happy. We have each other. That's all that matters to me."

"Well put, Thaddeus," I said.

"Feeling better, Daddy?" Rae asked him. Mack nodded.

"Good. On that note, dinner," Oliver said.

"Oh my God!" Olivia said. "I swear you have an eating disorder! How can you eat so much?"

"Easy! Open your mouth and chew. Wally brain! If I don't eat, it could ugly," Oliver said.

"It's ugly when you eat!" Bella said. "Do you take a breath?"

Lydia came in. "I've got a slight problem."

"You've lost your bottle of wine!" Oliver said.

"Sod off you. Maggie is coming home Friday. She has a friend, who's a boy. Joel doesn't know. He'll have a heart attack. Where's the good scotch!" Lydia said.

"This is going to be interesting," Mack said. "Tell me. Can you imagine what will happen if he turns up and Joel doesn't know? He'll kill him. Literally."

Joel walked in. "Thought you were here. What?"

"Honey. Maggie… has a friend. It's a boy," Lydia said.

Joel's eye started twitching. "Excuse me? What was that? A boyfriend. Hell no!"

"Joel, calm down. Please!" Lydia said.

"Calm down?" He was incredulous. "No fucking way! He's a dead man."

"Dad, are you going to be like that when I get a boyfriend?" Olivia said.

"He's going to be worse than that!" I told her. Her face dropped. "Come here for dinner. Saturday," I said. "Joel, Joel, I'll have the good scotch."

Saturday came around. We were all ready. Maggie came in. She saw Joel. "Dad, calm down. It's going to be OK. Sit down." She brought him in.

He was tall. About six two. Mixed race. Seemed OK. He looked nervous. She introduced him to Joel. "Dad, this is Max. He's a law student."

"Hello, Mr. Green. Why is his eye twitching?" he said.

"Why my daughter?" he said.

"Joel, scotch," I said. "Couch, now. Sorry about that."

Joel was mumbling.

"Shut up, Dad," Maggie said.

218

Dinner went well. Max left. He gave Maggie a kiss. Joel just looked at him. Max looked worried and left.

"That went well," Maggie said.

"Maggie, no boys!" Joel told her.

"I'm eighteen. It's not up to you. Mum, we're going to the pub. I'm buying. Grow up, Dad."

Just as they were about to leave, Maggie turned round and kissed his head.

We had scotch. "That went well," Mack said.

"Shut up, man! You've got this to come. Starting with Olivia," Joel said.

"No way. Over my dead body," he said.

"Hold that thought!" Olivia said. Mack's face was a picture.

"I'm off!" Joel said.

"Dad. I was asked to the pictures Saturday night by Thomas. I said yes," she told Mack.

He got up. "I want to meet him first."

"OK," Olivia said. She smiled at me. "Thanks," she whispered.

Friday came. Thomas came to pick her up. "Hi, I'm Michael. Olivia's Dad. This is Mack, her other Dad."

He looked surprised. "I thought Olivia was kidding when she said she had two dads."

Olivia looked at Mack.

"Have a good time. Thomas, straight home after the film. No arguing." He walked away.

"Yes, Mr Denton," he said. Olivia's face looked sad.

After the film. Thomas did as he was asked. Mack sat on the couch. Olivia sat next to him. "Dad, I know this was hard for you. Thank you. I love you." She hugged him.

"Love you too, Olivia."

She went to bed.

"You did well," I told Mack.

"I still see them as if they were little. Almost seventeen, Mike. Where's it gone? They won't need us soon." He had a tear in his eye. "After my crappy childhood, I want to give them the best in life. I know I'm overprotective. But after having no one in my corner growing up, with a sister that hated me for being different…"

"They are not like that. Look at how they annoy each other, look after each other. You took taught them that. You've done more than you realise. If you had your way, they would be indoors all day," I said.

"Not a bad idea," Mack said, scratching his head.

"I'm not staying indoors all day," Francesca said. "Can you hear yourself?" She sat next to Mack. "You listen to me, Mackenzie Denton. You're a good dad. So are you," she said, looking at me. "We're growing up. Get used to it.

"OK, OK," he said.

Olivia had her second date with Thomas. They went to have a meal. Her face dropped when she clocked Matthew.

"What?" Thomas asked.

"Wait here!" she said. She walked up to Matthew. "What are you three doing here?"

"Didn't think you'd notice?" Matthew was shocked.

"Really. You know Dad raised me with eyes in the back of my head," Olivia said. He couldn't say anything. "You take me home now. Don't call Dad." He did as he was told.

When they got home, she came in fuming. "Where is he?" she asked me. I saw Matthew come in. Mack came in too.

"How did it…" His face dropped.

"You are unbearable. Really! This is unforgivable. Why?" she yelled. He didn't have an answer. "You really don't trust me!"

"Yes, I do!" he said.

"You lying bastard! Jesus, Dad. You have no faith in me, you don't love me whatsoever. Do you?" Olivia was screaming.

"Olivia, take it easy!" I said.

"No way. I've had enough of this. You've done it now. I can't be here with you any more," she said to Mack.

"Olivia, please. No!" Mack was in bits. She went upstairs and packed a bag. She took her bear.

"I've called Grandad. Matthew, can you take me there, please?" she said. He looked at us. I nodded.

"Olivia, I'm sorry. Really. Don't go!" Mack was crying as he went up to her.

Olivia slapped him. "Don't talk to me ever. We're done. You never wanted me. I hate you! I will never forgive you." She was crying. She hugged me. "I will call you

She was gone.

"Why?" I asked. "Jesus. You may have lost her. I know you love her, but this…?"

"I just want them safe." He was heartbroken.

Everything and everyone was sad. Mack was a total mess. He didn't sleep, eat or wash. Olivia refused to talk to him.

Two months later. "I've had enough of this!" Oliver said.

He got his phone and took a photo of Mack. Joel was there. "Joel, can you take me to Grandad's? Dad, get him washed and dressed. Go to that place were Olivia likes. This has to stop, now!"

When they got to my dad's, Olivia was happy to see her brother.

"Ollie!" Olivia said and hugged him.

"Olivia, this has to stop, now. Look at this!" He showed her the photo of Mack.

"Oh God. He's so thin!" she said.

"What has happened, happened. You two are so stubborn. What he did was way out of line. Big time. He can't stop crying," Oliver said. "Can we go for lunch, please, Olivia?"

"OK, where?" she said.

"Your favourite place! That cafe you like! Come on. I want to spend some time with you, sis."

When they got there, Mack and Olivia clocked each other.

"Olivia!" he said.

"No. I want to go!" she said.

"No. Go, talk to him. Not asking. See you later," I told her.

She went to him, but she couldn't look at him.

"Olivia. I'm sorry. Really."

"Why, Dad? You do this all the time. You're a control freak!" Olivia said. "We go round in circles. You don't how bad you hurt me. I'm smarter than you think. You taught me to keep an eye out. Keep aware of surroundings. But yet you push all the time." Olivia looked at him. "You look like shit. When did you last eat?"

He smiled. "I got a lot to answer for, haven't I?"

"No shit. You are the most stubborn bastard, ever," she told him. "Tell me the truth, Dad. Why? We tell the truth."

"I want to keep you all safe. I couldn't bear if something happened to you. Any of you. I'm scared, Olivia. Scared of losing everyone. I can't help the way I am. Letting go just hurts. I fought for this. Now I'm scared it's going to be taken away from me." Mack got to the truth.

"Finally, the truth. Doesn't that feel better? Dad, Dad. We're not going anywhere. The reason why I went was because you pushed me away. I felt suffocated. I couldn't breathe." She paused. "I never meant those things. You need to eat. Please eat something."

The waiter brought them a menu. They had their favourite chicken burger salad and fries. Olivia looked at Mack.

"Can I come home, please, Dad?"

"Sweetheart, you never left. Fancy a walk?" he asked her.

They went for a walk.

"Dad, I'm sorry for all those horrible things I said to you. I felt guilty every day. It hurt me that I hurt you. Sorry!" She was crying her eyes out. Mack hugged her. "Dad I'm so sorry."

"Hey, enough, baby girl. I'm sorry that I hurt you. I should have learnt my last lesson. It won't happen again. Promise," he said.

She looked at him like she was six. "Promise?" He nodded.

"I'm hungry again," he said.

"Wait till dinner. Can we stay out a bit longer, please? Can we go to the market?" she asked.

They went to the market and made an afternoon of it.

"I missed you, Dad. I'll always come home to you and Dad. Promise me one thing," she told him.

"Promise. What is it?" Mack asked.

"Don't worry about losing us. We're not leaving. You and Dad are home. I remember my first day at school. I was scared. You said, it'll be OK, and you'll be here after school. I was so scared that you wouldn't be. When I saw you there, I was so happy. You brought me Georgia, my bear. You've been there every day. I was always worried that you wouldn't be there. I was wrong." Mack had tears. Olivia wiped his tears away.

We were all glad to see Mack and Olivia. Rae, was so happy. "Olivia. I missed you so much. Please don't do that again. Are you and Daddy OK now?" Olivia nodded. "Wait here. I have something for you." She came back with a card. Inside was a picture of Rae and Olivia.

"Rae, I don't deserve you as a sister. I love you." Olivia hugged her tight.

"Oliva, enough tears. Stop the tears. We're glad you're home."

Oliver sat next to her. "Glad you're home, sis."

"Ollie. Thank you, little brother." She took his hand. Oliver put his head on her shoulder.

"You two OK? Did you eat?" I asked him.

"Yes. Yes we are. I did eat. We had our fave. Then we went to the market," Mack said. "I better get dinner ready."

"I'll help, Dad," Olivia said.

She went and helped. Mack was a bit wobbly on his feet. "Dad, sit down on the couch. I'll finish dinner," Olivia said.

"Dad, please. It won't be long. Callum, can you help me with the plates?" Callum went and helped.

"This is good," Oliver said. "Better than yours. What's for dessert?"

"Got your favourite. Apple pie from that deli in the market," Olivia said.

"Did I ever tell you, you are the best sister ever!" he said between mouthfuls.

They went, cleared up and did their thing, either homework or bath. I was in the kitchen making tea. Olivia came up to me. Towel wrapped round her head. "Dad, I'm sorry for what happened. I was wrong!"

"Honey, it's fine. It had to happen. It needed to be done. Glad you are home. I hate not having you home. Don't do it again!" I told her.

She looked at Mack who was dozing.

"Is he going to be OK? I'm worried. He's thin. I did that!" She was getting upset.

"Hey, don't put that on you. Ever!" I raised my voice. Mack heard.

"Olivia, come here." She sat down. "Don't do that. It's done. I'm fine. I'm getting there. Don't worry. Come here." Mack hugged her.

"OK." She went and dried her hair. She came down with her teddy and her story book. She gave it to Mack, who smiled. "Please!"

"Aren't you getting too old for stories before bed?" Mack laughed.

"Never! I'm never too old for a story." Olivia sat next to Mack, head on his shoulder, knees to her chest. He read her story.

He looked at her at the end. She was asleep. Mack got choked up. He went to get up. "No, Daddy. Stay, please!"

He smiled. "OK, Olivia." He put his arm around her. "I'm not leaving, Olivia. I'm here for good. You're my daughter. I love you forever."

"I love you too. Always." Olivia fell back to sleep. Then Mack fell asleep. Oliver took a couple of photos then went to the computer and printed them out and put them in photo frames.

"Come on, wakey, wakey, you two," I said. "Bed, come on."

"Can't I stay here?" Olivia said, getting up.

"School in the morning," I told her.

"Do I have to go?" She yawned. She held her teddy and rubbed her eyes.

"Yes, you do," I told her. "Love you."

The next morning, everything was back to normal.

"Oh my God. Nothing to wear!" Olivia said. "Where my phone!"

"Where's the toast? I'm hungry!" Thaddeus said.

"Do I have to go to school? It's depressing. It makes it want to vomit," Oliver said.

"Where's my French homework?" Rae said.

"No one cares about French. Can't find my glasses!" Callum said.

Mack and I started laughing.

"Kids, come on, were late!" I said, getting the car keys.

"Don't you dare go out like that!" Bella said. "You're in your pjs, your hair ain't combed. You're in your dad slippers. Could you be any more embarrassing? Oh my god."

"Where's my bloody phone? Ollie, ring it," Olivia said. "There it is!" Then quiet. We smiled.

"So, aren't you glad we got kids?" Mack said.

I looked at him. "I was quite happy with a coffee and a biscuit."

When they came home from school, Oliver gave us the pictures he did of Mack, me and Olivia.

"That's sweet. Thanks, Ollie. You know you can be very sweet," Olivia said. She hugged him. Really hugged him. "Thanks, Ollie bear."

"Olivia, we wanted you home. I had to do something. The thought of our big sister not here. It hurt. A lot. I love you, sis. We all do." Then, in typical Oliver fashion, he farted.

"You smelly git!" Olivia said. "Dad. That's worse than yours. That smells like death!"

We laughed. We racked our brains to think of what to do for family day.

"What about that place you took us to when Rae was a baby? You know, the lakes and garden place?" Francesca said.

"Good idea," I said. "Didn't think you remembered that."

Francesca smiled. "Yes. I remember Rae getting out the pushchair and chasing the butterflies. She was so cute in her pigtails. Can we, please? It's not far."

It was agreed. We went. So did Lydia and the rest.

"I'd forgotten how beautiful it is here," Lydia said. "It's quiet. I wish Maggie were here. She loved it here."

"Mum. She's here. Always," Jack told her. He took her hand.

Lydia wiped her eyes. "Love you, Jack."

"You too, Mum. Always." Jack smiled.

Then Oliver shouted, "Food. I smell food. Let's go!"

Jack laughed. "Mum. He's so funny. I'm glad he's my cousin."

Olivia was very quiet. "Olivia, you OK?" Bella asked. "You look sad."

"I'm OK-ish. I'm still upset that I hurt Dad's feelings, and that I slapped him hard. I really screamed at him." She had tears in her eyes. "It's just that… sometimes, I think he hates me for what I did to him. I wouldn't blame them if they didn't want me any more." Olivia started crying.

Bella turned round. "Olivia. Dads want to talk to you."

We sat on a bench. "Olivia. I don't hate you. Ever. I screwed up. Big time. As for not wanting you, don't ever say that again. Ever!" Mack said.

"You're our daughter. Didn't realise it still worried you," I said.

"Listen. Don't ever put that pressure on you. It's OK, Olivia, always. Come on. Olivia, I was so happy to have you back," Mack said.

"That true," she said to me. I nodded and smiled.

"I thought that I would never become a father. That's what I always wanted. This little baby, just looking around. I just sat in the garden with you. You fell asleep and I cried. This perfect person, with those big brown doe-eyes, relying on me. That night, while your dad was sleeping, I sat in the chair, near your cot. I just listened to you breathing. Making sure you were OK. You took my breath away. I wanted you then. Always will. You are my baby. Don't forget that," Mack told her.

She hugged him. "Love you both very much. Sorry."

"Come on. Let's go. Before your brother eats them out of business," I

225

said.

Bella had ordered Olivia a chicken burger. Her favourite. "Thanks, Bella."

"You're welcome. You OK now?" she asked Olivia.

"Yes, I am. Can we go to the lake after? It's peaceful there," she asked. We went to the lake. It was beautiful.

"Daddy, butterflies." Rae smiled.

Even Oliver was enjoying it. "Forgot how nice it is here."

The drive home was different. They were quiet. So, when we got home and got changed, we sat on the couch.

"What's up?" we said.

"Nothing. It was just a nice day," Callum said.

"Just thinking about growing up, and changes," Bella said.

Mack got up and put on a DVD. It was all of the kids growing up, with us and their grandad.

"I didn't realise this meant so much to you two," Francesca told them.

"You have no idea," I said. "Callum?" He looked at me. I told him the story of when he came home. "You were a happy soul. You loved cake so much." He smiled. "You followed Rae everywhere. When she wasn't there, you looked lost. You, like Rae, have a kind soul. You laughed at the Road Runner cartoon. You have the same laugh as Francesca. You kids are wonderful human beings," I said.

"Even when do wrong things?" Bella said. I nodded.

"I feel better," Thaddeus said. "Can we watch a film now? Thank you for being my dads."

"Are you two happy?" Rae asked.

"Yes. Except when he annoys me. Then I rather have a cuppa and a biscuit," I told them. They laughed.

Olivia was asleep next to Mack.

Dad and Malek came round. Dad had a tear in his eye. He looked at us four. "You four should be proud of yourselves. Those kids are growing up to be the best versions of you. I'm proud of you. So proud."

They saw Dad and Malek. "Granddad Malek!" They ran in and all twelve of them hugged them. "We missed you. Here!"

Alice had made them a present from all of them. It was a bronze statue of them. Dad was choked up. So was Malek. Then they, as usual, started. Oliver and Jack farted. They gave each other a high five. Alice and

Thaddeus started karate chopping one another. The rest of them were arguing over the Easter eggs.

We just looked at each other.

"I need a glass of wine," Lydia said. "It's not even twelve! You alcoholic," Oliver said. We laughed. "Grandad?" Bella said. "Don't forget to say grace."

During dinner, Malek asked everyone what they were thankful for. The kids said the same thing. That they were grateful for this. Having a family around them. To have a home. Bella said, "It's nice to be in a family that cares about each other." She got up from the table, came back and gave Mack and me a present.

"What's this, kiddo?" Mack asked.

"Open it!" she said, smiling.

It a handmade card and a picture of all of us when she came.

"It's beautiful" was all he could say. She hugged us tight.

"Thank you for being my parents. I'm thankful I got a second chance. Just promise me one thing."

"What's that?" I said, wiping my eyes.

"You'll always be here," Bella said.

"Bella, We promise. Always," Mack said.

"Good. Can we play Twister. That's funny." She smiled.

"What about Operation and Hungry Hippos?" Emily said.

There it was. Family games. We did the usual. Family films. The kids had blankets and sat on cushions together. Oliver had a tear in his eye. He sat next to me.

"Son, what's wrong?"

"Just happy. This is something I will teach my kids." He put his head on my shoulder, and pulled his blanket on him. He fell asleep.

"Dad, what do you want for your birthday?" Callum asked me during dinner.

"Haven't thought about it. You want a drink? I don't need or want anything," I told him.

"You got to have something. It's a rule!" Callum said.

I smiled. "Callum, really. I got everything I need." I had a thought. "All I want is time with my family."

"We do that every weekend," Francesca said.

"I really don't want anything thing else. That's all I want. We'll have a takeaway, films. That will be enough for me. You know, Callum, you came to us the day before my birthday."

"Really? I never knew that. Dad, is that true?" he said to Mack. Mack smiled and nodded. Callum was happy.

"I got an early birthday present. I was so happy, everything else didn't matter. You were my gift thirteen years ago. This tiny little bundle of joy. I was always grateful for that. Always will, Callum," I told him.

Callum had a tear in his eye. "Thanks, Dad. That means a lot."

"So," Oliver said to me, "I take it you're nearly pension age. You'll be getting a bus pass, hearing aid, old man scooter. Oh, and a walking stick."

Mack was laughing. "I'm glad it's not me."

"I haven't started on you yet. Give it time," he said to Mack.

"You're a rotten sod. Besides, your dad is three years older than me!" I told him.

"So, he's like ancient beyond belief. Like you! Did you hear that? The pair of you. Can you hear me?" Oliver shouted.

"No desert for you. Holly can have it. Yes, girl!" I said.

"You're a bad parent. Depriving me of desert. I love dessert." Oliver was sarcastic. We laughed.

My birthday came around. It was a lovely day. Callum walked with me. "Dad, I'm glad I was a present for you."

"So am I, son," I told him.

"No. Don't get broody on me. Seven kids. Enough. Can't believe I said that," Mack said, smiling. I laughed.

"Who's getting broody?" Rae asked

"No one, Rae," I said, laughing.

"That's a shame. It would be nice," Rae said.

"Really. Why?" Mack asked her.

"Because, babies need a loving home and parents that love them." The simple truth from Rae.

"That's sweet. But no. No more," I said. It made me think though. Mack saw it and smiled.

That evening, all I could think of was what Rae had said. I couldn't sleep. Mack came down.

"I know what you're thinking," he said, yawning. "This is a big deal."

"I know, Mack. Can't think of anything else. I'm you, all those years ago," I told him.

He laughed. "Are you serious about this?"

"Yes, I am. I know this is a big deal, the kids are growing up. Olivia just had exams. What do think about this?" I made a coffee.

"I think we should do it. We have the room. Let's talk to the kids, your dad and Lydia first. Get their opinions. Take it from there. Then as a family, make that decision together. Agreed?"

"After almost twenty years. You always surprise me." I took his hand.

"We're in this together. Always will be. Decisions like this have to be made together." He smiled back at me.

The following week, we spoke to my dad, Lydia and Joel.

"Are you serious?" Joel said.

"Bloody hell! Are you sure? I mean seven kids, you want number eight?" Lydia replied. "Have you really thought this through?"

"We've thought of nothing else. I can't think of nothing else," I told her. "Dad, Malek. What do you both think?"

They paused. "I think, go for it," Dad said. "I'm behind you all the way."

"I agree," Malek said. "I believe that giving life is a gift from Allah. He is with you, my friend, as am I."

"Go for it. Family together, always," Joel replied, smiling.

"What the hell. If that's what you want. I'm with you," Lydia said. "You told the kids?"

"No. We'll tell them when they get in from school. I want to tell your lot too," I said.

Lydia rang Alice to come here with the rest after school. It was important.

When they came over, we explained to them what we were planning on doing.

"Go for it, Dad," Bella said. The others agreed.

"It's gonna be hard," Mack said.

"We know. We'll help," Thaddeus said.

That was that. It was agreed. Alfie hugged us. "Good for you."

Rae was a bit quiet. "Are you OK with this?"

"Yes, Dad. Will I still be your little girl?" she asked me.

"Always," I smiled. She hugged me.

We made the calls to start adopting. The wheels were in motion. We did the usual stuff, like we did before. It was now a waiting game. It was nerve racking, but there was no going back.

Then three months later, we got a call. A little boy. A month old. We all welcomed him home.

"What shall we call him?" Mack asked.

Francesca smiled. "I know. Leo Alexander Denton."

"Leo the lion," Callum said. "He's cute."

Later that evening, Leo started crying. We were just about to get him when Oliver beat us to it. He sat with him on the sofa with a bottle. We just watched. What Oliver said amazed us.

"You know, Leo, you are going to have one hell of a happy life with us. Your dads are the finest parents you could ever wish for. They will always be there for you, no matter what. You've got brothers and sisters that love you with every breath that we have. We will always, always have your back, kiddo. This is such a happy home. I love you so much Leo. I'm going to be the best big brother I can be to you. Right, let's burp you." Oliver kissed his tiny head. "You've got a life worth living."

Oliver changed him and put him down for a sleep. He turned round and saw us.

"What you said, Ollie, that was amazing," I told him.

"It's true, Dad. I meant every word. Leo will have the best life." He put the dirty nappy in the bin and washed his hands. "He's got good parents." He hugged us and went to his room, but not before saying, "I'm so glad I'm your son. Love you always."

We sat there in awe that a fifteen-year-old boy was so wise. We started crying.

We were getting the kids ready for school. The kids said goodbye to Leo.

"We love you very much, Leo," Olivia told him.

"What did we do to deserve them?" Mack said when I got home.

"I don't know," I told him. Leo was stirring.

"Come on, little man, let's change you and go for a walk, shall we?"

Life changed from that moment on. Everything and everyone pulled together. Leo made his mark on the family. As if he was always with us. He was now a two-year-old. Where did time go?

"Happy! Happy!" Leo said, dancing around. "Daddy, Daddy," he put his arms up for me to hug. "Beans. Books."

He loved Oliver. Vice versa. He loved them all. "Rae, Rae."

"Leo, you been good boy?" she asked him. He nodded and yawned, rubbing his eyes. "Want a story and your bottle?" He nodded. He put his head on her shoulder. "Love Rae."

"I love you too, Leo. Always," Rae said. Smiling. She saw me with tears and smiled.

"Thanks, Angel girl." Then, Leo farted.

"That's gross. Just like your brother Oliver. Dad. What did you feed him?"

We laughed. "Come on, Leo. Let's get you ready for bed."

"Story, Dada. Please. Night, Rae," he said to me.

Mack sat next to Rae on the sofa. "How's Rae?"

"I'm good, Daddy. Are you OK? I worry about you two." She rested her head on his shoulder.

"Hey! What did we say? Don't worry. You know, it's not your job. We are fine. Always will be. Rae, you are the best." She looked at him and smiled. She started yawning. She got her book. "Please, Daddy." Mack smiled, he read her story. She fell asleep.

"Oh my God! Oh my God!" Olivia was screaming.

We rushed in. "Olivia. You OK? What's wrong!" I said, panting.

She handed me her letter. "I done it. I got in. To Cambridge. Dad, I done it!" She was stunned.

"Olivia. I'm so proud of you. Wow. Our girl's off to uni." I hugged her tight. Mack on the other hand looked like he'd been kicked in the bullocks. He sat in the kitchen chair.

"Dad. Dad, say something?" She looked worried.

"Come here," he said. She went over. He hugged her. "I'm so proud of you. My baby. I never wanted this day to come, ever." He was crying. "It is hard, sweetheart, for us both. Letting go is hard."

"Oh, you two. Listen, you're not really letting go." Olivia was getting upset. "I'm not going forever. I'm always coming home. You're my home. Listen. There's an open day next week. Why don't the three of us go together? Make a day of it. Just us." She looked at me and hugged me too.

"I'm lucky. Without you two, I wouldn't have got this far. I'm scared too, you know. Really scared. But I'll always know that you all will be here. I'm a happy girl. Always."

We phoned and told the others. My dad was worse than Mack. "My God. I still see her as a little girl. We'll have to celebrate, like we did with Maggie."

Later that evening, we saw the kids together on the couch. "You know, Olivia," Francesca said, "I'm proud of you. I'm going to miss you very much. You're a wonderful sister. I'm proud to be yours. Just remember, this is where you'll always be. With us."

"I agree," replied Callum and the rest.

"And me," Leo said. "Pretty Olivia. Good sister."

Mack again burst into tears. I looked at him. "Right, kids. Dad's too hormonal to cook. He forgot his HRT this morning. Who wants a takeaway?"

"Yes. Thank God!" They all went.

"Shut up," I said. "Pull yourself together, idiot." They burst out laughing.

The time came when us three went to Cambridge university for the day.

"This place is amazing!" Olivia said. "So cool. Dads, what do you think?" We got a few funny looks and stares.

"What, never seen a kid with their parents before?" Olivia said. "How rude!"

We had a great day. On the way home, Olivia was asleep in back.

"How are you?" I asked Mack.

"OK. Feel better now that we did that today. At least it's only an hour away. Why's it so hard?" he said.

"Because they are our kids. We want the best for them. I still see her as a six-year-old. I found myself looking at their pictures the other day. I cried for an hour. These kids came into our lives and turned it upside down. But I tell you, I'd do it again. They are my life. The best gifts that we got. I'm proud of them all. These wonderful kids. I hope that I've been a good dad to her. Every day I pray I am a good dad and I'm not a disappointment."

I started crying. Olivia woke up.

"I need a wee," she said.

We smiled. "Ten minutes," Mack said.

Dad asked how it went. "Good day. Worth it. Why is it quiet?" I asked.

"Kids are in the conservatory, reading or homework," he said, smiling.

"Did you slip them something?" Mack asked. "Leo been OK?"

"Good as gold. He's such a character."

On that, Leo came bouncing in. "Daddy! Glad you're home. I've been good. Haven't I, grandad?" He started dancing around.

"Yes, Leo, you have. Want a drink?" Dad asked him.

"Please. Orange. Where Olivia?" he asked. Olivia scooped him up.

"Right here, cheeky boy."

He laughed. "Olivia. Read me a story, please. Pardon. I farted on your hand. It smells. Funny Leo." He hugged Olivia.

"Come on, farty pants. Get your book!" she said, smiling.

"Yes, we can. I'd like that." He smiled sadly.

"Don't look like that. I'm going to uni, not dying. So pack that in," she told him.

"Definitely a Denton," Dad said, making a drink. He looked at Mack. "Don't even think about it. You two didn't talk for two months. Do you want to lose her for good? No? Good."

The day came for her to go. We took her. "As it's only an hour away, we want you to come home for the weekend, when you're settled?" I asked. She nodded.

"Daddy, Daddy. I'm scared. Really scared."

Mack hugged her. "Baby girl. It's going to be OK. Me and your dad are scared too. Our grown baby, facing the world. You are our gift from god. Go, sweetheart. I'll call you tonight."

Off she went. She looked back and that was it. We were in bits and cried all the way home. Everyone was the same.

"Will Olivia come home?" Bella asked. We nodded through the tears.

She phoned later that evening. "Olivia, you OK?" Mack asked.

"I'm fine. Nervous. You and Dad OK?" she asked.

"We will be. Just want you to be happy and OK," he said.

"I am happy. Next weekend. Can I come home? Please?" Olivia pleaded.

"Course you can. We'll pick you up. Always. Love you, Olivia," I told her.

"Love you too. Always," Olivia told us.

I would say that it was quiet without Olivia. No chance. The others made up for it. "Thaddeus. Stop gluing sticks to Dad's head. Rae, get dressed for school. Bella, put your phone away. Leo, stop picking your nose." I felt like a broken record.

Olivia phoned every night. She was enjoying uni. She couldn't wait to come home at the weekend. "What time you picking me up?" she asked.

"About five. Knowing your dad, he'll be there at five in the morning," I told her. She laughed. "I'm surprised he didn't send Matthew to keep an eye on me," she said.

We picked her up. It was like her first day at school. She clung her arms around us. "I missed you," she said, smiling.

Mack was so happy. "Come on. Tell us how it's going."

"I'll carry your bag, shall I?" I said, laughing.

She told us everything. When we got home, Leo went straight up to her. "Olivia. I missed you. You OK?" He hugged her tight.

"I'm good, cheeky boy." She hugged him back. She started crying.

"Olivia," Leo said, "don't cry. Be happy. Can you read me my story before bed? But first, can you get me a drink. Then dinner."

Everything went quickly. The year went very quickly. We celebrated Emily's seventh birthday.

"Where the hell has time gone?" Joel said. "Maggie's in her second year. Alfie and Alice are just starting A levels. Jack's doing his GCSEs. I'm getting old."

"Tell me about it," I said. "Leo's five soon. They will be off doing their thing. We'll be a distant memory. I'll have to talk to Mack!" We laughed.

"Ah, good. You're here!" Lydia said. She looked at Joel. "Maggie's met someone at university. It's looking serious. He's name is Tom. There, I said it."

Joel's eye started twitching. "Pardon. A boyfriend. Hell no!"

"Calm down. It's fine. He seems nice," Lydia said.

"You've spoken to him?" Joel asked.

"Umm! Yes. Twice. Relax. It'll be fine. Help me!" she said, looking at me.

234

"You're on your own! Joel, chill out." I laughed.

Then Deja vu happened. Olivia phoned me to tell me she had a boyfriend, and could I tell Dad? He flipped out. Like Joel.

"My God. You are so overprotective. What is it so hard for you? Bloody hell!" I asked him.

"Just because. Why doesn't it bother you? Why are you so chilled out?" he said, annoyed.

"Of course, it bothers me. But it's not good going all guns blazing. Do you want that incident again? Didn't think so. If you go down that road again, you'll lose her for good. Good job I'm the sensible one?" I told him. "Lighten up a bit, for God's sake."

So, Mack and I, Lydia and Joel took Maggie, Olivia and their 'friends' for dinner. Mack and Joel looked like they were going to have a psychotic moment. The boys looked scared. They didn't hang around long.

"Thanks very much!" Maggie said to them. "How could you? You two are *ugh!* Stupid. Grow up! Leo and Emily are more grown up. Take us home. Now. Mum, Michael, thank you.'

The drive home was awful. Olivia slammed the door. "See you later, Maggie. I'll call you tomorrow," she told her.

"Dad, can you take me back to uni in the morning, please?" she asked me. I nodded.

"Olivia?" Mack said. She ignored him. "Olivia."

"Leave it," I told him.

As we were leaving, Olivia went to Mack. "Right now, I'm angry at you. I love you. But I'm angry and mad. I can't talk to you at the moment. I'll be home. But don't talk to me. Not yet. I'm not ready." She sat next to him on the sofa. "Stop with this shit. Dad, I get it. I do. Please, stop controlling. Why me? Why do you hate me so much!"

"I don't hate you. I don't want anyone hurting you. I thought I'd learnt my lesson." He told her.

"I get that, Dad. But there will be times in life that will happen. You can't always do that. You just have to be there. Look at me!" Mack looked at her. "Let go. Just a little. You're a prick, you know that?" She got up, turned round and hugged him round the shoulder. "You and Dad are the finest men I know. I love you. We're OK. Always. Leo, get your shoes on. We're going to the park."

"Yeah!" he shouted.

I looked at Mack. "Idiot. She's you. Don't fuck up again," I told him. "Tough as old boots and stubborn as hell. Wonder where she gets it from. Oh yeah. You!"

Every week was going too fast. Before we knew it, it was our favourite time of the year; Christmas. Leo loved it! He had to have his Christmas pyjamas, slippers and favourite teddy.

"Does Father Christmas come to everyone?" he asked Oliver, eating a biscuit while watching their programme. 'Ben and Holly's Little Kingdom'.

"Yes, he does, Leo. He comes to all that are good and kind. Want a drink?" Oliver asked.

"I'm OK. Will you always be my big brother?" Leo asked.

"Yes. Why? I love being your big brother," Oliver said.

"Just asking. I love you, Ollie bear. Always. Thank you for being my brother," Leo said, cuddling him. That brought a tear to Oliver's eye. "I'm a happy boy."

Christmas came. Leo was up with the larks.

"Thaddeus! He came. Santa came."

"Yes, he did. Merry Christmas, Leo," Thaddeus said.

"Merry Christmas, Thaddeus," Leo hugged him.

I don't know why, but Christmas meant something. Not that it didn't, anyway. It actually snowed!

"Oh my God!" Callum said. "Hey, it's snowing. Fran, your wish came true!"

Francesca's face lifted up. "If it settles, I'm making a snowman."

We all had a good day. Mack had a day off cooking. My dad and Olivia cooked. "I can get used to this. It's nice." Lydia brought round her famous Christmas cake. Oliver's eyes popped out his head.

"Right. You two need a hand in here," Lydia said. She was out on veg duty.

"Olivia, you OK in there?" Mack asked.

"Yes, old man. I'm fine," she told him.

Olivia and Maggie gave us and Lydia an envelope. "Merry Christmas, you lot. Love you."

It was a weekend away for us. "Olivia! Maggie," Joel said. "You can't afford this."

"I helped as well," Maggie said, "so did Grandad."

"You two! Naughty," Lydia said. "Why?"

"Just because. You've done so much for us. It's a thank-you," Maggie said. Lydia was about to say something. "Don't answer me back, woman. You and Dad are going."

Joel laughed. Lydia looked at him.

"Olivia," I said.

"Dad. Not another word. I swear if you argue with me, I'll slap you!" She looked at us. "Good. Dad, get the plates ready. Dinner in ten minutes. Come on."

"When did she get this bossy?" I asked Mack.

"I'm not bloody arguing with her. I've just got back in her good books," Mack said.

What a day! Everyone stayed as usual. "Come on, Leo. Bed for you," I told him.

"OK, Daddy. Read me a story. My favourite at Christmas." He ran to my dad. "Love you, Grandad. See you in the morning. Night, Grandad Malek."

"Goodnight, Leo," they said.

Dad had a tear in his eye. Before he could finish his sentence, Maggie brought him and Malek their favourite scotch. She hugged him. "Thank you. You too, Malek. Here, for you." It was a photo of all of them. At the bottom in Arabic was written *'Home is you. Life is what you make it.'*

They started crying. "Oh my God! You're worse than Mack. Jesus and Allah!" Maggie said. "Bloody hell!"

"Language, Maggie," Lydia told her.

"Really, mother? It's better than piss off. Don't look at me like that. I'm an adult. Wine? Good. That'll keep you quiet, for ten minutes," Maggie said. Again, Joel laughed loud.

"Olivia," said Rae. "Thank you. I'm glad you're home. I miss you!" She clung on to Olivia.

"I miss you too, Rae. You are so sweet and kind. You're a wonderful sister, Rae. You always think of others. I remember when you were six. Dad brought a lolly. You saw a bit crying. You gave it to him. Just like that. You're an angel, Rae. My angel," Olivia told her.

When Rae was asleep Olivia tucked into her. "Rae, bed."

"Five minutes. I want five minutes. Please," Olivia couldn't say no. Next thing, Olivia fell asleep too.

"Come on, bed," Mack told them.

"OK. Dad, I love you," Rae told Mack. "Merry Christmas."

"Merry Christmas, Angel girl. Thank you," Mack told her.

"For what, Daddy?" she said, cuddling Jonas.

"Being you," She smiled. He kissed her head.

"Same to you." She fell asleep.

"It's nice this," Callum said to us.

"What's that?" I said, passing him a drink.

"Us, extra-long family time. We're really enjoying it.

"Son, thank you. You know, all we want is for you kids to be happy, and be the people you want to be. I'm proud to be your dad." Callum smiled. He rested his head on my shoulder.

"Dad, I'm proud of you too. I couldn't wish for anything else. I'm here with a family that wants and loves me," Callum said. I was about to get up. "No, can we just sit here for a bit? You and me, and watch some TV. Holly, come on, girl." Holly jumped up and sat next to him. It was nice. "You don't mind, do you?"

"No, I don't mind at all. What shall we watch? Anything?" I said.

Dad walked in and saw Callum and I asleep on the sofa. "Michael, I've been calling for ages. That's a nice sight," he said.

"Everything OK?" I said, yawning.

"Just bringing stuff round for the do tomorrow night. Callum OK?" Dad asked.

"Yes. Just wanted to spend some time together. Even as they get older, they still want to spend time with us," I said.

"You know you were like that. Wanting to spend time with us. I think it's nice that it's been passed down," he said, putting the meat in the fridge.

"Grandad?" Thaddeus said. "How are you?"

"I'm good. Still helping me tomorrow with bringing stuff over?" he asked.

"Yes, looking forward to it. Shall I wake Callum up? He won't sleep tonight," he asked me. I nodded. Callum got up and yawned.

"Hi, Grandad. Dad, what's time's dinner? I'm getting hungry."

"Dad said about six. It's takeaway night." Callum and Thaddeus high-fived each other.

"Right, I'm off. Thaddeus, I'll be here at ten. So be ready. OK?" Dad told him. He nodded.

Mack walked in with Rae and Francesca. They all had bags. "What the hell is in there?" I said.

"These girls can spend," Mack said. "Stuff for the do tomorrow. Rae gave me her soppy-eyes look when I said no about something. I did a you and caved in." I smiled.

"Dad is such a soft touch." Francesca laughed. "The ladies in the shop were laughing when Rae got her own way. He couldn't say no. It was a good day. I enjoyed it. Dad, thanks for a good day. Rae, help me put this stuff away. Dad, sit for ten minutes," Francesca said.

Mack did as he was told.

I laughed. Mack smiled. "God, I'm knackered."

Rae brought us a cuppa. "Thanks for today."

"Dad!" Oliver shouted. "My stomach had no food in it. What time's dinner?"

"Ollie, Dad just sat down. Give him ten minutes. Pig!" Francesca said. I laughed.

Leo came bouncing in. "Daddy, you're home. Good day?"

Mack nodded yes. Leo rested his head on my shoulder. "You OK, Leo?" I said.

"Yes, Daddy. Can we watch 'Wall-E' later. What does happy mean?" he asked out of the blue.

"It means, you like what you have and you are lucky to have it," I said.

"Then I'm happy that I have all of you. You make me happy," he said.

Mack and I smiled. "Leo, what shall we have for dinner?" Mack asked him.

"Pizza Hut. Cheese and tomato stuffed crust and pepperoni and garlic bread. Better get extra, Oliver is a pig!" Leo said.

"I heard that," Oliver said, smiling. "Leo, you want a drink?" Leo nodded.

Mack went to get a drink.

"What do you want, I'll get it?" Francesca asked.

"Who are you and what have done with my kids?" He looked confused.

"Ah, look!" Francesca said. "He looks confused like he doesn't know if he needs a fart or a poo."

"I am confused. I'm not used to this. My job is to look after you," he said.

"We look after each. We're getting older. It's not just your job. Let us help," Francesca told him and hugged him. "Sit down."

He did as he was told. Mack and I smiled.

"Right, Leo. Bath before film," Francesca told him.

"Can't I stay here!" He whined.

"Come on. We'll put your favourite pyjamas on," she told him. That was it. He went straight up. Thaddeus smiled. He took my hand. " Everything OK?"

"Yes. Never better," Thaddeus told me. "Thank you."

"For what?" I asked.

"Being there and for being my dad," he said.

"You are more than welcome, son. I'm proud of you. Always." I hugged him.

That night, Mack and I heard screaming. It was Rae.

"Rae, Rae? Bad dream?"

"Daddy. The monster came back. Don't let him take me away. I don't want to go." She was crying like a small child.

"You are not going anywhere. They can't have you. You're a daddy's girl. This is your home, forever," I told her.

She smiled through the tears. "Really. I'm glad. I don't want to leave you and Daddy."

"Angel girl. You're never leaving us. Ever," Mack told her. Rae looked happy. "You're our daughter. That stupid monster can bugger off. You will always be our princess." Rae laughed.

"You're silly, Daddy. I feel better now. Are we still good to go on our walk tomorrow?" she asked us. We nodded.

"Good. I love those walks. Night, Daddy. Both of you." She fell asleep with Jonas.

"She's a delicate flower. She's a China doll," Mack told me.

"I know. I won't change her, for nothing," I replied. "I want to wrap her in cotton wool."

"She's definitely a daddy's girl with you." Mack smiled when he said it.

We had our family New Year walk. Always around the hills.

"Dad, why is family tradition important to us?" Bella asked us.

"Because," Mack and I said, "as a family, it's good to have those little things in place. No matter how busy we get. At least we have this."

"Good," she said. She looked at Oliver. "I'll bet you a cuppa and a biscuit he'll say I'm hungry, when's lunch?"

"You're on," I told her. Right on cue, he did just that.

"Told you. He's a Hoover." she laughed.

After New Year's, Rae and I went to get Holly and the cats their usual check-up. Then, we went to get some more food for them. As usual, Rae fell in love with the kittens. "They're so cute."

"Come on you home," I said. I paused. "Rae, choose another one."

Her face lit up. "Really, Daddy? But we have enough. I'll be fine."

"Rae, you never ask for anything. Go on. My treat," I said, smiling.

"Daddy, thank you. Are you sure about this?" she said. I nodded.

When we got home, everyone smiled. They saw how happy she was. "What's her name?" Olivia said.

"Rose. You don't mind me having another one?" she asked.

"Not in the slightest. Nice to see you happy, Angel girl," Olivia told her.

Alice got into Art college. Alfie got into Durham university. "Oh my god. My kids are growing up too quick," Lydia said over coffee. "Where did it go?" She was crying. "I'm proud of them. As this rate, I'll have to talk to Joel. That's pushing it."

I laughed. "We complained when they were too noisy, now we don't want them to leave. We're the weird ones."

She laughed. "We've come a long way, haven't we? In all these years. We've become stronger as a family. Family weekends are a god-send, Michael." She took my hand and shed a tear. "I am so lucky to have you all. Love you."

"Love you too, Lydia. Mack made me a better man. I adore that man. Even after twenty-plus years, I love him very much. That man is my life."

I didn't realise he was behind me. "I love you too. Always have. Can't be without you too." Mack kissed me.

"I think I want to throw up," Lydia said. She saw Rose the cat. "Don't tell me. Rae." I nodded. "Daddy's girl that one." Rose purred around her. Then Toby and George followed.

Rae came along and fed them. "Aunt Lydia." Rae hugged her tight. "Miss you lots."

241

"Miss you too, kiddo. I see Daddy bought you a cat." Lydia smiled.

"Yes. It was nice. Rose is a good cat. Are you OK, Lydia?" she asked.

"Yes, Angel girl. Don't worry about me," she replied. Rae started yawning. "Right, miss. Bath then bed," I told her.

"Will you read me my story?" I nodded.

"Night, Lid-lid," Rae said, hugging her.

"She hasn't called me that in years. She still likes her bed-time story?"

"They all do. They say it's the little things that make them happy. Even Olivia still has her story when she's home," Mack told her.

"Wow. You two have done a good job with those kids," she told us.

"Right back at you," I told her.

"I better go, before Emily beats up Joel again. See you Saturday. Love you," Lydia said.

"Love you too," I said.

Mack and I spoke for a while. "Twenty-plus years, Mike. The best years of my life. I don't know where I'd be if it weren't for you. I'll never stop loving you. I know we've had our moments over the years. Wouldn't change it."

"I remember when I first saw you in the hospital. Smart arse, opinionated. I fell in love with you there and then. That was it. I knew I didn't want to lose you. That was it for me. I couldn't lose sight of you. When you were away, I had to sleep on the sofa. Not having you next to me, it hurt." Mack took my hand. "I loved you then. I love you more now. I will always, always love you. We got eight wonderful amazing children. Three cats and a dog. You're everything and more." I was crying.

Mack was quiet. "You know how I feel. When I saw you, I fell in love with you. I knew I had to spend the rest of my life with you. I've never wanted anyone else. Married you and had our kids. I love you, Mike, so much."

We heard sniffling. We turned round to see Oliver and Francesca wiping their eyes.

"Oh my God. What's wrong? What happened!" I asked them.

"Nothing. We heard you two talking. It made us cry," Francesca said. She had Digby with her.

"Ollie, you OK, son?" Mack asked him.

"Dad, I'm OK. You two said nice things about each other." He put his head on Mack's shoulder.

"Because it's all true. Meant every word," I told them both.

"Do you regret having us?" Francesca asked.

"No way. My God. You kids are the most amazing people in our lives. You kids have changed us for the better. Don't ever think that, Francesca. We wanted you then, we will always want you kids. You kids are..." I couldn't finish my sentence through the tears.

"Dad. I'm sorry. I didn't mean to make you cry," Francesca started crying. "I'm putting the kettle on before I start," Oliver said.

"What you thinking, Ollie?" Mack asked him.

"It's nice that you feel like that. It's cool. Most of my mates' parents are divorced. I think I'm the only one in my class whose parents are still married after all these years," Oliver said. "Most of them don't talk to their parents like we talk. Can I have a biscuit. I'm hungry."

Mack and I smiled. "My god!" Francesca said. "Why are so hungry all the time? You're going to turn into Bigfoot when you're older."

"I just am. I was going to offer you one. I don't think now I'll bother," he said to her.

"Shut up and get me a jammy dodger." Francesca laughed. He did as he was told.

"Love you, Fran!" he said.

"Same to you with knobs on!" Francesca put her head on my shoulder. "Sorry I upset you, Dad. Didn't mean it."

"I know, sweetheart," I told her.

"Why is it important to talk about stuff?" Oliver said, passing out the drinks.

"So whatever is bothering you is out in the open and it's not going to worry you. It's good to do that," I said.

"Well, I've been thinking," Oliver said. "You know that work experience I did at that special needs school?"

We nodded. "I've decided I want to become a Special Needs teacher, not a footballer."

"Really. Are you sure. That's what you wanted," Mack told him.

"Dad, those two weeks made a difference to me. I want to help and do something special. I'll always play football, but this is what I want to do. You're not mad?" He looked at me.

"Ollie, I'm proud of you so much. If that's what you want, Dad and I will back you up," I told him. He looked at Mack.

"Good on, son. I agree with your dad. We'll always have your back," Mack told him.

"What do you think, Fran?" Oliver asked her. She was asleep on my shoulder. Oliver kissed her head. "I love you, Francesca, I like being your big brother. Come on, bed."

She woke up and went to bed.

"You've sacrificed a lot to raise us." Ollie rested his head on my shoulder.

Mack and I smiled at each other. "Ollie, you're welcome."

"Can we just sit here? This means a lot," he said. He looked at me, smiled and rested his head on my shoulder. "This right here is enough for me."

Mack went to get up. "I'll start dinner."

Oliver took his hand. "Dad, stay please. Five more minutes, please. I want to spend time with you." Mack sat back down. That made my day. Our son, instead of wanting to be either on his phone or out with a mate, just wanted to spend time with us.

"Can we watch Aladdin after dinner? I haven't seen that in ages," Oliver asked.

"OK. That was your favourite," I told him.

Mack cooked his favourite. Every week, Mack cooked the kids' fave dinners. Oliver loved Mexican food.

"Go have a shower before dinner," I told him.

"Oh. Do I have to?" Oliver said.

"Yes, you do," Leo said. "I have to have one too. Go on."

"OK, I'm going, bossy boots," he told Leo.

"Will you watch telly with me?" Leo asked. Oliver nodded.

"How was school today, Leo?" I asked him.

"Good. We did numbers today. Miss Dylan thinks I'm good at them." He did what Oliver had done, rested his head on my shoulder. "Dad, when I grow up. I want to be happy."

"That's what Callum said when he was your age. You're like him," I told him.

He smiled. "Dad? Is dinner ready? I'm hungry," Leo said. "Five minutes, Leo. Want to help set the table?"

"Yeah, I'm helping." He went and did as he was told. "Dad, why do you like cooking?"

"I just do. I'm better than your dad. He can't cook!" He laughed. So did Leo.

"You two are silly. When's Olivia coming home? I miss her."

Mack and I looked sad. "She'll be home in six weeks," I told him.

"That's too long. Can't you go and get her?" he asked innocently. "I want my sister home."

"So do we," Mack told him.

It was a long six weeks. When Olivia came home, we surprised Leo at school. She hid behind me.

"Leo, what's up?" Mack asked.

"I miss my Olivia. She should be home."

She stood behind him and put her hands over his eyes. "Here I am, cheeky boy."

He spun round to see her and cried, "I missed you, Olivia. All I wanted was you. I got my sister home."

When they got home. "Look in that bag, Leo," Olivia told him.

He looked. He took out the teddy bear he wanted, the story book and the slippers he wanted.

He ran to her and hugged her tight. "Thank you, Olivia. I love them. Dad, look. I didn't even ask for this. You're so kind. Like Rae."

Then Rae and the others walked in. They hugged her. Rae was so happy. "My Olivia. We've missed you."

"Look in the blue bag, Rae," she told Rae. She pulled out the pink and purple jumper she wanted. "Olivia, Thank you. It's beautiful. Just what I wanted. You need your money for school? I've got pennies," Rae told her.

"No, I don't. It's a gift to my little sister who didn't ask for anything, but does so much for everyone else." Olivia hugged her. Olivia got the rest a little present each.

"You spoil them," I told her.

"Dad, I saved up from my job. I worked it out. I've got enough saved for what I need to do. I love seeing their faces. Let me do it every now and then. Where are you going, Dad? I've got something for you both."

"Garden. Come on," I said.

We sat next to Mack on the garden bench. Mack put his arm around her shoulder.

"Here, for you two." She gave me the present. It was a photo of us three. The same in her necklace. "I've got one on my desk at my dorm. Every time I feel a bit sad, I look at this. It makes me feel better. Hope it helps you two when I'm not here. I know you miss me a lot."

"This means a lot, Olivia. Thank you." I wiped a tear.

Olivia looked at Mack. "Daddy!"

"I'm proud of you so much. My eldest daughter. When you kids go away, even for the weekend, it's odd. You kids are our lives. I'm OK. I'm just being soppy." He smiled.

"What's new?" Thaddeus said. He made us jump. "You better start dinner. Ollie is nibbling. It's not looking pretty in there. Come on. Chop, chop."

We laughed. "I'll cook," Olivia said.

"Oh no, you don't. First night home. Go and watch telly," Mack told her.

Leo was glued to Olivia's side. "I'm not letting you out of my sight," he told her. "You're not going back. I said so."

Maggie and Olivia went out that Saturday night.

"Dad, can you pick us up at ten?" Mack nodded. "Lydia is taking us."

"Where you going?" I asked.

"Only to that restaurant by the marine. Going to have dinner." Mack smiled. "What are you smiling at?" she asked.

"It's nice that you two are doing that. See you in a bit," he told her.

We had a call an hour later. Olivia and Maggie were having trouble. Mack went and got Joel. Matthew and Jacob met them there. It was getting rough in there. The girls were shaking.

"Dad, that's horrible," Maggie told Joel. "All we wanted was a nice meal and a catch up. Olivia, you OK?" she asked her.

"Maggie, I'm OK. Uncle Joel. You OK?" she asked him.

"Baby girl, I'm OK. Come on home. Your mum is ready to murder someone." He looked at Maggie. "It's not your fault. I've got fave ice cream at home. I hid it from your mother."

We took the girls home. "I'll call you tomorrow, Olivia."

"Love you, Maggie. Night, Uncle Joel," she told them.

Olivia was OK. She had a bath and came down.

"Better now?" I asked.

"Yer." She sat next to me. "It was scary. We just wanted a night out. A nice dinner and a catch up. A couple of hours. Then you get idiots that spoil it. It's not fair."

Mack brought her a bowl of her favourite ice cream. She smiled and said thanks.

"Thanks for getting me. I didn't mind Matthew and Jacob coming. Got any sprinkles?" She gave Mack her soppy look.

"Why do we cave in with you girls?" he said getting up.

"Because we are geniuses. And you can't say no. Isn't that right, Dad?" She looked at me. I just nodded.

Leo came down rubbing his eyes. "Why you up, young man?" I asked him.

"Couldn't sleep. I wanted to make sure Olivia didn't leave." He sat next to her and pulled the blanket over him.

"I'm not going anywhere for a while, cheeky monkey," she told him. "Five minutes then bed. OK, Leo?" Olivia told him.

"OK, Olivia." They were asleep arm in arm. Eldest and youngest.

In the morning, I was woken up by the smell of cooking.

"What the bloody hell?" Mack said. "Why are you cooking?"

"You needed a lie-in. I thought we could stay in today. It looks miserable out there," Olivia said.

We couldn't complain. Oliver and Mack were exactly the same. Eating like animals.

"I'll wash up!" Oliver said. Rae helped. The rest tidied up. Mack and I were at a loss.

"You both look confused. What's the matter?" Thaddeus asked.

"We're so used to looking after you, it's weird that you lot are helping," I told him. "That's weird, Dad. We like helping." He looked at Mack. "You look like you need a poo."

"I'm not used to this. I'm used to doing things," Mack said.

Thaddeus sat next to us. "You know, let us help you two. You need to chill out a bit. Dad, we're getting older. We're going to help you. Get used to it. Now you two want a cuppa?" He got up and made a drink.

I looked at Mack. "I can get used to this."

Mack looked at me and shook his head. "I can't. I love looking after my kids."

Rae came up to us. "We love looking after you two as well." She gave us a kiss and a hug. "Daddy. Let us help you."

We smiled. "Rae, you are going to have a wonderful life. When you're older, you are going to do great things."

"Thank you, Daddy. But my mind's made up." She smiled and went and played with Francesca.

"I think she will be with us," Mack said, smiling. "She's a delicate flower. But you're right. She's going to do great things. They all are. They are the most amazing people that entered our lives. Like you, I'm proud of my kids."

"You mean that?" Thaddeus said.

"Yes, we do," I told him. "If we didn't have you lot, I'd have to talk to your dad and I would to have to take medication."

"Hey, cruel git!" Mack said. The kids laughed.

"He's good," Oliver said.

"Have you always got on?" Callum asked.

"We've had our moments over the years, fair share of arguments. But yeah, we've got on," Mack said, smiling.

"It's part and parcel of being a couple. It happens. But we've talked things through and spoke the truth," I added.

"Right, come on. Get Holly, we need some fresh air. Well go to the market and get some stuff for tea tonight," Mack said.

Leo took my hand. "You OK, son?" I asked.

He nodded. "Yes, Dad. I'm happy, that's all. Will we always be happy?" he asked the same question the rest always did.

"Yes, we will. Just remember what we told you. We will always be here."

Leo smiled.

"Leo, get your shoes on. Take your teddy if you want," Olivia told him. He ran and hugged her tight. "What was that for?" She smiled.

"I felt like it. You're a good sister, like the others." He then went and put his shoes on.

I walked to Olivia, who had a tear in her eye. "Olivia. I'm proud of you. You help out so much when you're here. They look up to you more than you realise. You're turning out to be a fine young lady. I'm proud that you're my daughter. Olivia Anna Denton, you are truly a gift like the rest." She flung her arms around me with tears in her eyes.

"Daddy, that is the most wonderful thing you have ever said to me." She looked at me. "Just remember, you are a wonderful dad and a good man. I love you, Daddy."

"Love you too, my darling angel," I told her.

Mack saw us. "Everything OK?" She flung her arms around him. "You're wonderful too, Daddy. Thank you for being my dad and looking out for me. Love you so much." She wiped her eyes.

Mack was choked up. He nodded. "That was unexpected and very nice."

We went for our walk. Then the market.

"Olivia, sit down. I'm doing tea tonight. You choose a film. You've done enough today," Mack told her.

"OK, Dad. I'm sorry for the times I yelled at you. I didn't mean it. I know now you're looking out for me." She hugged him tight.

"I'll always look out for you and the rest of you till my dying day. Losing you kids is not an option." Mack hugged her. "Love you, kiddo. Always have, always will."

"Don't worry about that. I went on a date before I came home. He was an arsehole. Homophobic. I kicked him in the bullocks, and punched him in the throat, like you taught me." Olivia smiled.

"That's my girl." He smiled. "Go and sit down."

"I'll have a bath." She kissed the top of my head. "Love you, Dad."

"Love you too." I smiled.

She came a while later. Hair wrapped in a towel. I knew she was going to ask her usual. Instead, she sat next to me. I wrapped my arm around her. "You OK?"

She nodded. "I miss this, when I'm not here. I know it sounds silly, but I really miss it a lot. I even miss my stories," Olivia said.

"It doesn't sound silly at all. It just means that what we have is worth fighting for. Olivia, we will always be here." I looked at her. She was dozing off. "Don't fall asleep. Tea's ready."

That evening, she was quite soppy. It was nice. Mack gave her ice cream. "You forgot the sprinkles." she gave him her soppy look. Then the others did it.

"You girls have me wrapped your little finger." They all smiled.

"Tomorrow, can we go to the lakes?" Thaddeus asked.

We said yes. Olivia asked for her story. "Please?"

"You're over twenty," I told her.

She smiled. "I don't care. I miss it when I'm not here. Sometimes, I find to sleep at university. Dad, I don't want to stop having my story." She got a bit upset.

"OK, Olivia. It really means a lot to you."

"It means a lot to all of us," Callum said. "Can't explain it. It's like family weekends. It's nice. I'd rather have this than be out with friends."

"Yes. We can be ourselves, doing different stuff all the time," Bella said.

"Plus, we get to hang out. We actually get on," Francesca said. "You two done the right thing doing this."

The next morning, Olivia gave us an envelope.

"What's this?" Mack asked.

"Housekeeping money," she said.

"Olivia. We can't take this. You'll need it," Mack told her.

"Dad, you two taught me about money before. It's for just while I'm here. To help you. I have enough for the year. It's all worked out. I'll know if you've put it back," she told me.

Mack sadly smiled. "My little girl. Come on. Let's go."

On our walk, Mack said, "We can't take that. Mike, I don't feel right taking money from our daughter."

"I agree. We'll save it, and put it in an account for her. I think it's sweet that she wants to do that for us. I miss her lots," I told him.

"Well, you can tell her. We've been through enough, Olivia and I. We are getting back to the way it was. I can't risk it," he was getting upset.

"It's gonna be fine." I took his hand. "You really miss her, don't you?"

"That obvious? It'll be the same for all of them. Empty nest syndrome I think they call it," Mack said, smiling and wiping his eyes.

Olivia saw that. "Dad, are you two OK?" I smiled.

"Yes, love, we are OK," I told her. "Good. Can I have an ice cream? Please!" she did her usual at Mack. I laughed. "No. Not before dinner. I'm not looking. Mike, back me up!" I said no.

"Right!" Olivia was smiling. "Rae, Fran, Bella." They walked over. She told them. They all did it. They gave us their soppy looks. Rae looked at me. Her lip went.

"Why did we have daughters?" That was it. We caved in. The girls gave each other high-fives.

"Works every time," Francesca said, smiling.

"Love you, Daddy," Rae said to me, smiling. "You little moo."

The boys stood there and shook their heads. "You are wimps with those girls," Oliver said.

"Yeah," Thaddeus said. "So not fair. I wanted a computer game. I had to wait."

"Grow a pair. Why do you cave in with them?" Callum said. "Leo, what do you think?"

"I need a wee, bad," he said. We laughed.

"Come on," I said.

"What!" Mack said to Oliver.

He just shook his head and smiled. "I've got a list at home. I'm going to get Rae to do her soppy look on you," Oliver told Mack. Mack smiled.

When Olivia went back to university, it was quiet. Leo stomped about for days. "I want my sister! It's not fair! It's too quiet."

I sat him in the sofa. He put his head on my shoulder. "Dad, why does she have to go away? All I want is my sister home. Can't you stop her? Please!" he begged.

"Leo. We miss her too, so much. But she's learning at her school. But she'll be here for Christmas and your birthday. It's not right her not being here."

He looked at me. "I'm glad I'm home, Dad. This is a good, happy home. I feel better."

Just then, Mack and Oliver came from football practice. Leo ran to Oliver and hugged him.

"What was that for?" Oliver said to Leo.

"Dad told me what you said to me when I was a month old. That was nice. I love you, big brother."

"I love you too, Leo. Always," Oliver told him. "I'm going for a shower."

Mack sat next to me. "I take it Leo wanted Olivia home. That chat made him feel better."

"Yes, it did. I forget how quiet it is without her," I told him.

He took my hand. "I know. I don't like it either. Only eight weeks to go. I'll have a shower when Ollie has finished and we get a takeaway. Can't be bothered to cook tonight. I love you, Mike."

"I love you too, Mack. I always will," I told him.

During dinner, Francesca was quiet. We knew something was wrong, as she had Digby, her dog.

"Francesca, what's wrong, honey?" I asked after dinner.

"What do you care!" she said, walking away. "You don't care about me. You don't want me. I'm not Olivia."

I walked to her. She went to go round me. "Hey. Where did this come from? Sit down."

She sat down away from me. "Fran. Of course, we want you."

"Yer, right. Dad hardly talks to me. He never wanted me. He hates me. As long as Olivia is here, he's happy. But you don't want me. You should have given me back. I don't belong here any more." She was crying.

I went and hugged her. "Francesca Sophia. My god. Don't ever say that. We love and want you here. We're not giving you away."

Mack walked in. "What's going on?" He sat next to Francesca, who got up and walked away. I told him what happened. "Poor Fran. I'll talk to her."

He found her in the conservatory. "Fran. Fran. Come here."

She was crying hard. "Why! Why don't you love me? I'm sorry I'm not Olivia."

"No, you're not Olivia. You're my little girl, who always watched 'Scooby Doo' every Saturday morning with me. We had toast and tea. Your fave colour is purple. I love you, Francesca. We're not giving you away. Ever. You're my daughter. I always wanted to be your dad. When you came home to us, I held you for the longest time. You have the biggest brown eyes. I just sat there with you. I melted away when you were in my arms. You were so tiny. I can't be without you. They can't have you back. You belong here." Francesca got up. Mack followed.

"You don't talk to me. You don't want me!" she yelled. Mack went to her. "Go away."

"I'll never leave you." He hugged her. She was trying to get out. He repeatedly said I love you. "I'm sorry we got lost along the way. I'm your dad, forever. You know I still keep all your drawings from pre-school and school in a scrapbook. You love horses. *The Ugly Duckling* is your story. You still have your baby blanket as a comforter." She calmed down. "Oh, Fran, don't ever think you're not wanted. You're my baby. I remember your first day of school. You were scared. You clung on to me and Dad. We promised to be there. You were so happy when we were. You're beautiful, Francesca. I'm not letting go. I'll make a promise. We will talk more, we'll spend more time together. I'm sorry, Fran."

She calmed down. "Dad, I'm sorry too. I just thought…"

"Fran, it's OK. We just got lost, that's all. How about we spend the day together? You and me?" he said.

"What about Dad?" she asked.

"I think I can survive for one day. Besides, when you come home, we'll spend more time together. What do you want to do?" I asked her. She smiled.

"The horses. That place we went when I was little. I like it there. Please?" she asked.

"You got it, kiddo. Then we'll get you ice cream. I believe it's Raspberry Ripple." Mack kissed the top of her head.

"When you come home, we'll do something," I told her.

"No. I want to spend the day with you both. I miss it. Please, can I skip school tomorrow?" Francesca said, smiling.

Mack and I looked at each other. I nodded. "Just this once." I sat next to her. She put her head on my shoulder.

"Did you always want us?" she asked, yawning.

"Like you wouldn't believe," Mack told her. "Don't fall asleep, dinner soon."

She looked at Mack. "I missed you, Dad. So much. I thought I'd lost you."

"You'll never lose me. Princess. I'd miss you too." Mack shed a tear. She wiped them away. "It's OK, Dad."

We had a good day with the horses. She helped the horses. On the way home, Fran was asleep.

"You OK now?" I asked Mack.

"Yeah. I missed that a lot. I wish…" he trailed off. I looked at him.

"So do I. Fran. Wakey, wakey. We're home, sweetheart." She stirred. "Come on." She leaned on my arm.

"Thank you for today. It was good."

Mack went straight to the garden with his scotch and cigar.

Fran looked worried. "Go and sit with him," I told her.

She sat next to him and took his hand. "I'm so sorry, Fran," Mack said. She rested her head on his shoulder. "So am I. But it's OK. We should've talked. But we will be OK. Today was good. Forgive yourself. I have."

They sat for the longest time. It was lovely to see them together. After an hour. "You hungry, kiddo? Want to help make your fave dinner? Lasagne and garlic bread."

She nodded. "Dad. Thanks for choosing me to be your daughter." He hugged her.

"Dad?" Leo asked me. "Are Dad and my Fran OK now?"

"Yes, son, they are OK. They are better now," I told him.

"Good. I hate it when we fight. It's not nice," Leo told me.

He didn't even notice that Olivia had come home for a long weekend. She put her hands over his eyes. "How about spending it with me, cheeky boy?" she said.

His face lit up. "Olivia!" He hugged her. He told her about Francesca and Mack. She was sad.

She saw Francesca on the sofa and sat next to her. "Francesca. I love you just the way you are. You are wonderful. Dad loves you too. Look in that bag."

It was a picture of a horse and carriage. "Olivia, it's beautiful. Why?" she asked

"Because you're my sister. Forever," she said.

Later that evening, Olivia sat next to us. "Leo's asleep. He's had a bath so he's happy. You want a cuppa?" she asked us.

"Sit down, miss," I told her.

Fran sat next to Olivia. "Glad you're home, Olivia."

"So am I, sis." She put her arm round Fran. Mack was still quiet. Rae saw this and went to him. "Daddy. Don't be tough on yourself. What happened? You're soft. I wonder where I get it from. Come on. Stop it. I love you, Daddy." She hung on to him tight.

"Thanks, Angel girl."

Rae called my dad.

"Why did you call Grandad?" I asked.

"Because you and Dad are going for dinner. You haven't been out for a while, Dad. Go and enjoy yourself. Not asking," she said.

We went and had a good time. "You OK now?" I asked him, sipping my beer. "Yes. I'm OK. Just hurt, that's all. I didn't realise I hurt her that much. She really thought she lost us," he replied.

"I know. She's our baby. At least it's sorted. She knows we love her. We just have to try a bit more," I told him and smiled.

"What you smiling at?" Mack was confused.

"That grumpy woman who served us before is giving us dirty looks again." She looked at us with a dirty look.

Mack smiled. "Fancy a kiss?"

"Thought you'd never ask!" I said.

We made out in front of her. "Wow. That was good," I told him.

"Wait till we get home." He winked at me.

When we got home, it was quiet.

"Why's it quiet?" I asked my dad. "They are in the conservatory, reading, watching TV. Olivia is one tough nut. They started mucking about. I tried. She told them if they didn't start behaving, no family day and no film, no dinner. Ollie's face when she said no dinner. It was a picture. It's good to see them together. And no mobile phones. Look." He pointed to the room. We looked. It was quiet.

"Who are you and what have you done with our kids?" I asked.

"Olivia said no dinner and no family day," Oliver said.

She smiled. Fran looked at us.

"Come here," I said. She came over. "You choose family day and film. Never forget we love you and you're not going anywhere, ever," I said.

She looked at Mack. "All true, princess." She smiled and hugged us.

"I choose the lakes we like and the film 'Pete's Dragon'. Can we have popcorn?" she asked. We nodded. "Dad?" she said to Mack. "Can you read me my story, please?"

He nodded. "Go and get your blanket as well."

They went and spent time together. "Thanks, Dad. This is what we needed," she said.

"I know. You know, you're going to do amazing things with your life. I'm a lucky dad," he told her. Then they laughed.

"Where's my bloody dinner!" Oliver shouted. "I'm starving."

"That brother of your is a pig! Hang on," he said.

Fran held his hand. "Dad. Let's never get lost again."

"You have my word, princess." He kissed her head. "Hang on, Ollie, Mexican."

"You may be old, but you're a genius," he said. Oliver looked at

Francesca. "You and Dad OK now? I was worried."

"Yes, we are. We got lost for a bit. We're OK, Ollie. Don't worry," she said.

He put his arm around her. "I do worry. You're my little sister. Can't bear it when we get lost. Dad loves you. So do I." Oliver told her.

"Dinner! Come on!" Mack said.

"Thank God," Oliver said. "Come on, Fran. Sit next to me."

Leo and Oliver had an eating contest. "Slow down, you two!" I said. "Or you don't get pudding."

Oliver looked at me. "That's abuse! Depriving me of pudding. Cruel father. What pudding is it?"

"Apple pie and custard. From that deli you love." I smiled.

"I've changed my mind. You're a delightful man." He smiled. "Can you help me with my studies later? It's English. There's a bit I don't understand." I nodded. I sat with him.

"Get it now?" I asked. "Yes, thanks, Dad. I enjoyed spending time with you, even though it's homework." He got up and hugged me. "Love you, Dad."

"Always, son," I told him.

Mack gave me a cuppa and smiled. "What?" I asked.

"Nothing. It's nice to see that. This is what I wanted all along," he said. "Family day is my favourite."

"My friend Harry thinks it's weird we do something every weekend and like it. That's his problem. Before I forget. Here." Callum gave us his English homework. He got an A.

"Callum. This is brilliant!" Mack told him.

"I got it for writing about my family and what I've learnt from them," he said.

"What have you learnt?" I asked him. He sat next to us. "Well, I've learnt that even though we have our moments, we're still a family and we stick together. Dad? Promise me something?" he asked us.

"What's that?" Mack asked.

"Never leave each other. Always stick together." He rested his head on me.

"That's easy," I said. "We plan on staying together forever," I told him.

Callum smiled. "Good. I'll be lost without you both. Can you read me my story, please?"

"Go and have a shower, then I'll do it," I told him.

He did as he was told. I read the story to him. He was happy.

"Night. Looking forward to family day."

We smiled. Lydia came round. She put the meat in the fridge for Sunday dinner. "How's you?" she asked. "You and Fran OK, Mack?"

"We're good. I missed the time we lost. But we are OK, now. Wine?" he asked.

"No thanks. Tea!" she said. We were gobsmacked. I twigged. "How far are you?" I smirked.

"I'm not. I'm diabetic," she said.

"What! When?" I asked. I was shocked. Mack was taken aback.

"Three weeks ago. I wasn't feeling good. So…" she was sheepish.

"Lydia. You should have told us," Mack said. "Type 1 or 2?"

"Type 2. So not too bad. I didn't say anything as you had things with Francesca. Kids and Joel have been fussing over me," she said.

"Yeah well," I said. "Family sticks together. You're not alone in this, you know that," I told her.

Lydia was quiet for a moment. Oliver walked in. "Lydia. You OK?"

She nodded and wiped her eyes. Oliver gave her a hug. "Lid-lid. Whatever it is, it's OK. Don't worry. You brought cake, right?"

She laughed. "Cheeky sod. In the fridge. Not to be eaten till tomorrow."

His face fell. "OK. Love you, Aunt Lydia. It's gonna be fine."

"Love you too, Ollie bear," she told him.

"Dad, can I play football with Jack in the garden?"

"Yeah. Give him a call. That OK, Lydia?" Mack asked.

"Don't see why not. Hang on." Lydia called home. "On his way."

Ten minutes later, he was here. "Hey, Mack and Michael. Where's Oliver?"

"In the garden with the boys. Stay for dinner, Jack. I'll take you home later, OK?" Mack said.

"Thanks, Mack. Mum, that OK?" he said. She nodded and smiled. "Right, I'll see you lot tomorrow. Love you."

"Love you too, Lydia. It's gonna be fine," I told her. I turned around to see Rae and Thaddeus on the couch looking at a magazine.

"Who's Norman Wisdom?" Thaddeus asked.

We smiled. "He was an old funny actor. We liked his films. We spent our first night together watching his films," Mack told them.

"'On the Beat', I loved that one," I said, smiling.

"Can we watch it later?" Rae asked. I said yes. "Thaddeus, want a drink?" Rae asked.

"Yes, please. You want a biscuit?" She nodded.

"Dad, can we take George to the vet? He don't look well."

"We'll take him," I told her.

Mack got dinner ready. "Come on, dinner!"

"Mack, have you always cooked?" Jack said.

Mack smiled. "Yes, I love cooking," he said. "Helps me relax. How's school?"

"It's OK. I'm enjoying Chemistry a lot," he said, eating his lamb chops. "Rae, you OK?" he asked.

"Just worried about George," she said, looking at him.

Later on, Mack took Jack home. Thaddeus and Leo saw Rae looking sad. "George will be OK. How old is he?"

"Almost nine," she said. George was on her lap, purring away.

I sat next to her. She scooted herself under my arm, like she always had. "Don't worry. He'll be fine."

We took him to the vet. I was right. He was fine. Just had an infection. "See, told you," I said. She smiled.

"I know. He's my baby. He means a lot. You and Daddy got him for me when I was five," she said.

"I know. Shall we take him home, then we'll go for a walk? You, me and Dad," I told her.

She smiled. "Yes, please. Can Fran come too?" I nodded. "Daddy and Fran could do with it as well."

It was nice to get out for a bit. The others were round their mates' houses.

"This is what we need," Mack said. "Rae is such a sweetheart."

"You and Fran are getting closer. Nice to see that." I took his hand.

Fran screeched. We ran over. "Fran, what's wrong?"

She pointed to a dead rat on the pavement. "Gross. I was going to sit down. Disgusting." She went to Mack. "I was going to ask for an ice cream. Don't think I'll bother." We laughed. Mack hugged her. She looked at him and smiled. "Dad?" she asked us. "As everyone else is round their mates house, why don't the four of us go out for dinner? Make a nice change. Please?" Fran asked.

"Why not?" Mack said. "Rae?"

"Don't have to ask me twice! Daddy, come on," she said. "Can we go to that bistro. Their chicken risotto is nice. Fran?" she asked.

"Sounds good to me."

"Don't me and your dad get a say?" I said.

They both said no! Mack and I smiled. We actually had a good time. The girls chatted away.

"Can we have pudding, please?" Fran asked.

"Go on," Mack said. "We're not going to win."

When we got home, the girls were happy. George the cat was right as rain. We sat and watched TV. "

Dad, want a cuppa?" Rae asked. We said yes. "Thanks for today. It was good. Haven't done that in a while," Fran said giving us our cuppa.

"Why do you kids like spending time with us? You should be out with your friends?" Mack asked.

"You raised us to put family first. Besides, I'd rather be with family. When I do arrange to do stuff with mates, they cancel. This is important to me," Francesca said. She rested her head on Mack's shoulder. "I'll always remember the time spent with you all. It means everything."

"I agree with Fran," Rae said. "Being here counts. Family is most important. That's why we have family day. I don't want to change that ever. Does that make sense?"

"Yes. It does," I said. Mack and I looked at each other. Fran knew what the question was.

"No, it doesn't bother us that you are gay, and we have two dads. We don't care. Most of our mates' parents don't care what they do. You do. You care what happens to us." She started yawning. "We've got a good life."

Just then, the boys and Bella came in. Leo was singing away 'Because I'm Happy'. Oliver farted. Callum and Thaddeus were dancing. Bella shook her head. "I need new brothers."

We laughed. Oliver said his usual, "Where's the food?"

"You're a pig!" Bella said.

"Bothered. Not bothered," was the reply he gave. They smiled.

Rae and I nodded off. Oliver woke us up. "You two are well sweet. Rae, wakey, wakey."

"Don't want to. Want to stay here. I don't want to move," she said. "Come on, miss," I told her yawning.

"Please, five more minutes," she pleaded.

Oliver smiled. "You're the sweetest sister ever."

"Bed," I told her.

She got the hump. "Not fair," I smiled. "She's such a daddy's girl," Oliver said, smiling. I smiled too.

The phone rang and Mack answered. His face dropped.

"What?" I took the phone. It was my dad. Malek had had a heart attack. He was alive and stable but not to have visitors at the moment. I phoned Lydia and told her. They came to ours. We were all together. The man who was the heart of our family was in the hospital. Matthew went and sat with him, so Dad could come home and be with us. Dad was in bits, like us. "That man. I can't lose him. Sixteen years. God, I sound like you and Mack."

We smiled. Bella came to him. "Grandad, he'll be fine. He's a stubborn man. If he doesn't start looking after himself, I'll tell him off." Bella hugged him. "He's going to be OK."

True to her word, he made a good, steady recovery. Bella was there to help as were the rest of us.

"You lot are fussing too much. Allah help me!" he said.

Emily stood in front of him. "You listen to me, Uncle Malek. He wants you to get well. You are going to do what Allah and we say. You get me?" She folded her arms. Bella stood next to her.

"I'm not going to win. Am I?" he said.

"No. So get used to it," Bella said. They walked off. Malek said to the rest of us, "You are raising strong women. Good job. All of you."

Olivia and Maggie came home during the holidays. They, too, helped with Malek. Maggie was driving now, so she took Malek to his hospital appointments. Olivia went with her. When they got home. Malek was shaking his head. "Those two young women are two of the strongest, toughest women I've dealt with. Even the doctor was worried. They said if I don't do as I'm told, I'm in trouble. Good job, Mack and Lydia. The men that marry them. Good luck!"

They smiled. "I am blessed by Allah, with a wonderful life and family." He got upset.

Joel sat next to him. "Listen, we are the lucky ones. You keep in line.

You helped Maggie when she started university. Family sticks together. Always."

We had our family day at my Dad's. All nineteen of us. "Hang on. Everyone get together," Maggie said. "Family photo."

We all had our photo done.

"Look at us. How we've changed. But still the same," Alfie said.

"Wouldn't change anything. Granddad Malek, you say grace," which he did in Arabic. We all joined in. As over the years, we had learned the prayer she said. He was chuffed to bits.

The kids were watching TV and playing games. Maggie and Olivia were washing up and putting away. Rae was making tea with Alice and Leo and Emily.

"You have done well with your children," Malek told us. "Fine young people. I'm proud of them. Very proud to be a part of their lives. Allah blessed me. So very much."

Rae looked at him. "You know, Allah blessed us too. With you. Now stop being silly and drink your tea. No sugar."

He smiled and looked me. "Daddy's girl. But you've heard that a million times." I laughed.

"Daddy, we need to walk Holly. I'd think she's going crazy like Ollie," Rae said. We turned to look at Oliver, trying to add up and shaking his head.

"Come on, you lot. Walk, now." Holly was halfway to the door.

Mack was quiet. "What's wrong?" I asked.

He put his arm around me. "I was scared. That's all. Grateful for you and my kids. Love you."

"Love you, too. Silly sod. You know what day it is next month?" I smiled.

"Actually. It's two. Our twentieth and Rae's," he corrected me. "What shall we do? Make it a double celebration. She's fifteen."

"Good idea. I'd think she's like that. Have a party, Rae?" Mack called. He told her the plan.

"Yes, please. Can I invite Georgina and Poppy?" She pulled her soppy face.

"'Course you can!" I said.

"Can I have a fairy cake?" she asked.

"Anything else?" Mack said.

"I have a list!" she told us. We laughed.

Thaddeus said, "She's got you wrapped around your little finger. But it's sweet."

We walked for ages. The sea air did us good. We were knackered when we got home. We sat in our usual seats, with Rae next to me and Oliver next to Mack. "You know, Rae. You were brought to us when we renewed our vows," I told her.

She looked at me. "Really? I didn't know that."

"Thaddeus and Francesca, did you know that you two came not long after each other. You two couldn't sleep without each other. You were always together," I told them. They smiled. "Thaddeus, did you know that your dad would read you *Thomas the Tank Engine* every night? You would sit on his lap." I had a tear in my eye. "Bella. Did you know that you loved the sea, to calm you down, when you came to us? Leo. You would fall asleep to 'The Stable Song'."

"Why the tears, Dad?" Oliver said.

"Because I want you all to know that we wanted you all the moment you came through the door. Never forget that all of you are the reason why we breathe. Never forget that you are all loved." Leo hugged me tight. We were quiet for a moment. Then Leo made us laugh. "Can we have ice cream please? Oh, and the cake Auntie Lydia made?"

Mack and Rae got the ice cream.

Oliver sat next to me. "Thanks for what you said. I love you, Dad."

"I love you, son. Come here." I hugged him. "Who wants to watch a silly film?" They all nodded. I put on 'On the Beat' by Norman Wisdom. They laughed their heads off. Especially Oliver and Leo.

"That's hilarious. I nearly wet myself," Leo said.

Rae looked at me and smiled. "You and Daddy are the best." She rested her head on my shoulder.

"Rae, never change you. You're perfect, just the way you are. All you kids are."

Our anniversary came. So did Rae's birthday. Her friends Georgina and Poppy came. They spoilt her. We got a surprise when Olivia walked in the door.

"Surprise!" She hugged us. Leo was the happiest.

"Where's Rae?"

"In the garden," Mack said, smiling.

Rae was happy too. She opened her presents. "Olivia. These are beautiful." There was a bag, a jumper and a cardigan and shoes. "Thank you."

Then came our present. It was a night-out to our favourite restaurant. "Olivia. This is too much," we told her.

"Shut up. You're going. No arguing. God! You two deserve it. Now, where's the chicken salad. Oh, Maggie!" They hugged each other. They had a glass of wine.

"When did she get old enough to drink?" Mack said.

"She's almost nineteen, numb-nuts," I told him giving him a beer.

We called Rae over and gave her a box. She opened it. It was a necklace like Olivia. She opened it. It was the three of us. She had a tear. "Daddy. Thank you. Here. For you."

We opened the present she gave us. It was a painting of all of us, with the motto *'Those who are strong of heart, will weather the storm'*.

"Rae!" Mack said. "It's beautiful. Thanks."

She hugged us. "I love you both very much. You're welcome."

"One more thing for you, young lady." Mack gave her an envelope.

She opened it. "Daddies! This is way too much! I can't." It was a day out to her favourite place. The animal sanctuary, with the animals she loved. "Can we all go as a family? I'd love that. Family day."

We agreed. "Cake! Where's the bloody cake?" Oliver said.

Rae shook her head. "That brother is an idiot. Wait a minute, you pig. I'm surprised your bowels haven't rotten away."

We laughed out loud. Olivia started the night, much to the delight of Leo. "Leo, bath, come on. Pudding, then story."

He did as he was told.

"Dad. Can I keep Leo's birthday pressies here, please?" she asked. I said yes. She yawned.

"You OK, sweetheart?" I asked.

"Yes. Just tired. Can't wait for the holiday," she leaned into me. "I miss home."

"Home misses you too," I told her. She smiled. "When do you finish?"

"Two weeks. Will you help me with shopping?" she said.

"'Course, I will." I got teary again. Olivia looked at me. "Daddy. Daddy, what's wrong?"

"Nothing. Just glad I've got everyone here," I told her.

Two weeks went quick. We picked Olivia up. Mack and I had a row about who was staying where for Christmas. "For God's sake. Everyone to us on Christmas day. Then Granddad's for boxing day. Lydia's for New Year. There, sorted. Now shut up and drive. I need a wee." That told us. "Don't forget. Maggie and I are going for dinner tomorrow night. Maggie's driving."

We smiled. "Can't believe you're all grown up," Mack said.

"Well, duh! That's what's happens." Her phone rang. "That's her." She had a conversation with her. I smiled. Her face fell. "Hospital, now."

"What/" Mack said.

"Uncle Joel's had an accident."

We raced to the hospital. Turned out, he broke his ankle falling off a ladder. Maggie and Olivia gave him what for.

"Really, Dad?" Maggie said. "Thought it was serious. Jesus!"

"What were you thinking?" Olivia said. "Right before Christmas?" Lydia was laughing.

"Not funny, Mum." Maggie looked at her. "Dad, in the car now, move. And you too, Mum. Don't argue."

"Today would be good," Olivia told them.

Joel looked at them. Then us. "When did the roles reserve?" We shook our heads.

"Dad, get a move on!" Olivia told us.

"I'm not arguing with her," Mack said.

We followed and I smiled.

"What you smiling at?" Lydia asked.

"We've raised two young women that can hold their own. We should be proud. I am."

"Still on for tonight?" Maggie said to Olivia. She said yes.

"You're still going out?" Joel said to them.

"Uncle Joel, you broke your ankle. It wasn't amputated. Yes, we're going out. Seven OK?" Olivia said. Maggie's said yes.

We laughed. "Olivia takes after you, Mack. Smart mouth."

He smiled.

Olivia got ready and was waiting for Maggie. Mack looked sad. "Why so sad, Dad?" she asked him.

"You're growing up so fast. Soon you won't need me any more," he said.

She hugged him tight. "I'll always need my dad. Don't ever say that." Maggie beeped. Off she went.

When she came home, she found Mack waiting for her. She smiled. "You silly sod." She sat next to him.

"You will always be my baby girl. My first-born. I'm the same with the others."

She just stayed there with him. "What a drink?" he said.

"No. I wanna sit here with my dad. I miss you and dad when I'm gone. It's hard," she said. "I just want to be here always. I told Dad this too. You know I'm a lot like you and Dad, aren't I?"

"Sure are, baby girl!"

Just then, Leo came down. "I can't sleep. Olivia, can I have a drink, please?"

She smiled. "Come on, cheeky boy. Then bed."

"Are you two OK? You're not fighting?" He looked worried.

"We're not fighting," Mack said.

I came downstairs. "Hey, what's this?"

"I can't sleep. Dad and Olivia are soppy sods," Leo said. "When I grow up, I want to be a teacher."

We smiled. "Leo. Get that photo album. The blue one," Olivia told him.

It was pictures of him with all of us. From a baby till now. He cuddled up to Olivia with his teddy.

"That's my favourite," Olivia told him.

"Why that one?" He pointed to the one of him as a new-born.

"That's easy," I told him. "Because we wanted you. You settled in so well. Dad took you in the garden. You settled with me for your naps."

He was asleep by the end of it, ss was Olivia. Curled up together. We took them back to bed. We talked for hours, like we used to.

"We need a night out before Christmas," I said. "We need to chill out for one night."

Mack smiled like a Cheshire cat. "How about tomorrow night?" We agreed.

We went out and had the best time. A lot of people gave us a double take when they saw us holding hands and kissing. Even a couple of girls took a fancy to Mack who smiled and took my hand.

We got home and made love. "That was just what we needed. That was a good time." I smiled. "That t-shirt. Can't believe you still have it after twenty years."

Mack looked at me. "Yeah, well. Never going anywhere. Can't and won't throw it away."

We woke up to Leo jumping on our bed. "It's my birthday. I'm seven. Come on, Dads. It's also family day. Yeah!" We laughed.

"Come on, birthday boy," Mack said, scooping him up. I got his presents. He loved what he got. Olivia spoilt him as usual.

Lydia and the gang came round. They spoilt him even more. We all went for Leo's day out. It was simple. We went to the beach for a walk then the park. When we walked in our favourite pub, the ladies got our favourite table ready. All nineteen of us. Leo and Olivia sat with each other. He adored his big sister. "Love you, Olivia."

"Love you too, cheeky boy." She kissed his head.

On the way home, she walked with me. "You OK now?"

Leo chose his favourite film; 'Up'. He cuddled up to Olivia. Had his pjs on and his blanket.

"I'll never get bored with this," she told us.

Joel came round with his boys, looking bemused. "The smell, the noise. Too girly." We laughed.

Our girls were round at Lydia's having a girly night. Alfie said, "It smells like a tart's handbag in there."

Jack said, "Emily tried to put a face mask on me. Uncle Michael, it was horrible." I laughed. "Not funny. Alice wanted to put lipstick on Dad."

That was it; Mack, Thaddeus and I were hysterical.

"I need a beer," Jack said. We decided to go to the pub for lunch to have some guys' time."

"This is better," Jack said. "Dad, you OK? You look tired."

"I'm OK, son," he replied.

"Why don't you lot stay at ours tonight? Have some beers. Get a pizza in?" I said. Mack nodded.

"I'll phone Matthew and the guys. Like old days," Mack said.

Joel looked at the boys. They nodded. "Why the hell not. Tell Jacob to

266

bring that scotch we like."

We had a good night. Later, we got a call from Lydia. Someone tried to break in. The police had already been called.

We ran round there. "Oh, Joel. It happened while we were sleeping, Michael, Mack, I'm sorry. Really sorry. She was crying.

"Not your fault. It's OK," Mack and I said.

Our girls and Lydia were frightened. When the police left, we gathered them all.

"Come on. Ours. All of you. Ours," Mack said.

They hadn't taken anything. As soon as they saw that the house was full, they did a runner.

The girls were all together in the conservatory and slept there. Lydia's boys were in the den. We were in the living room.

"Just one night of fun," Lydia said. "That's all."

Joel looked worried. "I'm sorry I weren't there."

"Don't be daft. It was about time you did something for you. Been a long time. I'm going to bed. I love you, Joel." Joel followed.

Mack and I sat there. Rae came out and sat next to me with her blanket.

"Hey, Angel girl. How are you?" Mack asked her.

"I'm OK, now. Poor Lydia. I hope they find them and put them away. It was not nice. Glad we're all here, together. Can I have a drink?"

Mack got her one. "Thanks, Daddy." She soon fell asleep, curled up next to me.

The next morning, it was quiet.

"Right, Come on. We need some air. All of us," I said.

We went for a long walk, sea air always worked. Oliver was quiet. "What's wrong?" Mack asked him. He didn't answer.

"Talk to me. What do we say in this family?" Mack said.

"We always say what's on our mind. Truth, no lies," Oliver said.

Oliver told him what was on his mind. "My sisters were there. Lydia too. They are so important to us, Dad. No one is to blame, we know that." He went to Lydia and hugged her tight. "You are the most wonderful woman ever. Can I buy you an ice cream?"

Lydia cried. "What a lovely thing to say. Yes. You know my fave."

Oliver walked with Lydia. "You OK, now Lid-lid?"

"I am now. Don't worry," she told him.

His face fell. He had an outburst, which wasn't like him, ever.

"Don't worry?" he yelled. "The most important people in my life were in a house when some nutter tried to get in there. I'm supposed to make sure you're OK! I couldn't bear if he hurt any of you. It's not fair. You hear me!" He cried so hard. Lydia hugged him tight. "Ollie. Ollie. It's not your job. Us girls are OK." She held him tight.

"But, Lydia. I can't lose you all," he said.

"You never will," she said. She kissed his head. Mack and I had tears in our eyes. "Go to your dads."

We went home. Oliver was in bits. He was angry. The rest went to the den. Oliver was hitting stuff. Mack got hold of him. I was next to him as well.

"Ollie, it's OK. It's OK," Mack said.

"They're safe," I said.

Oliver hit the floor. "Dads. Those girls are everything to me." Mack hugged him. "Let me go."

"Never. We're never letting go. We're a tight family," I said.

The girls came out. "Ollie. We're OK. Look at us," Fran said.

"I'm your brother. I have to look after you," he said.

"We look after each other," Bella said. "Ollie, you are a good brother. Please don't carry that guilt with you. Please!"

Rae sat with him. "My Ollie bear. You will never lose us."

Olivia said, "We'll always be together. Come on, get up, let's all spend some time together. Oliver James Denton, you, like the rest of my family, are the best thing ever."

Oliver never left our side that evening. Mack kissed his head.

"Dads. I'm sorry."

"Never be sorry. It shows that family matters to you. That's the way we have always wanted it to be," I said.

"But I shouted in the street. Hope Lydia is OK," he said.

Mack stood there saying nothing. Then he said, "Ollie, you're like me. You are sensitive and kind. It proves that you care. Never be ashamed of that. I'm proud of you. So is your dad."

Oliver calmed down. Thaddeus came in with Ollie's favourite drink and biscuits when he's worried. "It's cool, Ollie. Come here," Thaddeus and Ollie hugged him. "Choose a film."

Leo was in bed. "Night, cheeky boy."

"Night, my Olivia," Leo said.

Oliver was tucked up with Mack. He looked at me and hugged me. "It's OK. It's OK."

He fell asleep. Mack looked sad. Fran sat with him. "Thanks, love."

The next day, Lydia came over and she and Oliver went for a walk.

"Lydia, I'm sorry for shouting like that yesterday."

"Oh Ollie, it's OK. I know you were worried about us. Everyone was. But nothing went wrong." She hugged him.

"I got scared that something could have. You, my cousins and my sisters, are my life. I didn't want you hurt. I want you all safe," he replied. Lydia smiled.

"You know, you sound like Mack. Joel is exactly the same. It's good that you feel like that. It shows that you care and family is everything to you. It's the way we want it to be. But never carry that with you. What happened, happened. I hope they cut his balls off, and throw him in the river. Dickhead."

They laughed. "Better now," Oliver said. "You're the best person ever, Lid-lid."

"I know. Something that can't be helped. Now how about fish and chips?" Lydia said.

"You read my mind. Genius." Oliver smiled.

They had a good time, then they came back. "OK now, Ollie?" I asked him.

He nodded. "Cuppa, Lydia?" she said. Just then, Joel and the kids came in.

"Everything OK?" Joel asked. Lydia said yes. Joel hugged her. "I love you, you mad old woman."

"Love you too, you bloody moron," she told him. Oliver and the boys were happy playing on the X-box. The girls were in the den.

"You know," Lydia said, taking her drink. "Oliver is so much like you, Mack and you, Michael. I can see the way that he spoke." We smiled. "He takes the weight of the world on his shoulders. Jack is exactly the same. Look at them." We watched them, playing on the computer.

"We can feel you watching us," Alfie said.

Joel said, "Just like his mother. They've grown up so quickly. Where did it go?"

"I know," Mack said. "Seemed like yesterday they were little. I'm getting old."

"Yeah, you are, old man," Oliver said. "You need to take your old-man pills. You too, Dad. Yes, one point for me. *Ha!*"

"Smart arse," Jack said. We laughed. Back to normal. "Mum, can we stay, please?" Jack asked. "I want to kick Ollie's arse on the computer."

"No chance," Oliver said.

"Stay," we said.

"We'll get a takeaway," Mack said. Joel and Lydia nodded. We heard a scream from the den.

"That's gross!" Emily said. "I feel sick. Slugs! Ugh!"

"It's a common garden breed," Olivia said. She got it out and cleaned up.

Leo was with Olivia, as usual. "Get your colouring book and crayons," she told him.

He smiled. "Can I get my blanket?" he asked. Olivia nodded. Off he went. Olivia looked up and saw me smiling.

"Hey, Daddy!" Leo said to me. "Love you. Always."

"Love you too, son," I told him.

As I walked to the door, Leo said, "Dad?" I turned round. "You're a good dad."

I wiped a tear and watched them colouring away.

"You OK?" Mack looked confused.

"Yeah. Everything OK."

"Really!" He cheered up. "Can we get lunch out and dessert?"

"You bet your rear end! You're a silly boy. Want pizza? It's your fave. Pepperoni. There's garlic bread with cheese." He hugged him tight. They went off.

"What's that?" I said.

"Let's never change this. Family, I mean. Being together. Talking and stuff," she told me.

"That's the easiest promise to keep," I told her.

We heard Oliver laughing really hard. He flicked pepperoni at Mack's face. It landed on his eye.

"Oliver needs medication. But that is funny."

Leo came and ate with Olivia. "Better now, cheeky boy?"

"Yes. I'm good. I love our silly family," he said, eating his garlic bread.

"So do I," Olivia said.

Christmas came and went. Then New Year was upon us. "Where did that year go?" my dad said.

"Haven't a clue!" I said, getting things ready for dinner at Lydia's. "Mind you, I think where has the last twenty-plus years gone? Dad, it's been so different, but good."

"I know. The best journey ever. Remarkable!" Dad said.

Malek came through the doorway. "The best. We are stronger than ever. Nothing will change that. Life has thrown curves, but we have come through."

"Sit down, Granddad Malek. You need your rest," Callum told him. "I'll make you tea. Come on. And you, Granddad." They did as they were told.

Rae came in with Alice. She was carrying something. "What's that?" I asked.

"Look, Daddy, someone left this puppy on the door. Look, he's so tiny. How could they do that? Can we look after him? Please! I've called him Harvey. We've got him milk. Didn't we, Ally Cat? Please, Daddy." She looked at us. We looked at each other. Alice smiled. Rae did her soppy eyes at me. Alice laughed.

"Mack, help me. God's sake. Help me," I said.

Then the lip went. "Daddy, please?" Mack laughed. "Please! Daddy."

"OK. OK. Harvey can stay. For good." I said. "I need a beer."

"Thank you, Daddy. Love you, Daddy." She walked away happy.

Alice looked at me. "My God, Uncle Michael. You cave all the time with her. She's such a daddy's girl. She looks up to you so much. Softie."

Thaddeus looked at me. "Wimp! This house will become the London Zoo at this rate. But he is cute."

Mack laughed. "My God. I thought I was bad." He looked at Rae.

"What!" I said.

"Wish I had the same relationship that you two have," he said.

Rae heard what he said. She put Harvey down. "Daddy. Don't be silly. I love you the same. Idiot."

I smiled. "Let's go for a walk before the party. Put your coat on, come on."

When they came back, Rae was shaking her head. "He's an idiot and a big softie. I wonder about him," she told me. I laughed. She hugged Mack. "You silly sod. I love you, too. Don't worry. Sort him out, Daddy," she told me.

"That told me," Mack said.

"See, told you. Idiot," I said, passing him a beer. "We've done a good job with the kids."

Mack smiled. "Yeah. They're all right, I suppose."

We watched them mucking about with Lydia's lot. It was funny. Joel came over and I gave him a beer.

"I'm proud of this family being together. This will never be boring," he said.

"What's wrong with them?" Joel said. "Why can't we have normal kids?"

"Uncle Joel. Normal is boring. This family is not that. You know that," Oliver said. Joel couldn't answer. He went to sit with the boys. "Here, rest your leg, Joel," Oliver said.

"You're a good kid, Ollie," he said.

"You're the best uncle I've got. Jack, thanks."

"For what?" he said.

"For losing this computer game," he said. "This game's so easy," Oliver said, laughing.

"You're an arse, you know that?" Jack said.

"Takes one to know one!" was the reply.

Mack and I laughed. Joel laughed too. That evening, we sat around watching TV. Mack asked them if they had one wish, what would they do?

They all said, 'family time'.

"Really?" Lydia said.

"Yeah, really," Maggie said. "Every weekend, we come together and just be ourselves. I love this. Us here. I loved it as a kid, I love it as an adult."

"You're still my little girl," Joel said. Maggie smiled.

They disappeared and came back five minutes later with three bags. The kids smiled. They gave Mack and I, my dad and Lydia and Joel a present each. When we opened it, we cried.

They had made us quilts of their stuff from when they were babies till now.

"These are beautiful," my dad said.

"We wanted you all to have something to have of us from over the years," Emily said. "I told my friend Lux what we were doing. She said it was silly. I said she was an idiot."

Lydia and Mack were crying like babies. Oliver looked at me. "Really? Can we swap him?"

"I've tried. He's like a stray dog and a boomerang. Keeps coming back!" Oliver laughed.

"Hey!" Mack said. "I'm not a stray dog. Kids, this is brilliant. Are we going to tell them? Joel, Lydia?"

"I guess so," Lydia said. "How would you lot like a family holiday for three weeks in the summer?"

"Really!" Leo said. "Where?"

"South of France," I said.

Olivia and Maggie said, "Our first holiday abroad. Oh my god! What are we going to wear? Then there's our hair, make up. Good job we've got a few more months. We need to plan now!" Maggie said.

Mack, Joel and I looked at Lydia. "You understand that?"

"Oh God, yes. You never know. They might even meet a nice French chap." She smiled. She was winding us up.

"Hell no," Joel said. "If Olivia meets a French man, I'll kill him and bury him in the garden," he said.

"Oh really?" Olivia said, folding her arms. Maggie stood next to her. "You never know, we might meet one and run off... into the sun."

"No way are you meeting some guy and running off." Leo got up and walked away. Olivia got worried and upset.

I went and saw him. "Leo! She was joking," I told him.

"I don't want my big sister going away. I'm scared of losing her, Daddy," he said.

Olivia came in and sat next to him. "Oh, Leo. I can never leave you. Any of you. You're my baby brother." She had a tear in her eye.

"Please don't cry, Olivia. All I want is all of you here. I don't want to be alone." He rested his head on her shoulder.

"You'll never be alone. Ever," Mack told him. "We'll always be together. Family is important."

Leo looked at Olivia. "You promise you won't leave me?"

"I promise, cheeky boy. Now how about that pudding you love? Just remember, Leo, no matter where we go, we will always be here for each other. You are important to me."

He smiled and hugged her. "I love you, my Olivia. Can I get the plates ready?" We nodded. Off he went. Olivia cried and I hugged her.

"That was very true what you said. Come on, before a riot starts over the pudding."

Maggie gave her a glass of wine. Mack looked at her.

"I'm old enough." She smiled. "Dad?" she said to us. "I'm glad we found each other. You two are the best parents we could wish for. I'm proud to be your daughter. Happy New Year."

The rest agreed with Olivia.

"We got what we wanted," Thaddeus said. "You're OK. Oliver, save me some of that bloody cake. Pig! How can someone eat so much? My brother the idiot. Joel, you want cake?" He nodded. Thaddeus sat next to Alfie. He gave a controller for the Xbox. "Cheers, buddy boy," Thaddeus said.

"Thaddeus, you still up for that bike ride next week? You gonna be OK with your asthma?"

"Yes, if we do what we normally do! That OK, Dad? Uncle Joel!" he asked. We said that's OK.

New Year came and went. Olivia went back to university, much to the annoyance of Leo.

"I'm living with Olivia," he decided.

"Oh really?" said Bella, while they were reading his book. "What about the rest of us, that will miss their baby brother?"

"Hadn't thought of that," he replied, leaning on her shoulder.

"I miss her too, you know. Listen, you want a biscuit before dinner? Don't tell Dad. Get your colouring book and crayons." She smiled. Mack walked in.

"Bella gave me a biscuit," Leo said.

Bella laughed. "You little monkey."

Leo giggled and Mack laughed watching them.

"Want some help?" Bella asked him.

"I'm OK, kiddo. It's your fave dinner tonight. Leo, you OK?"

"Yes, Dad. We still going to the aquarium on Friday?" he asked, jumping on the sofa.

"Sit down," Bella said.

"Yes, we are. Do as Bella says. No more biscuits. You got ants in your pants," Mack replied.

"Don't be stupid. Why would ants live in my pants? That's stupid," he said, sitting down.

"You sound like Ollie," Bella told him.

Mack got a call one day. "Shit! Shit! Mike! Mike!" he yelled.

"What?" I ran in from the garden.

Mack told me Thaddeus was in the hospital. He had an asthma attack. Alfie had a spare inhaler in his bag but called the ambulance to be safe. Dad came over with Malek to keep an eye on the kids.

We ran into A and E. We found Thaddeus and Alfie. Thaddeus looked tired.

"I'm fine, Dad. Alfie didn't need to call an ambulance. Good job he keeps a spare."

"You know I always do. I wanted to make sure you're OK. You're not just my cousin, you're my best mate. Like Maggie and Olivia. Sorry, Michael and Mack."

"Don't be sorry. You did the right thing," Mack told him. "You sure you're OK?" Thaddeus nodded.

Then the doctor came over. It was Dr Shaw.

"Oh my God!" Dr Shaw said. "After all these years. Michael. How are you?"

"OK. How's Thaddeus?" I was surprised.

"Well, Thaddeus is fine. Thaddeus, the last time I saw you, you were five months old. How old are you?"

"Fifteen. Can we go now? I need the loo." Thaddeus was impatient to go.

"Yes, you can go. Nice to see you again," Dr Shaw said.

We took Thadd home. "Thanks, Alfie, for looking out for me," he said.

Alfie smiled. "Family look out for each other. I always keep a spare inhaler with me."

When we got home, Dad and Malek were asleep on the couch with the kids. They woke up when we walked in. "What are you doing up?"

"Really, Dad?" Bella said. "Our brother was in hospital. We had to be together. You OK, Thadd?"

He had a tear in his eye. "I'm OK, little sister. I'm OK. Can I have a drink?" he sat down. Oliver got his drink. "You shouldn't have worried."

My dad put his arm around him. "Thaddeus. We will always worry about each other. You are important. Alfie did the right thing. Just to be safe. Now, go get your book."

Thaddeus had fallen asleep in his arms.

Before we knew it, we were on holiday in the South of France. It also fell in one with Maggie's twenty-first birthday.

"Twenty-one. Lydia. Our eldest is a woman. I'm so proud of her," Joel said. Lydia took as quiet.

"My baby. I still remember when I told you I was pregnant with her. You nearly died of a heart attack. This little tiny thing. Now look. You know she's just like you."

"Really? You know she's got your attitude. Never forget the time she smacked that kid in the face for picking on Alice. Kicked that boy in the nuts for saying stuff about Mack and Michael.'

They didn't realise that she was standing behind them.

She hugged them. "I'm both of you. Dad, I'll always be your little girl. Mum, you are an amazing woman. Here."

They opened the present she gave them. It was a picture of all of them. "That," she said, "is all I want for my birthday. A family day in France. Nothing fancy, nothing big. Just my favourite people and a good film."

That made us smile.

"Dad, can we go for a walk by the marina? It looks pretty," Francesca said. She looked at Mack and smiled.

"What's that for?" he said, putting his arm around her.

"Nothing. Just enjoying being here. Dad, thanks, for everything. Best holiday ever," Francesca told him.

"You're welcome, princess. You seem happy?" he asked her.

"I am, Dad. You remember what Olivia said? I'm glad we found each other too," Francesca told him.

"So am I. You know something? When you came home to Dad and I, You couldn't sleep without your pink blanket. You fell asleep in my arms every night. You were so happy just being there. I never wanted to let you go. Don't grow up. Francesca, you will always will be my little princess. I'm glad I found you too." Mack looked at her. She had tears in her eyes. I looked at them. He nodded to say they were OK.

We went and had dinner out. All of a sudden, Maggie went, "Oh my God!" She kept saying it.

"What!" Joel said.

"Pharrell Williams is sitting over there," she said. "Don't look!"

Leo looked round and saw a microphone. He smiled and got off his chair. "Back in a sec!" He walked over to Pharrell.

"Leo!" Mack said.

"Excuse me, Mr. Williams."

He smiled. "Sorry to be rude and disturbing you, but you sing our family song. It means a lot to us."

"What song's that!" he asked Leo.

"It's 'Happy'. It's our favourite. It's our family song. It means a lot to us. My family means a lot to me. Would you sing it for my family? It's my cousin Maggie's birthday tomorrow. I have some pennies for you."

Pharrell looked at us then Leo. "They mean that much to you?"

Leo smiled at him. "Yes, sir. They're everything. I can't be without them. Whenever we're together, that song gets played."

"My friend. Wish granted." He took the microphone and went to the stage. Everyone was stunned. The band got ready.

"I was asked a very special request by Leo over there. Very convincing. Maggie, Happy birthday. This is for Leo's family."

As soon as the song started, all the kids were up dancing away and singing with him.

"Again!" Leo said. We filmed it on our phones. It was brilliant.

"Leo!" Maggie said. "Best birthday present ever. I'll never forget that."

He came over and took a photo with all of us. Leo was happy.

"Leo," I said. "That was very bold of you. That was amazing."

Everyone got up. "Why?" they asked.

"As I told him, everyone here means everything. I wanted Maggie to have something to remember. It worked, didn't it/ That was my wish. It came true," he said, taking Maggie's hand.

"You, Leo, are so kind. You're like Rae. I'll always, always remember what you did for me. You're a wonderful boy." She cried and went to Joel.

"Hey baby girl. What's wrong?"

"I'm OK, Dad. That was a wonderful gift. The simple things are the best. You taught me that. Can we go back and have that film?" she asked. "Dad, what's the best thing that happened to you?"

"You kids. And your mum. Your lot are the best things that will ever happen to me. You're my baby girl. Come on." Joel was choked up.

We had the best three weeks. It brought us closer together as a family. We printed the photo of us and Pharrell Williams. Leo gave Maggie her photo.

"Thank you, Leo."

"You're welcome, Maggie May." He farted and walked off.

"Just like Ollie." She shook her head.

When I came in from shopping, I heard shouting. It was Oliver and Mack. "Oh my God. Did you have to do that?" Oliver said.

"Really! Those kids are idiots," Mack said

"What's going on?" I said.

Mack told me that a few kids on the team were having a cigarette. He told them off. "Really?"

"Yes and I kicked them off the team. Those kids have got to learn, Oliver," Mack said.

"I hate you. It was embarrassing. Don't talk to me ever again."

Mack was angry. "That can be arranged," he said.

Oliver's face fell. "Prick!"

Mack knew he had pushed it. "Ollie, I'm sorry."

"Fuck off!" Oliver yelled.

"Let him calm down. He's got your temper," I told him.

Half hour later, Callum came down. "Ollie's not in his room."

"What?" I said. I got a call. It was Devon's dad. He was there. His mum brought him home.

"Ollie. Why?" I asked.

"Really? Dad's an arsehole. Maybe I should find my real parents, maybe they would want me."

"That's not fair," Mack said. "We just had an argument. You're my son, Oliver. I'm never leaving you. You hear me?"

"Whatever." He got upset.

"Not whatever." Mack sat next to him. "What I said and did was wrong. Big time. Look at me."

Oliver looked at him. "I'm sorry. We're your parents. I'll be lost without you. When I first held you, I cried. My eldest son. I didn't want to let you go. I still don't."

"I hate you." He got up, crying. Mack got stood next to him. He hugged him. "I'm your dad, you're my boy. I'm sorry."

Oliver hugged him back tight.

"Dad, I'm sorry about what I said about finding them. You and Dad are my real parents. I'm so sorry." he hugged me.

"There's nothing to forgive, Ollie. Like we told you kids before, you lot are better than winning the lottery. If you lot weren't here, if I have to talk to your dad…"

Oliver smiled. "Hey! Not fair!" Mack laughed. "You kids are worth fighting for."

"Were we hard work when we were little?" he asked, wiping his eyes. The other kids were at the stairs.

"Come on, you lot." I nodded to them to sit on the sofa. "No, you weren't. We loved seeing all of you grow into the young people you are now. Thaddeus and Fran, you two were always pulling pranks on your dad. Like gluing his bum to the toilet seat, and putting a sign on his back saying 'I'm an idiot, kick me'."

They laughed their heads off. "Rae, I'll always remember how you bandaged my hand to my nose and walked off. Callum, you hid a frog in our bed. Dad screamed like a girl, I nearly wet myself. Olivia put those bloody spiders on my head and ran away. Oliver, you used to hide Lydia's bottle of wine. Bella, you ate a packet of biscuit and was sick as a dog. Leo, you ran away when it was bath time and said it was degrading."

They were in fits of laughter. "We won't change anything. Best times. I remember Callum saying he was going to eat Holly if I didn't get dinner ready," Mack said. Callum laughed.

"You really love being our dads, don't you?" Bella said.

"Like you won't believe," I told her, smiling.

Bella had a tear in her eye. "What's the matter?" I asked her.

She rested her head on Rae's shoulder. "I'm so glad I got a second chance at being happy and having a family that wants me."

"That will never change," Mack told her. "Bella, you're our baby girl, we'll never leave you." She went to Mack and hugged him.

"Plus," Callum said, "you've got brothers and sisters that love you and want to be there for each other. That's the most important thing I've learnt. Never give up on anything on anyone that means something. Where would we be if we didn't have each other? That's something I don't like to think about."

"Wise words, son," I told him. Mack and I smiled.

Leo was tucked under Rae's arm fast asleep. She smiled. "He's so cute."

"You know, Rae," Mack told her, "when we took you out, you were in your baby carrier. You would only go to your dad. You had your thumb in your mouth. Your head rested on his chest by his heart. When he tried to get you out, you cried and cried. You'd be so content just lying there, being with your dad. You'd wake up, look at him and go right back to sleep."

She looked at me." Really?"

I nodded. One by one, the kids fell asleep. We covered them with blankets. We left them and went to bed.

"That was interesting, but nice. They love hearing stories about them growing up. That's sweet," Mack said. "Mike, you OK?"

"Yes, I am. I wish we had them sooner," I told him.

"You're just as broody as I am. I know I'm tough on them but I don't want to lose them," he said.

"We won't. Tonight proves that." I started yawning. "Love you, Mack."

"Love you too. Always," he replied.

Leo jumped on our bed. "Morning, Dads. Breakfast, please. We need food. Come on. Then walk. Love you."

We smiled. We loved our live. The following weeks, months fell by. was finishing his A-levels. The rest were either doing their G.C.S.E.s or starting them. Leo was getting tall. He was now ten. Olivia was on a gap year. Rae came home from school with a friend, who was a boy. His name was David. I was shocked. They seemed to like each other. Mack saw it and smiled. I hated it. Rae saw it and I walked away.

"Daddy. He's just a friend. I'm nearly sixteen. Don't be mad."

"I know," I told her. "You're growing up," she hugged me.

"I'll always be your little girl, but I might have a boyfriend one day."

"That's what I'm afraid of. Then you won't need me," I told her.

"That's stupid. I'll always need you. Come on. He's nice. Don't do a Dad and Olivia." She smiled.

"Hi, Mr Denton. I'm David," he said to me. He shook my hand. "I thought Rae was joking when she said she had two dads. You have a nice home." He was too polite.

"What do you want to be when you leave school?" I asked.

"A vet," he said. He looked scared.

"Are you two just friends?" I asked.

Mack said, "Calm down. Don't do a me, for God's sake."

"Yes, sir. I'm gay," he said.

Mack and I looked at each other. We were shocked. We looked at Rae. She couldn't stop smiling.

"I—we didn't know," Mack said.

"That's OK. Rae's the only one that knows," he said. "She's the only one I trust. My parents don't know yet."

"It'll be OK," I said. "Tell them when you're ready."

"Were you scared? When you told people?" he asked.

"No," we said together.

"People sort of knew," Mack said.

"I never hid it," I told him.

"Best thing I did was meet Rae's dad," Mack told him. Rae's face beamed. "Don't worry. It'll be OK."

David went home happy. Rae hugged us. "Thank you. That meant a lot. He just wanted someone to talk to. I suggested you two. That meant a lot to me," Rae said. She looked at me. "No matter what happens in my life, I'll always be Daddy's girl." She hugged me tight. I had a tear. She looked at Mack. "I'll always be your Angel girl. Can I have a drink?"

We nodded.

"We have to do something special for her?" Mack said. "She never asks for anything, but does so many things for others. What do you think?"

I agreed. Lucky enough, the kids were out round mates' houses, so we picked Rae up from school. She was surprised.

"What are you doing here?"

"We're taking you out for the afternoon! You've got to get changed first," Mack told her.

"Where are we going?" Rae said.

"Wait and see!" I told her.

We got in the car. She got changed, then we were on our way. We took her to her favourite, Tea Room. She was happy.

"Anything you want, Rae," we told her.

"I couldn't," she said.

"Yes, you can," I told her. "You do a lot for others. You deserve to be spoiled."

"Can I have my fave teacake and a cuppa tea, please?" She smiled. "Thanks for this. I get to spend some time with you both."

"I know," I replied. "You are a special young lady. Never forget that. I'm proud of you," I told her.

"I try to be kind, and be nice." She ate her teacake. "This is good. Can we go to that shop I like afterwards? Please!"

"Anything for you," Mack told her.

We walked around, got a few things and went home.

"Thanks for a good day," she said, sitting next to us in her favourite pjs and blanket. "I'll never forget this. I'm a lucky daughter." She fell asleep in my arms. I had tears in my eyes.

"She is my angel. My baby girl."

Mack had tears too. "She's perfect."

She woke up. "Daddy. You OK?" She hugged me.

"Yes. Yes, we are. Where's your book?" She smiled and got it. "We'll have to get you a new one. It's ripped."

"No. Uncle Jacob got me that. It stays," she said.

Mack put his hand on his heart, and got up. She went to bed.

A few months later, over dinner, Leo said, "I've decided I want to be a big brother. I want a sister called Chloe. So, can I have one?"

We all looked at each other and smiled. He was so matter-of-fact.

"When did you decide this?" Mack asked him, taking his plate.

"A month ago. So? I don't want to be the baby of the family."

"Leo, you are not the baby," I said.

"But I'm the youngest, it sucks. Not fair!" He folded his arms.

"Hey," Thaddeus said, "Leo Alexander Denton, you are much more than being the youngest. You are the same as the rest of us. I don't care that you are. I think eight is enough. Come here, Leo."

Leo hugged him. "I'm sorry, Thaddeus."

"That's OK. Now go and have a shower," Thaddeus told him.

He did as he was told. When he came down, he face said it all. "My Olivia, you're home!" he cried.

"Come here, cheeky boy. I'm home for a little while. Go look in that blue bag." She brought him the book he wanted and another teddy bear.

They sat on the sofa. "Dad says you want another sister called Chloe?" He nodded. "Don't worry. It'll be OK. Where's your book?"

He went and got it. "Olivia, will all of us be together?"

"Like you wouldn't believe. Home is here. Forever," Olivia told him. The kids sat with them.

"Leo," Fran said, "we have a good life."

"But when you all leave, I'll have no one. I'll be on my own. I'll be scared." Leo had tears in his eyes. That's why, they now understood. "I don't want to be on my own. You lot will leave me and forget I exist."

That broke their hearts. "We will never feel that way," Callum told him.

Rae cried. "Come here." He hugged her. "You are so important to us. You do exist, so very much. Whatever happens. Look. Right here is what matters. Us, all of us. This is our happy ever after. Dad, tell him, please!" She looked at me.

"Leo. You're a wonderful boy. You know you're a lot like all of them, rolled into one," Mack told him. "You're like your dad in so many ways." He looked at me. "You will always be part of our family."

Oliver came back with a picture. "This I keep on my wall." It was a painting of their feet and hands. Leo was a baby. "This is our first picture."

Leo rested his head on Rae's shoulder.

Olivia was in bits. "I'm sorry, Olivia. Didn't mean to make you cry."

"You're my little brother, Leo. I love coming home and seeing you run down the road and hug me. That never gets old."

"Right, come on. Enough. I think we should get a takeaway for tea. Leo, you choose," I said.

We had his favourite. Pizza. We watched a film later. Leo, as usual, was curled up with Olivia. Oliver sat next to him.

Rae was tucked under my arm. "Dad. Is he going to be OK?" I nodded. "He's my little brother."

"He will be, Rae. He just felt lost."

Three days later, Mack got a letter from a solicitor firm informing him that his sister had passed away in a car accident. There is a will hearing the following Friday. He had been left something.

"After all these years," Mack said. "Part of me wishes. So many regrets." He cried really hard. I'd only seen him cry once like that before. The first time we nearly broke up, all those years ago. It broke my heart. The kids and the family were there.

"Daddy, we're sorry," Rae said.

The following Friday came. We went to the will reading. There was a letter from her saying how sorry she was for the way she treated him. That she wished things could have been different and she hoped he had a good life.

She had left him his daughter. She was eight months old. She had her later in life when she was forty-three. We were gobsmacked. Another child. We phoned home and told them everything. They agreed we Could bring her home. She was Mack's niece after all. It was settled. Family sticks together. Mack cried. "Leo's gonna flip out. He got his wish."

Nine kids. We had planned on six. Ironic.

"Uncle Mack, she looks like you," Emily said. "She's beautiful, like a dolly."

"Well, I got my wish," Mack said. "A very large family." I hugged him. "Leo, you know what her name is?" He shook his head no. "Chloe. Chloe Louise Denton."

His face lit up. He picked her up and sat with her on the sofa. "Hey there, Chloe. I'm Leo. Your big brother. You're my wish come true. I promise to be there for you every day forever. So will everyone. You are my angel." That was it, we were all in tears.

"What!" he said, when he saw us crying. Then he said, "Olivia. Does she know?" Mack nodded.

That evening, Mack and I spoke about what happened. "You know, I forgave her a long time ago."

"I know you did. How are you feeling about having your niece here?" I asked.

"I'm OK about it. I thought it would be hard, but no. I'm at peace. It's lovely having her here."

On cue, she cried. "Right, let's get her." He smiled when he held her. "Nine kids, Mike. Do you regret it?"

"No bloody way. The best thing ever. The other option, talking to you…" I laughed.

Thaddeus came down. "How's the little one?"

"She OK," I said. "What you doing up?"

"Worried about Chloe. Dad?" he asked Mack. "You OK? I'm worried about you." I took Chloe from Mack.

"Listen, I'm good, I'm fine. Thaddeus, I couldn't be better." He put his arm around him.

"Really? I know you've been sad about your sister. I couldn't imagine what it would like to lose one of mine. It'll hurt too much." He cried.

"Hey. Don't think like that," Mack said. "Your sisters will be around for a long time."

"But I got scared that when you lost Aunt Lucy, it hurt you a lot. I was worried that you might not come back to us," Thaddeus said.

"I'll always come back to you kids. Don't doubt that, ever. But I'm good. Don't ever think I won't be here. You're my son, my wonderful Thaddeus. Look, she's smiling at you."

"Come here, princess," he said. She went to him smiling. Then Chloe yawned. She rested her head on his shoulder and put her thumb in her mouth. She fell asleep. Thaddeus smiled. "That's made my day. That really has. She is a good girl. Welcome home, Chloe. You're with a family that will love you, always."

I took her to bed. When I came down, Thaddeus got up. "You are amazing parents. Thank you." He kissed our heads and went to bed. "Love you always."

Oliver and Rae were in the den with Chloe. They were looking at photos of us. "I'm feel bad that Daddy didn't have a nice childhood, like we have. It makes me sad. But at least he met Daddy. Are they happy, Ollie?" Rae asked him.

"I hope so. I feel sad too, that Dad didn't have a good time. He's such a good man. I'm sorry he was lost for all these years." He wiped away his tears.

Mack was at the door, listening. "I'm not lost any more. Listen, I was lost for years. But then I met your dad, fell in love and had you kids. We are happy, Rae. This family has given me hope. Don't worry."

Rae started crying. "I don't understand. You were sad, but yet you make us happy. I can see where I get my kind heart. Are you really happy?"

"Angel girl. Yes, I am."

Chloe farted just then. It smelled. "God!" Rae said. "She takes after you two. When she gets bigger, I'm going to the loo before her." They laughed.

Oliver asked, "Who wants dessert gets Rae's favourite."

When he came back, she said, "Daddy! Where are the sprinkles?" She pulled the same stunt on him. Soppy eyes then the bottom lip. He pulled a face and went and got them.

"Wimp," Oliver said and smiled. Chloe loved the ice cream.

"My God!" Rae said. "She's definitely related to you, Ollie. She is a pig." She leaned her head on Mack's shoulder. "I'm glad Chloe's here. She's lovely. Just like you, Daddy."

He kissed her head. "Angel girl. Chloe's going to learn so many wonderful things from all of you." She nested into Mack, yawning. "I think she needs her bed." Mack took her up.

Oliver looked worried. "Ollie bear. What's worrying you?"

"Dads have done wonderful things for us. We should do something for them. I don't want them to feel we don't care." He put his arm around her.

"I've got an idea. It's simple. It'll make them cry like babies." Rae smiled.

So, they ordered something for them. It arrived a week later. "Ollie, a parcel for you," I shouted. I was confused when the kids came in, smiling.

"Sit down, both of you," Francesca said. We did as we were told.

"Here, open it," Callum said.

We opened it. It was a teddy with all their names and dates of birth on it. Underneath it said, 'Love you, always'. We cried.

"Told you," Rae said.

"Why?" Mack said. Rae walked up to him. "Daddy, we want you to know that being together is important. We don't want you feeling lost any more." She hugged us tight.

"I'm not lost any more, Angel girl. I have a good life with you all."

Leo then made us laugh.

"Can we have Pizza Hut for tea. I'm hungry?" he said. We agreed. "This is brilliant!" Leo said. Chloe loved the garlic bread.

Olivia came home and met Chloe. "Hello you. I'm Olivia. Your big sister. Welcome home. Dad, pass me that bag, please?" I gave it to her. She got this beautiful pink quilt out.

"Olivia. You shouldn't have spent a lot of money." I told her.

"I didn't. I made it. I had material left over when I made the girls theirs at Christmas. It cost nothing. Daddy, I wanted to do it. We got one. She can have one. See, look."

She was curled up in her blanket. "Let me help from time to time. It's all down to you and Daddy. I want to help you. I'm cooking dinner tonight. I'm not taking no for an answer."

I kissed her head. "Thanks, Olivia. But we like doing it."

"It's not the point, Dad. I'm almost twenty now. I'm helping out. Like it or not. You two need a rest." She looked worried.

"What's worrying you?" I asked her. She leaned on my shoulder.

"Are we putting pressure on you and Dad? Are we too much?" she had a tear.

"Oh, Olivia. You kids are not too much, no way. Don't ever think that. You lot are better than winning the lottery," I told her.

"You always say that," she said.

"It's true," I told her and hugged her.

Chloe climbed back on Olivia. "She's cute. You've got good daddies, kiddo. They will always be there for you. Through everything."

Mack was behind us. "Love you, kiddo," he told her.

"Love you too, always. Right, better start dinner." She got up and started on dinner.

"Want some help?" Mack asked her.

"I'm OK, Dad."

Twenty minutes later, she called, "Dad, need your help?"

Mack smiled. "Coming, your highness."

She looked at him. "Really!"

A couple of weeks later, we had a call from Olivia, she was crying like mad. "Daddy! Daddy!"

"Olivia. What' wrong?" I was scared.

She explained that someone had broken into her room and stolen some things. A bit of money, etc. We raced up there. We got to the main entrance and explained who we were. She came running down, shaking.

"Daddy, I'm scared," she said.

"Right, come on. Get your stuff, we're taking you home. I'll drive you here every day if I have to," Mack said.

I sat with her in the back. She clung on to me. "Why, daddy? Why are people like that?"

"Dunno. But you are not staying there on your own," I told her.

She dozed off in my arms. "Olivia, we're home."

Maggie was already there, waiting for her. "Olivia. God, you OK?" She hugged her. "Come on, I'll make you a cuppa."

Joel helped us with her stuff. "Man, what's wrong with people? Jesus, she OK?"

"Give it a couple of days. All we saw was a little girl. They took almost a hundred pounds. That was food money." I lost it. "If I ever get my hands on—"

Mack stood in front of me. "What's that going to do? Right now, our little girl needs us. Shit, it's normally me that kicks off. Come on. Joel, beer?"

"Damn right!" he said. The girls were in the den, talking. "They're really close, aren't they?" Joel said.

"Yes, they are," I said. "Remember when they were babies, now look at them," I said.

"Jesus, that seems like a lifetime ago. Maggie's almost twenty-two. You know, she still remembers that bike you bought her."

"Maggie?" I asked. "Want to stay for dinner?"

"Dad, that OK?" she asked.

He nodded. "I'm off. Maggie, see you at home."

"I'll walk her home," Mack said.

After dinner and Maggie went home, Olivia came down in my old blue jumper and joggers.

"I wondered where they went."

"They're comfy. Thanks for letting Maggie stay," she said.

"She's family. How you doing?" I put my arm around her.

"Still scared. Happy I'm home. I am staying here?" She looked at me.

"'Course you are! We'll work it out. Me and Dad will give you the money. No arguing."

Mack walked in and smiled. "That's where they went," he said, looking at the jumper. "Want your favourite drink? Marshmallows too. It's going to be OK, Olivia," Mack told her. "We'll help you."

"That's what Daddy said. Glad to be here." She looked at me. She and Rae gave me the same look. "Go and get your book."

I read her her book. "Happy now?" I said. She nodded.

"Come on, bed," Mack said.

"Can we stay here a little longer. Can we talk?"

"What do you want to talk about?" Mack asked. We smiled at each other.

"Have you always been together?" she asked. We told her about how we met, and that we almost spilt up.

Her face was in shock. "Really! Why?"

Mack told her what happened. That it was his fault. "I nearly lost the one man that means everything, because I'm a stubborn man," Mack told her, he was upset. "The love of my life nearly walked away."

"But I didn't," I told him. "I stayed. I knew I couldn't be without you. Ever. I was as much to blame." Olivia smiled.

"You two, really love each other." We nodded. "You two are amazing. Do you ever wish things were different? Like how you raised us kids?"

"God, no!" I said. "We wanted to raise you how we wanted. We wanted to raise you to be independent, strong people. You kids certainly are that! Olivia, how come you like spending time with us?"

"That's so easy." She smiled. "Family day is the best. We love it. All of us together. Then Sunday dinner with everyone. You know, not a lot of folks have that. I'm so, so glad we found each other. I'm proud to be your daughter. Just promise me one thing."

"Anything," Mack said.

"Never let us go. Let's stay together forever," she said, yawning.

"You have our word. Always," Mack replied. When she went to bed, we cried for the longest time.

In the morning, all our kids were at the table.

"Oh my God!" Bella said. "Oliver James Denton. Save some for the rest of us. You look like you've never seen food before."

Even Chloe was eating for England. Then they laughed. Chloe and Oliver farted loudly at the same time.

"Dad, come on, eat, before these two eat it all," Thaddeus said.

We looked at each other. "How about an extra family day?" Mack said.

The kids looked at each other. "You know it's a school day. It's Friday," Francesca said.

"What's one day? Besides, it's half-term next week," I said.

"What's wrong with you two?" Callum said.

"Nothing. Look, you lot want an extra day or what?" Mack said.

They all said yes. "Can we go to the lakes?" Rae said.

"Yes. You love it there," I asked.

She nodded. "I heard you two talking last night." I nodded.

"Come on. Let's have fun. Oh, Chloe's shoes," Oliver said.

We did just that. We had fun.

"This never gets old," Bella said.

"You know, best days ever," Callum said. He took Mack's hand. "Thank you." Mack got choked up. "You know, for a guy that looks like a tough guy, you're a softie. You know, like Olivia said, we're proud to be your kids. My mates are jealous. I told them to piss off."

Mack laughed. "No swearing."

I looked at them. "You know, your dad changed his surname, to mine."

"Really?" Thaddeus was shocked. "What was it before?" Mack told them.

"Denton's better," was the reply.

"Dad!" Oliver shouted. "Chloe done a big fat poo. It smells. I feel sick. Hurry up!" I went over. Oliver saw Mack. He took his hand.

"You OK, son?" Mack asked him.

"Never better, Dad." He looked at Mack and smiled. "I'm hungry!"

"You and your bloody stomach." Mack laughed.

"Take after you, Dad." Oliver leaned into him. "Can we have a big family cookout, like we used to? The whole family. Uncle Matthew, Jacob and… I miss that. Promise me one thing."

"Anything." Mack said.

"That we will always be happy," he said.

"Always, Come on, let's eat," he told him. Before they went, Oliver just stood there and hugged Mack tight. He wasn't embarrassed. This twenty-five-year-old lad hugging his father in public.

We had our family cookout. Everyone was there.

"Good idea of yours to have this," Matthew said to Mack.

"Actually, it was Ollie's idea," I said.

"I'm a genius," Oliver said, eating a burger. He looked at Mack and me. "Can we talk for a minute?"

We went into the den. "What's the matter?"

He gave us a letter. It was from Cambridge. He got in.

"Bloody brilliant!" Mack said.

Oliver looked sad. "Dad, I'm scared."

I smiled. "Come here. It's going to be OK. You know, Olivia was the same. You should talk to her."

"I'm proud of you. We both are. Could be a new tradition. Cambridge for the Dentons," Mack said. "My little boy. It's going to be strange not having you around. Same with Olivia."

I'm going to be OK, right?" he said.

"Like you wouldn't believe." I told him. I started crying. "Soon you won't need us."

"Hey! I'll always need you. You're my parents. I'm going to find it strange. Listen, can I stay here, after what happened with Olivia?" he said.

"Er, yes," Mack said. "Come on, let's tell everyone."

We told them the good news. Mack and I were crying. Olivia was happy. Leo on the other hand, was not.

"Not fair. Everyone's leaving. At least I've got my Chloe."

She gave him a big hug. "Leo. Drink! Please."

"Come on," he said, picking her up. Olivia smiled. Leo saw it. "I'll always need you, my Olivia," he shouted. She wiped her eyes.

Fran had been quiet all night. Mack was worried.

"Fran!" Mack said. "Come here. What's wrong? Don't say nothing. What did we promise each other? Always talk. Talk to me."

She sobbed really hard. "Fran." He hugged her tight.

"No, Dad. Why does it have to change?"

He looked at her arm. "Please, God. You're not hurting yourself. Fran. Mike, get in here now!"

I ran down. "Shit. What!" He nodded at her arm. "Francesca Sophia Denton. What did you do? Darling!"

"I didn't do anything. I burned on the grill, cooking bacon. Really. You thought I would do that?" she said. We sighed.

"Dad, why didn't they want me?" She looked at me.

"Dunno. Does it bother you?" I replied. She sat up.

"Sometimes. I don't want to find them, ever. But it does hurt. I feel like I don't belong." She cried.

"You do belong. Here, with us. We're never letting you go. You're my princess. For ever. You're our daughter. You will never be lost again. Look at me," Mack said to her.

She did as she was told. He began to cry. "Life changes all the time. It's part and parcel of being who we are. But, what will never change is that you are family. You belong, always have, always will. You, like the rest, are our everything. Your dad and I are grateful that you came home to us."

291

She hugged him. "Thank you, Daddy. Both of you."

"Now, how about your favourite drink? Hot chocolate marshmallows and your favourite treat. Treacle sponge?" I asked her. She nodded. "Baby girl. You're home." She smiled.

We heard crying. It was Rae and Olivia. "Come on. Same for you." They nodded.

"Francesca," Olivia said. "Thank you for being my sister. I can't be without you. You want to spend the day together? Just us girls?" Francesca smiled. "What do you want to do?" Olivia said.

"Easy. Watching films and popcorn. Chill out day. That OK?" Francesca asked them. They loved the idea. We smiled.

"Dad, that OK?" Rae asked.

"No problem," I said.

They spent the day in the sofa. Blankets, pjs and loads of movies. "Thanks for this. Just what we needed," Francesca said.

Bella said, "It's nice not to have the boys here. It's so quiet. We need to do this more often. Who wants a drink?"

We came home to see them on the couch watching 'Inside Out'. We smiled.

"Having fun?" I asked. They nodded.

"Dad, can I have my favourite dinner?" Francesca asked. Mack nodded.

Oliver gave Francesca a bag. She opened it. It was a musical box that she liked from the market. "Thank you, Ollie."

He kissed her head. "You're my little sister. You'll never be alone."

"Fran?" Leo asked her. "Are you feeling better now?"

"I'm a lot better now, Leo. I just felt sad. But Dads and my sisters helped me," she told him. "I'm OK, now. Sorry." She leaned her head on my shoulder.

"Don't be," Mack said. "Here." We gave her a present. It was the same as Olivia. A necklace. "Together, always."

"Dad, thank you. It's beautiful. I've been spoilt rotten. So, you mean it. That we'll be together forever?" Francesca said.

"You have my word, princess," Mack told her.

"Come here." He gave her a hug. "How about your fave dinner? What is it? You want chips or wedges?" he asked. Chips was the answer.

She sat with me. "I'm thinking of entering the art contest at school. I've started my painting."

"Really. Go on and show us!" I said. She brought it down. It was really good.

"What do you think?"

Mack and I were amazed. "God, that's brilliant. It's like that artist your grandad likes. What's his name?" I said.

"Edgar Degas. I like the ballerinas. So?" Francesca asked me.

"If you don't enter, I'll do it for you. Wow! You should show this to your grandad. He'd love it," I told her.

She smiled. "Thank you, Daddy. I'm going to have a shower before dinner." She took her painting upstairs.

When they watching TV, Francesca came to us. "Here, for you two." We opened it. She had painted us a picture of Mack and I. It was in the style of the other one.

"This is beautiful. It must have taken you ages," I said.

"A couple of months. Dad! You like it?" she said to Mack.

"No," Her face fell. "I love it. It's the most wonderful thing I've seen." She smiled.

"You kids are really smart," I said.

"Well, they do take after me!" Mack laughed.

"I won't go that far!" Francesca said. I laughed.

"Dad, what's for pudding?" Callum said.

"We haven't had dinner yet!" Francesca said.

"Got to plan ahead. That's really good, Fran. I like that. You're well smart. Can you help me with my art homework?" She nodded.

"Dad?" Olivia said to me quietly. "It's Fran's birthday soon. Can we do something special? She, like Rae, doesn't ask for a lot. What do you think?" I agreed.

So, the girls organised Francesca's birthday. They took her shopping. We had a party all done up. She was spoilt. We got her one more present.

"Dad, too much," she said.

"Open it," Mack said. The trinket said, 'For what a princess needs'. It was a tiara to go with her prom dress.

"Daddy! It's beautiful. Can I go with Cameron? He asked me to go."

Mack and I were surprised. Mack did the usual. "I want to meet him before I say yes!"

"Your so protective of us girls." Francesca smiled.

"I'm protective off all my kids." Mack kissed her head.

Cameron came round and met us. Mack did the usual twenty questions.

"You know she's my princess, right?" He was scared.

"Mack, stop it." I said.

"No. He needs to know."

"Know what?" Cameron said. "Don't mess around with my daughter. She's my pride and joy," Mack said.

"Dad!" Francesca said. "Don't scare him! Hey! You do this all the time. I'm surprised you didn't get the clipboard out." Francesca smiled.

"Not a bad idea!" Mack said.

"I'm sorry. But I have to go," Cameron said. He left in a hurry.

"I don't think I'm going to prom," Francesca said.

She tried to call and text Cameron. He didn't reply. She was disappointed.

"Never fear, Ollie's here. I'm taking you, end of story."

They had a good time, but later they were getting bored. Just like when Ollie and Olivia went. Mirror image.

"Can we get a burger, please?" Oliver said.

Francesca smiled and shook her head. "Thanks for tonight."

"No worries," Oliver said, eating his burger.

The next day, things were back to normal. Fighting over food, looking lost. Chloe crying. We all stopped when we saw Francesca in her tiara.

"Your morning hair don't go with that tiara," Thaddeus said.

"Don't care. I'm a princess," she said.

Mack and I laughed. He shook his head. "Dad, can we go to the farm please?" We agreed.

Chloe loved the sheep. "*Baa, baa.* Daddy," she told Mack.

We heard this noise. It was this noisy horse in a pen. He looked unsettled. Rae walked up the pen.

"Rae, careful," I said.

She stood on the railing. He calmed down when he saw her.

The lady who worked there said to me, "That has never happened. He hasn't been here that long. He won't go near anyone. She's good."

We walked up to them. "Dad, he's scared. He's going to be OK though. I told him. Does he have a name?" she asked.

The lady said no. "Rocket. Your name's rocket. I'll see you soon."

"Listen," the lady said, "I'll talk to my manager, see if you can have a job working with him, if your parents don't mind?"

Rae's face lit up. "Please. Just one afternoon a week?"

We agreed. Two weeks later, she went to see the manager, with us.

"See how you go Wednesday afternoons," he said.

"What do you think?" she asked us. We agreed. Rae was in heaven. "Can we see him, before we go home?"

Rocket was happy to see her. He calmed down when he saw her. We looked at each other. Even the manager was amazed.

"Is she a horse whisperer?"

"She never ceases to amaze us. We're her parents," Mack said.

I was amazed. She loved it there. She really grew up. I felt lost.

"I'm going for a walk. Won't be long." She and Mack noticed. I walked for ages. I felt as if they didn't need me any more.

"Is Daddy OK?" Rae asked.

Mack explained to her that I felt lost and that I felt like they didn't need me any more.

"That's silly. I need him. Is it because I'm working with Rocket? I'll stop."

"Don't you dare," Mack told her. "Listen, you're good at what you do. Dad feels the way I did when Olivia went to university."

"Silly old man. He'll always be needed."

I walked in the door.

"Daddy!" She ran up to me and gave the same doe-eyed look. "Don't be sad. I'll always need you. Can't be without you. We'll spend the day together. Can I have my story?"

A couple of weeks later, Bella stormed in the house after school, with Callum and Thaddeus behind her.

"What's all that about?" I asked.

Callum and Thaddeus looked at each other. They didn't look happy.

"Spill. You know the rules," Mack said.

They explained that on the way home from school, in the distance, she saw her real parents with two kids, hugging them.

"Dad, that's not fair. What did she do? Nothing. My poor sister."

We heard things smashing in the den and screaming. "Why! Why!" She was screaming.

"Bella. It's OK," Mack said.

"It's not OK. What did I do? I want to die! They hurt me bad!" She kicked the table.

Mack got hold of her. "It's not your fault. It's not your fault."

She was still kicking and screaming. "Let me go. Let me go!"

"Never. I'm not letting you go," Mack told her.

She was punching him now. "I hate them. I didn't do anything wrong! Now they've got more kids." She collapsed into him.

"Hey," I told her. "I'm sorry. So sorry, Bella. You're home. Safe. It's not your fault. Dad and I are always here. Honey, you're OK. I'm sorry."

Callum came in. "Bella. I'm sorry it still haunts you. Look at me. They can't hurt you no more. Dad is right. It's not your fault."

"I hate them, Callum. I hate them. I hate me. I'm bad. I did something wrong," she said.

"No, you didn't, Bella. Don't ever think or say that," I told her.

Mack was silently crying. "My wonderful daughter," he said. "I'm glad I found you. You did nothing wrong. We don't hate you. Whatever you go through, we go through. We're a family. You are not bad. You're perfect. We'll talk to someone. All of us. Together. We're not letting go. You're my girl. Always."

She calmed down. "Promise me."

"You have my word," Mack said.

She looked at me. "Dad. I'm sorry."

"Never be sorry. We got you. We got you." She sat with us.

"Let's see that lady who saw me and when I was little." She took our hands. "Let's stick together. I can't lose you."

"Right back at you, Bella." He told her. We just sat there for the longest time. "Come on. Let's get this place tidied up and get dinner. Bella, go have a bath," I told her. "It's going to be OK."

She came down awhile later. She hugged us both. She looked at Mack. "God, you've got a black eye."

"Good shot. We got you, sweet pea. We will always have your back. Chicken and salad do you for tea?" he told her.

She looked at us. "You two are the greatest parents."

"You OK now?" Thaddeus asked her.

"I will be, Thaddeus. I got you lot behind me. That's what counts." She took his hand. "Love you, big brother."

"Love you too, Bella. You're stronger than you know." He had tears in his eyes.

We went back to counselling. It really helped. Chloe was stuck to Bella. "My Bella. Poor Bella. Ice cream please! Daddy love Bella."

We got home and Bella did an Olivia. She nicked an old jumper from Mack.

"Really?" he said smiling.

"Yes. It's comfy. I nicked it ages ago. Don't mind, do you?" She looks at him.

"No, sweet pea. How you doing?" he asked her. She was quiet for a minute. He put his arm around her shoulder. "Talk to me. You know I can take it."

"I'm OK. Still hurts a bit. But talking helps. Why are some people like that?" she asked him.

"I have no idea. But you're safe. We got you, kiddo," Mack said. "My old man was an arsehole. Couldn't accept me for who I am and made it rough for me. It took me a long time to accept who I am."

"What changed?" Bella was curious.

"I met your dad. First time in the hospital. Then a week later after that. Been together ever since. I accepted it, just like that. Twenty-two years."

She smiled. "I get it now. I can I have ice cream, please?"

He brought her some. "Dad, you forgot!"

He gave her the sprinkles. She looked at him with a tear in her eye. "You never gave up on me. Why?"

"You're my daughter, Bella. Through thick and thin; your dad and I will fight for you always. Bad and good. Whatever happens, we will never give up on you kids."

She smiled. "Can we go bowling? We haven't done that in ages. Get Aunt Lydia and Joel to come as well? I need my family around me. Then a burger."

"For you, anything." He kissed her head.

We went bowling and had a good time. Joel beat Oliver.

"For an old man, you're good," Oliver told Joel.

"Less of the old. Round two."

Alfie was laughing. "My God, you got your arse kicked. Good job, Dad."

Oliver looked at him and stuck his tongue out. I took Mack's hand. There was a few drunk idiots who saw us. "Queer bastard."

For once, Mack didn't bite back. He wanted to.

Malek looked at him and said, "Good job."

They saw Malek. We got up to protect him. They got the picture and soon left. Matthew and Jacob made sure if it.

"You OK, Granddad?" Leo asked him.

"Yes, Leo, I am," Malek told him. "How's your burger?"

"Really good," he said, taking a bite. "You're a good granddad."

"What about me?" my dad said.

"You're OK," he said. They laughed.

On the way back, we walked along the beach. Chloe was asleep in the pushchair.

"I'm not looking forward to Ollie going to university," Mack told me. "I know. It was bad enough when Olivia went. But the main thing is, they will be home during the week. Olivia has managed to get a lift for them both. We have to accept they're growing up."

When we got home, Maggie came round.

"Hey. How are you?" I asked, giving her a hug.

"Good," she said. "Olivia here?"

"No. Why?" Mack said. There was a pause. "Maggie. You know the rules. Speak the truth."

"Olivia has had a bit of trouble with a guy at university. Nothing major. Just being a pain. Uni is keeping tabs on him. I'm surprised she didn't say anything."

Just then, Olivia walked in with Leo. We looked at her.

"You told them?" she said to Maggie.

"Had to. You wouldn't. Don't be mad. I had to. We don't hide anything from each other."

"Why!" Mack said.

"Because this is how you react. Jesus. Dad, tell him," she said to me.

"I'm with your dad on this," I said to her. "You should have told us."

"I know. I know," she said. "Thought I'd handle it. I'm sorry."

"Come here," Mack said. He hugged her. "Don't be mad at Maggie. She did the right thing."

"I'm not. Don't know what to do," she said.

"Get a restraining order," I said. "That's what I did all those years ago. For God's sake." I walked away.

Olivia looked at Mack. She was scared.

298

"I'm sorry, Olivia," Maggie said.

"You did the right thing. I'm not mad," Olivia said. Maggie left.

"I'll talk to him," Mack said.

We talked for ages. "I know this brings back bad memories. Don't take it out on her," He told me. "She needs us."

She came down and found me. "Daddy. I'm sorry. I know you had a rough time."

"Olivia, come here. I'm sorry. We'll sort it out. I'm worried about you," I told her.

"I'm stronger than you think. You taught me to be strong. I'm going to be fine. I have my family. That's all I need," she said.

"You want a drink?" I asked.

"No. Can we just sit here for a while? Just you and me?"

That's what we did. Just the two of us.

Mack poked his head round the door later. "Dinner. Your fave, Olivia."

Before we left, Olivia said to me, "Daddy, it's going to fine. I know it is."

She was right. It was just that. Fine. He backed off. He was told that he could face prison time. He left there and went who knew where.

"I told you," Olivia told us. "I had faith. Leo, go and have a shower. I'll put Chloe to bed."

Mack and I smiled. "Where does she get her strength from?" I said.

"She gets it from you two," Francesca said. "We all do. We're tougher than you think. You two have done a good job."

"We did OK," Mack said, smiling.

She sat with us and gave us a deep, thoughtful look. "You did more than OK," she said. "I look at my friends. They never spend time with their parents. Or their parents don't care. Going from A to B. They don't communicate. They're on the phone or whatever. You two make the time. That's why we are the way we are. You care. You listen. It makes such a difference. Don't change that. Ever." She leaned her head on my shoulder. "You're bloody good at being our dads. We couldn't ask for more. I'm proud of you both, so much."

I kissed her head. "Thank you, princess."

"Love you always, princess," Mack told her. She smiled.

The following week, we heard a screaming sob. It was Rae. What we saw broke our hearts. She was on the floor, holding Holly, our Jack Russell. She had passed away in her arms.

"Daddy. Daddy." She was sobbing.

"Come on. Give her to me. Rae, sweetheart, Mack told her.

She gave him Holly and flung into me. "Daddy, will she be in heaven?" For fifteen, so innocent. She was so sensitive. The others came in and saw what had happened. Looking at Rae, it broke their hearts.

I sat with her. She sat there in my arms.

"My poor Holly. My poor Holly," she repeated. "I hope she had a happy life."

That made me cry. Mack came in. "Rae. We'll bury her. Uncle Jacob is going to say a prayer for her."

"He doesn't have to do that," she said.

Mack smiled. "Hey. He told me you're his favourite goddaughter. He will do it for you." Mack wiped her eyes. "Go and have a bath. You will have your favourite drink when you come down."

An hour later, she came down. She looked so sad. She dragged her blanket on the floor. "Come on," I told her.

She sat with me. She looked at me with the doe-eyes. "Daddy, so you think she was happy?"

I smiled. "Sweetheart. She was so happy." I was getting choked up. "Do you remember the time Ollie was being stupid with Dad? Then we laughed when she did a wee on Ollie's leg."

She smiled. Oliver came down and sat next to Rae. "I had to throw my shoes out. They smelt awful. I miss her too, Rae. We all do. So much." He took her hand. "She's in a safe place."

There was a knock at the door. It was Jacob. "How's my girl?"

I got up and Rae looked up to him. She started crying again. "Uncle Jacob. I miss her so much." She hugged him tight.

"She's OK. She's looking down thanking you for a happy life. It's OK. It's going to be OK."

It broke out hearts to see this young lady, so innocent and child-like, so sad. She fell asleep.

"That girl is so…" Jacob said. "She's so fragile. She's like you, Mack. She wears her heart on her sleeve. I don't mind doing that tomorrow. She is an angel."

We buried her the next day. Jacob did the funeral. That made us happy. Specially Rae. "Thanks, Uncle Jacob. That meant a lot."

"For my favourite goddaughter, anything," he told her. "It'll hurt for a little while. But it will be OK."

It was tough the next couple of weeks. We were sad. Then Jacob came round. "Where's Rae?"

She was in the den. We followed. We knew what Jacob had brought with him.

"Uncle Jacob." She smiled.

"How you doing?" he asked her. "I'm OK. What's in that box?"

We smiled. "Have a look."

She went over. Her face and the kids' faces lit up. It was a German shepherd puppy. "Oh, he's cute," said Leo.

"Good doggie," said Chloe.

"What are you going to call him?" Mack asked us.

"Barney," Leo said. "That OK, Rae?"

She nodded. "Thanks, Uncle Jacob." She smiled. Harvey liked him too. "Good boy, Harvey. That's your new brother." They fell asleep in his basket. "Daddy, I'm hungry."

"On it, Angel girl. Homemade burgers, OK?" Mack asked.

Jacob left us to it. Chloe liked Barney. "Good, Barney. Rae. Barney good boy."

"Yes, he is. Want a drink?" Rae asked.

"Orange, please. Leo, want juice?" Chloe asked.

"Dad, what are we going to do for Ollie's eighteenth?" Leo asked. "We have to do something special for him."

We planned a small family party. He was happy. When they left, I asked Ollie, "Aren't you going out with your mates?"

"No. I want to stay here with you and Dad. That OK?" he asked.

"Yes, if you want. I can't believe you're eighteen. I'll never forget when you came home. Our eldest son. I'm proud of you, son. So much." I had tears in my eyes. "This tiny little baby that cried, but when your dad took you in his arms, you stopped and fell asleep. You are a fine young man, Oliver James Denton."

We sat there for the longest time with his head on my shoulder. He fell asleep. I left him on the couch.

Mack came in. "Thought he wanted to go out?"

"He wants to be here with us," I told him.

"Our baby boy," Mack said.

Oliver woke up with Leo singing 'Happy' and Chloe dancing around in circles. It was funny. We all smiled.

"This is why I don't want to go out," said Oliver.

"Ollie bear. Dance." Chloe held her arms up. Oliver picked her up. She rested her head on his shoulder. Thumb in mouth. They danced away. "I love you, Chloe."

"Love Ollie bear." She looked at him, she then fell asleep.

"That was the nicest present ever. Cuppa tea?"

The next week, I came home from work early and saw Callum at the table. He looked confused. "What's up?"

"What does diversity mean?" he asked.

I explained what it meant.

"Oh. We're doing that at school. It's also LGTB week as well. Did you always know you were gay?"

I said next to him. "Yes, I did. So did your Dad. Does it bother you?" I asked him.

"God no. To me and the rest of us, it's OK. Never has been an issue. Being brought up by two dads, it's cool." He smiled.

"What do your mates think?" I was curious.

"Some think it's cool. When some asked me, ages ago, what my parents did, they thought I was kidding. When they saw you both picking us up from school, it shut them up. The rest don't care. You know, I'm the kid in my class whose parents are still married. How do you put up with that soppy sod?"

"Who's a soppy sod?" Mack asked, sticking the kettle on. Callum pointed to him. "Whatever." He smiled. "What are you talking about? You both look deep in thought." Callum told him what we said.

"I never knew that. Wow. The only parents that are married. What's the world coming to," he said.

"What's pride?" Callum asked. "It's a gay thing?"

We laughed. "Yes, it's a gay thing. It's a march and an event where you celebrate who you are," I told him.

He thought about it. "Can we go? All of us. You been before?"

We told him we hadn't. "Come on. Even if it's for a couple of hours. Listen, I'm proud of you. Please?"

"Yes!" he said. "You know, whatever happens, I want you to know that I am proud of you two." He smiled and made the tea. He was a good kid.

Leo came up to us. "What can we do for you?" Mack asked him.

"I would like a three-course meal and a lager." He sounded like Oliver when he was little. We had to laugh.

"You're funny, Leo," Callum said. "Hey, you know what we haven't done for a while?"

"What's that?" Leo asked.

"Played football in the garden. Want a game?" he asked.

"Let's get Thaddeus." His face lit up.

They were happy in the garden. Playing games. Chloe came in and held up her arms. "Daddy, hug." She gave me a lovely hug.

"How's Chloe?"

"Good, Daddy. Biscuit, please. One." She gave me the same look Rae used to. I gave in.

Mack shook his head and smiled. "I thought I was a softie."

We told Lydia what we had planned. "About bloody time. Pride. I've always wanted to go. I'm proud of you, Michael. You've always stood up for what you believed in. You're my brother. I'm looking forward to it."

Maggie was chuffed to bits. "Oh my God. Brilliant. Oh my God. New outfit."

"Is that what you are worried about?" Jack said. "It's a day out."

Maggie and Olivia were immediately on the Internet, looking for new outfits.

"You OK, princess?" Mack asked Francesca.

"I'm wearing my tiara when we go, 'cause that's what I am. Dad, will you come with me to get my GCSE results?"

"How are you feeling about it?" Mack asked Francesca.

"Nervous. I've worked hard. Afterwards, can we go to that place I like for lunch?"

"For you, my princess. Anything." Mack told her. She hugged him tight. "Love you, Daddy. Always."

"Good idea, Callum," I told him. "Should have done it sooner." Callum smiled.

Pride came round. Everyone enjoyed themselves. "Uncle Michael," Emily said. "This is a good day out. I'll always remember this."

"So will I," I told her. "Where's Rae gone?" I started to panic. "Mack, where is she?"

We found her at a safety point. "Oh my God. Rae, I'm sorry," I told her.

She was upset. She then said words I never thought I'd hear her say. "I hate you. I want to go home. I'm never talking to you again. You left me. I always knew you didn't want me."

"Rae!" I said.

"Don't talk to me." She went to Alice, who tried to talk to Rae, but she wouldn't have it.

When we got home, Rae went to her room and came down with an overnight bag.

"Rae, where you going?" I was hurt.

"Like you care," Rae said.

"Listen, let her stay with me. I'll talk to her. It was an accident," Lydia said.

The next day, I was sitting in the den. "There's someone here to see you," Mack said. Rae walked in.

"Hey, baby girl."

"I'm so sorry, Daddy. I didn't mean it. Please don't give me away. I don't want to leave you and my family." She started crying.

"Come here. You're never leaving here, ever. I'm sorry too. I missed you."

She ran to me. "Daddy. I was so mean to you. I hate being nasty. I couldn't sleep. I missed everyone. Please, please, don't give me away. Please." She was panicking.

"Hey, hey. Look at me. I'm not giving you away. God, no. You're my little girl." It broke my heart. "*Shh, shh.*" Barney came in jumped on her. She smiled.

"You know when you were a baby, I had to go to the loo, so your dad took you. You cried and cried. The lady in the shop thought it was sad. As soon as you saw me, your little legs went, you smiled and put your arms out. As soon as I took you, you rested your head on my heart, put your thumb in your mouth and fell asleep. That was so sweet. The lady gave you Jonas." She fell asleep in my arms.

"How is she?" Mack said.

"Sorry. Terrified we're going to give her away." I looked at her on the sofa, asleep. "She was so scared. Mack, she's so sensitive. She's fifteen and child-like."

"Listen, go have a shower, I'll cook. Go," he told me.

Then just as I finished, I heard screaming. "Daddy. Daddy. Where are you? What have I done?" Rae was crying.

"Hey. I'm here. I'm here. Told you I'm not going anywhere. I was in the bath," I told her.

"I thought you left me." She clung to me.

"Told you I'd never go. Nor will Daddy," I said.

Leo walked in. "Rae. You're my big sister. I will always be here. I know you will never leave me. It's bad enough that Olivia is at university. Ollie will be going soon. Can't lose you too. We need each other. Now go have a shower. Then let's watch the TV together. Please, Rae." Leo begged her.

She went and did as she was told. When she came down, she went to Mack in the kitchen. "For you."

He opened it. It was a photo of them at the beach. "Thank you, Angel girl. How are you?"

"I feel silly. I ruined the day," she said.

"No, you didn't. We found you."

I walked in with a box. Mack nodded. "For you," I told her.

She opened it. It was the necklace that Olivia and Francesca had. Her bottom lip went. "It's beautiful. Thank you."

Leo walked in. "You are aware we're missing our programme?"

"Daddy gave me a necklace. So there!" She told him.

Mack and I looked at each other and smiled. "You're bossy, Leo. Like Olivia."

"Back to normal," Mack said, chopping up the onions.

A few days later, Lydia came over in tears. "Joel may have cancer."

We were stunned. "What!" I asked.

"He found a lump in his... you know where. That man is my life. Oh God. Please no." She was sobbing. I hugged her tight.

"Do the kids know?" Mack asked.

"Yeah. They're in bits. Maggie and Olivia have been talking.

We looked at each other. Before we could say anything, Thaddeus went to her and hugged her. "Lydia. Uncle Joel is going to be OK. He's a stubborn idiot. Always has been. Family sticks together. We're here for all of you. You're my favourite people. Now when does he get his results?"

"Tomorrow," she told him.

"Good. It's Friday. You lot come here for family weekend. All of us together. For Joel. Love you, Aunt Lid-lid." Thaddeus had tears in his eyes.

"Thank you, you darling boy. You have a heart of gold." She wiped his tears.

"Learnt that from you, and Dads." He kissed her forehead.

When they came over, Joel got the call. Good news. It was just fatty tissue. But he was told to keep an eye and check regularly.

"Told you," Thaddeus said. He looked at Joel. "Uncle Joel. You are the finest uncle ever. Glad you're going to be around forever."

Joel was in bits. He hugged Thaddeus. "Thank you."

Malek and Joel spoke at length. "How are you, my dear Joel?"

"Every emotion you can think of, I have felt it. It changes you. Here." He pointed to his heart. "I'm lucky, man. Few can say they have this. A family who sticks together."

"Allah has blessed you with love and life. Do not change how you do things. But take stock in how you live your life," Malek told him. "I'm proud of you, Joel. Blessed to call you my brother."

Maggie walked in. "I shall leave, let father and daughter talk. Maggie."

"Grandpa!" She hugged him. "How are you, Dad?"

They talked for ages. "I'm proud of you."

"So are we," Jack said, with Alice, Alfie and Emily.

"I was scared that I was gonna lose you," Emily said.

"Listen, I've got a second chance. Not going to waste it," he told them. They smiled.

"Dad. I'm glad you're OK," Alfie said. "I'm glad we're here."

"Son. We're going to be OK," Joel told him.

"I know. I see many of my mates without a dad. I didn't want that for us. I am lucky, you know. Love you, Dad," Alfie told him.

"Love you too. All of you," Joel told them. Lydia was crying. They looked at her.

"Are you pregnant again?" Jack asked.

"Oh, give over," Maggie said. "His dick almost fell over. He's hardly going to get that old biddy pregnant."

They laughed. "Should have left you in Tesco's," Lydia said.

"Thought I was from Waitrose," Maggie said sarcastically. We couldn't stop laughing.

Francesca walked up to Mack. "Don't forget my exams next week. We're going for lunch after."

"Well." He laughed.

"Don't be a git. You promised." She smiled.

He smiled and said, "I hadn't forgotten. We're going to that little retro diner you like after. Just us three. OK?"

"Thanks, Dad." She hugged him.

The day came for her results. Francesca picked them up. Her face as a picture. "Please be good," Mack said.

She showed us. A*. All of them, like Olivia. "My princess is a genius," Mack said loudly. We smiled.

"You're embarrassing."

"I'm proud of you," I told her. "Lunch. Then shopping."

We had a good time and later went shopping. She stood outside this shop she liked. It was an old-fashioned one. She looked at this dress that she loved. A purple and pink dress. I nodded to Mack. We walked along the beach.

When we got home, we gave her the box. Her face was a picture when she saw it.

"Daddy! Too much. It's beautiful. Back in a minute." She ran into her room. She came in her dress and tiara.

"Wow. You definitely are a princess," Mack told her.

She ran to us. "Thank you. I love it. I enjoyed today." She started yawning.

"Early night for you," I told her.

"Please, let me stay up." She looked at Mack.

"Mike, help me."

"Please. I'm a princess," she said. Mack caved in.

"Thank you for my life. It's perfect." She leaned on my shoulder.

"You're welcome," I told her. "I'm glad we're making you happy."

"You are. I know we have our moments, but I wouldn't change it. It's wonderful." She was yawning. "Whatever happens, just remember, you are the best parents ever. You are and always will be my real parents."

She fell asleep on me.

"We done something right, Mike." He smiled at her.

"We certainly did. Come on, miss. Bed, no arguing," I told her.

"No. Do I have to? I'm a princess," she said. We laughed.

"Yes. Come on," Mack laughed. She leaned on him and put her arm around him. "Best day ever."

Mother's day was fast upon on. "I want to sit on my arse," she said.

We had a nice time. Olivia gave her a glass of wine.

"Enjoy. This is from me."

It was a photo of Lydia and Olivia as a baby in her arms, Lydia kissing her head.

"Oh Olivia. I remember this. You were the most curious baby. Always looking around. When you got unsettled, your dad," she pointed to Mack, "would pick you up and walk around with you in the garden. Then your dad would read you stories. Maggie kissed your forehead and said 'I'll always be there for you'. Now look at you two. Best friends. I'll treasure this."

Olivia wiped her eyes and hugged Lydia. Mack and I wiped our eyes as well. Olivia looked at us and sat with us. Leo and Chloe were cuddled up together in a blanket, asleep. "Mike, look at this."

I stood next to him and took his hand. "That's sweet." I looked at him. "Thanks."

"For what?" He was confused.

"Sticking by me. Just being there," I told him. He smiled at me.

"It was easy. I'd do it again." He kissed me. "Come on. Let's get these two to bed."

I scooped up Chloe, who like the others, was sucking her thumb. Leo complained. "It's an inset day tomorrow. Can't I stay up late?"

"No. You're only ten. Come on," Mack told him.

The following week, I came home to find Mack sitting stunned on the couch.

"Mack, what's wrong with you? Oh, numb-nuts!"

"Look!" He gave me the Euromillions tickets from Tuesday.

"This is a joke, right?" I just managed to say.

He shook his head. "No joke. We won the bloody jackpot. I just called the number. They had to repeat themselves. We won the rollover. Forty million. Forty million."

"I can retire. Oh my God." I just sat there, next to him.

Lydia and Emily walked in. "What's the matter with them?" Emily said.

We told them. "Fuck Off!" Lydia said. We looked at her. "Oh my god, you're serious!"

"Cool. Way to go!" Emily said.

"Don't say a word," Lydia told Emily. She nodded. She knew better than to argue. Lydia called the others. We told them. For once, our family couldn't talk. Mack looked at me. I nodded. "We're staying anonymous."

Everyone agreed. "This family never ceases to amaze me," Joel said.

Oliver and Mack were thinking. "What are you two planning?" I asked, smiling.

They both said, "Gaming room!"

"Really! You're off to university in a couple of weeks," Mack told him.

Oliver's face fell. "Thanks for reminding me." He walked off.

I nodded to Mack. "Talk to him."

"Ollie, I'm sorry. Didn't think," Mack said.

"I know. Dad, I'm scared. The thought of not being here for a couple of months…" He was getting upset. Mack hugged him.

"Son, I don't want you going either. My boy," he told him.

"I'm going to be OK, right?" Oliver asked.

Mack smiled. "Like you wouldn't believe. Now, what do you want for dinner?"

"My favourite, please!" Oliver said. "I'm glad I turned out like you." That made Mack happy.

After dinner, we were watching TV. We looked at the kids.

"I thought they would be making lists of what they want," I told Mack.

Rae looked at me. "Why would we write a list when we've got everything we need?"

"We agree," the others said.

"Really?" Mack said, smiling.

"Yes," Bella said. "We've got a roof over our heads, food on the tables. Clothes. Others don't have that. So, it doesn't bother me. But I do need some school shoes, though." She smiled.

We smiled. "You know. You two need a break," Francesca said. "You spend so much of your time on us. Go to that cottage you like."

We thought about it. Rae looked worried. "Will you come back?" She was still worried about her outburst.

"Yes, we will," I told her. "Always." That made her happy.

That weekend, we went away. Dad and Malek looked after the kids. Olivia was home for the weekend, so she helped. It was nice for us.

"I've missed this. I've missed you," I told Mack.

He looked at me. "Same to you."

We sat on the couch, holding hands. Next thing, we're asleep. We woke up with the sun blinding us. It made us smile.

"We're getting old," Mack told me. We took our usual walk and bought the kids some things and for my dad.

When we got home, it was quiet. Leo ran up to us. "Thank God, you're home. Olivia is so bossy." He paused. "Dad, I'm worried. She seemed stressed. Can you talk to her? Chloe has been good."

On cue, she walked in, saw us and went mad. "Daddy. Miss you. Chloe good girl for granddad."

"Dad, is Olivia OK?" I asked my father.

"She's been very quiet. Not herself," he said. "See you later. Malek, come on."

"OK, OK. You're bossy. Michael, see you soon. Don't look at me like that, Simon," he told him. I just laughed.

We found her in the den.

"Talk." Mack told her, putting his arm around her.

"I found a lump."

"Oh God," Mack said. "You been to the doctor?"

"Yes. Got a hospital appointment for Tuesday morning," she said.

"We are coming with you. No arguing," I told her. "Why didn't you tell us?"

"I was scared. Haven't slept properly." She yawned. "Daddy, don't worry. It'll be OK. I just need my family." She fell asleep in his arms.

We were in bits. Our baby girl was more worried about us. Mack couldn't stop crying. Not could I.

Tuesday came around. Maggie came with us to support Olivia. The tests were done. Good news. It was just an infection.

Mack and I wouldn't let her go. "I can't bloody breathe!" We let go.

"Come on. Let's go for lunch. Favourite cafe, do you?" I asked her. She nodded. "Maggie, you're coming too. No arguing."

"Dad, what's wrong?" Olivia asked Mack.

"Worried that I was going to lose my baby girl," he said.

"No chance. I'm going to make you a granddad." She laughed.

"Piss off you. I'm too young. Besides you're not allowed a boyfriend."
He laughed.

"Tough shit. Whatever happens, I'll always be your little girl," she told
him. "Can we go the market after? Need to pick something for Leo. I was a
bit nasty to him."

We went and got him something. Leo was waiting for us.

"I'm sorry, Leo," Olivia told him.

"You pushed me away. It made me sad. Are you OK!" He had tears in
his eyes.

"Yes, I am. Sorry I did that. Here, for you." She gave him the bag. It
was the book he wanted.

He ran to her. "Olivia, I've missed you. I love you."

"Same to you, cheeky boy. I promise I'll never do that again. Ever."
She hugged him tight. "Now, go and get changed and I will read your
book." He ran off and did as he was told. They were happy.

The next day, over breakfast, Callum, out of nowhere, asked Bella, "If
you had one wish, what would it be?"

"That's easy. I would like to put on a pretty dress and go to the Ritz for
afternoon tea with my sisters. You?"

"Watching footie and video games," he said.

We smiled. Over dinner, Callum said, "What's the matter with you
two? You're acting weirder than normal."

"Well, we have a surprise for you lot," I told them.

"Don't tell me," Callum said. "Dad's got you pregnant again! We're
having another brother or sister."

"Really?" Mack said. "No. Next Saturday, we're going to spoil you
kids. You boys are having a boys' day in. Computer and footie. Pizza, the
works. Then I'm taking the girls, wait for it! The Ritz for afternoon tea. So,
we need to get everyone a new dress, the lot."

They all looked at them, stunned. "Have you been drinking?" Rae
asked.

"What's wrong with you?" Thaddeus said.

"Nothing. So, girls, you up for some shopping?" Mack asked.

"OK. Who are you and what have you done with our real parents?" Oliver said.

"I get to wear my tiara," Francesca said. "Is Chloe coming? She'll look pretty in a yellow dress."

It was settled. We took the girls shopping. They were in heaven.

"Daddy, are you sure about this?" Rae asked.

"Yes, Angel girl. Go and get that dress you've been looking at," Mack told her. She smiled.

That Saturday, the boys were in their element.

"Dad!" Francesca said. "Close your eyes. We're ready!"

"Open!" Bella said.

They looked like angels. Chloe was so sweet. "Pretty dress, like Bella."

"You all look like angels," I told them. Even Mack looked good. He took Chloe. "You ready, girls?"

Off they went. Jacob drove them in style. Rae was happy. They had a really good afternoon. They were asleep in the car on the way home. Chloe was curled up in Mack's arms.

"You had fun?" Jacob asked him.

"Yes. Really nice, actually. The girls loved it. It's nice to treat them. Mike's having fun at home with the footie. I'll tell you one thing that was funny. When the matron asked where their mum was, they said, 'don't have one'. Their other dad was at home playing football with their brothers. She nearly shat himself." Mack laughed. "Want a cup of tea?"

He said yes. The boys were having fun. I was kicking Callum's rear in in some computer game. I won. "So unfair. Beaten by an old man. You don't play these games,"

Oliver was stunned. "Who are you and what have you done with my real dad?"

I was feeling smug. Mack kissed my head. "Chloe is in bed. Give me a few minutes. The girls will be asleep. How's it been?"

"Had a good day. Listen, you thought about what I said?" I asked him.

"Yes. It's a good idea. But they have to use it for stuff they need," he replied. We told them what we had done.

"Give over, Dad. It's your money. You always taught us if we want something, when we're of age to go and get a job and save up," Thaddeus said. He had us there.

"True. But this is a little nest egg," Mack told them.

"Thank you, Dads," they all said.

We checked on the girls. They were still awake.

"Good day out?" I asked. They all spoke at once. I laughed.

"It was nice to spend time with each other," Bella said. "I was joking about today. It was nice of Uncle Jacob to take us." She leaned on my shoulder.

"What's up, sweet pea?" I asked her.

"Absolutely nothing."

"Your birthday is coming up. Anything you would like?" I asked. She was already asleep.

Oliver was ready to go to university.

"Don't want to go," he said. We laughed.

"Most kids can't wait to see the back of their parents," Mack said.

"Listen, you'll be back tonight. We worked it out. Half hour in the car."

"This is different. Something new." He leaned on Mack's shoulder.

"It will be fine," Olivia said. "The first few weeks are always hard. Listen, I'm always around. Plus, we get a lift there and back, like dad said. You ready?"

Off they went. Like at school. It was sweet. I put my hand on Mack's shoulder.

"Look at them," Mack said. "How times have changed."

Oliver was loving it there. How three months had gone. "I love it there. The course is good."

There was something else. "What it is?" we asked him.

"There is this girl there. I like her," he said.

"Ask her out!" Mack said.

"Not that easy. She's a bit out of my league," he said.

"Give over," I said. "Look at us. Your dad is not someone I would've gone for."

"Oh?" Mack said. Oliver laughed.

"Seriously, though," I said. "Take your time. When you're ready, ask her out. It's going to be OK."

While I was working, I collapsed. Mack was called. I was in the treatment room, with wires on me. Mack walked in.

"I'm fine. I'm fine."

"No, you're not! You got wires everywhere. Jesus, Mike. What happened?"

My colleague had said I blacked out. The doctor came in. "Nothing to worry about. The tests say nothing. You're exhausted, Michael. You've been working your arse off for a while now. I'm signing you off for a month, no arguing. Take him home. If he moves, slap him."

Mack smiled. "Don't worry, I will. Come on."

When we got home, I sat on the couch.

"What are you doing home?" Callum asked. The others walked in. We told them what happened.

"Dad!" Francesca said. "You've got to look after yourself. We can't lose you."

"We've been telling you for ages to slow down. You've been told," Bella said.

Rae was quiet. "Come here," I told her.

"Please, don't leave us. Bella's right. You have to take it easy. Dad, tell him."

"You kids already have," Mack told them. "They're right, Mike. You have to. This is a wake-up call."

"OK, OK. I'm not going to win, am I?" I replied.

Olivia and Oliver came home to find me asleep on the couch. "Is he OK?" Oliver asked Mack. Mack told them.

"Bloody hell!" Olivia said. She was annoyed.

I woke up to them talking. "Hey, kids."

Olivia had tears in her eyes. I hugged her. "I'm OK. I'm going to be OK."

"Did we do this?" she said.

"No way! Never think that, ever. I'm tired, via work. Dad's looking after me."

"You sure?" Oliver said. He was worried too.

"Always." I hugged them tight.

Later that evening, we talked. "Sorry," I said.

"Don't worry," he replied. "We just want you safe for ever. You've always worried about us. Let me worry about you. I can't lose you. After all these years. No way. You're my life, my home. I think you should give it up. We've got the money. Just think about it. That's all I ask. Think about it. Now, dinner." He kissed my head. "For better, for worse. I take my vows seriously." He meant it.

My dad and Malek came over.

"How's he been?" Dad asked him.

"He's doing OK," he said.

"I'm sitting right here. Bloody hell," I said.

"Son. I lost your mum at a young age. I don't want that for my grandchildren. Look after you. We need you."

Rae stood at the door. "Please, Daddy. Do as Granddad says. This is my fault. If I hadn't shouted at you at Pride, this wouldn't have happened."

Malek walked to her. "My darling Rae. This is in no way your fault. Your daddy works too hard. He has to slow down. This is not your burden to carry, or your fault."

Her eyes were glassy with tears. She buried her head in his chest and cried, "Grandad."

"She's so fragile," my dad said. "She carries the weight of the world on her shoulders. Remind you of anyone?" he said to Mack and I. "Talk to her. Really talk to her. We'll stay for a bit."

We went into the den. "Angel girl. Stop worrying about Dad and I and everyone so much. You're a kid," Mack told her.

"But what if something happens?" she said.

"Then we'll deal with it," I said. "Why do you worry so?"

She paused. "I think it's because, I don't like bad things happening. I get scared, what if they come to get me."

"Who?" Mack asked.

"The people that made me. I won't see my family any more. Dad, it scares me," she said innocently.

We sighed. "Rae Morgan Denton. That will never happen. Why? Because you're our daughter. For life. I can't be without my little girl. The rest of them will miss you like crazy. Never think that. Ever."

Leo was at the door. "They can't have my big sister. Ever. It's bad enough that Olivia and Oliver go to university." He pointed his finger at her. "Not having you. You're mine. Always. Now, can we have a biscuit and a drink Rae, you're so sweet. Dad, drink. Biscuits."

She laughed. "You're like Olivia. Sorry, Daddy."

I kissed her head. "There's nothing to be sorry for. Just always remember, you're our daughter. You are wanted here, so much."

"How is she?" dad asked. We told him. "That girl." He had a tear. "She really thought that?" I nodded.

Malek was snoring in the armchair. "That man can sleep for Allah," my dad said. "Malek!" he shouted.

He woke up. "What!"

"You were asleep. Come on. Home," Dad said.

"Wasn't asleep. I was resting my eyes," he said.

"Really! You were snoring so loud, they could hear you in France," he replied. Mack and I laughed. They looked at us.

"You're worse than us!" I told them. I couldn't stop laughing.

"You're the worst son-in-law ever," Malek said, smiling. "You're cooking, Simon."

"What, again?" he said as they left. They were arguing down the road.

"Don't know why you're laughing," Thaddeus said. "That's you two in a few years."

"Thanks, Thaddeus," I said.

"You're welcome. What's for dinner? Barney looks good," he said.

"Leave him alone. Otherwise, I'll take your Xbox," Rae said. He looked at her.

"You wouldn't dare," he replied.

"Try me!" she said, folding her arms. He shut up.

"I better get started on dinner." Mack laughed.

Rae had a good time. We took Francesca with us. "She's really good with him, isn't she, Dad? She's so lovely, my sister. Always thinks of others. Never herself. I love being her sister. Can we take her for her fave afterwards? My treat. Please!"

I hugged her. "She'd love that. Come on, let's get her."

We drove to Rae's fave place. "What are we doing here?"

"I'm buying my beautiful sister her favourite teacake and a cuppa. You are the most amazing person in my life. No arguing," Francesca said. Rae smiled.

"This is lovely. This is nice. Thanks, Fran," Rae said. "We should do more things like this. I like spending time with you. Can we take Chloe to see the ducks at the pond she loves?"

Francesca had a tear in her eye. She took Rae's hand. "I can see why Dad calls you an angel. Rae, I'm so proud of you. I wish more people were like you. This world would be amazing."

The lady came over to us. "Thank you. Can I pay now, please?" Francesca asked her.

She smiled. "Today, it's on the house." She looked at me. "I wish there were more parents like you and your husband. You two have a good job. You should be proud."

The girls smiled at me.

"Told you," Francesca said. "You two are amazing."

"I agree. One thing that you taught us is to be yourself, speak the truth and be happy. Come on. Time to go," Rae said. "Thanks for a nice afternoon, Fran." Rae hugged her.

"You're more than welcome. My lovely sister."

I walked next to them. Francesca held my hand. "Proud of you, Dad."

When we got home, they hugged Mack tight. "What was that for?"

I told him what happened at the tea shop.

"You two should be proud of yourselves," Francesca said.

"Thanks, princess."

Oliver came storming in and went straight to the den. Olivia followed in.

"What's wrong with him?" I asked.

She explained that he asked that girl for coffee. They were talking. When she asked about family, and he told her about us. She paused. When she found out about Thaddeus, she walked off and said not to call her again. Thaddeus heard that.

"Thaddeus," Olivia said.

"Where's Ollie?" he said.

"Den," I said. Thaddeus sat next to Oliver.

"Thaddeus, I'm sorry. She was a cow."

"Not your fault. Makes me sad that you're sad."

Oliver started crying. "Thaddeus, I'm glad it happened. You know why? It made me realize that you are the most wonderful person ever. Your mates at school are OK with you. They don't see that. We don't. Not everyone is going to get along in this life." Oliver took his hand. "You are important to me. I will never lose you. I look up to you."

"Why?" He was confused.

"Because you treat people how you would like to be treated. You're kind, smart and most of all, you are the most amazing person in my life. Thank you for being my brother." Tears rolled down Oliver's face. Same

317

with Thaddeus.

"Right back at you, Oliver." They sat there for the longest time.

"Come on. Dinner. Your fave, Thaddeus," Mack told them.

They got up and Thaddeus hugged Oliver. "Love you, big brother."

"Love you too. Always," Oliver said.

Dinner was eaten in quiet. It was one of those dinners where nothing needed to be said. Then in true Oliver style, he farted out loud.

Then Chloe said, "Smelly Oliver. Dirty bum." We laughed.

"Can we watch a film?" Callum asked. "Please, it's Friday. Thaddeus, you choose."

He chose 'ET'.

Chloe sat with Francesca. "Hey, princess. Blanket. Chloe ballerina. Pretty dress." She cuddled with Francesca. Francesca looked at Mack. "You used to do that to me. So happy, I just wanted to sit."

"Can we make a trip to town in the morning? I want to get something for Chloe?" Francesca asked Mack.

He nodded. "You got enough, princess?"

She nodded.

They picked up a ballerina dress, tutu and shoes for Chloe. "You sure, princess? We'll go half." Before she could do anything, Mack paid.

"Dad, that's naughty." She looked at him. "I'm glad we recounted, Dad. We've got a lot closer."

He smiled. "Princess. I'm glad too. I'm so proud of you. I remember when you came home to us as a baby. When you were put in my arms. You looked at me with your brown eyes. You fell asleep in my arms. I cried. I was scared that a little girl who had a strong personality wouldn't need me. As you got older, you made yourself known. I'm glad I'm your dad."

She hugged him tight. "I'm glad I'm your princess."

When they came home, Francesca said, "Chloe. Come here." She took out the outfit.

Chloe's face lit up. "Ballerina for Chloe. Thank you, princess." She put the outfit on. She looked so cute. She was dancing around. "Beautiful Chloe. Princess, dance."

Francesca danced with her. We couldn't get her out of that outfit.

"Good job, kiddo," I told her.

Mack and I sat down to watch the telly, when Bella came in. "What's up, sweet pea?" Mack said.

Bella smiled. "You've got nicknames for us kids?" He smiled. "For my birthday, I only want to do one thing," she asked.

"What's that?" I asked.

"I want to go to the aquarium. It was the first day out I chose. Then a walk and then Dad's famous—"

"Steak and kidney pie, roast potatoes and veg. Then carrot cake for pudding," Mack finished her sentence. She had a tear. Mack and I looked at each other. I got up and got the box.

"Early birthday present," I said, giving her the box. It was the necklace. She saw the picture and burst into tears.

"Hey, it's not that bad," I said. She really was sobbing.

"Bella. Talk," Mack told her.

"It's beautiful. You really care about us kids," she said.

"Like you wouldn't believe," Mack said. "You know, you've grown into a wonderful young lady."

"I'm fourteen," she said.

"I remember when you came home. You wouldn't let Callum's hand go. You were so scared. Over the months, you came out of your shell. You loved playing with Rae and Francesca. Olivia loved reading you stories. Your face when we bought you easy-bake oven for Christmas. Priceless. My god, Bella, you are a gem. You are an amazing daughter. You will never be lost again," I told her. She took my hand.

"You've given me so much. I'm lucky. Most kids don't have that." She started yawning. "Can we go, please?"

"Yes, we can." Mack told her. She fell asleep in my arms.

On her birthday, she was excited. Callum gave her a present. It was a homemade photo frame with a picture of them together. He also brought her, her favourite book. *Little Women*.

She hugged him tight. "This is amazing, Callum. You are my guardian angel. You saved me. You gave me my second chance. I love you, forever."

He wiped his tears away. "Anything for you. One more thing. There was another present. It was a quilt. "Olivia helped me. I'm glad you're my sister and my best friend." We all cried.

The day was perfect.

"Good day?" I asked.

"Amazing."

"Almost done," Mack told her.

"Who's up for a film?" I asked. "Bella. Choose one."

She chose her favourite, 'Up'.

When we were clearing up, she hugged us. "Thanks for a wonderful life. I love you, always. Night, Dads."

"Night, sweet pea. Bella?" Mack said. She turned round. "Love you too. Always." She smiled and went to bed.

Mack and I spoke for a while.

"When was the last time we went out for a nice meal?" Mack asked. "It would be nice to spend time with you. Just you. Put a nice suit on and do what we used to."

"I like the sound of that. Be nice. Another thing we haven't done. Gone out on the bike," I told him. He smiled.

"So, how about twice a month, date night?" He was smiling. I agreed.

The following Friday night, we went for a meal together. It was nice. We got carried away. We got a bit drunk and stayed at a hotel. Didn't want to drive. We hadn't realised we spelt in. It was two in the afternoon when we woke up. Family day. Shit. We were in trouble.

The kids were mad. "Sorry," we said.

"Don't bother. We're going to Granddad's," Callum said. "We don't mind you two going out. Just be here when you say you are gonna be."

"How about a film tonight?" Mack said.

"Whatever," Francesca said. "We won't be here. Happy now?"

"Princess. It was one night," Mack was upset and sorry. Francesca looked at him.

Mack's face fell when she said that. When they were at my dad's, he gave them a talking to. "You kids. One night. They do everything for you lot. Give them a break. They deserve it."

When they got home, they were really sorry. Francesca avoided Mack for a while.

"Go and talk to him," I told her.

"Daddy. I'm sorry." She sat next to him. He just sat there and looked at her.

"I know you are," Mack said.

"Good. I've spoken to Granddad. So, every Thursday, you and Dad are going out. He's coming here. We were wrong. I've told the others. You do everything for us kids. We were selfish. I guess we're so used to having you here all the time."

Mack out his arm around her. "You wonderful little girl."

"I'm not little. I'm sixteen." She smiled. Later, she dozed off.

I walked in. Mack told me what happened and what she had arranged for us.

"That's a lovely thing to do. We better not mess up again."

"Dad, sorry about earlier," Leo said.

"It's OK," I told him. Chloe came in, in her ballerina outfit. "Daddy, I'm pretty."

We laughed. "Can't get her out of that outfit.." Leo smiled. "I'm glad I'm a big brother."

"Daddy. My tummy is empty. Making noises," Chloe said. "Fran, pretty girl." She kissed her nose.

Francesca woke up. "Sorry. Hello, Chloe. Look at you. Dad, she's pooed. That smells like Ollie when he's been to the loo. Gross! Can I help with dinner?"

"Come on, princess. Sausage and mash tonight, peas and carrots," Mack said.

Dinner was quiet.

"Right," I said. "What happened, happened. Let's not dwell on it. I would say shut up. But you're doing it. I hate the quiet."

Leo farted, loudly.

"Leo. That's gross," Rae said. "That stinks. God. What's wrong with your bum."

"I was enjoying my dinner," Callum said.

"I'd been holding it in for ages. Didn't have a choice," Leo replied.

"Could've left the table," Bella said.

"Dad, says it's rude to leave the table while eating your dinner," he replied, pointing to me.

I looked at Mack. "Back to normal. That didn't last long."

"Where's the air freshener?" Francesca said.

Mack was laughing. Then I started.

"Why is it quiet?" I said.

We turned around; they were reading books. They had turned off their phones and put them away, like on family day. "What's this?" I asked them.

"Bored of the telly," Bella said. "Reading *Little Women*." She looked at Callum. Francesca was reading *Wuthering Heights*. She looked at Mack. "Can we have pudding, please?"

He got them all some.

"Thanks, Dad. Thanks for everything. Don't change how you do things. You two have given us a good life."

"Princess, thank you. How about a walk tomorrow, to the lakes, then lunch at our favourite pub?" I asked them. They were happy.

Leo started yawning.

"Come on, mister. Bed," Mack told him. For once, he didn't argue. Mack carried him up.

"Fancy a game of cards, Dad?" Thaddeus asked me. We played for ages.

Fran had a bath and came down in one of Mack's old jumpers. "You know, Fran, he bought that just after we got married. Said it was lucky," I told her.

He saw it when he came down and smiled. "Why do you girls nick our stuff?" he said.

"They're comfy, Dad. I need my eyes tested. I'm getting headaches," Francesca said.

"How long this been going on for?" Mack asked her.

"A few weeks, now," she said sheepishly.

"Princess. Well go in the morning, before we go out," he told her.

She did need glasses. We got them straight away. "You should have said something," Mack told her.

"Didn't want to. Dad, look. That's what Dad's been after for ages. Can I get it for him? Please!" Francesca asked.

When we got home, she gave the book I'd been looking for, for ages. "Francesca, where did you get this?"

"There's a stall just outside the mall, near the market. Hope you like it!" she said.

I hugged her. "It's brilliant. Come on, let's go. You know, you're like Rae. Kind and very sweet."

She loved that compliment. This day seemed different. In a good way. Peace. That was what it was. Chloe loved the lakes.

"Pretty lakes, Daddy. Harvey liked it too. Butterflies. Blue, Daddy. Can I walk?" she said.

She held my hand and looked at me. "Love you, Daddy. You're a good daddy."

"Love you too, little bear," I told her.

She yawned. "Daddy, carry Chloe. Hungry too."

A few days later, we heard Rae and Francesca shouting at each other. "What the bloody hell!" I said.

"Did she tell you?" Francesca said. I shook my head. "Some kid in her class is stealing her lunch money. That's why she's hungry. I told the teacher, but they don't believe me. Dad, they're horrid. I've been getting her lunch. Dad, please help. They're so mean."

"Rae. This true?" I said. When she didn't answer, I said, "I take that as a yes then. Rae, you need to tell us. Remember when you were bullied? Alice told us. Fran did the right thing. Though you shouldn't have shouted."

Mack and Jacob walked in. I told them what Francesca said.

"Rae Morgan Denton," Mack said. "We're talking to the teacher. No arguing."

She looked at Jacob. "I'm with your dads on this one."

"I hate you all!" She stormed off.

"Dad, I had to tell you. No lies, remember," Fran said.

"You did the right thing, princess," Mack said.

Rae came down later, with Jonas. "Daddy, I'm sorry. I was scared." She sat in the middle of us.

"Angel girl. You have to talk to us. You know the rules."

"Maybe I should be like everyone else. Instead of being me," Rae said.

"Don't you bloody dare," Fran told her. "I love you just the way you are. Rae, they're jealous and mean. Stealing is bad. I will be with you at school. I should have tried harder. I'm glad I told. Rules are rules at home. Here." She gave Rae the money they stole.

"Put that away," I told her. "We'll make sure Rae's OK."

"It was Charlie Ross who stole my money. He's nasty. He picks on everyone," Rae said.

When we went to the school, as soon as they saw us, their faces fell. They knew they were in trouble, especially with Mack. He didn't take any shit from no one when it came to the kids. He demanded the money back; otherwise, he would have him arrested and charged with theft. If he came near Rae, he would also have charged with harassment.

"You can't do that," the head said. "We have to follow school procedures. It'll be dealt with."

"Fine. But this will happen if it fails. Keep him away from my daughter. Thanks for your time." Mack and I got up.

"Rae, go to class. Dad and I will pick you up after school."

Just then, Charlie clocked Mack and I. He shat his pants. Mack gave him his famous death stare. It gave me the chills.

"Go, Rae. Love you. Tell Francesca as well. Have a good day."

Rae smiled, knowing he won't come near her again.

Rae came to us after dinner. "Thank you, Daddy, for what you did. For you." She made us a box with a picture of us on it.

"Thank you," I told her. She hugged me and Mack.

"Where's Francesca?" she asked. I told her the den.

"Francesca?" Rae said. "Thank you. Here."

She gave her a picture frame with a photo of them, laughing.

Fran had a tear. "Rae, you didn't need to do that. I'll always defend you and everyone. You are an angel. You know, I would have kicked him in the nuts for you."

"No, you wouldn't. Dad would have grounded you," Rae told her.

"Yer, well. It would have made me feel better. He's an idiot. I've got your back. Always. I know you would do the same for me. Now, how about a cuppa and a biscuit?" Fran asked her.

I realised how proud of my kids I was. I was looking at their baby photos.

"Don't even think about it," Mack said, giving me my cuppa.

"Don't be stupid, you idiot. Nine kids, two dogs, three cats, a goat and a bloody horse."

"And a partridge in a pear tree," he sang, laughing.

"Look at Ollie. Chubby thing. Leo, same as. Where it gone? I'm glad we did it. Had them," I told him.

Leo waltzed in. In usual Leo style, he said, "I want to go fishing and have a beer."

We smiled. "Why fishing?" Mack said.

"Because it's relaxing," he said, like we were stupid.

"Well, perhaps I'll ask Granddad if he'll take you fishing, minus the beer," I told him.

"Really. I was joking. Cool. Does Grandad Malek know?" he asked.

"I think Grandad does it to have a break from Grandad Malek." Mack laughed.

"Are they like you two?" Leo asked. We said no.

"They act like it. Don't forget you're going tomorrow night. Night." Off he went to bed.

"He's definitely a character. He put me in mind of Ollie at that age," Mack said. He started yawning. "Fancy an early night?" He winked at me.

"Thought you'd never ask. Come on, before I change my mind and fall asleep." I smiled.

We went out that Thursday evening. Dinner and a movie, like we used to. "Brings back good memories," I said, yawning. "God, I'm old. Good idea of Fran."

"How was dinner?" Francesca asked.

"Why you up? It's eleven," Mack said. "School."

"Dad, couldn't sleep. Inset day. So?" Fran asked.

"Good. Really nice," I told her. "Come on, bed, missy."

"What's up?" Mack asked. "You look deep in thought?" He was worried.

"I've been thinking of giving up work, now we've got the money. It's been on my mind for a while now," I replied.

"Thank God for that," Mack said. "I was going to say something. You need to. I want you around." He took my hand. "Please do it. I have noticed that we're kind of drifting apart."

"I know. That's why I'm doing this. I'm not losing you. I do love you, Mack. More than ever. I'm sorry. I'll see them tomorrow. Come with me?" I asked him.

He smiled. "For you. Anything. I love you too. Always."

So we went to my job. I handed in my notice. They weren't surprised. They were happy and said I still had a load of holidays left, so that was that. I was gone.

"How do you feel?" Mack asked me. I looked at him.

"Actually, pretty good. Glad I've done it. Listen, let's pick Chloe up and go for lunch." I kissed him. "Mack, I'm glad we met, got married had our beautiful children. You are the best thing that happened to me. Always remember that. Sometimes, I don't deserve you."

He welled up. "I feel the same way too. You are my everything. Come on, let's get our little bear," Mack replied.

Chloe went mad when she saw us. "Lunch, missy."

"Yes, please, Daddy. Hungry bear." She made a bear noise.

When we got home, Chloe was asleep on the couch. We told the kids what happened.

"Really?" Thaddeus asked. "Are you sure that's what you want?"

"Yes, son. It's what I want. Dad and I spoke and we agreed. I feel better," I told them.

"As long as you're happy, that's good enough for us," Callum said. "Just be happy."

"I am. Always," I replied. "Rae, you OK with that?"

"Are you divorcing?" she asked.

We told her. "No, we are not divorcing. We spoke about what was bothering us. We are sorted now. So, no worries. OK? We promised and gave our word," Mack told her and the rest. "That's why we talk. To clear the air. We've always done this." Rae was happy.

Olivia and Oliver walked in. "What's going on?" Oliver said.

We told them too.

"About bloody time," Olivia said. "I've been worried for a while. But you've done it. Good."

Oliver hugged me. "Please be OK. I need my dad around. You are important to me."

"Son, I am. I will be. You have my word," I told him. "I'm not going anywhere."

"That's good enough for me," he said. "What's for dinner?"

"Thought we'd go to the pub for dinner," Mack said. They were happy.

Oliver was quiet, so we knew something was up. After dinner, we went for a walk. "Walk with me, Ollie bear," I told him. "Speak. Tell the truth," I said.

"Did we do this?" He was crying.

I stopped. "Sit down. None of you kids did this. You are the best thing ever. I was tired so I stopped work. I want to be at home to be with you kids and your dad. I'll always be here for all of you. You're like your dad."

"I'm like you too, you know." He leaned on my shoulder. "You are a bloody good dad. You've changed my life. Love you, Dad, always. Please be well."

"You have my word. Come on, before Chloe and Leo beat your dad up." We looked at them and laughed. "You used to do that. It was funny." Out of nowhere, he hugged me, tight. "It's going to be OK. I promise."

When we got home, Oliver gave us a present. We had mugs with 'World's Greatest Dad' printed on it. We had tears in our eyes.

Olivia said, "Very true. I'll put the kettle on. Go and sit down."

We did as we were told. Oliver gave Chloe a bath and put on her favourite pjs.

"Ollie, bottle, please. I like my milk." She sat with him.

"Can't wait to be a dad when I'm older. Where's your book, Chloe?" She pointed to the bookcase. He read her a story.

She yawned. "Again, please."

"OK, then bed for you, little bear." He kissed her head. She fell fast asleep.

"I'll take her," Mack said.

"No, I'll do it. You stay there," Oliver told him. We smiled.

"They all are. They are the most wonderful human beings that graced our lives." I started crying. "God gave us nine amazing people. They've changed my life for the better. They've made me a better man."

They were stood there. "You mean that?" Francesca asked.

"You bet your arse I do," I told them.

Rae ran and sat next to me and tucked herself under my arm, like she always did. Olivia was crying. "That's so sweet."

"Why are you crying? You never cry," Bella said.

"Time of the month. Where's the chocolate?" she said.

"Top corner cupboard," Mack smiled.

"My fave," she said when she saw the flavour. "How did you know?" she asked him.

"I just do."

Olivia was really crying now. She never did that. Mack got up and hugged her. "Baby girl. It's OK."

"Sorry. Don't know what came over me," she said.

"Girly hormones," Thaddeus told her. She smiled.

"I'm going for a bath." She went up.

An hour later, she came down and sat with Mack. "Better?"

She nodded. "I do feel sick. I ate all the chocolate in the bath. Thank God it's the weekend." Mack laughed. She leaned on his shoulder. "I'll get some paracetamol." He got up.

"You OK, Olivia?" I asked her.

"Yes, I'm OK." She sat with me. "Nice of you to say that stuff."

"I meant it. Come here." She hugged me. Mack gave her the tablets.

"Can we stay in for family day tomorrow? We haven't done that for ages?" Rae asked.

"Don't see why not. Mack?" I asked.

He was asleep. Snoring. Rae smiled. "He's silly."

Oliver did his usual. Our popcorn up his nose. Thaddeus was disappointed. "I wanted to put this breadstick up his nose." So, he stuck it in his ear.

"Why did Dad have a rough time with his dad?" Olivia asked.

"They never got on. Dad has always been strong-willed. When they found out he was gay, that was it. He felt like he didn't belong. He told me that changed when he met me. He wanted to change that with you kids."

Olivia got upset again. "Poor Dad."

Mack woke up. "Bloody kids. Olivia.?"

She cried and hugged him. "I'm sorry."

"For what?" he asked.

I told him. "Olivia. I told you I had a rough time. It's not your fault."

"But you're such a good dad! My God, what's wrong me?" she said.

"Told you. Girly hormones," Thaddeus said.

Mack smiled and hugged her.

"I'm OK. I got your dad and you kids. That's all that matters."

She started crying again. "I'm putting the kettle on. Who wants a cuppa?" I helped her. Once in the kitchen, I looked at her.

"No, I'm not pregnant. Don't worry. I'm not ready for that," she told me. I sighed. So did Mack. "I heard that!" she said. She gave us our drinks. She looked at us. "Don't worry, I'll talk to you first. OK?"

We agreed. "Not looking forward to that conversation," I said.

She soon fell asleep on Mack. "Can't believe she's twenty-one in a few weeks. We'll have to do something special for her," he said.

"I know. How's to quick." Rae was snoring away.

"Rae, Olivia, come on, bed."

"Don't want to go to bed," Rae said.

"Well, you're going," I told her. "We got you a puzzle to finish, tomorrow."

She yawned and smiled. Olivia followed.

Lydia popped over the next day. "What are we doing for Olivia's birthday? Can't believe she will be twenty-one. Can't believe Maggie is almost twenty-three."

"I know. Mack and I were talking about it last night," I replied, giving her a cuppa. "Knowing Olivia, she won't want to do anything fancy."

Just then, she walked in. "What?" she said.

"Nothing," Lydia said.

"Rubbish. I know you're planning my twenty-first. I'll tell you now, all I want is my family around me and to go to that cafe I like and have my favourite dinner. No arguing," she said.

"Are you sure?" Mack said.

She smiled. "Yes. Listen, I don't drink, I don't find clubs or pubs interesting. All I want is my family around. And it falls on family day. So, that's what I want. Please!"

So, it was agreed. That's what she wanted. I spoke to her again, "Are sure that's what you want?"

"Dad, it is. I don't want anything fancy. I want to be with you all. I know it's sounds silly to some. But you and Dad raised us to have our own mind and choose what we want to do within reason. it makes me happy and that is what I want to do. So, shut up. I do want a cake though."

I laughed. "Of course, you can have a cake." I paused.

"What's wrong, Dad?" she asked.

"I can't believe you are growing up to be a smart, wonderful, young lady. I'm proud of you, so much. It only seems like yesterday that you came home to us. This little bundle of joy. Soon you will make your own way in life, and we will be there."

"Oh, Dad. I'll always need you and Dad. This is home. So, you know how lucky I am. To have my parents still married and love each other. You now every day possible. I love you for that. You always believe that we can do whatever we want to do. I will always be proud to be your daughter."

She hugged me tight. "Love you always, Daddy."

"I love you too, Olivia, always," I replied. Mack started crying.

"You big baby," Olivia told him, smiling. She hugged him tight. "I love you too, you silly old git face."

"Hey, I'm not old!" he said.

"So you're a git then?" she replied back.

"Smart arse." He laughed.

Her birthday came around. We were up early with her presents.

"Our baby girl. Twenty-one," Mack said.

"Can't believe it. All grown up," I said. They came down to the smell of cooked breakfast.

"Happy birthday, baby girl," Mack said.

I got-teary eyed. "Happy Birthday, darling."

She saw the gifts. "You've overdone it. Dad. You're naughty."

She loved the gifts she got. The kids got her lovely gifts too. Chloe wanted to give Olivia her present. "For my Olivia."

It was a picture of them together at the park and a painting of her. She burst out crying. She hugged Chloe. "No tears, Olivia. Birthday girl."

Lydia and Joel came over with the kids. So did my dad and Malek.

She was spoiled rotten. "I don't deserve all this," she said.

"Yes, you do," Maggie said.

Malek walked over to her. "For you, dear child."

It was the most unexpected, unique gift ever. It was a copy of his Koran. Her face was a picture. "Granddad. I can't. This is your Koran. This is important to you."

"Child, you are as important as the morning sun that graces us with its beauty. This is something to cherish, just as I you," he told her.

She hugged him tight. She said in Arabic, "Those who are strong of heart, will weather the storm."

Lydia had made Olivia her favourite cake. Chocolate and vanilla.

"You wonderful woman," Olivia told her.

"I know. It's a gift. This is from Joel and me." Lydia handed her an envelope. It was three hundred pounds.

"Oh no, you don't," Olivia told them.

"You listen to me," Joel told her. "You are our eldest niece. You are good my to do so many great things with your life. Put this to use. Save it up. No arguing. Understand?" Olivia knew better than to argue with him.

We went to her favourite cafe. She had the famous chicken burger, so did Mack. She looked sad.

"I know what you're thinking," Mack told her. "It was here that we had our argument and made up. Don't be sad. That's the past. I'm proud to say that you speak your mind. That's what we wanted. I'll tell you this again. I was proud to have you come to us. My Olivia. I'm proud of you."

She was happy. We walked along the beach. She held my hand. "Thank you is not enough for what you all have done for me. Not just today, but for everything you have done. You're faultless."

"Don't know about that. The greatest gift was you kids. I'm glad you had a lovely day," I told her.

"It wasn't lovely. It was perfect." She smiled at me. That made my day. They all fell asleep on the couch. We let them have a kip.

We sat in the den. "That was a good day," I said.

"Yeah, it was. Look at them." Mack smiled.

Then Oliver woke up and farted. It smelt.

"Ollie!" Fran said. "Your arse is rotten. Do you have bowels."

"No, they rotted away with all that food he eats," Rae said. "You need to sterilise that arse."

"Nothing wrong with my arse," he said.

"Oh look," Thaddeus said. "There goes that flying pig. It sparkles too."

Mack and I laughed. "That never gets old," Mack laughingly said.

"Who wants cake? Olivia first," I said.

"This is so good," Oliver said between mouthfuls.

"Don't talk with your mouth full. You're not an animal," Callum said.

"Yes, I am. I have seven stomachs. Moo!" he said.

"Really?" Francesca said.

Mack looked at me. "Don't look at me. You wanted kids. Tea?" I said.

We told the kids Mack and I were going for a walk. We took Chloe. They didn't mind.

"This is nice," Mack said.

"I'd thought we should do this more often too." Chloe was singing away. "We should do more things like this. We did in the early days. Now I don't have to work any more. Kids are getting older."

"I'm not complaining. I've missed it too. It's nice," Mack told me.

"Daddy. I'm hungry. Dinner, please!" she chirped up.

"Come on, missy. Let's get you fed," Mack said.

We walked through the door. It was best and tidy and dinner in the oven.

"Is this the right house?" Mack asked. I looked confused.

"I think so. Can't be sure," was the answer I gave.

"Good, you're back," Olivia said. "Why do you look confused and constipated?"

"It's tidy and dinner's on," Mack said.

"Yeah, and?" Callum said. "We can help, you know. You'd be surprised of what we can do."

"Smarty pants," I said. Oliver and Rae were cooking. The rest were tidying up. "I'm so confused." I had to sit down.

"Dinner in an hour," Rae said.

"Told you he lost it," Oliver said, chopping carrots.

"Why?" Mack asked them.

"Why not?" Thaddeus said. "If you go out, and we're here, we're going to help. Deal with it. Shut up and sit down." A lot was made ready. It was really good.

"This is good," Mack said.

"We're geniuses," Rae said.

Bella and Olivia cleaned up.

"I can get used to this," I said.

Chloe started crying. She was tired. "Come on, missy. Bath then bed," Francesca said.

"OK. Princess. Story please," she replied.

That was that. Oliver made us a cuppa. "Here. You know we like helping you out. You can't do it all. It's not fair. We love you. We want to help. We're a family."

"OK," I said. "We'll let you. Right, Mack?"

He was already asleep, snoring.

"That didn't take long," Ollie said. Ollie kissed his head and mine. "Best dads in the world."

Dad came round the following week, "Dad, you OK?"

"Yeah, why?" he said, putting the kettle on.

"Surprised to see you here. That's all," I replied.

"Well, there is something. I'm thinking of sending Malek to Mecca. He's always talked about going again. He's stuck by me all these years," he replied.

"Do it. That man's a god send. Or Allah send. We'll all pitch in," I said. Which, we did.

They came round for dinner the following week. "For you, Grandad." Bella gave him an envelope. They had always been close. His face when he saw it! "Really. Great Allah. Too much."

"You deserve this, Grandad," Olivia said. "You're the backbone of this family."

Bella smiled. "You're going, Grandad. End of discussion."

He cried his eyes out. "Thank you, my family. Thank you. May Allah bless you and keep you safe."

Dad was lost without Malek. Like me without Mack. "Stay for a while. Till your husband comes home." I laughed. He looked at me.

"You know, we got funny looks in Tesco's last week," he said.

"I know, I was there," Bella said. "It was funny. They were arguing over Haddock. Granddad starting talking in Arabic. Granddad said, 'Stop yelling at me. After all these years, I still don't know what you're saying.' I couldn't stop laughing. The lady at the till asked if they were always like this. I nodded yes. They've been like it for years. Her face, Dad, it was funny."

Bella and I laughed. Dad gave us a funny look. "Sod off."

Chloe came bouncing in. "Look, Daddy, I'm dancing. Bella, dance." They danced. Chloe started laughing. "Silly, Bella. You're a good sister. You help me. You're kind and lovely. I'm glad you're my beautiful sister. Cuddle." She hugged her. Bella cried. "Bella, no tears. Kind Bella. I need a wee." Off she went.

"I'm glad I make her happy," Bella said.

"Tea, you two?"

She made us a cuppa. "Can I have a biscuit, please?" Chloe said. Before I could say no, my dad gave in. "Thank you, Granddad."

"No more. You spoil her."

"Sorry, can't hear you. Gone deaf. What did you say?" He smiled. I shook my head.

"Simon, you staying for dinner?" Mack asked him.

"Yes. How many times have I told you, call me dad. You're my son too. What is for dinner?" Mack looked at me. "Beef bourguignon." I smiled.

Dad was confused. "It's the first dinner he cooked for me. It's good. He was cooking for me when I got home from work," I told him. "Then he cooked it the night before we got married."

Mack kissed me. "It worked. You fell for me."

"I fell for you in the hospital," I replied.

Dad smiled. "You know when I first met you, Mack. I knew you were the one for him, that other one. That shit bag. Well, you made him believe that it's worth it. Here we are, twenty odd years later." he told us.

"How come you never became a chef, Dad?" Thaddeus asked.

"I don't know. It was a hobby that I enjoyed doing. Couldn't do as a living." Mack said.

Leo was quiet. "Take it you miss Olivia and Oliver?" I asked him. He shook his head and went to the den.

"What's the matter?" I asked him.

"I didn't make the football team. Coach says I have two left feet. I wanted to make Ollie proud of me. I look up to him. He'll be disappointed in me," he told me.

"No, he won't. He's proud of you no matter what." Just then, Oliver walked in. I told him what Leo had just said.

"Leo. It's nice to see you try. But I don't care about that. I care about you. My baby brother. You're better at maths than me. You love reading, you're good at so many things. Please don't worry. I love you just the way you are. You are silly," Oliver told him. "Have you eaten?" Leo said no.

"Good. I brought you a McDonald's. Your fave. Large cheeseburger, chips and a diet coke. Eat that you'll get your fave pudding. Jam roly poly and custard." Oliver have the bag.

"You're good," Leo said. "Thanks, Ollie. Can we play football at the weekend?"

"'Course we can. Jesus, take a breath," Oliver said.

"You were like that. Still are," I told him. I heard shouting from the living room. Francesca and Mack arguing.

"Why can't I go?" she yelled.

"You're sixteen. It's a late-night party on a school night. An hour away. There'll be booze there. I suppose that loser boy you like will be there? Andrew Phillips? A drug dealer. Beat his mate up for grassing on him. Good

334

choice. Real good. Thought you were smarter than that," he said. She realised what he did. He did a background check on him.

"Oh my god. You did a check on him? What's wrong with you?" Fran was horrified.

"Don't you dare. Don't you dare call me that again. If I were Olivia, things would be different. I always knew I was a disappointment. I hate you." she walked away.

"Princess!" he called after her.

"Fuck off, you arsehole," she screamed at him.

"Really Jesus, Mack. You know how to wind them up. But I agree with you on this. Hundred percent. Be a bit more diplomatic," I told him.

Mack knocked on her door. "Princess."

"Fuck off! Don't call me that. Leave me alone. Arsehole. I wish you weren't my dad," she screamed at him. Mack was heartbroken.

Family day came around. Francesca went to her friend, Lizzie's house.

"Princess. Please," Mack begged.

"Stay the fuck away from me. For good," she said.

"That's enough. I have had enough of this!" I said.

"Don't care. He started it. Hope you're happy. Don't expect me to be home, if he is here," she said, pointing to Mack. She was really hurting. So was Mack. He looked broken.

"She's my princess, Mike." He cried.

When Francesca came home, I told her, "This has to stop. Now!" Mack was sitting on the sofa.

"No way. He deserves it. He hates me. I really hate him." She wiped away her tears. "Can't wait to leave you behind. I'm off out. Not coming back. Bet you're glad, aren't you? Sorry I never lived up to the perfect other Denton kids. I will always hate you," she yelled at him.

Something else was going on here. Mack was in bits.

Mack and I went to Francesca's school and spoke to the head. "She never spoke to you? That's a surprise. We had the Phillips kid removed from school as he was selling drugs and," he paused. "Pushing Francesca around. Bulling her. I'm sorry. She said she told you. God. I'm sorry. I should have told you."

"Can we take her home?" I asked.

"OK. I'll get her." He went and got her. Her face fell.

335

"Come on. Princess." She didn't argue. We took her home.

"Why were you there?" She was in tears.

"We know the truth," Mack said. "All of it. You should have talked to us." He went to hug her.

"Get off me! Get off me!"

"No. Never," Mack said. "Fran, oh Fran. I'm sorry." We were crying.

"He made me feel so useless. He hurt me, Dad. I felt like the ugly duckling. He told me that you will never love me because I'm not your real daughter. You'll throw me away. I'm rubbish. I want to go to heaven." She was sobbing.

"Look at me!" I told her. "You're not going to heaven. Don't talk like that. You are our daughter. We don't throw things away that we love and you're not an ugly duckling. You're beautiful." I looked at Mack, who was trying to keep it together. Then he really cried.

"Princess. You will always be so loved. My baby. Fran, I'm sorry. So sorry." They cried together.

"What's going on?" Bella looked scared. I told her what happened. "Oh my God! Fran. Come here." Fran went to her. "That piece of shit. I'll kill him. He can't touch you ever again. If he does, I'll call the police. You need to talk to my counsellor. She's so nice. It'll help. Just remember, you're my sister. I love you." she at us. "Fran, go have a shower. I need to talk to Dad." Off she went.

"Let me tell you this, this is not your fault. It's his. You did nothing wrong. I know what it's like to be scared. Really scared. Blaming yourself doesn't help. I learnt that. He took advantage of the fact that she's kind. Cruel motherfucker," she said.

"Language, Bella," I told her.

"Sorry, Dad." She looked at Mack. "It's going to be OK. We're a strong family. We'll get through it. We always do." She kissed our heads.

Francesca came down an hour later. "I'm so sorry for everything I said to you both. It is unforgivable." She stood there.

I got up and hugged her. "It's going to be OK."

She looked at Mack. "Daddy. I'm sorry. Please don't hate me. I said so many wicked things. Please, don't give up on me."

"Come here," he told her, wiping away the tears. "I'll never give up on you. The words did hurt me. Now I know what you went through. You will always be my princess. That will never ever change. We're going to

336

counselling. You need to talk. I will never lose you. You're my precious child. All is forgiven."

She cried. "I don't deserve you."

"Francesca." Bella smiled. "We're in this together. Stick together. Stronger together."

Mack and I spoke that evening. "I wish I knew. I should have done something," Mack said.

"So do I," I told him. "But what's done is done. Let's move forward, go to counselling and help her and us. We have to. I feel guilty that I didn't stop it sooner, the pain she was going through. To think she wanted to be in heaven, that hurts the most."

"I know. She's here. That's what's important. I'll check up on her." He went to see her.

"Francesca?" he said quietly.

She woke up. "Daddy, what's wrong? I'm not going to hurt myself. You have my word. I was scared that's all. Can you read me a story, please?" she asked him.

He sat on the floor and read her a story. He cried. She sat on the floor next to him. She took his hand.

"It's OK. We will be OK. Just remember, you and Dad are my favourite people. You are my dads. I'm your daughter." She looked at him. "I'm sorry that I put you two through a lot."

"Princess. We will support you through heaven and hell."

"Can I speak to Daddy before I go back to bed?" she asked him.

"He'd love that. Come on," he said, getting up. They came down. She sat with me. "Daddy, thank you for being there. I know I have not made it easy. But I'll try. Promise."

"I know you will. As a family, we'll stick together. No worries. Now, don't tell the others. How would you like your favourite drink?" She grinned like a Cheshire cat.

"Yes, please. Then bed. Promise," she said.

The next few months were good. We went to counselling, which really helped. It did us good. Francesca changed a lot. She looked so happy.

The counsellor spoke to us, "She's really doing well. She's been through a lot. She's got mild PTSD after what that lad did, but, in time that will go. She speaks highly of you two and her family. She's very well adjusted now, so is Bella. You've done a good job as parents. I would like to see you all once a month now. Anything changes, come back. You know, I see a lot of parents that don't take this seriously enough. You two are an exception. You should be proud of how well you're doing. Good job." We walked out of there proud of ourselves.

When we got home, we watched them play around. Then there was a knock at the door. It was a lovely bunch of flowers. The card said, *'To the most wonderful parents ever. Thanks for never letting me go. Always, your princess.'* That got us.

Fran saw our faces. "Glad you love them. Tea?" We couldn't talk.

"Leo, Oliver. Jesus, your arses. Your farts could stop wars," Fran yelled. "Where's that air freshener. Dirty sods." We laughed.

"Right, can we have Pizza Hut for tea? Please?" Leo asked.

We said yes. "Can't be arsed to cook," Mack said.

"Dad, where's Olivia?" Francesca asked me.

"Loo, I think. Why?" I asked. Olivia came out.

"Olivia, close your eyes. Give me your hand, please," Fran said.

Olivia did as she was told. "Open your eyes."

Olivia opened them. "Fran. This is beautiful." It was a painting of Olivia that Fran did of her.

"You've always been there for me. I've been a cow towards you lately. This is a sorry," Fran said. Olivia hugged her. "This is the most wonderful thing ever. Never worry about that. I told you before. I love you, beautiful sister. I'm proud that you've come through that rough patch. This painting means everything to me. I'm here for you always. You're so bloody talented. You should do this for a living."

"She's right, you know," I told her. "It's stunning."

"Well, I'm looking into Art history, instead of becoming an architect. I like this more," Fran said.

"Follow your dream, beautiful sister. Thank you," Olivia said, crying. "I'm a lucky sister, to have you and everyone."

"Me too," Chloe said. "Cuddle."

Olivia picked her up. "You're getting heavy, missy." Olivia smiled.

"I just had pizza with Leo. He's greedy. But he's funny, like me." Chloe giggled. "I want to dance." She was dancing. We had to laugh.

"Dad, she's so Diddy," Callum said.

She started yawning.

"Bed for you, missy," Olivia said. "Come on, let's get you into bed."

"Bath, please. I want a bath," Chloe said.

Olivia caved in. "Say night to everyone." She said it and waved.

Mack caught me looking at some brochures. "What's this?" he said.

"You know how many years we've been together?" I said.

"Twenty-five," he said, smiling.

"I want to do something special for us. From me to you. Mack, you're the love of my life. I loved you the day we met. I love you more now."

He smiled. "You've given me everything I wanted. Kids, home, love happy ever after. I can't ask for more. You are home."

"Please. How about updating our album?" I said.

"OK. Jacob is good at that," Mack said.

So that's what we did. Jacob took beautiful ones of us. In black and white. Our favourite. Just us. Together. After all these years, we hadn't changed much.

Rae looked at them with us. "You know, for old men, you're handsome." We smiled.

"Thank you, Angel girl." Mack smiled at her.

"Look at this one." I showed her one of us when she was a baby. Lying on my stomach, asleep, with her thumb in her mouth. "Uncle Jacob took that. My favourite," I told her.

She smiled. "We mean a lot to you, don't we, Daddy?" she asked.

"Yes. You do," Mack told her. "How about your fave dinner?"

"Yes, please, Daddy," she said.

Leo sat with us. "Rae, will you read me a story please?" He leaned on her shoulder. "Go on."

"Why are photos important to us?" Leo asked, looking at them.

"It's nice to look at them and how we've changed. How we've grown over the years," I told him.

"I don't want to grow up. It's sounds boring!" he said.

I chuckled.

"Dinner! Come on," Mack shouted. Everyone was talking and laughing. Fran was drawing away. Deep in thought.

"Fran, that's brilliant," Thaddeus told her. She smiled.

"Dad, I'm applying for university. I'm thinking of Oxford. That OK?" Fran asked us.

We were chuffed. "That'll be cool," Mack said. "Our kids going to good schools."

"You're not going to university," Leo said to Fran.

"And why is that, young man?" Francesca smiled.

"Because I said so. You need to stay here. I don't like my family leaving. I said no!" Leo was upset.

"I'll always come home, everyone," she told me.

"Promise?" he asked. Fran nodded.

Rae asked her usual. Ice cream. Mack got it. "Daddy!"

"You and your bloody sprinkles." He laughed.

"Can't have ice cream without sprinkles. It's the law!" She laughed. She looked at me. "How do you put with him? He's hard work."

"Tell me about it. He's a nightmare. Always has been. Do you think I need a medal?" I asked her.

"Damn right you do. Pain in the bum." She laughed.

"Really! I thought I was the favourite?" Mack asked.

"Not by a long shot," she said between mouthfuls of ice cream. "But you make good burgers." I burst out laughing.

"Fran, you got a letter!" Callum shouted.

She was confused. It was from an art contest. "Who entered me into a contest?" She read the letter. "Oh my God!"

"What!" I asked. I read the letter. She had won first place. It was going on display at the Tate with other winners from other counties. It was the painting like Degras. Ballerina.

"Who did that?" She was confused.

"It was me!" Olivia said. "You are so talented. A day out to an art gallery." Fran ran to her and flung her arms around her.

"Thanks so much. Dad, I need a new outfit, shoes. Please!" She gave me her doe-eyed look. "OK, OK." She jumped up and down. "I'm wearing my tiara."

I took her shopping with Olivia.

"Can I see?" I asked.

"Not until the day," Olivia said to me. "I'll give you a clue. She looks beautiful."

We got ready. "Close your eyes, you two!" Olivia told us. Fran came down. "Open! What do you think?" she asked us.

"You look like Natalie Wood," Mack said.

"Who's that?" Fran asked. We couldn't believe it. She had this beautiful long ruby red dress on. She looked older than sixteen. "My princess. Bloody hell."

"Come on. Let's go," I said. I took Francesca's arm around my elbow. "We're going in style."

They was a beautiful car outside. "Daddy, it's beautiful. Look, Olivia."

Mack and I were chuffed. Taking our girls out for an evening.

"Daddies, you both look handsome," Olivia said.

"This place is amazing," Olivia said looking around. She took Francesca's hand. "Dad, can we look around? We won't go far."

I nodded. "There's her painting."

"Bloody hell. She's so good," Mack said.

"Yes, she is. Miss Denton is very talented," the man said. "You know Miss Denton?"

We smiled. "Yes," I said. "She's our daughter. Who are you?"

He looked surprised. "She's good. I'm Dr Andrews, the curator here. It's nice to see young artists trying. We run a scholarship to help kids get into university."

Just then, the girls came over. He looked at Francesca. She looked nervous.

"It's OK. This is Dr Andrews. He's the curator here. He likes your painting."

"You look like Natalie wood," he told Fran.

"I don't who that is," Fran replied. "It's good here. Thanks for liking my painting. I want to go to Oxford."

"Here's my card. I know the head there. I can put in a word. Nice to meet you." Off he went.

Mack was on the phone. "Don't worry. I'm just checking. Old habits."

"Can we get some dinner soon? I'm hungry," Olivia said. "Sorry, Fran. This is your night." She smiled.

Fran leaned on me. "I can't believe I won. Do you like it?"

"No. I love it. You have a good eye for this. I'm proud of you. So proud of you." I had a tear.

"Daddy, don't cry. No tears. Daddy, what do you think?" she asked Mack.

"It's amazing. Stunning. My princess." He took her hand. "Who's up for dinner?" We nodded. We took them to a fancy old-world French restaurant we knew they would like.

"Table for four. Denton," Mack said. "Come on."

Olivia and Francesca looked at each other. "You two are naughty," Olivia told them.

"It's lovely though. You spoil us," Fran said.

We smiled. "Listen, we will spoil you from time to time. So, behave." Mack smiled. The waiter came over to us. He took our orders and left.

"Dad, it's expensive in here," Fran said. "I'd be happy with a pizza like Leo."

Mack looked at me and nodded. He saw some roses. The waiter came over and Mack asked for two roses for his daughters. "Here, for you two."

"Daddy. Thank you," they said. Fran had a tear.

"After…" she started.

"Stop. All forgotten," I told her. She nodded.

"This food is amazing. Oh my god!" Olivia said. "I love it here. It's very cosy. Can I have that coffee? Smells lovely."

When we got ready to leave, we put our jackets round them. They looked so little. When we got in the car, they fell asleep on us.

"Girls, we're home. Come on," I told them. They took each other's hand.

"Daddy, Thank you for a lovely evening. Olivia, Thank you for entering me. Thanks, sis. Love you."

Olivia told her, "I'm glad I did it. To see that smile was all worth it. Fancy a drink and a chat before bed?" She nodded.

Off they went. Bella and Callum were up.

"Good night?" Callum asked.

"Yes, it was," Mack said. "You been OK?"

"Yes. Granddad let us watch 'Lord of the Rings'. It was good," Bella replied. I handed her a rose. We got one for her and Rae. Her face lit up. "Thank You. It's pretty. I'll put it in water."

Callum smiled. "That made her day. Hey, why don't you take her and Rae out one day?"

"Good idea. How's my boy?" Mack asked.

"Cool. Got a school trip next month. Science Museum. Sounds interesting. Hey, they're asking for volunteers to help out. Fancy coming along?" he asked Mack and me. We said yes.

"Bella, you coming for a chat and drink?" Fran asked her. She went with them.

"That's sweet," Callum said. "It's nice, how we all get along. Fran's picture was brilliant. If she doesn't get in to university..." He leaned on my shoulder. "Thanks for everything you do for us, Dad. I don't say it often enough. I'm glad I've got this life. I'm glad you gave up work. I missed you when you were at work."

"You're more than welcome, son. You know when you were little, you were so curious. Always looking around. You love books with animals in them. You're a kind soul, Callum. What you did for Bella, that was the right thing to do," I told him.

"You and Dad taught us to always do the right thing, no matter how tough the problem is. I couldn't sit by and watch that happen to another human being. That was wrong. Bella has a kind heart, always helping others." He wiped his tears away. "I'd never forgive myself if I didn't do anything. I'm glad she's my sister. You know I'd do it again."

"Thanks is not enough for what you did for me," Bella told him. "But you gave me a second chance. And a family that wants me."

Mack burst out crying.

"Are you hormonal again?" Callum asked him.

"My God, Mack." I looked at them. "You know I swear he was a bloody woman in a former life. Oh, shut up, pull yourself together."

They laughed. "Idiot," I told him.

We took Callum to the science museum with the school. There were other volunteers there. "This is cool," Mack said. "Wish I came here when I was a kid."

Callum and I smiled. When the teacher was asking questions, Callum knew the answers. We were impressed. So was the teacher.

On the way home, Mack fell asleep. Snoring. "Dad!" Callum said.

"What!" he said.

"You're snoring. Embarrassing sod," Callum told him. The teacher smiled. So did I. "Don't you nod off again," Callum said.

"You are aware I'm the parent. If I want to nod off, I'll nod off. You hearing this, Mike?" Mack looked at me. I just laughed. "Fat lot of good you are." Then Mack smiled.

"Are you and your family always like this?" the teacher asked me.

"Yes, we are. Mack and I wanted it like that," I told him.

"He's a good kid. Very respectful," he told me. I turned round to see them arguing over Spider-Man. "Sometimes I do wonder who's the bigger kid. Pack it in, you two. I want a divorce."

"Can't have one. Told you that years ago. Tough," he told me. Some of the kids were laughing. Callum shook his head.

As we got off the coach, a kid in Callum's class said, "Your dads are really cool." Callum smiled.

"See, I'm cool." Mack looked smug. "I enjoyed that, son. Sorry if I embarrassed you."

"No, you didn't. Not by a long shot," Callum said to us.

That made us happy. "Come on. Let's get dinner."

We got home. It was quiet. "I don't like it when it's quiet," I said.

"Hey, good day out?" Leo asked.

"What's going on?" I asked.

"Grandad is in the den, telling us stories of when he was growing up, it's interesting," Leo said. We walked in.

"Ah, you're here. I've been telling them stories of when I was a wee lad in Scotland. I was a bit of a rogue." The kids were really interested.

"Where were you born?" Bella asked him.

"I was born in Edinburgh. The capitol. It was so different."

Mack's phone rang. It was Jacob. "Calm down. Shit. Jacob, I'm on my way."

"What's going on?" I asked. Mack told me that Niamh, Jacob's wife, was rushed to the hospital. She tried to hurt herself. "Don't tell Rae. Jacob doesn't want her to know. Not yet. See you in a bit." He kissed me.

A couple of hours later, Mack came home with Jacob. Thankfully, the kids were in bed. I hugged Jacob. He was crying.

"You're staying here. Family sticks together."

"I knew she was hurting. She stopped seeing the counsellor. She became more irate. They've sectioned her."

"Why didn't you tell us?" Mack asked.

"Felt like a burden," Jacob told him.

"You're not a burden," Rae said.

"Rae!" Jacob said.

Instead of getting upset, she did something unexpected. "Uncle Jacob, she's in the best place. She's needs looking after. You are staying here. You can't be alone. I don't want to see her. It's not because I don't care. I want to remember the way she was. When she gets better, I'll come with you. I know she'll get better. Have faith. Now put that beer down, I'll make a tea. Alcohol at this time. No good."

She put us all to shame. "I'm going to bed. Uncle Jacob. Pray. You're a man of the cloth. God will hear you. Talk to him. Daddy, look after your brother." She told Mack. He nodded.

"You should be proud of her," Jacob told us. "I'm glad I'm here. Thank you. It means a lot to me."

"You're my brother. Family sticks together," Mack said.

There was a knock at the door. It was Matthew. He hugged Jacob. "Sorry, brother. How is she?" Not good was the answer.

"Tea? Where's the beer?" He was confused. I explained that Rae told us off for drinking at a time like this. It wouldn't do us any good. "Remind me never to get on the bad side of the Denton girls."

We had to laugh. "It's true. Jacob. We're here for you. Niamh's family too. We got her back. Anything you need we're here," he said.

We had a laugh and a joke. We stopped in our tracks when the girls stood at the stairs. All five of them. "Really. Do you have to be so loud? Keep the noise down," Olivia said. We gave them a look.

"Don't look at us like that!" Francesca said. "You're the adults. You should know better."

"Bed. Now. All of you. Matthew, home, before Anna calls," Bella said.

"Do we have to?" Mack asked.

"Really. You need sleep. Besides, you have to take Jacob to see Niamh. God, do us girls have to think of everything?" Rae said.

Chloe said, "Naughty. Bed, now! Move!"

"Are you going to stand there until we move?" I said.

"If it takes all bloody night. Move!" Olivia said.

We were up, quick sharp.

"Excuse me. Cups. Dishwasher," Bella said. Matthew was about to say something. He thought better of it. They stood there with their arms folded.

"Come on. Bed. Move," Fran said. "No arguing." We didn't argue.

"Night, Daddy. Love you, Daddy," Rae said.

The next morning, we woke to the smell of cooking. "You're late. Sit, eat," Olivia told us.

345

The girls were busy. "You don't mind missing family day?" I asked.

"It's for two hours. Jacob needs to be with Niamh. Dad, we don't mind. Honest," Bella told us.

"You kids are amazing. Thank you," Jacob said.

"Dad, don't forget to bring the deli I like and pick up some of apple pies Ollie loves," Fran said. Jacob smiled.

"What?" I said.

"They do you proud. We need to go," Jacob said.

Rae hugged him. "Tell Auntie Niamh, we're not going anywhere. We're here for her. Tell her I love her." Jacob had a tear in his eye. He couldn't talk.

It was a hard morning for him. She was diagnosed with schizophrenia. She had to go to a hospital. He cried. While they were saying goodbye, Jacob said, "Niamh. Hey, you remember Rae?" There was a spark in her eye. She knew. "She says she loves you and she misses you."

"Tell her, she's a good girl. See you soon." Off she went.

Not a word was said. What could you say. We got the apple pie for Oliver.

"Hey," Jacob said. "I want to get this for the kids. If know they would love this." It was the game Twister. They loved it. It made them laugh.

When we got home, Bella smiled. "Don't go in the den."

"Why?" I asked.

"Fran is nearly finished doing something. So please wait. Uncle Jacob. How are you!"

He nodded.

Fran came in. "Good. You're here. Don't move," she told Jacob.

She came in with a picture for him. He looked at it. It was him and Niamh. He cried. "Uncle Jacob. I'm so sorry. I didn't think."

"It's OK, Fran. This is beautiful. Thank you. Your Aunt Niamh is beautiful. I'll always love her."

"Princess. That's a lovely thing you did." Mack put his arm around her shoulder.

She looked at him. "He's family, Daddy. He needs us. So does Auntie Niamh."

Lydia and the family came in. Lydia went to Jacob. "Jacob." She hugged him. "How is she?"

Jacob told her. She gasped. Joel was crying, so were the kids. Emily walked to Jacob.

She said something so wonderful. "Uncle Jacob. She may have schizophrenia, but she's my auntie, I love her just the way she is. She's family. We will always be here. Now enough of being sad. Let's get rid of these cobwebs and go for a walk."

We smiled and did as we were told.

"Just what I needed. Thanks, Emily."

"You're welcome."

"Oh no," Mack said.

"What!" Jacob said.

"Watch this," Oliver said to Jacob. "This is classic."

"Daddy, ice cream, please!" Bella asked Mack.

"Not before dinner," Mack said. He knew what was coming.

"Watch!" Oliver was smiling.

"Please!" Rae said. The girls all looked at Mack. They gave him the doe-eyed look. Rae's bottom lip went.

"Mike, for God's sake help me. Please. This is kryptonite."

"You're on your own." I laughed. So did everyone.

"Shit! What's wrong with me?" he said. "Come on. You girls drive me crazy."

"We always win, though," Olivia said, smiling.

"They're good." Jacob laughed. He looked at Mack.

"Shut up!" Mack told Jacob.

"You know you and Michael are damn good parents. Give yourself a pat on the back," he said.

Then out of nowhere, all the kids started singing 'Happy' at the top of their lungs. Everyone looked and smiled. Jacob got choked up.

"It's going to be OK," Joel told him. "Brother, keep the faith."

It wasn't OK. A month later, Jacob got the call no one wanted. Niamh took her own life.

"No! No! Why! God, no!" he screamed. All we could do was be there. Malek and Matthew stayed with him.

When we walked in, Mack grabbed hold of me and cried. "Not fair. My sister-in-law. Mike, if anything happened to you…"

"Hey. I feel the same." We stood there, just holding each other. This had made us stronger. The kids were there in bits.

"Come here, kids," I said. We hugged them. They were all crying.

"Daddy, how's Uncle Jacob?" Bella asked.

"Not good, baby," I told her. "Not good. Uncle Matthew and Granddad Malek are with him."

"Poor man," Thaddeus said. "Is Auntie Niamh at peace now?"

"I hope so, son. I really do," I said.

Mack was crying really hard.

"Excuse me." He got up and walked to the den. We could hear him.

"Oh Daddy," Fran went to him. He was on the couch. She took his hand. "You were there for me. I'm here for you."

The funeral came around. It was a beautiful service. Bush's family was there. When it came to the eulogy, Jacob couldn't talk. It was hard. Before we knew it, Rae went to him and he sat with his dad. What she said was amazing, beautiful. If was off the cuff. We were so proud of her.

"Our beautiful Auntie Niamh was a beautiful and kind soul, who lit up a room without even trying. She was a good daughter, sister, wife and an aunt and a friend. We were lucky to have her for the shortest time. But she's at peace. Jacob, we are sorry. She will always be here in our hearts and minds." Tears poured down her face, but she held her own. She sat with us.

Mack kissed her head. "I'm so proud of you. Beautiful."

The wake was at ours. Jacob walked up to Rae. He hugged her tight. "What you said up there, perfect. You are a credit to your dads. Thank you."

Even Niamh's family thanked her. "Your daughter is a credit to you both," Niamh's mother said.

After everyone left, Mack went to Jacob. "Stay?" Mack asked.

"My parents are staying with me for a few days. But thanks. Thanks for everything, brother." Jacob hugged Mack and me.

Lydia, Joel and the kids were clearing up. It was very quiet.

"Mum," Emily said. "Why do some people take their own lives? I'm not being horrible. Poor Aunt Niamh."

"I know you're not. I don't know why, baby. She must have been in so much pain. It must have felt like the only way out. Yes, poor Aunt Niamh. What we have to remind ourselves is that now she's in heaven. I believe the pain has gone. She's free."

"I'll miss her very much, Mum. It must have been hard for her to go through that," Emily said. She hugged Lydia, crying. "She was a lovely aunt. She had a funny laugh. I'm glad I knew her."

"So am I, Emily," Lydia told her. We were all crying again.

"Why does it hurt so much?" Jack asked Joel.

"Because we are not going to see her any more. That person that was here for a long time is no longer with us," Joel told him.

"Will the pain go away?" Jack asked him.

"In time, son." Joel wiped his eyes.

We spent the evening together as a family. Mack held my hand. I looked at him. "I love you, more than ever."

"I love you, more than ever. Always. I'm glad we have each other," he told me.

A few weeks later, we held a memorial for Niamh. We went to the lakes. We let lanterns go and said a prayer and went and had lunch.

"Thanks for everything," Jacob told us, sipping his pint.

"No problem," Matthew said. "Family sticks together on everything."

"I agree," I told him. "This is what we do. Whilst we're here," I paused. I looked at Mack. "Mack, I know we've done this a lot over the years, but with everything that's gone on…" I took his hand with the wedding band on. "I want to renew my vows again."

"Yes," he said.

"So are we!" Lydia said. We looked at Jacob. "My honour."

There it was. In a time of sadness, came happiness.

"Party time!" Leo said. We all laughed.

It was done. The following month, we celebrated love.

Fran came up to us. "Daddy. I have a present for you both. You two have stood by me through my toughest times. You never let me go. This is my thank-you."

We followed her to the den. There was this amazing picture of Mack and me.

"Fran," I said. "This is amazing."

Mack couldn't talk.

"Daddy! Don't you like it?"

"Princess. It's the most wonderful gift ever. This is beautiful. Just like you." Mack loved the picture. He hugged her.

"Careful, Daddy, my tiara." She smiled.

The few weeks went by. Jacob came over. He was struggling a little. "I hate being in the house on my own. It's tough," he said over coffee. He looked at me. "Really! Where's the beer?"

"If Rae walks in, sees us, we're in trouble. So, coffee it'll be," I told him.

Jacob smiled. "I'll never forget the eulogy she gave. That was beautiful. I'm thinking of selling and buying something smaller. What do you think?" he asked, sipping his drink.

"Might be an idea," Mack said, eating a chocolate biscuit.

"Do you ever stop eating?" Jacob asked Mack. "In all the years I've known you. You are a pig."

"No, I'm not," he said. Oliver walked in and started eating. Jacob and I looked at them.

"What!" they said together.

Jacob and I laughed. "Like father, like son," Jacob said.

"You want to stay for dinner?" Oliver asked Jacob. Jacob looked at us. We nodded.

"OK, I'll stay."

"Dad, can I help you?" Oliver asked Mack.

"Come on then. Peel the spuds and carrots," Mack told him.

Jacob and I sat on the sofa. "Those two are so alike," Jacob told me.

"Yes, I know. They are two peas in a pod," I replied.

"I'm like you too, Dad. You taught me that first aid stuff and basically taught me to be a decent human being." He kissed my head. I smiled. I went to put my feet on the table.

Bella looked at me. "Really. It's not a good stool." I didn't do it.

"I'd rather be in Afghanistan than argue with your daughters," Jacob told me.

"I feel the same sometimes," Mack told us.

"That's nice," Bella said. "How rude! When's dinner?"

"An hour." Mack looked nervous.

"Love you, Daddy." She smiled.

"I feel sorry for the blokes that marry my sisters." Oliver laughed.

"They're never getting married. Ever!" Mack said, not realising Olivia was standing behind him.

"Since when do you make that decision? When I get married, it's going to be the most expensive wedding ever. By God, you're going to pay," she told him.

"Man, those girls are tough. You should be proud," Jacob told us.

Mack smiled. Oliver said, "Yes, Dad, give yourself a pat on the back. Uncle Jacob, want another coffee?"

He nodded. "How come you kids still call me Uncle Jacob?" he asked.

"You're family. You're the closest person Dad has to a brother," Oliver said, peeling the carrots.

That made him smile.

"Right. Dinner. Come on," Mack half yelled.

After dinner, the kids cleared up and went to the den to let us talk. Chloe started crying. She was tired.

"Stay there, Dad. I got this," Fran said. "Come on, miss. Say night." She was already dozing off.

"Daddy, is Jacob going to be OK?" Rae asked Mack after Jacob left.

"He will be, Angel girl. You worry too much, darling," he told her.

"I know. I just don't like seeing anyone in pain." She curled up to him. "I don't know what I'll do if I lost you and Daddy and my brothers and sisters. I have such a happy home. It makes you realise how lucky we are," Rae told him.

"It does, indeed. If you had one wish, what would you wish for?" Mack asked her.

"For the world to be happy. That was easy. Daddy, can you and I spend the day together? I'm always with Daddy. We don't spend a lot of time together. Please! Daddy won't mind, will he?" she asked him.

"I'm sure he won't mind. You really want to spend the day with me?" He was surprised, as she was always with me.

"Yes, I do. I want to go to the lanes, that oldie shop I love, then the tea house. I miss you, Dad," Rae told him.

"OK, Angel girl. You and me. Tomorrow. It's half term. I miss you too," he told her.

They had a lovely day. "Daddy, that was fun. Just us. It meant a lot to me to spend the day with you," she told him.

I smiled. It was nice to see them enjoying the day. She looked at me. "Daddy, you don't mind, do you?"

"No, sweetie. I don't. It is nice to see you having a good day. Don't forget, we've got to take George and Rose to the vets. George isn't looking too good," I told her.

"I know. He is old. I don't want lose him." She looked sad.

"I'll come as well," Mack told her. She liked that.

I was right. George wasn't well. We had to put him down. She was heartbroken. "My poor George. Did I make him ill?"

"No, you didn't. It was his heart. Rae, he's in heaven with Auntie Niamh. She'll look after him. She always liked George."

That made her feel better.

"Where's George?" Thaddeus asked when we got in. We told him. He went and hugged Rae. "Sorry, Rae. I liked him. Is Rose OK?"

She was fine. Toby looked for him. Rae picked him up. "Sorry, Toby. Your brother has gone to sleep." He purred.

"Rae, cuppa tea and a biscuit?" Thaddeus asked her. She smiled sadly at him.

Matthew and Anna came over. "Hey, what's going on?" Mack asked them.

"Yes. We wanted to talk to you first. We're planning our anniversary party. Twenty-five years," Matthew said.

"Poor me. People get out of prison quicker," Anna said.

We laughed. "Really. It hasn't been that bad?" he asked.

"'Course not, dear. The meds haven't helped either. Nor did therapy." She patted his knee. That was funny.

"Anyway," Matthew said, "we want to do something for Jacob too. It's been hard for him. Any ideas?"

Fran came in and suggested putting pictures around of everyone on their wedding day. Lydia walked in. We told her. "That's a good idea. It'll be good to remember the good times." We phoned and told Jacob. He liked the idea as well.

"Good," Fran said. "I'll do it."

"You sure?" I asked her. She nodded.

"We'll help her," Thaddeus told them. Settled.

Then Oliver said to Lydia, "You can make my fave cake, you delightful old woman."

"I'm not old, you little shit!" she told him.

"You're not delightful either, but I still want that cake. Get baking," he told her. We burst out laughing.

When the day came, it was a mixture of happy and sad tears. The photos were beautiful. All in black and white.

"These are wonderful," Anna said. "Good job, kids."

"Jacob. How are you?" Anna asked him, taking his hand.

"Sad and happy. Niamh will always be the love of my life. She's so beautiful." He looked at the photo of their wedding day. Rae looked sad.

"You OK, Angel girl?" Mack asked her.

"I just miss her. I remember she bought my fairy wings, and she used to swing me around, making me laugh. I'll never get rid of them. Chloe can have them," she said.

"We could never get you out of them," Mack said. "You cried when we had to." Jacob cried.

"Sorry," Rae said.

"Don't be," he said. "I know she's better with God. It's sad she's not here."

"Yes, she is," Anna said. "She's family. She's always with us. She was more than a friend to me. She was the sister I never knew. You know that! Even in her saddest days, she was there. I will love her for that. Always will. We're here to celebrate her life. She had you. She had us. God bless that beautiful woman. Now, let's toast to us. Family, friends, life."

We raised our glasses. Matthew hugged her. "There's a reason why I married you," he said to her.

Lydia made Oliver's fave cake. He hugged her. "Thanks, Lid-lid." She smiled.

Maggie and Alice asked Jacob if they were happy.

"Yes. Yes, we were. When you meet someone that changes you for the better, never let them go. It's the best love ever."

Lydia and Joel, Matthew and Anna and Mack and I looked at each other.

We talked, laughed, cried. We were cheered up by Chloe running in with Rae's fairy wings and her ballerina outfit.

"I'm a fairy ballerina. Don't I look fantastic?" When we laughed, she said, "Not funny. I am fantastic." She got upset.

I scooped her up. "Little bear. You are beautiful and fantastic. Would you like a biscuit?"

Her face lit up. "Yes please, Daddy. Where is Rae?" Rae walked in. "Thank you for my wings. They're pretty. You want a biscuit, too?"

"Go on then. You want to watch Ben and Holly?" Rae asked.

"Yes, please." They went off happy.

When everyone left, Mack and I spoke. "You are the love of my life, Mike."

I smiled. "So are you. Don't know what I'll do if I lost you. We have a good marriage. I'll never stop loving you." I grabbed his hand. "Thank you."

We sat there. Hand in hand. Then we heard arguing. Over the remote.

"I want the footie on!" Oliver said.

"No, there's a documentary on," Francesca said.

Mack got up. Did what he does best. He picked the telly up and walked out. "Read a bloody book and shut up," he said. I laughed. So not subtle. For once, they did as they were told.

I checked on them. Fran was reading *Wuthering Heights*. "You love that book."

She smiled. "It's my fave." She had my old jumper on.

Oliver was reading about the war. "This is good, Dad. Sad. But interesting." Mack walked in. "Dad, when you were in the army, did you fight in a war?"

He never spoke about it. "Yes, I did. I was in Afghanistan. With Jacob and Matthew. I did three tours. It was hard. I'm glad I got out. But glad I did it. Taught me a lot. Too much fighting." He looked sad.

"Sorry, Dad," Oliver told him. "I'm glad you came home to us." He leaned on his shoulder.

"So am I, son. Right, who wants ice cream?" he asked.

"Lydia's cake as well," Oliver said. "I'll help. Dad, I'm proud of you for fighting for us. I'm proud of that. That means a lot to us." He then said something that made Mack proud. "Dad, you're my hero for doing that. I'm proud to be your son."

"That means a lot, son. It really does." Mack held him close.

Mack brought the TV back.

"Can we talk instead?" Francesca asked.

"What do you want to talk about?" I asked.

"How you two met?" she asked. I told her the story.

"Really. You've been together since your first date? Wow. That's amazing. You've never been apart?" She was interested.

"Apart from the odd job I've done, no," Mack told them.

"Wow. You two are really devoted to each other, aren't you?" Oliver asked. We nodded.

"I hope I find someone like this when I get married," Fran said.

"Told you before, you're never getting married," Mack told her.

"Shut up. I'm going to make you a granddad," she told him.

We smiled. "Dad, cake, ice cream. Empty hands," Olivier said.

Fran shook her head. "Dad," she said. "You know I don't consider myself as adopted any more. You are my real dad. Always will be. So is Dad. Thank you."

I was about to say something when we looked at Oliver and Mack eating and farting.

"This is good cake," Oliver said, eating.

"I know. Bloody brilliant," Mack said.

We looked at each other. "I wonder about them," she said.

"So do I, princess. So do I," I said.

They looked at us and in unison said. "What!" We smiled and left them to it.

"Dad, hurry up!" Callum shouted. "'Harry Potter' is on in a minute."

Thaddeus smiled. "What's that for?" I asked.

"This. All of us. Movie night, can't beat it. You forgot the pop—" He didn't finish his sentence when Mack gave him a bowl of his favourite popcorn.

"Thanks, Dad," Thaddeus told him.

"Can we watch another one? Please!" Thaddeus asked me.

I looked at Mack. He nodded. "Go on then."

"You really enjoy movie night, don't you, Thaddeus?" I asked him.

"Yes. I get to watch movies I like and be with the people I like. My family. Family is important," Thaddeus told us. He looked at me.

"Son, what is it?" I was concerned.

"Nothing. I'm just happy that we're together. We should count ourselves lucky," he told us. "Thanks for this and for being my dads."

"You're welcome, son," Mack told him. "More popcorn."

"Thought you'd never ask." He smiled and gave Mack his bowl.

Thaddeus looked at Rae tucked under my arm. As usual, she was snoring away.

"She's the sweetest sister ever. She makes me laugh. I have lovely brothers and sisters." He shed a tear.

"I'm glad you're happy, son. That's all we want for our kids. To be happy," I told him.

"You have. Can we go bowling next weekend? I want to kick Dad's arse again. That was funny," Thaddeus asked.

"You bet. I want to see that too." Thaddeus looked at Mack, who was asleep with a breadstick up his nose.

"You kids torture him. But it's funny," I laughed.

Joel came round with Jack.

"Hey, you two. What's up?" Mack asked.

"I need your opinion, Mack," Jack asked. He had his guitar. "Can I play this for you?" I stood next to him.

"Go for it!" I said.

He sang 'We'll Make It Through' By Ray LaMontagne. My fave song. I cried.

"Jack, that was amazing," Mack said. "Your know that's Mike's favourite song. It was playing the night I cooked for him. Our first date."

"Really? There's a contest at school," he said.

"Go for it. If you don't win. I'll punch them in the bullocks," I said. "You are so talented. Really. That song means a lot to me. As Mack said, it was playing the night he cooked. To me, it's our song." I was choked up.

"Want to stay for a drink?" Mack asked. They stayed.

"When's the contest?" I asked. A week from Friday.

"We'll be there. All of us. Then out for dinner," Mack said.

"Thanks. I'm glad I'm singing that song," Jack said.

The night of the contest came. Jack came on, with a band behind him. "This is for my two uncles, Mack and Mike."

He sang it beautifully. Lydia cried her eyes out. So did Joel.

"Proud of you, son. So proud," Lydia and Joel said. Jack won the contest.

We took them for dinner. "That was amazing, Jack," Mack told him. I was quiet.

"That was the most amazing thing ever. To get up and sing so gracefully. That meant a lot, to us. Thanks, Jack," I told him.

"Well, I do have the coolest uncles," he told us.

Mack looked smug. "I'm the coolest," he said smugly

"Oh, shut up. I married a twat!" I said. Jack laughed.

"But Jack said I'm cool," Mack said, smiling.

"Jack, for over twenty years, I've had to put up with him. But I love him very much," I said. Mack smiled.

We dropped them off home.

"How did it go?" Leo asked. We told him. "I knew he could do it. He's smart."

"Just like you," I told him. "How did you get on with your maths test?"

"Promise you won't get angry?" he asked. I nodded.

"Got you! Ha! I passed. All correct. It was so easy. Harvey could do it." I looked at the question. They looked hard and he was ten.

I showed Mack. He looked as confused as I did. We gave him some really hard maths questions from one of Olivia's old textbook. It was for a sixteen-year-old. He worked it out.

"That was easy," he told us. We checked. We were confused.

I phoned his teacher and told him.

"I agree with you. He's very good at this. Look, I'll put in a call to someone I know about getting a proper maths exam and see his standard."

Which he did.

"Am I in trouble?" Leo asked.

We told him what was going on. He sat down and took the tests.

"How was that?" Mack asked.

"A little bit easy and hard," Leo said.

We waited a couple of days. We got a call to say that Leo was a maths genius. We weren't surprised.

"Our son is a genius," Mack smiled. "I'm proud of him," I replied. Leo came in.

"You two OK?" he asked. We told him we were.

"How do feel about the test?" Mack asked him.

"OK. Don't feel any different. I've always liked numbers. Can I have a drink, please?" he asked. I smiled and got him a drink.

"Where's that giggling coming from?" Leo asked.

We went to the den. The girls were laughing and joking.

"What's so funny?" Mack smiled.

They told us they thought boys were silly.

"So, no boyfriends to worry about then?" Mack asked them.

"Dad! No," Francesca told him.

"Thank God," Mack whispered.

They saw this. "But you need to get used to the fact that we will, Dad.

One day, we'll get married," Rae told him.

"I know. I just want you lot to be safe," he said.

"We will. Don't worry, Dad. We're good at judging who's right. You taught us that," Olivia said. He smiled.

"Rae, shall we all go to your fave tea place for afternoon tea?" I asked. She smiled. She looked at everyone. They nodded yes.

"Tiara!" Francesca shouted. We laughed. Mack was quiet. Olivia could read him like a book. "You know, Dad, no one will ever replace you, don't you?"

"Yes, I know. As a dad, it's hard seeing your kids growing up and being independent," he told her.

Rae made us laugh. "We won't replace you. But if it was a contest between you and this teacake, the cake will win. I'll never get bored of a teacake and tea. Love you, Dad."

I looked at him and smiled. Chloe got out of her pushchair, got on Mack's shoulder and smiled. Then she had her nap. Right there on his shoulder.

"See!" Thaddeus said to Mack. "Soppy sod."

The lady came over. "You never get bored of that teacake, do you?" She smiled. Rae shook her head no. "How would you like a job here?" She looked at us. "Two hours. Once a week. I can teach you how to make those teacakes."

"Daddy, please. It's two hours. Please!" she pleaded. I looked at mack. He nodded and smiled. "OK. Two hours. Mondays OK?" They both agreed.

On the way home, Fran looked at me. "She's going to be OK, you know. It'll be good for her. That and looking after Rocket. It's what she needs. Don't worry, she'll still be daddy's girl."

Fran was right. It was what she needed. She came home with a box of teacakes. "Wow. Lizzie gave them to you?" Leo asked her.

"No. I made them. You can have one after dinner, not before." She smiled. "OK, bossy boots," Leo sounded disappointed.

"Rae, these are well good. Bloody delicious," Mack told her.

"Here. Try this. I made this too." It was homemade Apricot jam. Her favourite.

"OMG. Rae. You can really bake," Thaddeus said. "I love the jam."

She looked at me. "I love them."

"You haven't touched them." She walked off. Mack nodded to me.

"Rae, I'm sorry."

"You're finding it hard, me growing up?" she asked me. I nodded.

"I'm afraid of this, but you have to accept it." I was worried. She hugged me and gave me her soppy look.

"I'll always be a daddy's girl. Now eat your bloody teacake," she told me. "Oliver, put that down. You've had two. They're Daddy's." His face fell. Mack laughed. "Daddy, wipe your beard, you've got jam on it. You look like a tramp. My God! Tea, Daddy?"

I hugged her tight. "Don't grow up, please."

"I have to, Daddy. I don't want to, either, but I'll always have you," she told me. "Oliver, put it down. Don't make me come over there."

"Damn it. She's good." Oliver had the hump.

"That's my girl," I told her, smiling.

I sat next to Mack. "She's growing up differently. She's still the same. Changing the subject, what do you want to do for date night, on Thursday?"

"How about that fancy French restaurant we took Olivia and Francesca to? I love it there. If we book an early time, we can catch a movie," I told him. He agreed.

"Mack, come on. We're going to be late!" I shouted to him to get a move on.

"All right, all right. I'm coming," he told me. "What do you think!" He had a new suit on. A sleek black suit.

"Wow! You look good." I smiled.

"You don't look bad yourself." He kissed me. "I look forward to this. You and me."

Dad was here to keep an eye on the kids. "You two look sharp."

We had a good night. We talked, laughed. "Remember when we did this every Friday?" Mack asked me.

"Yes, I do. Brings back a lot of good memories. Funny how our lives changed for the better. Kids, marriage," I told him.

"Wouldn't change anything. Worked out just liked I hoped. You make me happy," he said, scratching his beard. "Come on. Fancy a walk instead of the movie?"

"I like that," I told him. We walked hand-in-hand, talking about everything, like we used to. I mean, really talked.

"Promise well never stop talking?" Mack asked me. I promised.

We got home to peace. Dad was asleep. "Dad, we're home." He woke up. "Good night?"

"Good as gold. Rae's been a star with Chloe," he told me. "She's either going to be a baker or work with kids. I hope a baker."

"Come on. I'll drive you home," Mack told him.

On the drive home, my dad told him. "You are the best son-in-law. You've made Michael very happy."

"You OK? You're not sick?" Mack was worried.

"No, you silly arse. I'm too stubborn. Scottish through and through. I'm just saying, you've been good for my son. Thanks for my grandchildren. Don't look at me like that. I'm fine. Had a check-up. Fit as a fiddle," my dad told him. He smiled.

"Your dad's a puzzle," Mack said as he walked in. He told me what he said.

"He's always been like that. Man of few words. When he does, we think there's something wrong." I passed him a cuppa.

"Any of those tea cakes Rae made left?" he said.

"Didn't you eat enough when we were out?" I asked.

"I've hidden them, even the pope can't find them," Rae told him.

"It's two in the morning. Why are you up?" Mack asked her.

"Can't sleep," she said. We knew she as fibbing, as she had Mack's rusty-coloured jumper on and she had her comforter.

"Tell the truth!" he said.

"OK." She sat to me, in her usual place.

"Talk to us," I said to her.

"Daddy. What will happen when I do grow up? I don't want to get lost in the world, and for you two to forget about me. And Olivia and the others forget me too. Dad, I'm scared. That's why I want to be at home. I don't want to be forgotten." She was crying.

"Hey. We won't forget you. You're our Angel girl. I know you're scared. We will always be with you. If you want to be here, that's fine by us. We won't make you do anything," he told her.

She looked at me all glassy-eyed.

"Dad's telling the truth. We are always here. You will always be a daddy's girl."

She smiled, pulled her comforter up and fell asleep. We smiled, watching her.

Lydia came round the next morning in her dressing gown and messy hair.

Oliver did his usual. "Oh, lady. Homeless shelter's two streets away. They got soup and directions and a hairdresser," he told her.

"You little shit," she said, smiling.

"Why are you here? It's just gone eight. Dads are still in bed," Oliver said.

"Lazy sods. Get them up. I have news," she said.

We came down to see her there.

"What! You look like a bag lady," I told her. Oliver smiled.

"Jack got invited to play Glastonbury festival with Ray LaMontague. He heard about the song he did. He loved it. He wants him to play a couple of songs with him." We got tickets to the biggest festival. We were gobsmacked.

"Dad, can we go. Please?" Oliver asked.

"Damn right we are," I told him. "I've always wanted to go."

Mack was chuffed to bits. "Tell him, we're proud of him."

So off we went to Glastonbury. We got backstage passes to Ray LaMontague's set. Jack went on and sang his heart out. The audience loved him. He then sang a song for Lydia and Joel. "This song is for my mum and dad. You are the best thing." It was brilliant. The crowd wanted an encore. They did one more. 'Crazy'.

Lydia and Joel hugged him tight. "Proud of you, son," Joel told him.

Lydia couldn't stop crying. "My baby."

"I'm almost seventeen. I'm hungry. Can I have a burger?"

"Come on?" Joel smiled.

We enjoyed the rest of the day. The kids loved it. They thought it was bloody brilliant, according to Maggie.

"Can I have your autograph, Jack?" Thaddeus asked him.

Jack smiled. "Why?"

"When you become famous, I can say that my cousin gave me his first autograph. I'm proud of my Jack," Thaddeus told him.

Jack hugged him tight. "I'm proud of you too, Thaddeus. Come on. You know I look up to you. Why, because you are the kindest person that

I've ever met. I'm glad we're family." He smiled.

"Thank you, Jack." Thaddeus smiled.

Then typical Oliver. He had Chloe. "Oh my God! Dad, she's done the biggest poo ever. It's World War Three in there. Help! I need a lie down."

I laughed at him. "Give her here."

"Your brother is silly." I told her.

On the way home, they were all asleep on the train. All of them together. Lydia's lot too.

"That is the first time they've all shut up at the same time. And fallen asleep. My god. Quiet."

"I think it's sweet that these kids all get along and like each other. Our eldest daughters are best mates," I told her.

Lydia looked at them. "I think that is wonderful. Oh my god. Look at our husbands." They were asleep and snoring like the kids. Lydia smacked their legs. "Will you wake up? Embarrassing sod."

"What! Are we there yet?" Joel said.

"No, we're pissing not. Look at the kids. They're behaved," she said.

"They're asleep," Mack said.

"You're a genius," she said. I laughed.

We woke them up before we got our stop.

"Dad?" Oliver said. "Thanks for a good day. Chloe, come here. Hey, biscuit."

"Ollie. No. She'll go bang," I told her. She looked scared.

"Don't want to go bang, please," she said.

Oliver told her she wouldn't.

"OK, Ollie bear. Biscuit."

He caved in. I shook my head. "Dad! She's cute. Sorry!"

I put Chloe to bed.

"Who wants a teacake?" Rae asked. Mack smiled. "Take that as a yes. Ollie?" He didn't answer. He ran to the loo.

"Ollie?" Mack asked. Oliver wasn't well.

"Dad, I threw up. Bad!" Oliver said, curling up on the sofa. Then Chloe came downstairs and threw up. Mack was gagging.

"Weirdo," Thaddeus told him. "You were in Afghanistan; you can't handle a bit of vomit?"

Chloe went to Oliver. "Little bear and big bear not well."

"Come here, Chloe," Oliver told her. She curled up next to him and

362

they fell asleep. Mack put a blanket over them.

"They'll be OK in a couple of days," I told him. "Something they ate. I'll keep an eye out."

True to form, they were. All they wanted was food.

"Back to normal. Slow down, Ollie."

"OK, Dad," he told me. "Thanks for looking after me."

"I'm your dad. It's my job. Drink some water," which he did.

"Dad." He looked at me. "You're the greatest." He hugged me.

That meant a lot. Mack smiled.

"Don't worry, I'm not going to vomit," Oliver told him. "A tough nut who hates vomit. That's funny. You will always be a giant softie." We smiled at that.

Three days later, we got a call from Francesca's school. She, Bella and Rae were in trouble.

"What happened?" I was annoyed. They all spoke at once.

"Dad, that kid came back that picked on Fran. He started pulling on her arm and calling her names!" Bella said.

"So, Bella punched him in the throat and broke his nose. I smacked him round the head with my French textbook. No one touches my sister," Rae said. Mack smiled.

"Was this on school grounds?" I asked.

"No," the teacher said. "It was across the road."

"Then it's not a school matter. We will deal with this. Girls, car, now," I told them.

"Dad!" they said. They got in the car.

"Good bloody job, girls," I told them.

They were stunned. So was Mack.

"That shit hurt our princess, Mack. The thing you lot should have done, you should have hit him harder. Girls, Friday night, we're taking you out for dinner." They smiled. So did Mack.

"Girls. What you did, protecting your sister. I'm proud of you all," I told them.

"Seriously! You're not mad?" Francesca asked.

"No, I'm not. I'm glad you lot stuck together," I told her.

They smiled. The girls started whispering. "Dad, can we stay in, instead? Have a movie night?" Francesca asked us.

"You sure?" Mack asked. They nodded. We smiled.

When they walked in, the boys were waiting. "He didn't hurt you, did he?" Callum asked her. She shook her head.

We told them what happened. "Good!" Thaddeus told them. "Promise me you're OK?"

Francesca hugged Thaddeus. "I'm OK. I'm going to take a shower."

The girls were waiting for her in the den. "Fran, we're in here. Cuppa tea and a biscuit," Shouted Olivia. "Come here," she said.

She sat with Olivia. "I'm OK, Olivia. Promise."

"Good. If I had been there, I would have ripped his throat out," she said out loud. She cried. "I should have been there."

"Don't worry about it. I feel better now I twated the bastard," Fran told her. They smiled. I let the swearing go on that one.

Then Mack shouted, "Mike, where's my red jumper?" He walked in and saw Fran wearing it. "My God. I'm going shopping. My girls keep nicking my sodding clothes." He smiled.

They laughed. "Dad, what's for dinner?" Francesca asked him.

"Your fave!" he called back. She smiled.

Later that evening, Fran came down and sat with us. "Hey, princess. What's up?" Mack asked.

"Dad, I want to get Bella, Rae and Olivia something for being there for me. Can you help me?" she asked me. He said yes.

"What else? Tell us," I told her. "Sit down."

"When he was being mean and horrible…" She paused. "I nearly, you know. I almost took some pills." She was devastated to tell us.

Mack got up. He was mad as hell. I was upset. Fran got up. Mack looked at her. We hugged her.

"Glad you didn't. So glad."

"Counselling did help."

"Princess." He just stood there with her. "I can't lose you. Ever. You are my life. Please don't ever think about that again."

"Promise. I looked at a family photo of us and I realised I couldn't do it. I felt like an ugly duckling. I'm not, am I?" she asked.

"No, you bloody are not!" Oliver said. "You are my beautiful sister." He was crying. "Please don't leave us, Fran! Please!"

"I won't. I promised."

The rest of them all came in. "Dad, put the kettle on," Olivia said.

"We're going to be OK. We're going to talk, all of us," Which they did. For two hours.

"They're close, aren't they?" Mack smiled.

"Yes, they are. They stick together. I'm proud of them," I told him, handing him his tea.

Then, "Dad, I'm hungry! Dinner. Takeaway. Well help with money!" Oliver said loudly. We laughed and shook our heads.

All night, Leo, Oliver and Callum had a farting match.

"My God, you three are disgusting," Bella told them.

"Can't we have normal brothers?" Rae said.

"What about me?" Thaddeus said.

"You're OK!" Chloe said, eating a chip.

"That bloody stinks!" Francesca shouted. "Stop it!"

We laughed at them. "Don't laugh," Olivia said. "Dirty buggers."

Lydia came over. Her face! "Oliver. Your arse."

"Oh, you crazy old lady. It's not me. Leo and Callum as well. Mad old biddy," he said.

"I'm not old!" she replied.

"No, but you are mad, crazy and a biddy! What do you want? Got no booze." He smiled.

"Well, I was going to invite you all for dinner on Sunday, instead you can sod off. No cake!" She looked at Ollie.

His face! "You cow! How Joel puts up with you, I don't know."

She clipped him round the head.

"He's just like you, Mack. Annoying!" We smiled.

We told her about Fran and what the girls did.

"Good for them! Where is she?" Lydia asked. We called her and the girls.

"Good job, girls, for sticking together. That's what family does. Fran, I'm sorry you felt like that. But you were strong enough not to do it. Proud of all of you. Come here!" They all hugged her. "I can't bloody breathe!"

Oliver went to Lydia. "You know, I don't mean the stuff I say to you."

"I know. You're so like Mack. Very sensitive. Don't worry. I'll make the cake you love," she told him.

Over dinner on Sunday, while we were having dinner. Emily was worried about us.

"Spill, kiddo," I told her. "You know the family rules."

"Why don't you want to find your real parents?" Emily asked the kids.

Olivia smiled. "We" — pointing to Oliver and the rest — "decided that we didn't want to as we are brothers and sisters. And they are our real parents. We don't want to. We're home, Emily." She smiled.

We smiled at that. "It's true," Rae told us, taking our plates. "For a long time I was scared they would find me. But you two are my real parents. We got what we wanted. But Emily, do not go in the bathroom after Dad," she said, pointing to Mack. "You'll need medical attention if you do. Disgusting!"

"Oh. It ain't that bad, missy," he told her.

"Really? I lost vision in my left eye. I had a migraine for three hours," she told him.

"Why do you kids pick on me?" Mack said, sipping his beer.

"Because we don't have anything else to do," Thaddeus said.

"Shit bags," He replied. Then Chloe started saying it.

"Look at what you've done, twat!" I said. Chloe started saying it.

We shook our heads. Then Olivia looked at her. "No, Chloe. No cake."

"OK, Olivia. Please, can I have cake? I'll be good." She gave Olivia a soppy look. She caved in.

"Now you know how we feel." I laughed.

"Go sit with Leo." Chloe did as she was told. Leo smiled and helped her.

"Leo, I want a dolly and a pink bike. I'm a good girl. Please," she begged him.

"Soon." He kissed her head.

The next day, we got her home from nursery. There was a dolly and a pink bike for her. The note said *"You bought our Maggie a bike. Now let us treat Chloe. — Lydia and Joel."*

Chloe was so happy. "My pretty dolly. My pink bike. Look, Daddy. I'm a good girl."

She got on her bike and clapped. After an hour, she started yawning. "Come on. Dinner. Bring your dolly," I told her. She named her princess. After Fran. She was chuffed.

Leo helped with the dishes. "Dad, I'm glad I'm a big brother. She's lovely."

"I'm glad too," I told him. "It's your birthday soon. Can't believe you're going to be eleven. What do you want to do?"

"Easy. As it's family day. I want to go the lakes and then have fish and chips for tea. Then 'ET' for movie night." He smiled.

"Is that all?" I asked.

"Yes. I've got what I want. A little sister. That's all I wanted. Oh, I do need new shoes and trousers though."

I hugged him. "You know, you're so much like the rest. Thinking of others."

"Learned from the best, Dad," he told me.

The next weeks went by quickly. We took Dad out for his birthday. "I'm getting old," he said.

"How old are you, Grandad!" Francesca said.

"Seventy-five." he replied.

Leo's face. "God, that's so ancient. How are you still walking?"

Oliver burst out laughing. "God, I nearly said that. Good job, Leo. Don't look at me like that. It's true."

Dad couldn't help but smile. Malek was asleep in the chair as usual. "That man's snoring could bring a house down!" my dad told us. "Malek! Wake up!"

"I was resting my eyes," he started mumbling something in Arabic.

"Pardon. What was that?" my dad said.

The kids looked at my dad. "You're worse than these two! You sure you're not gay?" Bella asked him. Mack laughed.

"You kids are something else. God, Oliver, what is wrong with your arse?" Dad asked him.

"It's called a fart. Have you heard of them? I said, have you heard of them! Deaf old man," Oliver said.

Malek laughed. So did Mack and I.

"You're so much like that one!" he said, pointing to Mack.

"At least it ain't me for a change!" Mack said.

"Give it twenty minutes," Thaddeus said.

Thaddeus got up and walked to the cupboard. He pulled out a nicely wrapped present for my dad. "Open it."

It was a photo of those two when he was a baby. My dad was chuffed. "Pop, pop," he had called my Dad that as a kid. "You are a good man. I'm glad you're my pop, pop." He hugged him.

Olivia looked sad all night. She was in the den, in my blue jumper and joggers. "What's wrong?" We asked her.

"Nothing," she replied.

Mack looked at her. "You're not pregnant, are you?"

"Oh, yes. I'm having triplets. I'm calling them you bloody idiot." I laughed. "I'm just tired. Told you before, I am not ready for all that. But, how did you know? That you were ready for that stuff?" she asked us.

"Are we really having this conversation?" Mack looked uncomfortable.

"Mack, come on. We just did, sweetheart. Don't rush into anything. If it's not right, it's not right," I told her. I looked at Mack.

"I'm not ready for this." He walked away.

Olivia looked at me. "This is hard for him. Us growing up. Can't fault him for that," she said.

"It's hard for both of us. You know, a parent is never ready for any conversation that is difficult. Mack, get your arse in here," I shouted at him.

He came back in the room. "Dad, I'm sorry," she said.

"I know. I don't want you growing up," he said.

"I'm twenty-one. Not four. But don't worry. I'm not rushing into anything. Not for a long time. Now, can I have a cuppa and a biscuit, please?" she smiled.

"Not a bloody problem," Mack told her.

"Dad" she said to him. "I'll always be your little girl."

"I know. What is that? Can you smell cake?" Mack went to the kitchen. Rae and Bella were making a large vanilla and chocolate sponge cake.

"What?" Rae said. "I wanted to make a cake. Bella wanted to help. That OK? It's nearly done."

"Fine by me. That looks good." Mack smiled.

Then Oliver shouted, "Who's making cake? Is Lydia here?"

He ran downstairs, saw Rae and Bella. "Can I lick the bowl when you're finished?"

"Oh my God. You're eighteen, not five. Grow up," Bella told him.

"Please! Lydia lets me. Please!" he begged.

"You're not to stop until we let you, are you?" Rae asked him.

"Let him," Mack said. "It'll keep him quiet."

"Why didn't I think of that?" Rae said.

True to form. It did. For ten minutes. "That's good. You two should open a cake shop, Rae. You're really good. I mean that." Rae smiled.

"I could help you both," Mack told them.

"It's OK. We wanted to do it. Besides, Ollie was quiet for ten minutes," Bella said.

"Heard that!" Oliver said. "I like baking, Dad. It's like you with cooking," Rae said. He smiled.

After dinner, they had Rae and Bella's cake. "My God, this is lovely," Thaddeus said.

"You two have done a good job," I told him. Then we heard screaming. It was Francesca. She had a letter in her hand.

"What is it?" I said. She showed me a letter. It was a conditional letter to Cambridge. "I thought you wanted to go to Oxford?" I asked her.

"Their art history programme is better. Besides, I want to be near Olivia and Oliver. I've been predicted four A*in my A levels," she replied.

Mack was over the moon. So was I.

"Save me some cake, Ollie."

"Ah, man!" he whined. Olivia was so happy. "Can't wait. Fran, you're going to love it there. Promise. I'll look after you." She hugged her.

"That's why I want to go!" She smiled.

Chloe came bouncing in with her dolly. "Princess!" She ran to Fran. "Playing hide and seek with Leo. Hide me!" She put her hands over her face.

Leo came in. "Where is she? I can't find my little bear. Uh, there she is. Hiding with Francesca." He tickled her.

She giggled, loudly. "Funny Leo. Please read me my story. Please. Biscuit and milk. Just one."

Leo looked at me. "Just one. Go on." Leo smiled. He loved his little sister.

There they were. Happy, reading. Olivia looked in with me.

"That's sweet, Dad. Soon, He won't need me any more." She had a tear in her eye. I put my arm around her. "Sweetheart. He'll always need you. He idolises you. You know, he packed his little red bag and told Bella he was living with you. He hasn't accepted you gone. He cried every night. He was sad. When to walked in, it made his day."

Chloe started rubbing her eyes and yawning. "Right, come on, missy. I think a bath then bed for you," I said.

"No, Daddy. Another story." She cuddled up to me.

"Come on, sleepy head."

Leo looked at Olivia. "Are you OK?" he asked her. She nodded. "You look sad. You're not leaving, are you? Please don't." He was worried.

"Hey. I'm not leaving you. I'm just tired. You know what we haven't done in a while? Watched our fave film. What do you think?" she asked him. He beamed.

"I'd love that. I've missed doing that. I've missed you," he told her.

We heard Mack scream. "No! God damn it! No!"

I rushed in. "What!"

Jacob was in the hospital. He had tried to take his own life. He missed Niamh that much. Mack rushed to the hospital. Matthew was waiting.

"How is he?" he asked Matthew.

"Not good. Does Rae know?" He shook his head no.

"Good. Not a good time," Matthew said flatly.

They spoke to Jacob for a long time.

"Sorry. I should've talked. I didn't know where to begin. I miss her. I miss her."

"Calm down," Matthew said. He looked at Mack. "We're here. Family sticks together."

Mack was crying. Jacob and Mack were always close. They always considered themselves brothers.

"Mack," Jacob told him. "Sorry, brother."

"Should've been there. I'm sorry, brother." They cried.

The doctor came in. "Hello. Could I have a word?"

They went outside. "We're going to keep him for a few days. He's got by to be someone."

"He'll stay with Anna and me. You've got enough on your plate," Matthew said.

"Make sure he comes three times a week for counselling. Otherwise…"

"Got the idea." Mack told him.

"He needs to rest now," the doctor told them.

They said their goodbye and came home. Mack told us what happened. We couldn't believe it.

Rae came down. "What's wrong with Jacob?" she asked us. When we didn't answer, she yelled, "Daddy! Tell me! No lies."

"Come here, Angel girl," Mack told her. He told her the truth. She was in bits, sobbing away.

"Not fair. So not fair. I've already lost my Auntie Niamh. I want to see him."

"Not a good idea," Mack told her.

"Not asking, Daddy. Tomorrow. He's my uncle. Family sticks together. Remember?" She sat on the sofa with her blanket.

Matthew left. Mack and I sat with her. "Daddy. I can't lose any more family. My heart hurts so much." She sobbed into Mack's arm.

"Angel girl. I'm sorry." Mack cried.

The next day, they went and saw him. She ran to him. "Uncle Jacob. Why? I can't lose you too. That's not fair. I know your heart has broken. Mine's breaking. Jacob, please stay."

"Rae, I'm sorry. Really. I'm getting help. I promise," he said.

The doctor came. "Mr Ripley. You ready?"

"Excuse me? Are you the person that's going to help my uncle with his broken heart?" she asked.

"Yes, I am." He smiled.

"Good. You hear that, Uncle Jacob? Talk about how you feel. Please. Get better. I need my uncle," she told him.

Off they went. On the way out, Mack put his arm around Rae.

"Good job in there," he said.

"I'm stronger than you think, Daddy. I'm just sad, that's all," she told him.

"Want an ice cream?" He tried to cheer her up.

She shook her head. "Just want to go home. I'm tired," she said.

Matthew dropped them off. She took Mack's hand. "Please don't leave me. I can't lose you or Daddy. That would really break my heart, for good."

"That won't happen! I promise you that. Come on, let's get in."

She ran in to me. "Daddy. He's so sad. I've never seen anyone so sad."

"It's going to be OK. He's going to stay with Matthew. He's promised. Come on, bed," I told her.

"I'm not ready for bed, yet. Can I stay up for a while. Please!" she asked. She went and got changed. She sat with us for a long time. Talking. She fell asleep on Mack.

Lydia called. We spoke for a while about Jacob. "That poor man. Hope he's going to be OK. Rae OK?"

"She'll be OK. She's stronger than we think. We need our family together at a time like this. Everyone together."

We arranged for us, including Matthew and Jacob, to spend time together. After a month, that's what we did.

Rae was with Jacob. "You OK, Jacob?" she asked him.

"Getting there, Rae. Getting there. Talking helps. The doctor says I'm making progress. So, it's very good," he told her. She smiled.

"That's good news," she told him.

That evening, us adults spoke about everything. Mack was quiet.

"Spill. Come on. You know the rules," Jacob told him.

"I'm angry, Jacob. I already lost my sister-in-law. Losing my brother is not an option. I'll nearly died when I heard. I'm there for you always. That's what family does. I love you, brother," he told him.

"I'm sorry. I couldn't find the words. After everything, I thought I could handle it. I'm sorry for not speaking to you. All of you," Jacob said. He got up. Mack got up too and walked to him and hugged him.

"I can't lose my brother. Not ever. You hear me?" Mack said.

Mack and I talked and talked. "Mike, losing what I have is not an option. You know that. My family is number one." He started crying. I took his hand. "That's why I find it hard letting go. Mike, we nearly lost him. I couldn't bear it if it were you. That would kill me."

"It's not going to happen. We will stick together. We have to talk more. All of us. Mack. We're going to be OK. I love you so much," I told him. We fell asleep hand-in-hand.

Chloe woke us up, jumping on us. "Brekkie. I want breakfast. My tummy making noises." Mack and I smiled. She hugged us. "Daddy. I love you. Uncle Jacob will be good. Now, I want toast and jam. Please?" she asked.

It was quiet over breakfast. Mack saw this. "Right, after breakfast, we're going out. All of us. The farm, then the lakes. No arguing."

We looked at him. "Don't look at me like that. For once, I'm making a decision." The kids looked at me.

"OK. On one condition, you, Jacob and Matthew go to football. You guys haven't done that in a while." I hate football.

"Deal," Mack agreed. "Thanks." He kissed me.

We had a really good day out. The kids and us loved it. Then Mack went to football. He, Jacob and Matthew had a good time. Jacob took a break. So did Matthew and Mack.

"This was a good idea of Michael," Matthew said.

"Just what we needed," Jacob said. "Oh God!"

"What?" Matthew said.

Jacob asked if the guys remembered a girl that liked him when they used to come down here. They smiled.

She came over with a friend, who took a shine to Mack. They said hi. The guys smiled.

"Sorry. I'm married," Mack told one of them. She looked disappointed.

"Married long?" she asked.

"Twenty-three years. Nine kids," he said, smiling.

"Bloody hell! Your poor wife," she said. They laughed.

"What's so funny?" she asked, confused. Then I walked in. He came over and kissed me.

"That's not fair!" she said.

"What did I miss?" I asked.

"Nothing. Didn't miss a thing. Want to go for a drink?" He smiled.

"Not when you stink. Come on," I told him.

When we got home, Maggie was there, having a cuppa with Olivia.

"Hey, Maggie! How you doing?" I asked.

"I'm OK. Tell them!" she told Olivia.

"Tell us what?" Mack said.

She paused. "Thanks. I have a boyfriend!"

"Doesn't that better. He's really nice. He's studying law! He's name's Benjamin," Maggie said.

"Thanks for talking for me." She looked at us.

Mack looked like he was having a heart attack. I was stunned.

"Dad, chill out. I've invited him for dinner Friday night. You" — pointing to Mack — "you are going to behave yourself. You" — pointing to me — "you are going to be nice. Maggie, you're coming too for dinner. No arguing!"

"Shit. Should have kept my mouth shut," Maggie said.

Olivia looked at us. "Dad. He's nice. Just be fair. That's all I ask."

"OK. Fair point," I told her. "How long?"

"Three months." She looked sheepish.

"Why didn't you tell us?" I asked.

"Because I knew how you would react. Especially Dad." She looked at Mack. "Look at him. He's having a heart attack. You two will never change."

Maggie left and Olivia went for a bath. When she came down, she made tea and went to the den, ignoring us.

"Olivia, talk to us," I told her.

"Why? You never listen. I'm twenty-bloody-one. If you had your bloody way, I'd still be rains. Let me grow up, Jesus. I want to be independent." She got up, but Mack stood in her way.

"Piss off, Dad, can't be arsed with you right now." She went to go past. He went to hug her.

"Let me go! Leave me alone. I hate you." She went to her room.

"Olivia. I'm sorry," Mack said.

"Don't give a shit. Don't bother about dinner," she shouted.

She ignored us for two days. Then she left and went to my dad's.

My dad called. "I'll talk to her."

"Please. Leo's in bits. He think it's his fault. Poor sod," I told him.

"She's so like Mack. Stubborn as hell. She's a tough nut. She'll come round," he told me.

True to word. A week later, she came home.

Leo shouted at her. "You left me! I thought it was me. I missed you so much!" He smacked her. "Why? Family sticks together."

She hugged him. "I'm sorry, Leo. I'm so sorry. I never meant to hurt you. We will make it up to you. I promise," she said.

"You better, miss. I'm counting on it," he said.

She looked at us. Mack went to her. "I'm sorry. We both are."

"Whatever. You always say it. I like him, Dad. Make the effort. You're a stubborn prick." I smirked.

"What!" she said.

"You two are so alike. I wonder if I'm actually a parent. I'm sorry, Olivia. I am. Friday night, we're going out. Call Benjamin and Maggie," I told her. She hugged me.

"You're such a good dad. I'll always remember when you brought me Georgia." She wiped her eyes. "All I ask is to let me grow up."

"Deal," Mack said.

374

Rae stood at the door. "Daddy! Don't say things like that. You're a good parent. Silly sod. Olivia Anna Denton. Stop running away when things get tough. You should know better than that. You acted like a spoilt little girl. Dad." She looked at Mack. "Let her grow up. Don't be afraid. Now, who wants a tea cake?"

Olivia hugged her. "I'm sorry. Really."

Friday came along. Mack was pacing.

"Jesus, Mack. Anyone would think you were dating him," I told him.

Maggie and Olivia looked lovely.

"What's wrong with him?" Maggie asked.

"Need you ask?" I told her.

"True. He's here. He's just got out of the car. Mack, breathe. Breathe!" Maggie told him.

He walked up the path with a bunch of flowers and a bottle of wine. I answered the door.

"Hi, Mr Denton. I'm Benjamin." I shook his hand.

"Come on in," I told him. "This is my husband, Mack. Olivia's other dad. You know Maggie."

"Hi, Benjamin. I'm Mack. How are you?" He shook his hand.

Olivia was surprised. So was Maggie.

He gave the flowers to Olivia. "Thank you, they're lovely."

"Drink?" Mack said. He gave him a beer. "Olivia tells us you're studying law."

"Training to be a barrister. I've never met same-sex parents before," he said.

"We get it all the time," I told him.

Oliver walked in. "Shit, sorry."

"Don't worry. This is Oliver. My brother," Olivia told him.

"How many brothers and sisters do you have?" Benjamin asked.

"I have four sisters and four brothers." His face was a picture.

"Nine of you. Bloody hell. I thought a brother and sister was bad enough. How do you cope? It must be a mad house," he said.

"We also have two dogs, two cats, a horse and a goat," Olivia said.

"I'm surprised you lot ain't in therapy. I would be." We laughed.

"Ollie, stay for dinner," Olivia said.

"You sure? What are you cooking, Dad?" he asked.

375

"Roast chicken and all the trimmings. Apple pie for desert."

"Did I ever tell you, you're a lovely old man," he told Mack.

"I'm not old!" he replied.

"Yer right!" Oliver said.

"Are you two always like this?" Benjamin asked them.

"You have no idea!" I said.

Dinner went well. Oliver turned and said to Benjamin, "Please don't hurt my sister. She means a lot to me. She's the best person I know. I'm lucky to have a sister like her."

Olivia smiled. Mack and I smiled too. "I'll do my best. I like your sister."

When Benjamin left, Olivia hugged Oliver. "Thank you, that meant a lot."

"I meant every word. Thanks for dinner." He looked sheepish. "I'll clear up and put the kettle on. Olivia, you looked very pretty tonight."

Olivia went and got changed after Maggie went home.

"Thanks for tonight," she said to us.

"I like him," Mack said. "Good for you."

"OK. Who are you and what have you done with my dad?" Olivia said. Even I was confused.

"What? You never seen a hypocrite before?" he said.

We shook our heads at him. "But, if he makes you cry, I'll kill him and bury him in the garden. OK?"

"And, there it is!" I said. Olivia just smiled.

On that note, she went to bed. "Love you, Olivia," we told her.

"Love you too, always," she said.

As promised, she took Leo out for the day to the farm then lunch.

"Hope you didn't spoil him," I asked her. She said nothing. I looked at her. "You're naughty."

"He's my baby brother. I did hurt his feelings. Leo, go and have a shower before dinner," she told him.

Benjamin popped round. "Hi. Can I talk to you and Mack, please?"

"What is it?" Mack looked nervous.

"Can I take Olivia to the theatre on Saturday night? In London. Then dinner. I'll have her back by midnight," he asked.

Olivia came down.

We told her what happened. "OK. Can Uncle Matthew take me and bring me back?"

Mack smiled. "Who's Matthew? Benjamin asked.

"My brother," Mack told him. His face! "Matthew said yes. He can take you."

Olivia felt better. "Do you feel comfortable with that?" I asked her.

She nodded. "Will he wait?" Mack said yes.

"You are a tight family?" Benjamin asked us.

"Yes, we are. Family first. So, if Olivia wants to come home early, you do as she says," I told him. He nodded.

Leo came in. "Who are you?" Benjamin introduced himself.

He looked at Olivia. "He hurts you. I'll punch him in the bullocks."

"Leo. Language," Mack said.

"You say it all the time. Don't give me that," he told him. He looked at Benjamin. "Be nice to her. Can I have a drink?"

Benjamin smiled. "You're lucky you're close."

"Aren't your family?" Olivia asked.

"Not by a long shot," he said.

"That's so sad. I don't know what I'd do without my family," Olivia said. Mack and I smiled. "What about your parents?"

"Too busy with work. Both are lawyers." He left us to it. "I'll be there at seven. That OK?" She nodded.

She sat with us later that evening. "Dad, that's sad about his family. I'm glad I've got all of you. I'd be lost."

"I know how he feels," Mack told her. "That's why now family is everything." We looked at him.

Chloe came bouncing in. "Daddy, I need a new ballerina outfit. Mine's too small. I'm getting big. Olivia, why tears? Did that boy make you cry? He's naughty."

"No, he didn't." She scooped up Chloe and tickled her.

She laughed. "You're pretty, Olivia. Can I have a biscuit?"

"You and your biscuits. Can she?" We nodded yes. "If you're good, I'll get you a new ballerina outfit."

Chloe started clapping. "Yeah. I'll be good. I promise."

"You spoil them," I told her. Thaddeus came in.

"Dad, can I go to Alfie's tomorrow night? Want to watch some films.

377

Lydia is giving me dinner," he asked.

We agreed. It was good he was getting out. "Don't forget your inhalers."

"I won't. Got a school trip next week. To Kew Gardens. Don't forget. I'm looking forward to it. Dad, can you come? They want a volunteer," he asked me. I agreed.

Chloe started jumping on him. "Calm down, your silly billy."

"You're funny, Thaddeus. Can you read my story at bedtime? You are good at it," She asked him.

"For you. Anything." He smiled.

She hugged him. "I love you," she told him.

He had a tear in his eye. "I love you too."

I went to the trip with Thaddeus. We had a good day. I enjoyed more than I thought.

"Dad, before we go home, can we spend time together? I miss it. Can we have a walk along the beach, like we used to?" he asked. I said yes.

"Dad, what was I like as a baby?" Thaddeus asked me.

I smiled. "You were funny. You were always smiling." I paused. "When you came home, it was the best day. You were asleep. I held you and just sat with you. Your dad took you, like with the others, and went in the garden. You and Fran were always teasing your dad. You always liked just relaxing with us. I'm proud of you so much. You have the kindest heart. You're a good soul, my son." He took my hand.

"You're a good dad. Thank you for being there for me. I love you, Dad. Can I have an ice cream?" Thaddeus asked me.

"Come on. Don't change who you are. You're a good kid. I'm proud of you," I told him.

When we got home, we heard shouting. Bella and Mack were arguing. "What's going on?" I asked.

"Dad's being an arsehole. I want to go the pictures on Friday with Jessica and Lucy. I said I'd be back by nine. He said no. But yet, Olivia can go out till midnight? So unfair. What's wrong with you? Why are you so anal. Sorry I'm not perfect. I hate you." She walked off.

"Why can't she go?" I asked. "Nine is early. She hardly goes out."

"Last time she went out with her mates, they ditched her. She cried for

378

378

two days. I don't want to happen again," he said.

"Bloody hell. She's going. If anything happens, I'll pick her up. Bella, come here," I told her. She was mad. "You can go. But if they stand you up, call me. Text them to see if they are still going. OK?"

She nodded. She looked at Mack and walked away.

She texted them to check as I said. Turned out, Mack was right. Change of plan. She was upset. She had been looking forward to it.

Mack went and saw her in the den. He had her favourite drink and a biscuit.

"I'm sorry, Dad. I should have listened." She leaned on his shoulder.

"It's OK. Don't worry. I've got an idea. Why don't we all go to the pictures?" Mack asked her. She smiled.

"Good idea," I said. "Haven't been for ages. Then we'll go for dinner after." Everyone heard this.

"Yeah!" they went.

"Thanks. But don't fall asleep," she smiled. "Sorry for shouting at you."

"It's OK, sweet pea. You know you have changed so much since coming home," he told Bella.

"Really. Don't feel like I have. I've got you all to thank for that. Callum especially. He's my angel. I am glad I got you. I'm a lucky girl." She remembered something. "Hang on!" She brought out a present. "Callum!" she called. He walked in and sat next to me. "Here." She gave him the present.

"Bella. This is beautiful." It was a photo of an angel in a frame. "You didn't have to do this."

"Yes, I did. You are my angel. My best friend," she told him.

"Bella. You are my best friend too. I'd do it again. Why don't we go out? I'll treat you," he told her.

"You sure? I'd like that. Dad, that OK" Bella asked me.

"No problem with that," I told them. Mack smiled.

Then Francesca came in, looking smug. She handed us an envelope. Her A levels. Three A's and a B.

"We're a bunch of smart arses," Callum said. We were chuffed. Mack looked at her. "I'm very proud of you, princess," he told her.

"Can we have pizza for tea. Please!" She gave him a soppy look.

"For you, anything. Then how about your fave pudding?" he told her.

She nodded.

Leo heard pizza. "Yes. My fave. Fran, here, for you. I'd knew you'd pass."

He made a card for her. "Thank you, Leo. You are so sweet." She went and got a bag. "Here. For you."

It was the jumper he wanted. "Thank you. You lot spoil me."

Olivia took Francesca to the university to see what it was like. She loved it.

"Oh my God, it's brilliant. Can't wait. I need to get a load of art stuff. Olivia, will you come with me?"

That night, we more or less had the house to ourselves.

"So, this is what quiet is. Don't like it. Not normal," I told Mack.

He smiled. "Yes. This is weird. I would say let's have an early night, but we've got Chloe and Leo in. Gogglebox is on later. Better check dinner. Listen, the kids ain't back till tomorrow night. Fancy taking Leo and Chloe out for the day? Get your dad and Malek to come along."

"As long as they don't argue. They're worse than us. You know, they had a row in Asda over a packet of pasta. Bloody pasta. Oliver was hysterical. He couldn't stop laughing. They hate pasta. Malek asked what he was laughing at. Oliver told him. This woman's face when Ollie called Malek granddad. I started laughing," I told him.

Just then, Oliver walked in. "Thought you were round Josh's house?" I asked him.

"His parents had a massive argument. I didn't feel comfortable. So, I came home. Any dinner left? I'm starving. You and Dad ever had a bad argument?" he asked.

"No. We've had a couple. But that's all," Mack told him.

"I hate arguing," he said, leaning on my shoulder.

"I know you do. Here you go," Mack gave him some dinner.

"Thanks, Dad. You know, I still want to be like you. Both of you. I look up to you two. Any pudding, please?" he said, putting his plate in the dishwasher. Mack gave him his fave. Apple pie and custard.

"Son," I said, "you're a fine young man. You're a good lad." I told him about tomorrow.

"Cool. As long as Granddad don't argue about bloody pasta. That was so funny."

The next day, as we were getting ready for our day out, I got a call from the hospital. Callum was in there. He had broken his leg playing football. When we got there, he was upset.

"Dad, I'm sorry. Didn't mean to scare you. It was an accident."

"Don't worry about it. It's OK. These things happen," I told him.

"I get to sign your cast," Leo said. "I'm going to put you're an idiot on it."

"Thanks, Leo. Oh god. I've ruined family day. I'm sorry." He was getting upset.

"Hey, we can still have the day. We'll get home and have a good day," Mack told him. "As long as we're together. That's what's matters. I've called the others. They're on their way home. Grandads are coming as well."

Callum nodded. Everyone was at home.

Bella was worried. "Callum!"

"I'm OK, Bella. Honestly. Went for a dive with Elliot and broke my leg." he told her.

Callum rested his leg in the stool. "God, I've got an itchy bloody leg now!" He smiled. Fran got him a knitting needle.

We ended up having a good day. It rained most of the day anyway. Bella kept an eye on him. "Bella, don't worry. I'm OK, really."

Mack and I smiled at each other.

"Dad, come here!" Fran asked from the den. "What do you think?" she asked us.

It was a large drawing of all of us. "That is so beautiful, princess. No wonder you got into university. When you've finished it, I'm buying a nice frame and hanging it up." He kissed her head. She looked at me. "Dad. What do you think?"

"That is the most amazing thing I've ever seen in my life. I'm proud of you. You're so talented. I agree with your dad. It's going on the wall." Fran beamed.

Then we heard Callum say, "Let me do it. I can get a drink. I broke my leg, not my head!" Bella was trying to help him.

"God, you are so stubborn. You're like Dad. Idiot. Talk to me like that again, I'll break the other one. Now sit down!"

He did as he was told. We laughed.

"Dad?" Fran said to us.

"Yes, sweetheart?" I replied.

"Thank you for encouraging us to become the people we are. You really do believe in us. You never give up on us. I love you both very much." She hugged us.

"We believe in you kids, so much. All we want is for you to be happy. Be who you are. Not what others see. We know your upbringing had been unconventional, but we're proud of you so much," I told her. She was glass-eyed.

"I love my unconventional life. Best one I'll ever have. Two parents that care," she told me. Then she said, "What's for tea? I'm really hungry."

"You kids and your stomachs. Anyone would think we don't feed you," Mack told her. "You're a fine one to talk. You're always hungry," Fran replied. He couldn't answer that one. I just smiled.

Jacob came over to see us. We were pleased to see him. He was looking a lot better. Rae was happy to see him.

"Uncle Jacob. I missed you. We all have. You OK?" Rae asked him. "Honey, I'm getting there." He smiled.

"Good. Stay for dinner. Stay with family. Please. Dad, that OK?" she asked us. We said yes.

"Truthfully, how are you?" Mack asked him.

"I'm OK. Still have my moments. But seeing the counsellor is helping. What's for dinner?" he asked.

"You're as bad as the kids," I told him.

We spoke to Jacob for the longest time. He seemed a lot happier. It had been six months since Niamh passed away. Jacob had tears in his eyes.

"I shall miss her every day. I'm slowly moving on. I know I won't meet anyone else. I can't do that to her memory. For me, that's a betrayal. But, I have you all and Matthew and Anna. That's enough," he told us.

We had tears in our eyes. "Right, enough." Jacob wiped his eyes. "When are we playing football next?"

Mack smiled. "Next Monday. Usual place. Well make sure that our fans ain't around." They laughed.

"Tarts!" was all I could say. Oliver came down and sat next to Jacob. "Uncle Jacob. Can I ask you a question?" He nodded.

He paused. "Can we go to see Auntie Niamh? I want to see her and see how she is. Is that OK?"

"That is OK by me, Oliver. She'd like that and so would I. Do you miss her?" he asked Oliver.

Oliver wiped his tears away. "All the time. She always made me laugh. She was a kind soul." He hugged Jacob tight. "She was one of a kind."

"Yes, she was. She made me very happy. Tomorrow, we'll all go. As a family," Jacob told us. We agreed. Rae was happy too.

So, we went and saw Niamh. We all had a cry. We laughed as well. We went and had lunch out.

"Thanks for today. All of you."

"Family sticks together. Never forget that," Thaddeus told him.

On the way home, I looked in the rear-view mirror and saw Oliver crying. When we got home, and it was just us, I said to him, "Ollie. Talk to me. I know you've been crying."

"I'm fine," he said.

"Liar. You're not going anywhere until you talk to me," I told him.

He hugged me. "Dad, please don't die and leave us. I'd miss you so much. I want you to see me get married and have kids. Couldn't bear it if I lost you like Auntie Niamh. Dad, please don't." He was really sobbing.

"Hey, hey. I'm not going anywhere. Not for a long time. Oh, son. I'm so not going to leave you," I told him. "You're my son. I love you. Please don't worry."

Oliver looked at me. "I do, Dad. I do worry."

"You know, when you were a baby, all we did was worry. Sorry if we were doing things wrong. But you kids turned out good. I always remember you loving toast and boiled eggs for breakfast. Your chubby hand with the toast. You shoved it in so much, we thought you were going to choke. You always loved watching TV with Olivia. Cartoons. I'm so glad you came home to us. I waited a long time to meet you, son. I'm not letting you go now," I told him.

We sat there in the sofa. Not saying a word. Oliver looked at me. "Thanks for everything. I'm proud to be your son."

"And I'm glad I'm your dad." I kissed the top of his head.

Rae came down and sat with us. "Did you really mean about what you said, waiting to meet us?"

"Yes, Rae. I meant it. I've been waiting to be a dad," I told her.

She smiled. "I'm glad too, Daddy. Want a cuppa? Oliver?" We nodded.

Mack came in and sat next to Oliver. Then they had a farting match. "Really. You two are gross. God, grow up, Dad. Last time you did that. You pooed yourself," Rae told Mack.

Oliver laughed. "Don't know why you're laughing. You are as bad as him," Rae told him. "I was gonna go to get you two a teacake. I'm not bothering now."

Oliver's face! "Oh please! They're well nice. I'll behave. I promise. You are my favourite sister." He started tickling her.

Rae started laughing. "OK, OK. Stop it. You're an idiot."

We smiled at each other.

"Here you go!" She gave us all a plate.

"Bloody brilliant," Mack said, with a mouthful.

Rae laughed. "I've got the weirdest family."

"We're not that weird," Oliver said, copying Mack. Rae and I smiled.

A few days later, Mack was quiet. He wasn't feeling well. He hated doctors.

"Come on. Tell me," I told him.

"I'm getting a load of headaches. Don't know what's wrong," he said. "Haven't had a panic attack for ages."

I took him to the doctor. We ended up having a scan. There was nothing. "It's migraines. You need medication. Nothing to worry about it."

"There! Glad we went? Idiot. You married a bloody nurse of all things. Dickhead," I told him.

The kids were worried. We told them what happened.

"Are you sure, Dad?" Callum asked him. He told him he was.

"Right!" Olivia said. "Dad, sit down. I'm cooking. No arguing," Olivia told him. The girls helped. The boys got the table ready. Thaddeus made drinks. Then after dinner, they all cleared up. Fran did some washing. They all did their homework.

"Dad. Don't worry," Bella told him. "We'll help. So, shut up."

Thaddeus made a cuppa for everyone. "There, old man. Drink. We're going to look after you. You are too important to me. You hear me? We want you around for a long time. You too, Dad. We're nothing without you."

He smiled at that. Our of the corner of my eye, I saw Fran with Didgy her dog under her chin, swaying. Something she hadn't done in years. She was crying.

"Hey, baby girl. Come here. Daddy is fine. Please don't worry," I told her.

"Oh Dad. I am worried. We've been through so much. It breaks my heart." She sobbed. Mack came through. "Princess. It's OK. I promise. Come here. I'm not going anywhere." He hugged her. She looked at him through glassy eyes.

"Promise me, Daddy," she told him.

"You have my word, Princess. Come on. How about you and me watching an episode of 'Scooby Doo'?" he told her. She nodded.

"Daddy, you too. Family sticks together. Please. Blanket," she said. We smiled.

"She really worries about us. Just like the rest of them," I told him.

"Dad, come on. Scooby waits for no one," she shouted.

Leo came running in. "Did someone say Scooby Doo? Please Fran. Can I watch with you? I promise I'll be quiet."

"Come on, Leo," Fran told him. He got under the blanket.

"Love you, princess," Leo told her.

"Love you too. Always," she told him.

Thaddeus came in with a letter from the local college. He got in on the course he wanted. "Thadd, I'm proud of you," I told him.

"Mack, our kids are geniuses."

Mack looked at the letter. "Good job, son. You worked really hard. Come here."

"Dad, I can't breathe. You're squashing my insides." Mack let go, smiling. "Thank God. I thought I was going to pass out. Can we go shopping for supplies soon?" he asked us.

"While we're out, we'll have lunch," I told him.

"You read my mind, old man. Sounds like a plan," he told me and walked off.

"Our kids are a delight, aren't they!" I said to Mack. He laughed.

Joel came round and helped himself to a beer. "Do come in and help yourself to a beer," Leo told him.

"You sound like Oliver. Where's your dad?" He smiled.

"Dad, Uncle Joel is here. He's drinking. How are you, Uncle Joel?" Leo smiled.

"I'm OK, kiddo." He smiled. I walked in. Joel asked if we could have

Alice and Emily for the night, as he's taking Lydia for a night out. The rest were at mates' houses. I said yes.

"How is Lydia?" I asked him.

"She is OK. She's thinking of giving up work. She wants to spend more time at home," he said.

"Good for her. What about you? You OK?" I asked.

"I'm good. Just thinking how quickly the kids are growing up. Emily's almost fourteen. Where's that gone? Man, I hope I've been a good dad. That's all I ever wanted," he told me.

"You're a good dad," Leo told him. "A lot of kids don't have a dad like you. You're always there, you sit with Emily and help her with her homework. You're a good uncle too. Give yourself a pat on the back."

"Thanks for that. You're a good kid." Joel's phone went.

"Jesus, woman. I'm having a drink with Michael. Don't you put a tracker on me. You're bat shit crazy. I'll be home soon, old bag." That was Lydia. Leo was laughing his head off.

"What's so funny?" Joel asked Leo.

"The way you talk to her. You know she'll beat you up. You're whipped. Bad!"

I had to laugh too. Leo was so on the mark.

Alice and Emily came over for the night. Rae was really happy. "Ally Cat, I'm happy you're here. You too, Emily."

Alice smiled. "I'll never get tired of you calling me that."

"Here you go. I made you my famous teacakes," Rae told them.

"My God!" Emily said. "Rae, these are amazing. You're clever. Thank you." Rae smiled.

"Oh, Ally Cat. I have a pressie for you." Rae gave her a scrapbook of Rae and Alice over the years. On the front, it said, *'To my lovely Ally Cat. Love, Rae.'* Alice cried.

Alice looked though the scrapbook. It was filled with photos of them through the years. "Rae, this is wonderful. What did we do to have someone like you! You are the most amazing girl I've ever met. We are lucky to have you. I thank God every day for you. I do believe that you are an angel. You're not just my cousin, you are my sunshine. You're everyone's sunshine. You're a gift from God." Alice wiped her eyes, so did the rest of us.

Rae hugged Alice tight. Rae wiped her eyes. "Love you, Ally Cat. Now,

I've made your favourite cake. Vanilla and Banana cake. After dinner, we can all have a piece. The reason why I do what I do is because you are my family. Family sticks together. I was given a second chance at a happy life. I choose to have that. Not everyone has that chance in life. I am a lucky girl. I have everything I need, Alice. My parents love me for who I am. I don't need anything else." Rae looked at us, she ran and hugged us tight as a button. "Thank you for being my dads." We couldn't stop crying.

"I'm ordering a takeaway. He's in no fit state to cook," Callum said out loud. We laughed.

Chloe was now three. She was as cheeky as ever. "Daddy, can I have a dolly's house, please? I am a good girl. I want to have dollies too."

Callum smiled. "She's so cute. Go on, Dad. She is good."

We got her what she wanted. "Look, Callum. My dolly house. What's in that bag?"

"Open it," Callum told her. "It's for you."

Her face was a picture. "Another dolly!" She hugged him. "Thank you, Callum. Will you play with me?"

"Yes. How about a tea party?" Callum asked her.

She jumped up and down. "Yeah!"

"Can I join in?" Bella asked her. She had an old dolly and fairy wings. Chloe was in her element. She bossed them about. They didn't mind. After two hours, Chloe started yawning.

"Come, little bear. Let's get you changed for bed," Bella told her.

"Can I have my story before bed, Bella? I love you, Bella. You make me smile," Chloe told her.

Bella was happy. "Love you too, little bear. Come on, get your book."

They had a good time playing. Callum brought her some lights for her house. It really did look pretty. Chloe loved it. "Callum. Thank you. It's very pretty. Can you play?"

He nodded. They were laughing. Callum put Rae's old fairy wings on. She giggled loudly. Then Olivia came in with Maggie. Olivia was crying like mad.

"Olivia. What's wrong?" Callum was really worried.

"I'm getting Dad," Thaddeus said.

I came in and she ran into me. "Baby, what's wrong?"

Maggie told me that she and Benjamin had broken up because he wanted to go a step further. Olivia said no, so he dumped her, by text.

"That bit of shit," I said. "I'll kill him."

"Don't worry, Uncle Michael. Olivia punched him in the face when she saw him. She broke his nose," Maggie told me. "Olivia, I've got to go. I'll call you later. Love you, always."

"Right, go have a shower. We'll talk more when you come down," I told her.

Mack came in with Francesca and Leo. I told him what happened. "She broke his nose."

Mack said, "Good."

When she came down, she had her teddy Georgia. Fran and Leo gave her a hug. "Come on, Olivia. I'll make us tea," Fran said. She looked at Mack, he hugged her.

"Good for you. Sticking to your values. Glad you broke his nose. I'll make you your fave dinner."

"I'll help Dad," Thaddeus said.

The girls were in the den, having their usual cuppa and a chat. Chloe sat with Olivia. "Please don't cry, pretty Olivia. Stupid boy."

Olivia smiled. "You're cute."

"I know," Chloe replied. Mack called to say dinner was ready.

Oliver took Olivia's hand. He looked at her. "Olivia. I'm sorry you're sad. You are the most wonderful person in the world. He didn't even deserve you." He kissed her head. "Love you, Olivia. Always."

Olivia just looked at him and told him, "Oliver, I love you too, little brother. You're a lot like Dad. I'm proud of my brother."

Mack as usual cried his eyes out.

"Pull yourself together, you hormonal twat," I told him. "Good God. What did I marry? Silly bitch!"

They all laughed. "Can we swap him?" Leo said.

"Tried it. Don't work. He finds his way home." Leo smiled.

"I'm not that bad," Mack said.

"Really!" Rae said. "You cried when we watched 'Bambi' and 'Snow White'. You sure you're not a girl? I've been wondering for years. Silly sod." I had to laugh.

"Now, who wants a teacake?" she asked. Everyone put their hands up.

"I'll help," Bella told her. She got a baking book out. Rae and Bella looked through it and found two cakes they wanted to make. "Dad, can we go shopping for baking stuff tomorrow!" I said yes.

"When you're older, you should open a cake shop. You two are well good," Leo told them.

Thaddeus had settled into his gardening course at college. He loved it. He came home with a leaflet. They needed some volunteers to help maintain the gardens. He asked Malek. Malek loved gardening. "My grandson, for I accept. We must go to see your tutor tomorrow."

They went and Malek loved the gardens. "Thaddeus, who is that man?" his tutor asked.

"My granddad. He's funny."

Malek was in his element. He started talking to Thaddeus in Arabic about the cucumbers.

"What's he saying!" he was confused.

"I think he's saying they need a good feed, like you do the tomatoes. Is that right, Grandpa?" Thaddeus asked him. He nodded yes. Everyone looked confused to see Thaddeus and Malek together.

"Good job I'm here. I made it in time. When can I start?" Malek asked the tutor. Thaddeus laughed his head off.

We asked him how it went with Malek. Thaddeus told us. "Dad, it was funny. Hearing him in Arabic. My tutor was impressed that knew about it and how good Grandpa is. I'm glad he was there. He's been helping me a lot. I want to do something nice for him."

"We'll think of something. I'm so glad you're enjoying it," I told him.

Fran was enjoying university. She was looking at an art catalogue for supplies. "I'll have to save up for this."

It was an easel, paint brushes, and a large painting book. Mack and I looked at each other. We knew Thaddeus needed stuff for college too.

"Thadd, Fran. Come in the den, please," I called to them.

They were gobsmacked when they saw their stuff.

"Dad, you're naughty. You know we were saving up," Thaddeus told us.

"Dad, this is just what I need. I'll pay you back," Fran told us.

"Absolutely not!" Mack told her. "This is from us both. You two, we did this for Olivia and Oliver. So shut up!"

They hugged us. "Thanks. I have an idea for Grandpa," Thaddeus said. "There's this open day at this large garden place. He always wanted to go.

Can we take him?"

We agreed. Malek loved it. "My grandson. Today was a wonderful day. You are a good soul. The world has great things in store for you. Never forget that. Now let's get you a drink," Malek told him. Thaddeus took his hand.

"Grandpa. I'm glad Allah gave us you to be our grandpa. You are a good man." Thaddeus was proud to have him. Malek put his hand on his heart and shed a tear.

Rae stomped in from school. "Boys are so bloody stupid. I want to slap it out of them." She sat on the kitchen table.

"Hi, Rae. How was school?" I asked sarcastically.

She smiled. She told me about a boy called Liam who kept being stupid in her French class. "He doesn't take it seriously. But you get people like that. It's sad. I like French and cooking. There the only two things I am good at."

"You're so much more than that," Oliver told her. He walked in, listening in. "You're kind, helpful. You're the sweetest person ever. Your teacakes are to die for. Never forget that."

"Thanks, Ollie. For a brother, you're OK." She smiled. "Daddy, for family day, can we watch old movies and stay in our PJs all day? Bella and I were talking. We'd like to bake with Daddy and just chill out for the day. Lizzie gave me Friday off. So, we could do the baking then. Please!"

Mack walked in and asked what was going on. He agreed. Rae was happy. She told Bella who got her favourite baking book out. Oliver smiled. "Dad, I'm glad we found Rae. She's the glue in this family. I'm glad we're together, Dad."

"So am I, Ollie," I told him.

Rae and Bella were in their element, baking. They gave their orders to Mack, who did as he was told. They had made a cake, three loaves of bread and tea cakes.

"All we need is that nice butter and cheese that everyone likes," Bella said.

"Don't forget we got a lasagne in the freezer for tea," Mack told them. We smiled at them.

Olivia, Oliver and I went to the shop to get what they needed. We came

390

back. "Bella, Rae, Dad, close your eyes," Olivia said. We had got them a bunch of flowers each for what they did.

Mack kissed me. The kids went, "Er, gross. Parents kissing." We laughed.

Oliver said, "I would say that would put me off my food, but that won't happen."

Rae and Bella hugged us. "Thanks. Very pretty."

Fran didn't look too good. "Daddy. I am freezing." She was coughing. I took her temperate.

"Honey, I think you may have the flu. Come on, bed."

"I'm missing family day," she said. She leaned on me. "Daddy. Can I have my favourite drink?"

Mack checked on her later that afternoon. She was asleep. She woke up when he came in. "Daddy, I'm poorly."

Mack smiled. "Oh, princess. You sound like when you were little. You OK?" Mack told her.

She nodded. "Where's my blanket? I want my blanket."

Mack got it for her and put it over her. He read her a story. "Have some water, come on."

"Daddy. Thank you. I love you. You're a wonderful man. I'm glad you're my dad. Never forget that." Fran fell back to sleep with her blanket and Digby. Mack kissed her head.

"I love your too, princess. You're a wonderful daughter." He was chuffed to bits.

Over the next couple of weeks, we all came down with the flu. Lydia came round. "Oh my God. It's like death warmed up in here. What the hell! Chicken soup and salad."

Mack went to hug her. "Don't you bloody come near me. You're diseased. I don't want it. You've tried Joel's cooking? Listen, I'll pop round in the morning. Give me that washing. I'll do it. Kids, Michael. Eat something. Love you."

True to word, she came round. Her, Maggie, Alice and Jack came over to help out. Jack wore a mask. "No way am I catching that. I don't want a sore throat."

When we got better, we invited Lydia and the gang for dinner. The kids got her a bunch of flowers.

"Lid-lid." Thaddeus told her. "Thanks for your help."

Rae and Bella made them cakes. "Why is it when they have sweet stuff, they shut up?" Lydia said.

"Because these cakes are better than yours," Alfie said. "God, they're good. Cheers, Rae and Bella."

"Cheeky git!" Lydia told him. "How's your headaches?" she asked Mack.

"Not bad. Haven't had one in a long time," he told her.

"I wonder why" she smiled and winked at us.

Oliver cottoned into what she said.

"You dirty old cow. At your age, you shouldn't even be thinking those things. You shouldn't be doing it! Pervert!"

She was about to say something. "Don't bother saying anything, you only call me that when you ain't got a comeback."

She smiled. "Look in the fridge," Lydia told Oliver.

It was his fave Lydia cake. He hugged her. "Thank you, you wonderful woman. I will always love you, Aunt Lid-lid."

Chloe turned four. She had a lovely day. "Daddy! This is lovely. Look, I got dollies."

"Chloe, look in the box," we told her. Her face was a picture. "A real bunny. Look, Leo. A bunny." Leo smiled. "I'm calling her—"

"Him," I said.

"I'm calling him Lovely. That what he is; lovely." Chloe cuddled him. "Come on. We need our you in your home. Thank you."

She sat with Leo. He gave her a present.

"Thank you, Leo." It was a book, teddy and a new book she wanted. She cuddled him. "You're a good brother to me. My presents are good."

He had a tear in his eye. "I'm glad you like them," he told her. "I'm glad you're my sister."

She smiled. "I'm glad you're my brother. No more tears. It's my birthday. I'm having my favourite dinner and pudding. Then cake that Rae and Bella made me."

"Come on, missy. Let's get you a drink." He took her hand. "I love you, little bear."

"Love you too, always, my lovely Leo," Chloe replied. I put my hand on my heart.

Later that evening, I heard noises from downstairs. It was Rae looking at a cookbook and going through a cupboard.

"What are you doing?" I asked her. "It's two in the morning."

"Can't sleep. Keep thinking of baking." Rae started yawning. "We're raising money at school for families that don't have a lot. Daddy, that's not fair. I want them to have a happy life." She wiped her eyes. "I want to raise as much as I can for them."

"We will. Even Daddy and I will help. Anything for my little girl," I told her. She smiled and we both went to sleep.

Rae and Bella has raised three hundred pounds for the needy families. Mack and I donated two grand to help. The teacher was very grateful.

On the way home, the girls were quiet. "What's wrong?" I asked.

"I hope what we raised will help," Bella said.

"You have no idea. Girls, we have made a donation too," Mack said. We told them how much.

Rae cried, "Daddy, thank you. Do you know how many families that will help? I was worried that it wasn't enough. Families can have food, clothes. Makes me realise how lucky we are. Thank you for what you have done for us, Daddies."

"Yes. Thank you. Words aren't enough to say what you have done for us. Rae, thanks for being my sister," Bella told her.

"Same to you, pretty Bella. You're going to achieve wonderful things," Rae told her. They fell asleep.

Fran was waiting for us. We told her how much they had raised. She was so happy. "Dad, why don't you two take them out? They raised that money to help. Take them to that place you took me and Olivia. They are so selfless. Dad, they're lovely. Please, Dad."

We told Rae and Bella. "Are you sure, Dad?" Bella asked.

"I'll be happy with a burger and chips," Rae told us. We laughed.

"I'm with Rae. I want a burger too. Just us. Family. Can we watch 'Up'." She smiled.

"If that is what my girls want. No problem. Anything for you two," Mack told them.

Bella shed a tear. "I've got the most wonderful parents who have given me more than I ever deserved. Thank you for being my dads." She hugged us both tight.

"Sweet pea. We'd move heaven and earth to make you happy," I told her. "Now go and get that film."

Thaddeus looked at us. "Thought you were going out?"

We told him we changed our minds. "I don't mind. Can I go out with Grandpa to the garden centre? Got to get bits for college." We said yes. "Good. I think he enjoys college more than me."

We laughed. Chloe stomped in. "Daddy, I've got spots and I'm itchy." We smiled. "Thaddeus Look at me. I'm ugly."

"Chloe, you are beautiful. Never say that again. Now you want a biscuit and a tea?" Thaddeus asked her. She hugged him.

"Yes, please. Thaddeus, you're beautiful too. You have a face of an angel," Chloe told him. He cried. "Don't cry. It's true. You are a beautiful brother with a beautiful face." Mack and I wiped our eyes.

"Come on, miss," I told her. "Let's get some camomile lotion on you. You got chicken pox. Then you can have tea and a biscuit."

"OK, Daddy. Can Thaddeus have a drink with me?" she asked. I agreed. She clapped her hands.

"Daddy. It's nearly Christmas. Will Father Christmas come and see me? Have I been good?" she asked me.

"Yes, you have. What would you like Father Christmas to bring you?" I asked. She thought about it.

"Dollies." She leaned on my shoulder. "Can I have my biscuit, please?"

Fran came stomping in. Sat next to Mack and rested her head on his shoulder. He smiled. "What's up, princess?"

"Boys are idiots," she told him. "I thought this guy liked me. He asked me out, then didn't turn up. I asked him where he was, he pretended he didn't know me. So, I punched him in the nuts."

Mack put his arm around her. "Good girl. Don't worry. There will be someone who will want to take you out."

"Nope. I'm staying here for good, like Rae, and be a princess forever," Fran told him.

"I can live with that. But there is a world with your name on it, Fran, it's princess," Mack told her.

"But if I did that, I won't be your princess any more," she said.

"Oh Fran. You will always be my princess. You were my princess when I held you in my arms, when you came home. I'll tell you something. Your dad and I loved you kids the moment we knew you were coming home to us. To be your dad is my greatest achievement." He kissed her head. "You are my pride and joy. My greatest achievement. I remember when you said 'Dada'. I just fed you your bottle. You were getting sleepy. You put your hand on my face and said 'Dada'. You put your head on my chest, thumb in your mouth, yawned and fell asleep." He looked at her. She looked at him with tears in her eyes and smiled. I sat next to her. "It's all true," I told her. She took my hand.

"Thank you for that. I feel better. I still think boys are stupid. Want a cuppa?" she asked. We said yes.

Lydia popped round. "Maggie is getting her university diploma next month. Can't believe she is finishing. Joel's finding it hard. So am I."

"What is she going to do next?" I asked.

"I think she said she wants to work for a while. She was offered a job in a philosophy department. I remember when she wanted to be a police officer. My baby. All grown up." She wiped her eyes. "She won't need her mum any more. I'm so proud of her."

Maggie walked in and heard that. "Mum! I'll always need you. Bloody hell, woman!"

Mack laughed. "You sound like your Dad."

I got up and got my cheque book. Mack nodded. We gave her three grand.

"Michael! Mack! No. I can't." Maggie showed Lydia.

"Guys!" Lydia said.

"Listen," Mack said. "Maggie, you are our eldest niece. This is a gift from us to help you, the way you've been there for Olivia. You've made us proud. Love you, kiddo."

She hugged us. "Thank you for being there for us. Olivia is not just my cousin, she's my best friend. Mum. You are the most wonderful woman ever. I'll be lost without you. I love you. You've always stood up for me." She hugged Lydia.

"Maggie Anne Green. I will always be here for you. You are my first born. You are a fine young lady. Love you always." Lydia told her.

Rae came in. "Maggie! Lydia. Where is Ally Cat?"

Maggie and Lydia smiled. "She's coming over in a minute."

Just on cue, she walked in, with a box. "Hey, Rae, this is for you."

Rae opened the box. It was a picture of them. "Ally Cat. It's beautiful. I love it. Thank you." She hugged her. "You're so nice to me, Ally Cat."

"Rae, you're everything to me. Like Olivia and Maggie, you're my best friend," Alice told Rae.

Rae smiled. "Just for that, you can have a teacake. Lydia and Maggie, want a tea cake?" They said yes.

"That was nice, what you did for Rae," I told Alice.

"She does so many things for others. I wanted to make her smile. "She's an angel. Look at her. She's happy helping others." Alice wiped her eyes. "You sure, she's not an angel?"

Rae brought the cakes over. "Where's mine?" Mack asked her.

"You got legs! We got guests!" she told Mack. We laughed. Rae went to get it.

"Rae, sit down. I'll get it." He kissed her head.

"Daddy, I was joking. I'll get it for you," Rae said

"Angel, it's fine," Mack told her.

Olivia and the rest came in, followed by Joel, Jack, Alfie and Emily.

The girls went to the den. The boys played video games on the computer.

We sat round the kitchen table. I smiled. "I'll never get bored of this," I said, passing everyone a beer. Lydia showed Joel the cheque for Maggie.

"Man, you serious right now!" he said to us.

"Hey, she's our niece. It's a gift," Mack told him.

"Man! Thank you. She's all grown up. This little girl fought for what she believes in. Shit, that reminds me. Maggie! You got a letter."

She opened it. "Oh my God! I got in. I got an internship at Kew Gardens. Look!" She showed us.

"Congrats!" we said. Thankfully it wasn't too far.

Lydia burst out crying. "My baby. My little girl."

"Mum!" Maggie told her.

"Maggie," Joel said to her. He was choked up. Something he rarely did. "We tried for a couple of years to have a kid. We nearly gave up when your mum fell pregnant with you. It was the best day ever. She knew she was having a girl. We spoke to you every waking minute. When you were born, your mum, named you straight away. 'Welcome home, Maggie Anne Green. We've been waiting for you'."

Maggie wiped her eyes. Joel continued. "When I held you, wow, I knew I was gonna try to be a better father than my old man. Then the rest is history. We were blessed with four more beautiful kids after you."

Maggie flung her arms around them. "This is hard for us as your mum and dad, seeing you as this young woman. But we know you'll be home every night. Baby, I'm proud of you. You're the first of my family to get into university," Joel told her.

That was it. We were all crying like babies.

"Can we have a takeaway please?" Oliver said. We all chipped in for pizzas and the works.

"This is brilliant, Dad," Olivia told me. "All of us together. I missed this."

I smiled. "Rae, Bella, where are those bloody teacakes?" Oliver shouted.

"My God! You've just eaten almost two pizzas. Where do you store it/" Bella told him. "Wait! Pig. No wonder the toilet stinks when you've been in it!"

We laughed. "It's not that bad!" Oliver said.

"Really! I went in there after you. I needed medical attention. I had to borrow Thaddeus' inhaler," she said.

That was it, we burst out laughing. "That's so true!" Mack told him.

"That's rich coming from a man who farted then shat himself!" Oliver told him. "How old is that!"

We really laughed. "But I will say this," Oliver said to us, "you and Dad are the best dads in the world. Thank you for being there for us kids. I hope when I'm a dad, I'm just like you both. Auntie Lydia and Uncle Joel, I love you two very much. You guys don't realise how lucky us kids are to have you in our lives. Please don't leave us." Lydia hugged him tight.

"We will never leave you, Ollie. This right here is what we wanted. To have a big family. Now, stop the tears. Guess what's in the fridge. I've named it Ollie's cake. Come on, you soppy sod. you're like your dad."

Rae was getting excited. It was her sweet sixteen and our anniversary. We decided to take her out for her birthday.

"Where we going, Daddy?" she asked me. I told her it was a surprise and that Alice was coming. Olivia helped her get ready.

"Close your eyes!" We did. When we opened them, our little angel looked beautiful. I burst out crying. "My little girl!"

Fran shot up. "Hang on!" She ran upstairs. She came down. "Close your eyes, Rae." She put her tiara on her.

"Francesca!" Rae told her.

"Shut up! You are wearing it. You always think of others. Never yourself. You're so beautiful. I love you, my baby sister." She kissed her head.

We had a good time. We went where we took Olivia and Francesca.

"Daddy, here, for you." She gave us a present; a photo of all of us together at the lakes.

"Thank you for that."

"Here, Rae. Open it." Alice gave her a present. It was the bath scent and perfume she really wanted. "Ally cat, thank you. I'm so lucky. I would have been happy with a teacake and my favourite drink."

"Rae, tough," Mack told her. "We wanted to do it for you."

When we got home, the girls for changed, came down. Rae's face was a picture. The table was covered with presents. She burst into tears.

"Why the tears?" Olivia said.

"Because I don't deserve it." She sobbed.

"Oh yes, you do, madam," Oliver told her.

Jacob walked in. "What's wrong?" Leo told him. "Oh sweetheart. You do deserve this. You know, your Auntie Niamh would have loved to be here with you." He started to get teary-eyed.

"Jacob, she is here," Mack told him.

"Here. From me and Auntie Niamh." Jacob gave her a photo of them when she was little.

"Uncle JJ. I miss her too, so much." She hugged him.

We all had ice cream. "Daddy!" Rae told Mack. "What's wrong with you? You forgot the—" Mack gave her her fave sprinkles.

Jacob said to Rae. "He's silly, your dad."

"No. He's the best daddy ever." That made him smile. "Thank you, everyone, for this. It's been lovely. This is all I ever wanted. My favourite people under one roof. A dream." Her favourite song came on.

Oliver walked to her. "I would like a dance with my sister."

Mack, as usual, cried. Maggie got out a tampon and threw it at his head. "Here! You hormonal bitch." I burst out laughing.

Three days later, we got a call to say Malek had a bad angina attack. "That bloody man!" Bella said. "He hasn't been taking his pills."

The girls were mad. When we got to the hospital, Malek could hear the girls. "Oh, Allah!"

My dad laughed. The nurse looked confused. "Our grandkids are going to kill him."

"So, you two are...?" Before Dad cold answer, the curtain was pulled back, and all the girls and Lydia's girls stood there, arms folded.

"Hey, my beautiful granddaughters." Malek was trying to butter them up.

"Really!" Emily said. "Not taking your pills?"

"What's wrong with you?" Maggie told him. Dad was laughing.

"Dunno why you're laughing, Granddad. You should have made him take his pills," Fran said. He stopped.

The nurse was gobsmacked. Then Bella said, "How many times have I told you to take your pills? If you don't take them, I will shove that broom up your arse and Allah won't find it. I know where you keep the scotch. Good luck finding it."

"Wow!" the nurse said. "Tough crowd."

"You have no idea!" my dad said.

Mack and I walked in. "Oh good, you're still alive," I told them. The girls looked at us.

"Dad. I'm staying at Grandpa's when he comes out for the night," Bella told us. "You are going to take them," she said, turning back to Malek.

"If he doesn't take them, Granddad, you'll have us to answer to. We won't be so polite next time," Rae told them. Dad opened his mouth to say something, but thought better of it.

I smiled. I thought of my mum. Just as strong. My dad knew what I was thinking. "You know you girls are like your nan. Didn't mince her words. No one messed with her. Isn't that right, Michael?" I nodded. "Strongest woman I knew. Family meant everything to her. Then you girls came along. The strongest woman I know. She's here, in all of you. Malek, we better do as they say. Otherwise, we'll be where Mary is."

Mack and I were really proud of them. "Is that true about Nan?" Olivia said.

"Oh God, yes!" I told them. "You're so much like her. All of you. She would have loved you lot so much."

When we got home, I showed them photos of my mum. "I wish she could have met you kids. She would have adored the lot of you. Especially you, Ollie. Giving as good as you get." He smiled.

"Do you miss her?" Oliver asked me.

"Every day. She died a year before I met your dad. Broke our hearts. But I met your dad. I'm sure your nan had something to do with it." Mack smiled.

The kids went to bed, Mack and I spoke about my mum. "You never really spoke about her," Mack told me.

"Too hard. She would have loved you. A gorgeous bit of stuff, she would have called you." Mack smiled. I hugged him tight.

"Mike! Hey. What's wrong?" He was really worried.

"I'm so glad I found you. You've given me a bloody brilliant life. No, I'm not sick. You are my everything. I'll never stop loving you, ever," I told him.

"I love you too, like you wouldn't believe."

We heard sniffling. It was Olivia. "That's sweet. I'm OK," Olivia said to us. We smiled. "I'm hormonal. I'll be OK in a minute. Where's the chocolate?" we laughed.

"Stick the kettle on, Dad. I want a cuppa," she told Mack.

"Yes, your highness. Anything, your highness!" he told her.

"Sarcastic git! No. I'm fine," she said. I laughed.

"That's what your nan was like. You know she threw a saucepan at the next-door neighbour for saying 'shit'. Literally, the word 'shit'. Knocked him out cold. Dad shat himself. No one messed with us," I told Olivia.

Olivia was amazed. "What a woman!"

"When I saw you girls giving Malek a hard time, it was like seeing mum. We raised really strong women," I told her.

"Tell me about Nan?" She leaned on my shoulder. I told her everything. So I did. She never let Dad get away with anything.

"She was the best mum. I miss her." I was choked up. Then we heard a scream. It was Rae. She showed us a letter she forgot to open. It was a cooking college. She got in. "Rae, that's brilliant!" Olivia told her.

"I'm not going to college," she said.

"Why?" Mack asked her. When she didn't answer, he said, "Spill, you know the rules."

"I will be on my own. Thadd's got grandpa, Olivia, you got Fran and

Ollie. I hate being alone. I'm scared. Olivia, I'm scared." She looked scared.

"Dad, give us a minute. Rae, I'll stick the kettle on, we'll have a chat," Olivia told her. We left them to it.

"Rae, come here," Olivia told her. She put her arm around her. "I know it's scary out there. I was scared when I stayed at university on my own. But, the fact that here is everything, coming home was—is the best."

"I don't like being on my own, you know that," Rae told her.

"No one does. But we have to try. It's not far. You'll be home for dinner. Rae, what else is bothering you?" Olivia was like a mother to her.

"I'm really growing up, aren't I? Will I still be a daddy's girl? I hope I don't change. I like who I am." Rae cuddled up to Olivia.

"Yes to both. Don't change. I love you just the way you are. Rae, you're going. Grab this chance, don't let good it. It might surprise you. You know, when I first met you as a baby, I knew that you would do good things. OK, I was only five. But I knew then you would be the sister you are today. Go get that life, you deserve it. You are brilliant. They say, no one's perfect. Rae, you are. Now let's have that tea and a cake. Don't move, I'm getting it."

They chatted about everything. "You'll be a good mum, Olivia," Rae told Olivia. "You're kind, patient and a wonderful person."

"Right back at you. God, is that the time? Rae, bed, come on. It's midnight. Thank God, it's the weekend," Olivia said

"Olivia, when I start college, will you be there when I go?" Rae asked her before bed.

"You have my word. Always." Olivia hugged her.

Mack, my dad and I were nursing hangovers. Dad had come round for a drink. Well, little more than one.

"Serves you bloody right," Fran told us. "Why did you get drunk, anyway?" She gave us a cuppa.

"Tell her," I told Mack. "Fran, get the others."

She looked worried, but did it.

"What's going on?" Leo asked us.

The kids looked worried. Mack paused. Then Oliver said, "Oh my God. You're splitting up? I knew it."

"Hey, hey!" I said. "We're not splitting up. Bloody hell. Mack, tell them."

"I applied for a culinary course at the local college. I got in," he said.

They were stunned.

"Dad, that's brilliant," Leo said. "You deserve it."

They agreed. "About time," Rae said. "You've done so much for us, it's about time you did something for yourself. Proud of you, Dad."

"Thank God," Olivia said. "For once you're looking after yourself. Good on you, Dad."

Mack was chuffed. Oliver was relieved. "Ollie," I said, "OK?"

He nodded. "I really thought, Dad" — he looked at Mack — "I'm so proud of you. Doing something you love. Don't know why you didn't do it sooner. Dad?" He looked at me. "Why don't you do something like that? We're older. Please, Dad. You've given us everything. Take some time for you. Right, everyone?" The kids nodded.

"You don't mind?" I was shocked.

"Do we look like we mind?" Olivia said. "You two are idiots. We will all pitch in and help. You know, you've taught us to do what we enjoy. Get an education. Now, it's your turn. We know you will be here. So, if you don't do it, I'll drag you by your shirt and curlies and make you do it." My Dad chucked. "What's so funny?" Olivia asked him.

"You're just like your nana, Olivia. I can see her in you. She would have said the same thing. You're just like her."

Olivia hugged him. "That means a lot. So, Dad, good for you."

"Thanks, kids. Mike, I applied for you to do that English language course. You got in too." He smiled.

"Sneaky bastard. Thank you." I laughed.

Then Chloe said, "What's a bastard?"

"You've done it now!" Mack laughed.

A month later, Mack was out with Jacob and Matthew when the phone rang at two a.m. It was Matthew. Mack has been arrested for drunk and disorderly. I was livid.

"Are you crazy? What?" I shouted at him when I saw him. "After twenty-six years? Jesus, Mack. Stay at my dad's. I'm too mad at you." I walked off, leaving him there. When I came back, he was gone. The kids were mad that he left and that I had asked him to.

"Go get him," Fran told me.

"Fran! It's not that easy," I told her.

"I want my dad!" she yelled.

Three days later, Mack came in. The kids were so happy.

"I need to talk to Dad. Go on." They left us to it. "Mike, I'm sorry." He explained they were having a laugh; they were talking about how much he loved me. One guy overheard about us. One thing led to another.

"Why didn't you walk off, like you always do?" I asked.

"I'd had too much scotch. My own fault. I'm sorry." Chloe ran to him.

"Daddy! I've missed you. Please stay. Daddy, don't make him go." She hugged him.

Mack got up and hugged me. "I've missed you," I told him.

Oliver didn't talk to him for a couple of weeks. He stayed at my dad's. "Ollie, you need to talk to your dad," my dad told him.

"No way. I hate him. He could've died," Oliver told him. "I never want to talk to him. So don't make me."

Mack was behind him. "Son, I'm so sorry."

"Piss off." Ollie couldn't look at him. "I never want to see you again."

"That's a lie. We're a family. I screwed up, big time. Your dad and I want you home. I know what I did was wrong. My ego got the better of me," Mack told him. "You are so like me."

"I'm nothing like you," he said.

"Oh yes, you are." Mack stood in front of Oliver. "Look at me. I need you at home."

"You should have seen Dad's face when he got that call. I thought you had died. I don't ever want to see that look again. It scared me, Dad," Oliver cried. "Don't do it again. I missed you Dad, so much."

Mack hugged him. "I'm sorry I hurt you. My little boy, who always followed me around to make sure I was OK. Who sat with his dad and watched old cartoons. Your dad misses that. Come home."

Oliver wiped his eyes. "I'm sorry too. Shouldn't have yelled. I was mad. Granddad, thanks for letting me stay."

"You're welcome, son. Go home. I'll see you Saturday for family day," my dad told him.

When they got home, Ollie ran to me. "Sorry, Dad. Shouldn't have left. Dad says you miss watching old cartoons with me."

I looked at Mack. "Yes, I do. I'm glad you're home. You want to watch some now? Your dad and I are OK."

"Good. I'd like that. Can Dad come? I want to spend some time with you both. Please, Dad."

So the three of us together watched cartoons. Soon, we heard Ollie snoring. He woke up when he smelt food. "Sorry, Dad."

"It's OK, son," I told him. "Come on, let's get dinner."

"Dad. I'm glad you're my dad. You're a good man. I'm glad we found each other. I can't think of a better place to call home," Oliver told me.

"That means a lot. You're as soppy as your dad. You have my determination," I told him. Mack called us for dinner.

Chloe was happy to see Oliver. "Don't leave again, Ollie. I missed you. I don't like it when we fight. I got sad, we all did. Can I have a chip?" She took one.

"Chloe. Come here." Ollie hugged her. "I promise I won't leave again."

"Good. Can I have another chip?" Ollie smiled. "What's for pudding?" she asked, then farted.

"Oh my God. That stinks! Gross!" Oliver said.

"Now you know how we feel when you fart and shit," Bella told him.

"Language!" Mack said.

"Oh my God. You let Ollie say that," Bella told him.

"Yes, 'cause I'm older than you," he told her.

"You're an idiot!" she replied. Back to normal.

Then Thaddeus wiped his eyes.

"Thadd. What's wrong?" Francesca asked him.

"Nothing." He got a tissue.

"That's a lie," she told him. "Thadd. You know the rules. We have to talk about what's bothering us. Talk to us."

"What's the point!" He got up and walked to the den. He never did that. Ever. He was mad.

"Thaddeus Matthew Denton," I told him. "Talk. You have to talk."

Mack looked worried. We sat next to him. The others followed.

"Whenever we argue, someone leaves. We fight, make up and pretend nothing happened. What happened hurt. You hurt me, Dad, by being stupid," he told Mack. He was really hurting. "You always taught us to walk away from violence. Yet you smacked someone in the face. Hypocrite. I got scared that you weren't coming home. I need you, Dad. Why!" He was sobbing. Mack sat next to him.

"I am so sorry. Thadd, I screwed up. I didn't realise I hurt you that much," Mack told him.

"Well, you did. It's not fair. Please stop this." He collapsed into Mack, crying.

"Kids, leave us to it," I told them.

"Thaddeus. I'm sorry we did that to you. We were wrong," I told him.

"I know. It doesn't stop that it hurts. We seem to go in circles. Dad, you let the drink get the better of you. Have you learnt your lesson? Did the police tell you off?" Thaddeus said.

"Yes, on both counts. It won't happen again. I'm sorry I hurt you though. I shouldn't have done that. I'm glad you told me that. I'm not mad," Mack told him.

"Dad, losing you two is not an option. You two are so important. We need to talk more, instead of doing stupid stuff like that. Promise me that," Thaddeus told Mack.

"You have my word, son, always." Mack hugged him tight.

"OK now, Thaddeus?" I asked him.

"Yes, Dad. I had to say it. It was bothering me a lot. I'm happy now." We smiled. Mack looked at Thaddeus.

"How about you and me watching your favourite film later? Just us, popcorn, the works. It's Friday night, we can stay up past bed time?" Mack asked him.

"Cool. Can't wait. Let me have a shower, then dinner. Can we have chocolate chip cookies as well?" he asked.

"Not too much, it makes you sick," I told Thaddeus. "Try two films. Stay up late," I told him.

"Thanks, Dad. It's just what we need. Right, old man?" Thaddeus told Mack. He smiled.

Olivia made me a cuppa. "They OK in there?" She sat next to me. I said yes. Good. We're a right old lot, aren't we? Good though."

"Don't grow up," I told her.

"Tough. I'm almost twenty-two. So there. You really want us to stay little," she said.

"If I had my way, yes," I replied.

She smiled and looked at me. "Oh, Dad. I'm not going anywhere. I love being at home." She started yawning and cuddled me. "You're soft as shit. I wouldn't have it any other way. You and Dad have made our lives wonderful. You've given us everything. Most don't have that. Our lives are perfect."

I put my arm around her. "Honey. You're welcome. I'm proud of you so much, Olivia. You do so much."

"Right back at you, Dad. Nan would be so proud of you, the way you turned out and brought us up. You're the best daddy ever. Never forget that," she told him. "Can you and me go out for dinner? Just the two of us?"

"Yes, we can," I told her. So, that's what we did. We got a couple of funny looks. "He's my dad."

We talked for ages. Laughed, joked.

"Thanks for this," I told her.

"Yes, it's been a good night."

"I never thought I'd be going to dinner with my daughter. I'd still think of the day you were put in my arms, the young lady before me. Twenty-two years. This little bundle of joy. I'm glad you were put in my arms, Olivia. I'm glad you found your way home to Dad and I. You are a wonderful daughter. Love you," I told her.

She flung her arms around me. "Daddy. Thank you. My life is better." She wiped her eyes. "Come on. Let's go home."

When we got home, Mack was making a drink. Olivia ran to him and hugged him. "Thank you, Daddy. Thank you for being my dad."

He cried. "Olivia. You are life. You are the strongest woman I've ever met. You have put me in my place more times than I care to remember." She smiled. "I'm glad you are my daughter. Don't change who you are. Now, go get changed. I'll make you tea."

I hugged Mack. "What happened?" Mack said, wiping his eyes.

"We just talked about everything. It was nice."

She came down with her teddy. "Come on, miss," I said.

She sat next to me. "Dad, what was dad like when you met?" she asked me.

"Pain in the arse," I said. She laughed. "Got on my bloody nerves. No really. He's all right." She burst out laughing.

"I'm not that bad," Mack said, sipping his tea.

"You cried for two hours before we got married. I thought you didn't want to marry me," I told him, forgetting she was there. She was laughing.

"Really! That's what girls do on the day. Tell me more," she said.

I told her what we went through. How we promised to stand by each other.

Mack spoke. "Your dad is my soul mate. I knew as soon as I saw him. I fell in love there and then."

"I hope when I get married and have babies, I'll have a happy life like your two," Olivia told us and yawned.

We smiled. "You're never getting married," I told her. "I want you home with us forever."

"You're so silly. Dad, read me my bedtime story. I'll never be too old for that."

I read her her story. She fell asleep in my arms.

Over the next few months, Maggie graduated university, so did Alice and Alfie. Oliver got a girlfriend. Malek was enjoying college more than Thaddeus. Leo decided he wanted to be a mathematician. Chloe just wanted to have lots of dollies. Callum got into college. He wanted to be a mechanic. Our kids were so talented.

Joel came round to borrow Callum to look at his car. "Damn piece of shit."

"Uncle Joel, stop swearing. Let's have a look," Callum told him. Five minutes later. "All done. Spart blub. Bring it in tomorrow, we'll get it checked over. No cost," Callum told him.

"Did I ever tell you, you're my favourite nephew? Come, let's get you home. You enjoying that?" Joel asked him.

"Yes," Callum said.

Bella and Rae were happy cooking. "Uncle Joel!" Rae beamed.

"Baby girl, I'm moving in. You know Callum is a genius. Fixed the car in five minutes," Joel told them.

"Told you," Bella told him. "Stop putting yourself down, Callum. I'll never stop reminding you what you did for me. Go have a shower and I've made you favourite dinner and pudding. Uncle Joel, you want a drink?"

"Go on. Can I have a piece of pie?" he asked.

"Not before dinner," Rae told him. Rae looked sad.

"Baby girl. What's wrong? Remember, truth," Joel told her.

"I just a bit lost at college. I like it, but..." she paused.

"It's scary, right?" Joel said. She nodded. "You'll be OK. Life's like that sometimes. You'll be OK. Can I have that pie?"

"Not before dinner. I'll tell Aunt Lydia," Rae told him.

"You wouldn't dare!" he said.

"Try me." Rae folded her arms.

"Damn you Denton girls."

Rae hugged him.

Jack came in. "Dad, there you are. Listen, where's Uncle Michael and Mack?"

Rae called for us. "Listen, it's Mum's birthday next Saturday. I want to play her a song. Can I play it for you? It's her favourite."

He played it. Acoustic version of Stereophonics. 'Just looking'.

"Jack, that's brilliant!" Rae said.

Joel paused. "Son, that's wonderful. I'm proud of you. She'll love it." He paused. "You know you were born early. Your mum worried like mad about you. When she held you, she told you that you would wake the world up. She named you after your Uncle Matthew's brother. He was a good man, like you will be. You always think of others. Son, I'm proud to be your dad, so proud." Jack hugged him.

"Next Saturday, family day, Lydia's party here. Stay the weekend. Come over Friday," I said. "Jack, that was amazing. You're so good."

Bella and Rae were happy with their baking books out. Mack sat with them. Bella leaned on his shoulder, yawning.

"You like baking with Rae, don't you, sweet pea?"

"Yes, I do. It makes me happy," she told him.

"I'm proud of you, Bella. I'm proud to be your dad. You've been through so much, but yet, you have proven to be a strong young woman. I'm a lucky dad to have a daughter like you. Love you very much," he told her.

"Thanks, Dad, that means a lot. I learnt from you to stand up for what I believe in. I've learnt so much from you and dad. You two are wonderful. Can we make bread and Lydia's favourite pudding?" She paused. "You know I don't have a middle name."

"That was random. What name would you like to have?" Mack asked her.

"That's easy." She looked at Mack. "Mackenzie."

Mack was chuffed. "That's a lovely thing to do."

She fell asleep on his shoulder.

Lydia had a lovely day. Spoilt as usual. She cried at Jack's song. Maggie surprised her by coming home. That set her off again. We got her a weekend away gift for a spa treatment. "Thank God."

Alice was ready eyes when she saw Rae.

"What's the matter, Ally Cat?" Rae asked her.

She told Rae she got a job about an hour away. She was worried that Rae would be upset. "Will you be home for family weekends?" Alice said yes. Rae was happy. "That's all that matters; that we're together at the weekends. Don't worry, Ally Cat."

Mack was snoring as usual. Leo looked at him. "Dad, what's wrong with him? He's so old. How do you put up with him!"

I smiled. "I love that silly old bugger, very much. For God's sake, Ollie," I said.

Oliver was putting twiglets up his nose, and popcorn in his ears. Oliver was laughing. Then Mack sneezed. The twiglets shot across the room. We laughed really hard. "You git," Mack told Oliver as he woke up.

"Barney did it!" Ollie always blamed the dogs. Mack just smiled. "Love you, Dad." Oliver told him.

"Love you too, son."

"Auntie Lydia. What was Dad like when he was young?" Leo asked her.

She smiled. "Always helping out."

That made Leo smile. "Are we like Dad?"

"Yes. You all are." She had a tear in her eye.

"Are you OK?" I asked her.

"Yes, I am. Just thinking of how we got here. Enough, where is the cake? Ollie, don't even think about it!" He handed her a slice.

"You lovely boy!" she told him.

He kissed her head. "You're the best auntie a boy can have. You're very special to me, Lid-lid. "

That was it. Mack and Lydia were in tears. "Dad, are you a woman with a beard?" Leo told Mack. "You act like one."

Date night for Mack and I came around. "Were not going out tonight," Mack told me. "The kids are at Lydia's and your dad's. So, the place is ours." We smiled.

"We haven't done this in a long time," I told him. "This is good. Real good."

He cooked our favourite dinner. Beef oregano. I kissed him hard. "I'm glad I married you. So damn glad. You've made so happy."

"Right back at you. This is what I wanted. You, the kids. Everything. I love you, Michael Andrew Denton. Shit, the dinner."

I laughed. Rae made us our favourite pudding.

"That girl can bake," I said.

We fell asleep watching the telly. It was only nine. How old were we! The kids came in, saw us and smiled. Leo and Fran put blankets on us. We woke up to breakfast being made.

"What time is it?" Mack asked. "Shit school."

"Dad, it's Easter," Fran said. Then the penny dropped.

"I forgot. You want to come with me to get the food for Easter Sunday? Perhaps get a coffee after?" he asked her.

"Really?" Fran asked him.

"Yes. Call it a father and daughter day. We'll even go to that oldie art shop you love. Then that book shop you love. We haven't spent a day together in a while. I miss it," Mack told her.

She hugged him. "Thanks, Dad." She looked at him with those soppy brown eyes. "I'll get ready. I'll leave my phone at home."

They had a good day. We always had chicken and lamb for Easter dinner. They went to Fran's favourite places.

"Daddy. Thanks for today. I've enjoyed it. I remember doing this years ago. I wanted an espresso, you said no. I was six. I got the hump. You know you and Dad always make time for us. Days like these are really special. You and I have been through a lot. I wouldn't change it. You know why? Because it made us stronger as father and daughter. I'm proud of you and Dad for sticking by us kids. When people ask me who my parents are, it makes me proud to tell them who you both are. Can we go for a walk? Maybe an ice cream?" she asked.

"Come on, princess. I would give you the world. You're right, we've become stronger. But never stop questioning or challenging. That's how Dad and I raised you kids. Fran, I'm proud of how you've grown into a strong young lady. I will never stop fighting for you. Come on. Let's get your favourite ice cream," Mack told her.

"Daddy, when I'm older, will I still be your princess?" she said, taking her ice cream.

"Always. You will always be my princess." That made her smile.

When they got home, Fran ran to me and hugged me.

"What's that for?" I asked, smiling.

"Just because," she told me. "We got the food. Dad, don't forget to phone Joel to remind him to bring the veg and spuds over," Fran told Mack.

He smiled. "Yes, your highness."

Chloe came skipping in. "Princess." She ran to Fran. We smiled.

"Look in that big yellow bag," Fran told her. It was a dolly and drawing book and pens. "Thank you, princess. You're so lovely. Can we draw, please?"

"Come on then. How about, let's see, your favourite biscuit and a drink?"

Francesca asked her. Chloe hugged her tight. "Yes please. You're a lovely sister. Pretty too. Love you."

"I love you, too. Come on," she told Chloe.

Off they went. "Daddy?" Chloe asked me. "Will the Easter bunny come and visit us?"

"I think he will. Have you been good?" I asked her.

"Of course, I have. Silly man!" she told me. Mack laughed.

Chloe was up early on Easter Sunday. She jumped on our beds. "Come on. Let's see if the Easter bunny had come. Move!" It was like when the kids were little. The kids found loads of eggs and toys. "Look Daddy." Chloe said. "He did come. Yeah! I'm going to save these."

We got each of the kids a small present.

"Dad!" they all said. "This is too much. "We got them what they wanted.

"Hey," I told them. "You kids don't ask for anything. This is something from us."

"Wait there!" Thaddeus said to us. He got us something. We opened it.

"Kids!" Mack said. They booked us a table at our favourite restaurant and brought us a bottle of wine.

"Shut up!" Thaddeus said. "We wanted to do this. Now, let's have our Easter day brekkie. I'll help."

Lydia and everybody came round and helped.

"We haven't done this for a long time," Lydia said. "Look how far we have grown."

"Jack," I told him. "Family film. You choose."

He paused. "Can we watch 'Pinocchio'? Haven't watched that in a long time."

Chloe loved it. So did Leo. "Dad. Can everyone stay the night? I miss it when we're not together."

"I'm not moving," Lydia told us in her pjs.

"Really!" Oliver said. "I think the pjs gave it away," he continued, eating his cake.

The boys played video games and the girls had tea in the den. Leo came in and sat with Olivia. "Can I stay?" They said yes. Leo had a tear. "I love all this. Family together. Rae, can I have a tea cake?"

Leo as looking at the photo albums with the girls. I sat with them and smiled. "I remember these as if they were yesterday. All of you that came into our lives and turned it upside down for the better, you all know your stories. Leo, when you came home to us, Fran named you. Oliver took you in his arms and you looked at him and smiled. You loved your milk." I cried.

"Oh Dad, you soppy sod," Fran told me. Rae cuddled up to me.

"You really wanted us, didn't you?" Leo asked me.

"Like you wouldn't believe. Don't grow up!" I told them.

"I won't," Chloe said, eating a biscuit. I smiled.

Oliver came storming in and threw his bag.

"Hey!" I said. "What's eating you?"

Oliver explained that he and his girlfriend had an argument. "Her parents had found out that you were gay. That won't let her see me any more. So fucking homophobic."

"Language, Oliver," I said.

"Well, Dad, this pisses me off. I just don't get it. Really, I don't. Arsehole." He was mad.

Mack walked in and I told what happened. "Shit. I'm sorry."

"Why aren't you mad?" Oliver asked.

"What's the point? We live the life we want. I feel sorry for them. Can't please everyone. Right, get your footie gear. We're going to play football with Uncle Matthew and Jacob. Blow some steam," Mack said.

Mack was right. It helped. "Cheers, Dad. That helped." Oliver leaned on his shoulder. "I'm starving. Can we get a burger?"

"Come on, son. Proud of you, son. Sorry that it happened to you." Mack put his arm around him. "Let's get everyone a burger."

"I just don't get it. Why are they like that?" Oliver asked him.

"Honestly. I don't know. Really, I don't. Come on. Leo's probably eating Toby." Mack smiled. So did Oliver.

When they walked in, they heard singing. We were watching 'Sister Act 2'.

"The right house?" Oliver said.

Mack scratched his head.

"Dinner! Burgers!" Mack said.

Leo ran in. "Thank God. I thought I was going to eat Toby."

"Don't you dare!" Rae told him. "Give me that burger."

"How rude!" Leo said.

Mack and Oliver laughed. "Don't know why you are laughing," Rae told them. "You're not eating till you've had a shower. You both stink. Move! Or no pudding after."

"Back in a bit!" Oliver said. Mack didn't move.

"Daddy. Move! Now." Mack moved. I laughed.

"I'm so whipped by my daughters."

Fran asked if she could go out Friday night to the pictures with a boy called Ryan.

"Dad, he's in my art lecture. He's asked me out for dinner. I want to go. Please?" she asked us.

"OK. We'll take you and pick you up," we said.

"Thank you, Daddy," Fran said.

"But if anything happens, phone me, princess. Not asking." Mack told her. She nodded.

The evening went OK for her. Mack and I were waiting for her. Ryan's face was a picture when he saw us.

Fran beamed. "Daddy!"

Mack walked up to him. "I'm Mack. This is my husband, Michael. My princess is very important to us. So, what are your intentions?"

"Daddy!" she smiled. "We went out for dinner. He was a gentleman. I'm sorry, Ryan. He's over protective."

"I can see that. Mr. Denton, can I take her out Saturday night?" he asked.

"Sorry, Ryan. Not Saturday," Fran said. "Friday would be better."

"What Fran says goes," I told him. He nodded. "Mack, come on, give her a minute. We're by the car," I told her.

"Your dad is scary," Ryan said about Mack. She smiled.

"He's ex-military. Thanks for tonight. What?" she asked. She looked to see Mack staring at him. I walked him on. "Dad! Sit in the bloody car, embarrassing shit." she shouted.

"Do you always talk to your parents like that?" he asked her.

"Yes. He does as he's told. Dad, car, now. One minute." Mack did as he was told.

Ryan was shocked. This tall military guy doing as his nineteen-year-old daughter said.

She walked to the car. "Friday, seven p.m. Here. Dad, you're so embarrassing. Behave."

As we drove home, Fran smiled. "Thanks for letting me go out. I know it's hard for you two to see us girls grow up. I appreciate it." She yawned.

We smiled. "Princess," Mack said, "I like him. But if he hurts you..."

"I know. You will kill him and bury him in the garden. Don't worry, I won't put up with that. You two taught me to stand on my own two feet. Can I have a cuppa before bed?" she asked.

When we got home, the girls were waiting for her, to gossip.

"Well? How did it go?" Olivia asked her.

"I'll go and get changed, then I'll tell you." Fran smiled.

"We're in the den. Hurry up!" Bella said. We smiled.

The girls chatted and laughed. We stood at the door. "Dad! You two are OK?" Rae asked.

"Yes, we are. Nice to see you having a good time. Come on, bed," I said.

"Please, Dad, ten minutes?" Bella asked.

"No. It's almost midnight. Plus, it's family day tomorrow," I said.

They slowly got up and Fran hugged us both tight. "Thanks for being there for me."

Callum was quiet over dinner. He went to the den and turned the telly on. I turned it off. "Hey!" Callum said.

"Talk to me. You were quiet at dinner," I told him. Mack came in with a drink.

"I'm fine," he said.

"You know the rules," Mack told him.

"Dad, why aren't I smart like the others? I feel stupid. Oliver is going by to be a teacher, Olivia a doctor. They must be so embarrassed that their brother is training to be a mechanic." He wiped his eyes.

"Hey, never ever say that again. You hear me?" I told him. "I'm proud of you kids doing what you love. Look at Dad. He can't even change a lightbulb without having a nosebleed."

"That happened once! Listen, you fixed my bike, uncles Joel and Matthew's cars. You're not stupid. You even fixed Dad's computer."

Olivia stood at the door. "I'm not embarrassed by you, Callum. Not now, not ever. My God, so what if you're a mechanic. It's a good job. I always remember you wanted to be a vet. You threw up when you saw a cow giving birth and changed your mind. Callum, never say that." Callum smiled.

"You're sure?" Callum asked. Olivia nodded.

Bella walked in. We told her.

"You idiot! You fixed Chloe's bike. She was well happy. She hugged you so hard, I thought your head was going to fall off."

We laughed. "It know what we haven't done in a while. Go Karting. I want to go. Callum, you need cheering up. I want to kick Dad's arse in beating him." She pointed at me.

Bella sat next to Callum. "My wonderful brother, you're the smartest person I know. You're the kindest soul ever. I will never stop reminding you of what you saved me from. You are my best friend. Dad, can we go out for a walk? All of us. We could do with it."

Before we left, I sat with Callum. "You were the best birthday present I ever got. Your dad asked me for weeks what I wanted. I didn't know. Then we got a call to say you were coming home. It was a miracle. When you were placed in my arms. I knew then that it was you that I wanted. I held you for the longest time, thanking God that you were here. I'm so glad you're here. I know that you are going to do so many wonderful things. You are a miracle to me. I love you, son, now and forever. Come on, son."

Callum hugged me. "Thanks for that, Dad. I'm glad I'm home with you and Dad."

"You will always be the greatest gift a dad could wish for," I told him.

Callum wiped his eyes. "You know something, Dad? What we have is so special. I'm the lucky one, to have you as my dad. I want to be just like you."

The next couple of years went quick. Chloe was at school. Olivia was in her last year at university.

Leo sat with Olivia. "Olivia. What are you going to do when you leave university? Are you going to leave us and move away?"

"Haven't decided. I'm never going to leave you and move away. Leo, why are you so worried?" she asked him.

He cuddled up to her. "Because I just want us all to be together. Losing you would hurt."

"Let me tell you something. Wherever we go in life, we will always end up here. This is home. Leo Alexander Denton. What we have is wonderful. I'll always be your big sister. I love you so much. I will always be here for you. Always. Night and day. Now, don't tell Dad, but how about your fave pudding and drink?" She smiled.

"Really? Cool. I love you too, Olivia," Leo said.

They never noticed me standing behind them. "Can I have some too?"

"Dad, eavesdropping. How rude!" Leo said. "Can I, please?"

"Just a small bowl. Olivia is right. This is home. We'll always be a family," I told him.

"I know, Dad. It's just the big wide world is scary," Leo told him.

"I get scared too. For you kids, your dad," I told him.

"Why?" he asked me.

"Because you are the most important people in my life. It's part and parcel of being who we are. When your dad went away for his job, I couldn't rest or sleep. I slept on the sofa, not in our bed. I hate him not being here."

Leo smiled. "That's sweet, Dad."

"I hated not being here too. That's what family does. Give us a bit." Mack went to grab Leo's pudding, when Rae hit him high on the head with a cushion.

"How rude! Not even dinnertime. Whose idea was this then?" We all pointed to Olivia. Rae shook her head. "You should be ashamed of yourself. Put that spoon down, Leo."

The time came that Olivia graduated Cambridge. We were proud of her. Mack was quiet. Olivia and I noticed and she came to sit with us.

"Mack, talk to us," I told him. I knew what he was going to say.

"Olivia, your dad and I are so proud of you." He went quiet.

I took over. "We waited our lives to have you. This tiny little person, placed in our arms. Now you have grown into this beautiful young woman that has done us so proud. Olivia Anna Denton." I cried.

"Dad!" she said. "I'm not going anywhere."

416

Mack came back with her baby album. "Look. This was the day you came home. We loved you from the moment we knew you were coming home. You had this little blanket. We could hear you crying from the car. When they placed you in my arms, you stopped. We sat with you for a long time. Bloody hell, you melted our hearts." She cried her eyes out.

"You know, Dad." She couldn't find the words. She leaned on me. "Haven't decided what's next. But I'm so happy. Really happy."

"We want to take you out for dinner," I told her.

"Can we stay in? I would like my fave dinner and pudding and watch an old movie, that's all I want. Can Maggie come over? My favourite people under one roof. Please, Daddy!"

I caved in. She looked at Mack.

"You are the most important people. Can I stay at home until I get married?" she asked us. We smiled. "I'm not ready to go out to be on my own."

"You are more than welcome," I told her. "If that's what you want."

"Daddy, this is where I want to be. I'll get a good job and help out with bills and food. I want to be with my family. Is that OK?" she asked us.

"Honey, that has made our day," Mack told her.

Leo was happy. "Thank God. I thought I was going to lose you."

"That will never happen. Come here, cheeky boy." Leo sat with her. That made his day.

Alfie came in. "Hey guys! Miss me!" We were glad to see him.

"How you doing?" I asked him. "Good. That smells good. I'm home for Olivia's graduation." Alfie had grown into a nice young man.

"Stay for dinner," Olivia said. "There's plenty. Want a cuppa?"

"Go on then. What are we doing for Dad's birthday?" he asked.

"What about a family dinner?" Olivia said. "I know he likes them. Then a couple of old movies and games. He's a man of simple tastes."

"Sounds good. Mum will be happy. She won't have to cook," Alfie said.

"So, I'm cooking!" Mack smiled. "Nice to see you two organising it all."

"Come on, Uncle Mack. We love your cooking. And Rae and Bella's. Come on, please!" he pleaded.

So that's what we did. Joel was chuffed to bits. He got quiet.

"Dad, what's up?" Emily asked him.

"These days are wonderful to me. Growing up, we didn't have much. My parents weren't much to write home about. I had the chance to come to England for work, I took it. I'm so glad I did. The rest is history. That's why family is so important. This means so much."

Emily hugged him. "I'm sorry that your parents weren't there for you. You are not them. You are a good man. Love you, Dad."

"Love you too, baby girl," Joel told her.

Then Leo and Oliver farted. "That's better," Oliver said. "When can we have food? I'm dying. I'm wasting away."

Lydia looked at him. "You're like your dad. There's people out there with no food."

"I'm one of them. You senile old bag. Here! Look, it's a bowl of shut up." We laughed.

"I'm not old!" Lydia said,

"No, but you are senile," Oliver told her. Lydia couldn't help but smile. "Just like your Dad. Love you, Ollie."

"Love you too, Aunt Lid-lid," Oliver told her.

Mack and I came in from shopping. The boys looked bewildered.

"What's going on?" I asked them. It took them a while to speak. "Don't go in the den. It's not pretty!" Thaddeus told us.

We heard crying. "What's wrong with the girls?" Mack asked.

"I think it's the time of the month. I don't know," Callum told us. We checked on them. They had their blankets, crisps, chocolate everything.

"You OK, girls?" Mack asked.

They started crying. "Dad, this film is sad. The fish." They were watching 'Finding Nemo'.

Mack had to smile. "It's good."

"But Nemo loses his daddy," Rae said. Her bottom lip quivered.

"It's a happy ending," I told them.

"That's so not the point!" Fran said. "He lost his dad. No one should be away from their parents." She wiped her eyes. We smiled.

"We have your favourite," Oliver said, trying to cheer them up.

"Why do girls go through that?" Leo asked. "It's scary. I don't like it."

I smiled. "When you're older, I'll tell you." I looked at Mack. "You girls need anything?" They gave us their hot water bottles. Olivia was asleep. When we came back, they were all asleep. We pulled their blankets over them and left them to it.

"That was the strangest thing I have ever seen," Leo said.

"Girls go through it every month. It's a sign of them growing up," I told him.

"Are they going to be OK?" he asked. I nodded.

They walked in and sat with us. "Sorry, Dad," Fran said. "Got a bit emotional." She leaned on Mack's shoulder.

"It's OK, princess."

"We're just feeling really soppy," Olivia said. Leo sat with Olivia.

"You girls OK now? You had me worried." He was really worried.

"Don't worry, we're fine. Come here." She hugged him tight. Rae tucked herself in usual place under my arm, and fell asleep.

"Rae, don't fall back to sleep. It's almost dinner time."

"Daddy, I'm tired." She yawned. "Come on, eat your tea," I told her. Rae did as she was told.

Later that evening, Callum sat with Leo. "How you doing?"

"I'm OK. Callum, do you like being my big brother?" Leo asked him.

Callum smiled. "Yes, I do. I love being your big brother. I remember when you came home, it was brilliant. I held you and you looked so happy. Then you did a poo, and it smelt awful." Leo smiled. "I was really happy. You loved your stories. Fancy spending the day together?"

Leo's face lit up. "Really? You and me. I'd like that."

"Fancy going fishing? Lunch. Hey! I think Dad's got an old barbeque, that small one. Burgers and sausages," Callum told him.

"That's a good idea. Can we go by the lake?" Leo asked.

Callum nodded. "You know, Leo. I was so happy when you were here."

They had the perfect day together. Leo was on cloud nine. "Thanks for the day, Callum. It has been brilliant."

"You're so welcome," Callum said.

When we got home, we heard screaming. We ran into the den. Bella and Rae were jumping up and down.

"What's going on?" I asked.

Bella showed us a letter. She got into the same college as Rae, to do the same course. "This is brilliant news, Bella." I hugged her. I had a tear in my eye.

"Dad, what's wrong? Why are you crying?" Bella asked.

I smiled at her. "I'm so proud of you. You have grown up so much. What you've been through, you are a special person. You are so wonderful and strong."

She cried and hugged me too. "Couldn't have done it without you. I'm glad I am here. Always." That set Rae off crying.

A few months later, Mack and I were sorting out our closet when we found the boxes of the kids when they came home. We smiled. One for each of them.

"Oh my god, look at this," I said. "Where did the time go?"

Mack was quiet. We heard Leo and Fran calling us. Then ran upstairs.

"What are you doing?" Leo asked, plonking himself on our bed.

We showed them. "You kept this stuff?" Francesca asked.

"Yes, we did," Mack told her. "Couldn't throw it out. Look how tiny you were." He showed her the baby clothes she came in.

"I was that tiny!" She was amazed.

"You all were," I replied. I showed them pictures of them as babies. They smiled.

"Dad, why didn't they want us? Were we bad?" Leo was upset.

"No, you weren't." Mack told him.

Mack and Michael explained to them what happened to each of them. Olivia and Fran were both left at Church doorways. Every effort to find the parents were Made but failed.

Oliver's parents died in a hit-and-run accident. Both sets of elderly grandparents were too old to care for him.

Thaddeus was given up because he was Downs.

Callum's dad had left, mum couldn't cope on her own.

Leo mum was a single parent who had mental health problems, who loved him enough to give him a new life.

Rae's had drink and drug issues.

"See." I told them. "They loved enough to give you a new life. We are so blessed that you all got to come home to be with us. Always remember that. Your dad and I are so grateful for that, Leo. You being here are miracles. Don't ever think that, son. You kids…" he couldn't finish his sentence.

They love hearing stories of when they were younger as they like to know what they were like. For instance, Oliver thinks it's so funny that he had a tantrum as he couldn't bring home a donkey as a pet. Oliver thinks this is funny.

As a family they enjoy spending together as a unit. But they also like having time outside. As a family they always talk openly and honestly about how they feel as to not bottle it up. Family weekend is a time when they can spend together as they are all busy during the week. So it is, either going to the lakes, the farm or just spending time at home. Sundays, they all come together. Lydia's family as well. To have dinner. They are a close family. They have their moments. But are close.

"Sorry, Dad," Leo told him. Then the rest of them came in. We showed them their boxes.

"Bloody hell, Dad. This is amazing," Callum said, smiling.

Mack and I looked at each other. "For you." We gave Bella her box.

She opened it. "I never thought..." She was lost for words.

Callum sat with her. "Here, for the box." It was a picture of them when they were at school.

"I didn't think you remembered that day."

"Always," he said. Then as usual, Ollie and Leo farted under the covers. "We won't open the covers. We could kill you. Plus, I think we put a hole in the mattress," Ollie said. He opened them a little. "Nasty smell, Dad." He opened them in front of Mack. "*Ta da!*"

Mack face fell. Ollie smiled. "Love you, Dad!"

Jacob came round a few days later.

"Hey. I know that look," Mack told him. "It's a year since losing her. We know."

Jacob cried. "I miss her, Mack."

"Hey, I know. I'm sorry," Mack told him.

Rae heard him and ran to him. "We need to see Auntie Niamh. Dad, get your coat."

Off they went, picking up flowers on the way. When they got there, Rae talked to her headstone. "Hi, Auntie Niamh. I brought uncle Jacob and Daddy. We miss you so much. I can't believe it's been a year. I miss you so much." Tears were running down her face. "Please look after my Holly. I miss her too. Jacob, talk to her. Daddy, let's give them a minute." She took his hand.

421

Ten minutes later.

"You OK?" Mack asked him.

He nodded. "Thanks for that, Rae. Come on."

Rae got a call. "Uncle Jacob, you're coming to ours for dinner. Olivia said so. No point arguing with her, she'll kick you one."

When we got home, Fran pulled us to one side. "Dad, I'm worried about Olivia. She's looking pale. She's over-doing it." Then we heard a thud. Olivia has collapsed on the floor. We took her to A&E.

She was exhausted. "That's enough, Olivia," I told her.

"Dad, I want to help." She cried.

"Listen to me. You are going to do as you're told," Mack told her. "You're resting. End of discussion, Olivia."

Later that afternoon, Olivia was resting. Thaddeus sat next to her and took her hand. "Olivia, please rest. I got scared when they took you to the hospital. It was like when Dad was there with his panic attacks. I need you to be well. You are my big sister. Let us look after you."

She lent on his shoulder. "I'm sorry Thaddeus. All I want is to do is help Dad. They've done so much. I want them to slow down."

"What about you? Please stop. You're so tired. I hear you sometimes at night, crying. Please, I need my sister." H was really crying.

"I'm sorry. I'm sorry. I didn't realise. I'll stop. Promise," she told him.

We walked in. "Come here, Thaddeus," I told him.

"Why are you crying at night?" Mack asked her.

"Because I want to look after everyone. I feel like it's not good enough." She sobbed.

"Honey, it's not your job to look after us," I told her. "We look after each other. We're the parents. No more, Olivia. Rest. How about some tea and honey?" she nodded.

"I'm sorry. I wanted to make it easier. Daddy." She hugged Mack.

"Baby, I know. It's OK, really." He wiped her tears away.

The others followed. They all sat on the sofa and chairs.

"Olivia," Fran said. "It's OK. Don't worry. You worry about us so much. Just because you are the eldest, doesn't mean you have to put the weight on your shoulders."

"It's my job," she said.

"No, it's not. Just be yourself." Oliver said.

"You need a night out with Maggie," Rae told her. "Olivia, have one night for you. Please. And stop stressing. Dad, where's that tea! Bring the cakes too! Chop! Chop!"

"All right, bossy boots. Come and help, then," I called after her.

She got up. "That man's useless. Coming!"

They all laughed. "What are you doing!" she asked me. "You can't put that lot on one tray. Good job I'm here."

We heard them really laughing when we came in. "What!" we said together.

"You two are so alike and funny," Leo told us.

We smiled at that. Olivia smiled. "Glad to see you smiling," I told her. Chloe started yawning. "Come on, your bed."

"No! Want to Stay with Leo." She cuddled up to him. He smiled. "I want to stay here. Please, Leo." She gave him the same look as Rae used to give me.

"Dad, help me. She's too cute. How about I take you to bed and read you your story? he told her.

She smiled. "OK, Leo. In five minutes, OK?"

"Five minutes," he smiled. Chloe was asleep in two. Leo took her to bed. "Dad, she's lovely."

A few days later, Callum came home from college. He was quiet. "Dad, can we talk?" he asked us.

We sat in the den. He seemed nervous. "Come on, spill," I told him.

"Dad, um. I've kinda met someone. We've had a coffee," he said.

"That's good. What's she like?" Mack asked. He was really quiet.

"She's a he…" he said. Callum looked at us. We were shocked.

"OK," I said and smiled.

"You're not disappointed?" he asked.

"No bloody way. Why didn't you tell us?" I asked.

"Not sure how I felt. I like him, Dad. So, I'm gay." He was relieved. "You OK with that?"

"Callum Theo Denton. I'm so proud of you for telling us. We're not disappointed. We raised you to be true to yourself. Be happy with who you are. We love you the same. Thanks for telling us," Mack said.

Oliver called to see where we were. "You OK telling them?"

He nodded. Everyone came in and Callum told them. "Callum, so you're gay, we don't care," Fran said.

Then Leo said, "Can we still go fishing?"

Callum smiled. "'Course we can."

I phoned Lydia and my dad. They came over and Callum told them. They were cool with it. My dad got up. "Callum, let's talk."

They went to the den. "I'm so proud of you," he told Callum. "I always had an idea. Never let anyone change who you are."

"Thanks, Grandad. I was scared," Callum said. Malek came in.

"My child. Never let fear overcome who you are. That stops you from being the true you. Be the man that you are. Stay true to you. Follow the path of happiness and joy," Malek told him.

Callum had tears in his eyes. "I wish I said it sooner. Now is the right time. Thank you both and everyone. Come on, before Lydia throws a coming-out party." They laughed. Callum was right.

"Lydia, no sodding coming-out party. You hear me? I'll settle for fish and chips," Callum told her.

"Really! OK. I was looking forward to a knees up." She was disappointed.

"You're paying for the fish and chips," Callum told her.

Her face was a picture. Joel laughed.

"Last time she got her purse out, Moses was alive," Oliver said. We laughed so hard. Callum was happy.

Bella and Callum were washing up. "Are you OK with what I said?" Callum asked her.

She paused, put the plate down and hugged him. "Callum, I couldn't care less. You're the same. I love you just the way you are."

"Thanks for that. I was worried," Callum said.

"Really! You know are parents are gay and no one cares. Come on. Dad, stick the kettle on! Make yourself useful," she said to me.

"You girls are so bossy! Anything else?" I asked her.

Rae came in. "I'd like to talk to Callum."

They went and spoke for a while. They spoke about everything. I walked in with their drinks.

"You two OK?" I asked.

"Yes, Dad," Callum said.

"I'm proud of my brother," Rae replied.

"You know, Callum, Rae was very protective over you as a toddler. You two were like two peas in a pod. She always made sure you were OK," I told them. Callum had tears in his eyes.

"No tears, little brother," Rae told him. "Don't tell Ollie, but you want a tea cake and jam!"

That boy's good hearing. "Did you say tea cake!" Ollie said.

We laughed. Rae looked at Callum. "Love you, Callum. Dad, you want one?" I said yes.

"She's amazing. Kind and sweet. Always sees the best in everything," Callum said. "She's like you. I'm glad I've got this family. Dad, I'm glad you're my dad. You are a wonderful man. You've done a bloody good job raising us kids. You and Dad should pat yourself on the back for what you've done for us. I'm so incredibly lucky to be here. You've made me very happy."

Then we heard Oliver and Mack singing 'Last Christmas'. Callum looked at me. "Can we swap them?"

"Can't. Lost the receipts," I said. We laughed.

"Shut up in there. You sound like dead cats! Bloody hell." Callum burst out laughing. "Mack, stop singing. Otherwise, I want a divorce."

"Tough shit. Can't have one. Love you!" Mack called back.

I looked at Callum who was laughing so hard. "What have I done? I need my meds."

Rae walked in, shaking her head. "Those two are a right pair. Dad, I need some for college. Can we go shopping?" I nodded.

"Thanks. Chloe, come and get your tea!"

Chloe came running in. She sat with Rae. "Thanks, Rae. Lovely is OK. Leo helped me change his stuff. I love Leo."

Leo smiled. "Dad, I need shoes for school and trousers," Leo said.

We decided to go shopping that Saturday morning. Olivia was happy. "Good. I can get out and help."

"You're not overdoing it, miss," Mack said, sitting next to me and taking my hand. I agreed.

"I know. I just want to do a little bit. Please!"

"OK. But if it gets too much, you're not allowed," I told her.

She smiled. "Promise. I'm sorry I worried you both. I just like helping you."

Rae passed Olivia her tea.

"Can we have a girls' afternoon soon, like we did with Bella?" Francesca asked. "Can we invite Maggie, Alice and Emily for the night?"

Then Oliver said, "Boys day out! Come on. Football then bowling." Everyone agreed. "Do we get a say?" I asked them. They all said no.

That Saturday, we did just that. The girls came round. They were in the den all ready. Mack took the boys to football with Joel. Lydia and I stayed at home. We sat in the living room, feet up, watching TV.

"This is nice," Lydia said. "I never thought our kids would get on so well."

"We have done a good job with them," I told her.

"You girls OK in there!" Lydia shouted to them.

"Yes," they replied. We smiled.

Maggie and Olivia went to make more tea. "Mum, can we stay the night?"

"Yes, you can." I said.

Lydia was happy. "I'll call your dad to bring dinner home," Lydia said.

"Dad, Lydia. You want another cuppa?" Olivia asked.

"You OK, Olivia?" I said, passing her my cup.

"Dad, I'm fine," she whined. Then she wrapped her arms around my neck and kissed my head. "Dad, I'm going to be fine. I love you. I promised to take it easy. I will. You're a good dad. Stop worrying."

As they went back to the den, Lydia looked at me. "She's going to be OK. She's right. You're a good dad."

Then the boys came home with pizzas and the works. Mack took the girls their pizzas. Then we heard Olivia say, "For God's sake, I'm fine. Jesus." She stormed to her room.

Mack looked sheepish. Maggie went after her. Ten minutes later, she came down and hugged Mack. "I'm sorry."

"It's OK, baby girl," he told her. "Just worried."

"I know, Daddy. I shouldn't have done that. Love you." She hugged him tight. "Go on, go watch the film."

"Hurry up, Livvy!" Emily said. "Your tea's going cold. Uncle Mack! Let the reins off! Bloody hell!"

We looked at Lydia. "She's so you!" I told her.

Lydia smiled and drank her tea. "That's my girl." I couldn't stop smiling.

Chloe sat with Lydia. "Hello, my little Chloe. What can I do for you!"

"I just want you to know," Chloe said to her, "you are lovely. You are a nice auntie." She leaned on her arm. "Can I have a biscuit?"

Lydia had a tear. "For you, anything. Come on, beautiful." Mack and I smiled.

Leo sat next to us. "You OK, son?" I asked him.

He nodded. "Dad, what was I like when I was little?"

I smiled and put my arm around him. "You were very funny. You're a lot like Ollie. I remember when Olivia went to university, you packed a bag and wanted to go and live with her. You always loved when she came home. You loved helping Dad with the garden. You are the kindest person ever. Chloe looks up to you. Dad and I are glad we found you." Mack sat next to him.

"I remember when you came home to us. I loved you the moment we knew you were coming home. When you were placed in our arms, my god, I vowed never to let you go. Same as the rest. You know Fran named you?"

Fran smiled and nodded. "You looked like a Leo. I remember when I met you from play school with Dad, you ran to me shouting 'Princess, I need a wee'." We couldn't stop laughing. Leo laughed. "You held my hand all the way home. I brought you a lolly."

"Princess?" Leo asked Francesca. "I think you're lovely. You're a lovely sister. Night." Leo kissed Fran's head. That made her cry. She tucked Digby under her chin.

"Sweetheart," I told her. "Why the tears?"

She looked at me. "That was sweet. Dad? Tell me a story about Nan."

"Hang on." I got up and got a photo album of me and Dad and Mum. "That's your nan." I pointed to one with her and Dad.

Francesca smiled. "I've got the same hair and eyes. Look."

She was right. "You know. She was very protective over me, Auntie Lydia and your granddad. She was the boss. We didn't argue. Dared not to. We liked walking." She laughed. "She would have loved you lot so much. She would have loved your paintings. You have the same twinkle in your eyes. I wish you could have met her, Fran. She was amazing," I told her. "I remember there was this kid in my class that didn't like me. She rolled up to his parents' house. Told his dad that if he didn't leave me alone, she would bury his dad's arse in the backyard, with his dick hanging out his eyes."

Fran laughed so hard. "Oh my god! Really!"

"Yes. It worked. Never bothered me again. That's where Auntie Lydia gets it from. Those two were like two peas in a pod."

Just then, Lydia popped in. "Oh my God. I remember that. Bloody hell." I told her the story. She looked at Francesca, then at mum's photo. "You look like her. Eyes and hair. We had a good childhood. We were lucky."

Mack got up and walked away. I cottoned on to why. So did Fran. "I'll go," said Fran. She followed him. "I know why you're sad, Dad. I'm sorry your dad hurt you. But he should be proud of you. I am. You're a wonderful husband and a damn good dad. You've got nine kids that love you so much, Dad. Now, want a cuppa?"

Mack hugged her and nodded. "Fran. You are a wonderful daughter. I'm so proud of you. I'm never letting you go. I'm proud to be your dad." She smiled through her tears. Then they heard me say, "For God's sake, Ollie, stop hitting me with the cushion."

"It's fun. Besides Dad's not about. Lydia, do something useful. Put the kettle on, you daft old cow. Dad, you OK now?"

"I am." Mack smiled. Lydia put the kettle on.

Oliver came back with a bag for Lydia. "What is this?" she asked.

"Open it." Oliver smiled.

She opened it. It was a photo of them together. She put her hand over her mouth. "Oh, Ollie. It's wonderful. Why?"

"Because you are the most amazing person ever." He had tears in his eyes. "I know I tease you like mad, but you are the most important aunt. I love you so much." He hugged her tight.

"I remember when you came home. You were the most gorgeous little thing ever. When I held you, when I held all of you, I knew this was where you belonged. I will always, always love you." She wiped her eyes. "You want to help me?" Oliver nodded.

Mack and I smiled. "See, Dad?" Fran said to Mack. "Just like you. All of us. And you too, Dad. Aunt Lydia. Can I have my favourite drink?"

"You bet you can, princess. I'll never forget when you glued his arse to the loo seat. Brilliant," Lydia told her.

"Dad?" Fran asked us. "When I'm older, can I still be your princess?"

"Always," I told her.

Joel and the kids came in. Alice had a box in her hands. She asked for Rae. Alice gave her the box and out came a kitten. Rae's face was a picture. She beamed. "Oh, Ally Cat! She's beautiful. Why?"

"Alfie and I walked past the pet shop and saw her on her own. We knew what you would do. We never leave anyone behind. What are you going to call her?" Alice said.

"That's easy. Niamh," she said. She looked at us. "Can I keep her? Please!" As usual, we caved in. We all smiled.

"Thanks, Ally Cat. Dad, can everyone stay?" she asked.

"Go on then," I said.

"Cool," Alfie said. "Get the pizza leaflet while you're up, Alice. Bottom drawer. I'm starving."

Olivia was really quiet. "Talk," I told her.

"Can I start helping out again? Doctor says, I'm fine. Just little things. Please?" She gave me her soppy look.

"OK," I said.

"You can take the rubbish out and wash up once a week," I told her.

"Deal." She leaned on me. "I'm sorry for stressing you two out. Didn't mean to."

Mack sat next to her. "You will never stress us out. You're our kids. We love you lot very much. You lot are our world."

She smiled and took his hand. "Right back at you."

Then the boys were having a farting match. It stunk. Jack won. Fran walked in and said, "You dirty shit bags. Your bowels are rotten. Just for that, you lot are clearing up."

"That's not fair. Dad?" Leo said.

All the girls got up and looked at them. "I suggest you do as you're told," Maggie said. They did as they were told.

Lydia smiled. "Good on Maggie."

"Damn my sister's and cousins." Alfie said. "I'm never arguing with them."

I looked at Mack at smiled. I said to Lydia, "You know, Bella wants to legally change her name. She wants to change it to Bella Mackenzie Denton."

"Wow, Mack," Lydia told him. "How does that make you feel?"

"Proud as a punch." He smiled. "To have my kid to choose my name. It's makes it worth it."

Just then, Bella walked in. "It is worth it. You're wonderful parents."

"Hurry up with the sprinkles!" shouted Olivia.

"Chill out. I'll be there in a minute. Bloody hell," she replied. We laughed. She got the sprinkles and kissed our heads while passing. "Love you both, always. I'm lucky to have you."

"See? Worth it," I told him. I took his hand. "Never forget that I love you. I'm so glad I met you. You're my life. I love you."

He smiled. "Love you too. Always." Chloe walked in with her teddy, rubbing her eyes. "Daddy. I'm tired." She yawned. She sat on my lap.

"Come on, miss. Bedtime story." She nodded. Joel smiled.

We took Bella to change her name. She sighed in relief.

"You OK?" I asked her.

"I am now. A weight's been lifted off my shoulder. I know I'm your daughter. I hated my other name. This was important to me."

We walked past this book shop. "I had that book. I loved it. I lost it," she said.

"Stay there," Mack said. He came out and handed her the bag. It was *Charlotte's Web.* "Dad. Thank you."

"Read inside." He smiled. It read, *To my beautiful daughter. Love you always, Daddy.* She hugged us both. Later that evening, after dinner, Bella came down. She had her book. "Please!"

"Come here." Mack smiled. She sat with him. Bella was happy. She started dosing off. "Hey, don't fall asleep, got your fave pudding." We heard Chloe scream in the garden.

"Daddy, Lovely won't move. Has he gone to heaven?" She clung to me. Mack checked. He nodded yes. She started crying her eyes out.

"Come here," Rae said. She went to Rae. "When Holly our dog went to heaven, I was very sad. But I know she's happy in heaven, with Auntie Niamh. Lovely will be OK there too. I promise."

"Really promise?" Chloe asked.

"Really promise. Come on, let's get you inside, it's cold."

We buried Lovely and said a prayer. Thaddeus came and asked if we could help him and Malek pick some fruit and vegetables from college, as there was a lot going on. We jumped at the chance.

"Blimey. You've done a good job with this lot," I told him.

"Oh my god, this is well nice," Mack said, eating a plum. Thaddeus laughed. "Glad you like it. There's more where that came from," Thaddeus told us. We were amazed of the hard work they had put in.

His tutor came over. "Hi, I'm Mr. Andrews. How do you know Thaddeus?"

Mack and I smiled at each other. "We're his parents. I'm Mack. This is Michael."

He was taken aback. "I thought he was kidding. He's really good at this. We've entered him in to younger gardener of the year. He doesn't know. It's a surprise."

We told Thaddeus, "Really! Wow. Where is it?" Mr. Andrews told him here in three weeks' Saturday.

The day came, when Thaddeus was up for the award, which he won hands down.

"Couldn't have done it without Grandpa." He took Malek's hand. "Thanks, Grandpa."

"My child, helping was easy; it has given me great enjoyment to watch and help you. Mack, Michael, let's go! We're hungry and I need the loo!" We laughed. So did Mr. Andrews.

When we got home, the kids had brought Thaddeus some presents. It was a nice gardening set and a nice outdoor warm jacket. Just what he wanted.

"Brilliant, just what I needed. Can we go for a walk along the beach? I need a walk." He took our hands. "Dads, thank you for everything. I love you two very much. You have given me so much."

"Right back at you, kiddo," I told him. "You're very talented at what you do. You're very gifted. Proud of you so much, Thaddeus."

That made him smile. He turned to Mack and asked for his dinner.

"You got it, son. Very proud of you, always have. Always will."

Thaddeus held our hands. "I just want you to know, you are the best parents ever. I'm proud of you. I love you very much. Dad, I want my fave too, tonight."

"You got it, son," Mack told him.

Rae and I had a row that evening.

"Why can't I go on the trip? Bella's coming with me. It's for four days.

431

It's only France," she said.

"What's going on?" Mack said. "I could hear you from the shed."

Rae told him about the trip to France. "Good idea. When do you go?"

"See. Dad thinks it's a good idea. It'll do me good," Rae told me.

"Come on, Mike. Why?" Mack asked me, sticking the kettle on.

"Because she's never gone away on her own," I told him.

"I'm right here. Dad, please. Bella!" Rae called.

Bella came in. "Dad, come on. It's four days. My tutor thinks it will do me good. He thinks I should be in Rae's group. Please," Bella pleaded.

I caved. "I'm not happy. OK, OK. You can go."

They were happy. They started planning on what to wear. Mack handed me my tea. He just looked at me.

"Shut up!" I told him.

He smiled. "I agree with Rae. It will do her some good. Having a break. At least, Bella will be with her. She needs this. They both do. She stood her ground with you. But she didn't push her luck. Rae gets that from you." He kissed my head. "You're a good dad."

"You too. She's my little girl. Our little girl. Almost eighteen. Jesus," I told him. Mack shook his head. "Daft old git."

Rae and Bella couldn't wait to go. They went happy as Larry. Mack took my hand. "Come on," he said. "I'll get you a coffee. I miss them too."

It was quiet without them. Chloe didn't like it. "When are they coming home?"

"Tomorrow. It's your birthday," I told her. She smiled.

True to word, they loved France.

"Chloe!" Bella told Chloe. "Look in that big pretty pink bag."

Rae and Bella couldn't stop smiling. Chloe started smiling too.

"It's beautiful." It was a lovely dress and a doll she wanted. Plus, they got her another book and colouring book and pens and new shoes.

Mack did to them. "That's too much."

"Don't care. She's our little sister. There was a lovely market there," Rae told him. She was really spoilt. They made her a lovely cake. She fell asleep in Lydia's arms. "Come on, miss, bed."

The next morning, I came down to Mack shouting in the garage. "Shit, fucking thing!" He hurt his hand on his bike.

Callum walked in. "What's the yelling?" He looked at the bike. "I can fix this. I'll do it in a bit, I'm hungry. Brekkie first. Go fix your hand. Idiot!"

I smiled. "Come on. I'll get you one of Rae's teacakes."

"Really! It's eight in the morning." He chirped up.

As I gave Mack a teacake, Rae's face was a picture. "Oh no, you don't. It's eight in the morning. That's for after dinner. You will have your fave. Bacon and eggs."

"Dad gave to me," he grassed me up.

She looked at me. "Really! Dad!"

"He hurt his hand on his bike," I told her.

"Don't care if he picked his nose. You're not having it." Rae took it from him and made tea. Callum laughed. Rae looked at us. "Idiots." And walked off.

"She's mean." Mack said.

"No, I'm not!" she called back.

"Here, Dad." Callum gave him his bacon and eggs.

"You're a good lad," Mack said, eating.

Callum and I smiled at each other. Callum fixed his bike. "Sorted. You need to take care of this bike. Take it out every now and then. It's a cool bike."

A few days later. "Callum!" Mack called. "Get your coat."

Callum looked confused. "Where are we going?" he asked. Mack chucked him a spare helmet. "Really?"

They had a nice ride on his Harley. They pulled in to an old country pub. "This is a good day out, Dad," Callum said.

"Good. One more surprise. Your dad and I have been talking. When you're older, the bike's yours," Mack told him.

Callum's face was a picture. "Dad, that's too much. Dad bought you that."

"Son. No more. The bike's yours. What do you want for lunch?" Mack asked him. When they got home, Callum hugged me. "Thanks."

"You're welcome, son. Good day?" I asked him.

He nodded and yawned. We sat on the sofa.

"Let me tell you something," Callum told us. "You two are the most amazing people in my life. You have given me more than I could ever imagine. I'm glad I've got you as my parents. Thank you. Cuppa. Promise I won't give you a tea cake. Don't want Rae telling me off."

"Callum," I told him, "we're proud of you so much. Never stop being you."

We heard banging and Fran saying "Shit!"

"What's going on?" I asked her.

"I'm trying to work on my art project for uni. It's not going very well. Got no bloody room." She scratched her head like Mack. We both had the same idea.

A few weeks later, Fran had been at university late every day.

"Close your eyes, princess!" we told her.

"Got no problem with that," she said, yawning.

We walked her outside. "Open them," I said.

Her face was a picture. "Daddy!" We had built her a little sun house, but big enough to get her art stuff, everything. "You should not have done this."

"Listen. You can do this at home. We want you safe and well. The idea of you being out late is not good. So, this is a present," Mack told her.

She hugged us both. Then she clocked the old radio she always wanted. "You spoil me!"

We smiled. The others came in.

"This is amazing," Thaddeus told us.

Fran was in awe of it. "This is beautiful. Thank you is not enough."

I put my arm around her shoulder. "Fran."

"Princess," she corrected me, smiling.

I smiled back. "This is a gift from Dad and me. We wanted to do this. All the others did something too."

Olivia walked in. "This is beautiful. Fran, it's you."

At that moment, Fran burst into tears.

"Fran!" Olivia hugged her.

"I'm OK. I'm just so grateful. Really I am. I love it." She hugged Olivia back. "I'm a lucky princess."

Mack and I smiled.

"Right, come on." Mack said. "Early night for you, miss," he told Fran.

"After one cuppa with my sisters. Please? And a choccie biscuit." She looked at us.

"Just one." I kissed her head. "You need to rest." She nodded. Ten minutes later, she fell asleep on Olivia. Olivia smiled and woke her up. "Come on, bed."

She yawned. "Can you read me my book, Olivia?"

"For you. I'll give you the world, my wonderful sister," Olivia told her. That brought a tear to our eyes.

Leo saw this. "It's OK, Dad," he told us.

"I know. It was a sweet thing she said," I told him. He smiled.

Olivia came down. She looked at Leo. "Tomorrow. You and me are going out for lunch. We haven't done that for ages. Then the market." He was so happy, he hugged her. "Thanks, Olivia."

"For my Leo, anything. Now, get ready for bed," she told him. He did as he was told. "Don't look at me like that," she told us.

"We'll give you the money for tomorrow," Mack told her.

"Like hell you will," she told him, putting the kettle on.

"Olivia," he said. I smiled at them.

"Now, you two, listen to me." She pointed her finger at us. "How often do I take out my brother? Not another word. Understand?"

I laughed. "What!" they said together.

"You sound like so much like your nan. She would have backed you up. Your dad and I would have lost. You win," I told her.

"'Course I'm going to win. I'm a Denton girl," she said, sipping on her tea. Mack shook his head, smiling. She looked round the corner. "Do you think Rae will notice a missing tea cake?"

"Yes, I will! Don't even think about it!" Rae yelled from the den.

"Damn it!" Olivia said. We had to smile. "So not fair!"

I burst out laughing. "You always said that when you couldn't get your way. You used to fold your arms and storm off. Like your first day at school. You said to us, 'Don't make me go! I'll eat my carrots'."

She smiled. "No, I never."

"Yes, you did," Mack said, smiling. "When we told you to go, you did what your dad said. It was funny." She laughed. We sat on the sofa and she leaned on my arm.

"You always had a good sense of right and wrong. Like your dad." I told her, pointing to Mack. She smiled at Mack.

Leo came down and sat with us. "Everyone OK?" We nodded.

"We're just talking about when Olivia was little." I looked at Olivia, she was asleep, snoring.

"Why do the girls snore?" Leo asked.

"You should hear your dad," I told him. "He's like a tractor. Olivia, bed. Come on."

She got up and yawned. "I don't sound like a tractor," Mack said.

"Liar. I had to kick your shins, I had to sleep on the couch." I told him, putting the cups in the sink.

"Wouldn't do that if I was you, Leo said. "If the girls catch you, you're doomed. Put them in the dishwasher." He went to bed.

"I'm not that bad," Mack said. He had the hump.

"You snore badly. Always have done. Now fancy an early night?" I asked him.

"Thought you'd never ask!" Mack grinned like a Cheshire cat.

A few days later, we got a surprise. Alice came in. She had just got back from her job that had taken her to France for a month.

"Alice!" I said. She hugged me. "Does your mum know you are here?"

"Yes. Got in this morning. Where's Uncle Mack?" she asked.

I called after him. He was pleased as a punch to see her. Then Rae walked in. Her face was a picture. "Alley Cat! Oh my God!" They hugged each other.

"I missed you," Alice told her. "We got a lot to talk about. Plus, got you a load of gifts. Couldn't help it."

"You're naughty. Come on, den. Dad, stick the kettle on. Have you eaten?" Rae asked her. Alice said no.

"Right. Dad, start cooking. Alley Cat is staying for dinner. Call Auntie Lydia. Tell them they're coming here for dinner!" Rae said. Alice laughed.

"Anything else, your highness?" Mack asked her.

"Hurry up with that tea. Alley Cat, I'm sorry, he's an idiot."

Alice couldn't stop laughing. Mack smiled and did as he was told.

Lydia and the crew came round.

"Thank God for Rae," Lydia said. "Couldn't be arsed to cook."

"You never can," Emily told her. "What is for dinner, anyway?"

"Roast beef, all the trimmings," Mack told her.

"Mum, I'm moving in," Emily told her.

"Fine. One less mouth to feed," Lydia said, sitting on the couch next to Oliver.

"Sit down, Auntie Lydia. Make yourself at home. Oh look, surprise! Pyjamas. Do you actually own clothes?" Oliver said sarcastically.

Mack and I were laughing. She didn't have an answer. "A glass of wine? Or would you like the bottle with a straw, because you're a lazy old moo?" he asked her.

That was it. We couldn't stop laughing. Even Lydia laughed. Oliver got her a glass.

Thaddeus walked in and shook his head.

"What's the matter?" Joel asked him.

"Do not go in the den. The girls are going hormonal again and they are looking at the Avon book. Plus, Bella says she wants to marry the bloke who plays Captain America." Thaddeus shook his head.

"Bella isn't marrying no one," Mack said. "Not even spider man."

"Funny enough. That's who Fran wants to marry. The bloke that plays him. My sisters are weird," Thaddeus said.

Just then, Dad and Malek came in. "Ah, Thaddeus. I have a present for you," Dad told him.

Dad gave him an envelope. Dad and Malek smiled. It was an allotment plot. He always wanted one. "Granddad. Too much."

"You always wanted to grow your own veg. It has a shed too. It's a good size for you. We'll help. Call it an early birthday present."

He hugged them both. We smiled. Thaddeus had tears in his eyes. "This means so much. Dad, you hear that?"

"Son, good for you. We'll help as well," I told him.

"Saves going to Asda for the stuff," Mack said.

"What am I, a delivery service?" Thaddeus said. We laughed. "Can we go and have a look, please?"

We went and had a look. It was beautiful. Thaddeus took Dad's hand and said the most wonderful thing to him. "Granddad. I just want you to know that you are the most precious Granddad that I will ever have. What you have done for me is wonderful. I hope I can be half the man you are when I'm older. You are the best thing ever. I love you so much, Pop-pop."

For the first time since Mum's funeral, he cried. Lost for words. Lydia and I looked at each other, knowing that meant everything to him.

On the way home, Lydia asked him. "You OK, Dad?"

"Yes. That was the most wonderful thing. It meant a lot," he told her. "He looks up to you. Always has. Always will. Just like Michael and I. Love you, Dad," Lydia told him.

"Love you too," he smiled. He looked at Malek and Mack trying to plan the allotment. "For God's sake, you two. This is Thaddeus' plot. Let him organise it. Bloody hell." Lydia and I laughed.

There was a lady next to us who smiled. "Hi. I'm Charlotte. I can help out every now and then."

"Thank you," I told her, looking at them all.

"That's your wife and kids?" she asked.

I smiled. "I'm here with my kids. That bloke with the blue t-shirt, and tattoos is my husband." Mack was scratching his head.

She smiled. "Sorry. How long you been married?" she asked.

"Twenty-five years. Nine kids," I told her.

She was gobsmacked. She then laughed. Mack walked into a tree and got a nosebleed.

Olivia turned round and said, "You're an idiot. How can you not see a tree?" She stuck a tampon up his nose.

"Who's that?" Charlotte asked, laughing.

"That's our eldest, Olivia. She gives him what for,"

With that, Olivia looked at me. "Dad, what's wrong with him? How can he not see a bloody tree?"

I laughed. Mack said to her, "Excuse me! I'm the parent. Mike! Tell her."

Charlotte was in fits of laughter. I was laughing so much. "Charlotte. Thanks for your help. Right everyone, come on home. Olivia. Leave your dad alone."

Mack had the hump. When Oliver saw him with the tampon up his nose, he was in fits of laughter. "Oh my god! Dad, look at me!" Oliver took a photo on his phone. I shook my head, laughing.

On the way home, I saw that Fran had tears in her eyes. I tapped Mack. He looked and noticed it too. When we got home, we had a chat with her.

"Honestly, Dad, nothing is wrong. I'm just happy that Thaddeus got something. He's such a kind soul and a good brother. I just got choked up he got what he wanted."

"That's sweet, Fran," I told her.

She looked at me and said, "Oh my God! How many times do I have to remind you? I'm a 'princess'. Dad! Tell him. Do I have to keep wearing my tiara?" She shook her head.

Mack laughed. "Mike, she's a princess."

"See, told you. Now put the kettle on. There's a good lad," she told me. That made Mack really laugh.

"You girls are so bossy," I said, getting up. "Anything else you want?"

"'Scooby Doo'!" she smiled. "Chop chop with that tea!" She then remembered something. "Back in a sec."

When I sat down, she gave us a present. "What's this?" I asked.

"Open it." She was smiling. It was a painting of us, gold by her as a baby.

"Princess," Mack said. "It's beautiful."

I couldn't talk. She looked at me. "Dad. You OK?"

I was choked up. "You are so smart. This is beautiful. Thank you. Just remember, your dad and I will always be your biggest fans."

"Glad you like it." She started yawning. "I'm going for a bath."

"Yeah." I put the photo down and took his hand.

"You are damn good at being a dad," Mack told me. "And a bloody good husband. I know I don't say it a lot. It's true."

I was quiet for a moment. "Am I enough for you and the kids?"

"Damn right you are. I will never stop being in love you. Why?" he asked.

"In all the years we've been together, it still baffled me that you and I find each other. I love you so much," I told him. We heard the stairs creak. It was Callum.

"You two OK?" Callum asked. "Your marriage isn't in trouble?"

"Callum, no, it's not," I told him. "Not by a long shot. Come here."

He sat with us. "Dad, you are more than enough. For all of us." He leaned on my shoulder. "The greatest gift you gave us kids is knowing that you wanted us and that you love us and Dad. So, stop being over-dramatic. Don't forget you lot are going out for date night tomorrow. Uncle Joel is coming over later. Cuppa?"

Just then Joel walked in. "Man! That woman is a nightmare on two legs!"

"What's my sister done now?" I asked him.

"Not her. Emily. Jesus. We got a call from her school, saying she kicked the crap out of some kid who picked on someone with autism. When they asked her to apologise, she told him he's got more chance of his dick falling off and that Everton'll win the cup. Lydia is over the moon."

Callum was laughing. "That's funny. Come off it, Uncle Joel, she is a Denton."

"Shut up and make me a coffee. And a tea cake," Joel said.

"No, you can't. Ally Cat said you didn't eat your veg. I know it's broccoli. Suck it up," Rae called.

We laughed. "Those girls. Ah, Olivia. Call your Aunt Lydia, tell her I'm here," Joel said.

She stood there and glared at him. "Really! What's wrong with you doing it, you lazy git. Jesus, the men in this family. Useless!"

"Mack, tell her. Can't be arsed," Joel told him.

"Piss off. I ain't telling her," he told her. "Besides, you're scared of Maggie."

"Am not," Joel told him. Oliver looked at him.

"Really!" He smiled. "When you came home from the pub pissed as a fart with Dad" — pointing to me — "it wasn't Lydia that kicked your arse. Maggie let rip." Lydia laughed. "Maggie sent Olivia the video of you doing shit karaoke and bad dad dancing. Olivia's face when you walked in."

"That wasn't funny," I said. Rae smiled.

"No. It was hysterical." Oliver laughed. "The video was funny. You're not a bad singer, by the way."

Mack smiled. "That was funny. You came home singing Stevie Wonder's 'Superstition'. Then you threw up."

"Wasn't that bad," I said.

"That was a good night," Joel told us smiling. "My fave was when we sang 'Easy Lover' by Phil Collins and Philip Bailey."

"I saw the video.," Alfie said. "It was so funny. It got loads of views on YouTube. I think there hundred thousand. Drunk Dads singing."

Mack was laughing. "It was really good."

Then out of nowhere, we heard Bella and Rae shouting. "Oh my god!"

"What's wrong?" Joel asked.

"Michael Roux Jr is coming to our college to judge our cooking contest in a few weeks." Bella was so happy.

"Who?" Joel was confused.

"Oh my God!" she replied, yawning "He's the best. We got to do something amazing. Where's our cook book?"

Rae started yawning too. "Right, you two. Take a break," I told them. "You two are tired."

"But, Daddy!" Rae said.

"Do as Dad says," Mack told them. "You can cook over the weekend. You two need a rest. Go and get changed."

They were about to say something. "No arguing. Go on," I told them.

They did as they were told. When they came down, they were still yawning.

"I'll put the kettle on," Callum said, smiling.

"I'll help you," I told him. I looked at Callum. "How are you, son?"

"I'm good. Tired. But OK," he told me, pouring the water in the teapot.

"Tomorrow you, me and Dad, day out. Don't argue. I know you haven't got college. Mack! We're taking Callum out for the day," I told him.

"Where are we going?" he asked, yawning.

"The lakes," Callum said. "Then the pub for lunch. You're not going to argue with Dad?"

"No chance," Mack said. "I do as I'm told."

I smiled. "After all these years, it finally sunk in. Why did it take so long?"

The kids laughed. "I'm too tired to argue," Mack said.

"You're always tired," Thaddeus told him, looking at the paper.

We took Callum out for the day. Then Olivia phoned me to ask if we could get her a chocolate and tissues.

"What does she want that for?" Mack asked. In all the years, he still hadn't worked it out.

Callum had to tell him. "For God's sake. Hormones."

"You're a fine one," Callum told him. "You're worse than the girls. I swear you're always on." Mack looked at me.

"He's right," I told him. Mack just smiled.

"You better get the good chocolate. Otherwise, you're a gonner," Callum told us.

When we got home, Maggie was there crying her heart out. "Maggie!" I was concerned.

"Dad!" Fran said. "Get Aunt Lydia and Uncle Joel here now!"

They ran over to see their baby crying. "Maggie!" Lydia said. "What's wrong? God, you're shaking. Joel?"

"Talk to us," he told her.

"You'll hate me. You will kick me out." She sobbed.

"Maggie. Whatever it is, we can fix it," Lydia told her.

"Really! Mum, I'm pregnant. The guy I was dating left when I told him. He doesn't want to know. Oh God. Mum." She fell into Lydia. We were stunned.

"Maggie Anne Green," Joel said. "Look at me. We don't hate you. We love you. I'm sorry that prick left you. But we will deal with this as a family. I'm going to be a granddad."

"Dad's right," Lydia told her. "We are with you all the way. I'm too young to be a nan."

"You're not ashamed of me," Maggie asked them.

"You listen to me!" Lydia told her. "I am not. Have I ever been ashamed of you? I know you are scared. But we" — pointing to Joel — are going to help you. Maggie Anne Green. I'm proud of you."

Alfie sat next to Maggie. "You listen to me," he said. "Whatever happens, you are going to make one hell of a mum. Us four will help. You're not alone. Not now, not ever. This baby is going to be so happy, Maggie." He hugged her tight.

That made her cry even more. "I'm scared."

"Oh, honey," Lydia told her. "Even now, I get scared when you kids do your own thing. Doesn't matter how old you are. It's worth it. If I ever find that piece of shit. I will kill him and make it look like an accident. Then I'll tell the police your dad did it."

"Bitch!" Joel muttered. We laughed.

"Thanks, Mum. Dad. I was worried that I would disappoint you."

"You will never disappoint us," Joel told her. "When you'll get this baby in your arms, it'll all make sense. Lydia, call your dad."

Which she did. He came over with Malek.

"Maggie, let's talk." Dad never gave anything away.

"Grandad," Maggie cried.

"Hush. I love you, Maggie. Do not fear. I'm not disappointed. I am going to be a great grandad. My eldest granddaughter. When you were put in my arms, my God, I was so happy. You looked at me for the longest time. I cried so hard. I'm a proud man to have you as my eldest. You know you have your nan's smile and laugh. When you and Olivia get together, it's your nan in one. I love you so much. If it's a boy, call him Simon."

She hugged him. "Love you, Grandad. Grandpa."

"Allah has blessed you with life, your child will be loved. Never fear, Maggie." He hugged her. He said the family motto in Arabic.

The next few weeks went by. Maggie was showing. Fran and Mack had a blazing row. She wanted to go to a party with a few mates and come back in the morning.

"You are not going. There will be drugs and stuff," Mack told her. "You are not staying overnight. End of discussion. Fuck's sake."

"Don't see the problem," Fran shouted back. "You let the others go to parties. Jesus. You're an arsehole. I'm going."

"Like hell you are! Jesus, princess!" Mack yelled.

"I'm not your princess. Don't ever call me that. I wish you weren't my dad. You're a prick." She stormed past him. "Rot in hell. I'm leaving." He tried to stop her.

"She's mad. I'll check on her later."

When I did, but she was gone. "Shit, shit," I called the police. Mack was beside himself. Everyone tried ringing. Three days later, the police found her at her mate Abigail's.

We rowed when she got home. "You scared the shit out of us," I yelled at her.

"Whatever!" she said. Then out of nowhere, Mack lost his temper. In twenty-six years, I'd only seen it once.

"You listen to me!" he screamed. "Anything could have happened. I didn't want to get a phone call to say you were on a slab, dead. Get to your room. Now."

She did as she was told. She was shocked. She cried and ran to her room, slamming by the door shut.

"Mack!" I said.

"Don't" he said. "Anything could have happened. That's our little girl." He walked off, and had a scotch and cigar in the garden.

They didn't talk for three weeks. Callum had had enough. "Will you talk! Jesus, you're both so stubborn."

"No fucking way!" Francesca said. "I wish he was dead."

I exploded. "That's enough. Both of you. We hate this. Cut this shit out now!"

"Fine," Fran told us. She went and packed a bag. Our faces fell.

"Fran!" I told her.

Dad came and picked her up. Mack came in and saw her bag. His face fell. "Oh, princess. We had a bad row. We need to sort this out." He went to her, but she went to the door.

"Grandad. Can we go, please?" She walked out.

"I will talk to her," Dad told us.

Mack burst into tears. "What have I done!"

A few days later, Fran and my dad came back. We all were a mess. Fran had lost weight. Olivia hugged her. "Oh Fran. Right, you three, den, now."

Fran burst into tears. "I'm sorry. So sorry. Don't throw me away. I'm so bad."

"We had a row," Mack told her, with tears running down his face. "They can't have my princess. I love you."

"No! No!" She was crying, hitting him. "I was so wrong. I shouldn't have done that."

We talked for a long time. "Are we OK now, Dad?" Fran asked us.

"Yes, we are," I told her. "You need to eat."

The others came in. Chloe ran to her. "I've missed you so much."

We got a takeaway. Olivia and the girls talked about everything. "I'm sorry I did that to you all. I felt bad about what I did."

"What's done is done," Bella said. "Main thing is your home, where you belong."

Later, she came to us with her book. "Please, I've missed this."

I read her her book. She fell asleep in my arms.

The next morning, Mack and Fran went out for the afternoon. "Are we really OK?" Fran asked.

"Yes. Always. I shouldn't have exploded like that," he said.

"I understand why, now. You were protecting me," Fran said. "Hang on. Look. That's that picture Dad wanted."

She gave me the picture. "Thank you." I hugged her tight. "Honey, losing you would break my heart. Never again. OK?"

"Daddy. I was scared. We got lost again," she told me. "I'm to blame as well. Promise me you won't give me away!" she said.

I smiled. "Bit late now. You're twenty. Never in a million years can they have my princess. You are our baby. Forever."

"Thanks, Daddy." We sat there for ages.

Thaddeus came down and sat with us. He took Fran's hand. "I'm glad you're home. I missed you very much. I felt like I wouldn't see you again. We are close. Please don't leave me again. You and Dad are so stubborn.

You brightened up my day. We did so many silly things to Dad. We need to keep talking. Running away's no good. Promise me."

She cuddled up to Thaddeus. "You have my word. I promise. Dad, promise!"

"Always," I said. "You know you two were always lost when the other one weren't there. You always cried."

"Really!" Thaddeus asked.

Fran was confused. "Why?"

Mack sat next to Thaddeus. "I think because you two came together. I remember when secured to put you both for a nap, you two always held each other's hands. It was the most wonderful thing ever to see. When Dad used to come home from work, you used to hide behind the couch and make Dad jump. Then you would give him the biggest hug ever."

They smiled at that. "Tomorrow," Mack told us, "we're going to Fran's fave place for dinner."

She looked at him. "No arguing." He kissed her head.

"You two are real angels," Thaddeus told us. "Fran. Tea and a biscuit?" She had missed this.

Later that night, we heard screaming. It was Fran. Olivia was with her. "It's OK."

"It's not." Fran sobbed. "I hurt them bad. They look at me differently. I'm not their princess any more. I'm stupid and ugly. I don't want to live any more. Let me go, Olivia. Let me go."

"Never. Fran you're not stupid nor ugly. You're so beautiful. I love you. Please don't say that." Olivia started crying. We came in.

"Princess," I told her, "you are our everything."

Mack sat on the bed next to Fran. "Come here. Come on."

She cuddled up to him. "What happened, happened. I admit I was harsh on you. I shouldn't have done that. I felt really bad. You are still my princess. Always. I am sorry, so is Dad. I don't want to hear that talk any more about you not being here. I love you. I love you." She calmed down.

"Love you too, Dad. Always," she said, dozing off.

"I'll stay with her tonight," Olivia told us. "She'll be fine."

True to word, she was. "Sorry about that," She told us and Olivia.

"All is good." Olivia kissed her head.

Maggie came over to see us. "I'm well fat!" She said sitting on the couch.

We laughed. "You sound like your mum when she was pregnant with you lot," I told her.

"Whatever." She moaned. "Can I have toast and marmite, please?"

"You hate marmite," Oliver told her.

"Pregnancy does weird things to a woman," she said. Oliver smiled and made it for her and a cuppa. They talked for ages when Lydia and Joel came in.

"There you are. I was worried."

"Mum, I'm fine. You still coming to my scan later?" she asked.

"Damn right, we are," she told her. "You know when I went to my scans with all of you, I was so nervous. This tiny person growing. I was so blessed, Maggie. Dad and I are always with you. I can't wait to see my grandchild. You are a wonderful daughter. You are going to make a damn good mum."

"Just like you, Mum." Maggie leaned on Lydia's shoulder. "What's it like being a parent?"

"Tough, hard," Joel told her. "But it's the most amazing thing ever to see this little person grow into an amazing person. We got you, Maggie. All the way." She wiped away the tears.

She had the scan. Maggie was having a boy. When they came to tell us the news, I asked her if she had thought of names.

She told us, "His name is Joel Simon Green." Joel and Dad were chuffed. Joel had to walk away. Maggie followed. "I named my son after the best man I knew. You, Dad. I'm proud of you so much for being there for me." They hugged.

Lydia told Joel, "See. You are an amazing man and father."

She asked Alfie and Jack to be godfathers and Olivia and Fran to be godmothers. Fran was surprised. "Really! Yes."

Olivia gave Maggie a bag. It was a baby blanket she had made for baby Joel. "Olivia. It's beautiful."

Olivia had a tear in her eye. "We all had one growing up. This baby has got an amazing family. Lydia and Joel. You are going to be bloody good grandparents. Damn good. You two," she said, looking at us, "are going to be amazing great uncles."

We were gobsmacked. "Stay," Oliver said. "Let's have an early family day. It is Friday. Please, Dad." We said yes.

446

Dad was quiet. "What is wrong?" Lydia asked him.

"Nothing," he replied. "Flattered that I'm his middle name. Lydia, you listen to me. You are an amazing daughter, mother, sister. I am so proud of you. Your mother would be proud of the woman you are."

"Thanks, Dad," Lydia cried. Then we cried.

"My God!" Emily said. "We're all so weird. Can I see the picture of the baby?" Maggie showed her the picture. "Beautiful. Can't wait to meet my nephew."

Five months later, Joel was born. Healthy, eight pound nine. Good set of lungs.

"Hello, my beautiful boy," Maggie told him. "Welcome home. I love you very much. Grandpa?" she told Malek. We all listened. "I've added an extra name for Joel. His name is Joel Simon Malek Green."

He was taken aback. "Thank you for that, my child. This child is a gift. That is a wonderful gift." The tears ran down his face.

Dad stood with him. "You are a wonderful friend and part of this family. Never forget that. Allah is proud of you."

That was it, we were all in tears. "I need a drink!" Lydia said.

"Oh no, you don't," Emily told her. "Really! In a hospital. Bloody hell."

"I've got a Ribena," Chloe replied. "He's wrinkly. Like granddad."

"I'm not that bad," Dad said.

"Keep telling yourself that, old man." Jack said.

Oliver and Jack high-fived each other. Dad looked at them. "Love you," Oliver said.

"Shut up. No Apple pie for you," Dad told him.

"Wicked old man," Oliver told him.

"Oh, Joel," Maggie told him. "You've got one weird family. But it's a happy one.'

"We're not weird," Emily said. "Different. Not weird. Come on. Let's get you home. You need rest, Maggie." She looked at Joel. "Just so you know, you've got one hell of a good mum." Emily kissed Maggie's head. "Proud of you sis. Really proud." Lydia and Joel smiled at each other.

"Amazing." Joel said.

"Were we like that when we came home?" Callum asked.

"Yes," Mack replied. "Would you believe that Ollie was the smallest?"

"Shut up!" Callum replied.

"Really." I told him. I was getting choked up.

"You OK?" Thaddeus asked.

Mack smiled and said, "Yes. Having you kids was a god send. Any parent will tell you that. We waited so long to have you. We wouldn't swap you for *anything*." He looked at Fran.

We stopped at the lakes. "Why we stopping?" Leo said.

"To get some fresh air," Mack said, taking my hand.

We saw our kids being who they were.

"Princess. Come here," Mack told her.

"What happened, happened. Just remember this, you are my daughter. I'm proud to be your father. You're a special person, just as important as the others."

Then Chloe shouted, "Princess, can we feed the ducks? Daddy, the bread."

"I love you two. Coming, little bear." She took her hand.

Chloe looked at Fran. "Can we draw when we get home? Can Leo help?"

Fran nodded. Leo came and helped with the ducks.

"Dad!" Oliver shouted. "Dinner!"

"Why don't you cook for a change? You're twenty-three," Mack called after him.

Oliver laughed. "Yeah, like that's going happen. Really. Getting your kids to cook. Not normal." I had to laugh.

"How about burger and chips?" Fran said. We agreed.

"Apple pie for pudding," Oliver said.

"Really! Pudding before dinner?" Thaddeus said.

"Why not!" was the reply.

After dinner, the kids were in the den with their blankets, reading and watching the telly.

"What?" Oliver said.

We shook our heads and smiled. "You should be out with your mates, having a laugh," I told them.

"Can't be bothered," Callum told us. "Besides, we like it here. Right?"

448

he asked them. They all nodded yes.

Olivia was showing Chloe how to do a blanket she was making for her. "Go on. You do it," Olivia told her.

Chloe did just that. Mack got a tear in his eye. Then we heard, "Hello. It's Jacob."

"Den," I called.

He smiled and looked at Mack. "You big poof. Put the kettle on." I laughed.

"What do you want?" Mack asked, smiling.

"I heard that Rae and Bella got that contest next week. Got a recipe for them." He gave it to them. "It's Auntie Niamh's recipe. You loved it when you stayed at ours. She made it just for you. It's yours. For keeps." Rae and Bella hugged him.

"This means a lot, Uncle Jacob," Rae told him, wiping her eyes.

Thaddeus looked at the ingredients. "I've got this in the allotment, apart from two. Well go there on Saturday. Jacob, you're coming too. Call Uncle Matthew and Auntie Anna. Make a day of it."

We knew better than to argue with the kids.

Anna loved the allotment. "This is wonderful. Thaddeus, good job. Smart boy."

"Here." Thaddeus handed her a bag. It was filled with fruit and vegetables.

"Oh, Thaddeus. Thank you. Here. Make yourself useful." She handed Matthew the bag. "What else you got here?" Off they walked.

"And you say I'm whipped," Mack told him, laughing.

"Shut up!" Matthew said. "We're having a party week after next. Thirty years of marriage. Come over the lot of you. Lydia and the crew. Stay."

"You sure?" I asked.

"Yes, we are," Matthew said. "Besides, Anna told me to." We laughed. Olivia was giving Mack what for.

"Are you really that bloody stupid? How can you not see that? Jesus, idiot."

"May I remind I'm the parent!" he replied. "Mike, tell her."

"Then act like it. Git face!" she told him. Matthew, Jacob and I were laughing so hard.

"Oh my God! Stand on your own two feet. At the moment, you're

449

going to hobble on one," she told him. That was it. She looked at me.

"You better drive home. We'll end up in Bridgend at this rate," she told me.

"When will you stop picking on me?" Mack asked her.

"When you grow a pair!" she told him. Mack looked at me.

"Don't look at me like that. You wanted kids," I told him.

Jacob told Mack, "She gives you what for. Jesus."

"What is this? Have a Go at Mack Day?" He grumbled.

"God's sake! Shut up!" Olivia told him.

I smiled. So did Mack. "She's so like my mum. It's uncanny. I'm glad she's as tough as old boots. I'm proud of her and all of them."

"I know," Mack said. He showed me his arm. Another tattoo. It read Mack and Mike forever.

"I love it. And you." Then we heard singing. "Because we're happy!" They were singing their song. Anna put her hand on her heart.

"You all right, love?" Matthew asked her.

"Yes. I still can't believe they still call me Auntie Anna. I'm not their real aunt," Anna said.

"To us, you are," Callum told her. "Uncle Matthew and Dad are like brothers. That makes you our aunt. Come on. Tea. You're family, Anna. Always." That made her day.

I got in from shopping. It was quiet. Something smelled great. Mack looked amazing. "What's going on?" I asked.

"Get changed. Kids are at your dad's." He went back to the kitchen.

When I came down, the table was looking good. "What's the occasion?" I asked, taking a glass of wine.

"Do you remember what day it is?" Mack asked.

It then twigged. It was the day we met at the hospital. "Twenty-seven years ago. Best day of my life," I told him. He smiled. "Best years of my life. This is to say thank you for that."

"Mack!" I said.

He put his wine down and kissed me. "I don't know what or where I'd be without you. You and the kids are..." he trailed off.

"I know. Beef bourguignon. Our favourite. Suppose the kids were in on it?" I asked. He smiled.

We talked and laughed. It was good to do that. The next morning, the kids came in with Dad.

"So!" Callum said to me. "Did you get him pregnant again?" he asked.

"Callum!" I told him. Dad chuckled.

"Well. Every time you are two have a night in, we end up having another brother of sister," Callum said, going to the fridge.

We were lost for words.

Olivia came down. "Dad, can we look after little Joel today? To give Maggie a break?" We agreed.

"You sure?" Lydia said.

"Why not?" I told her. "Maggie can have a break. You lot have a rest. We'll bring him back tomorrow."

"Can't let you do that," Maggie told us.

"Tough," Olivia told her. "It's one night. It'll do you good. Now bed, miss. Love you."

"Love you too." Maggie did as she was told.

Little Joel made his mark at home. He was now almost a year old. He slept through the night and woke up at eight. When we took him home, we told Maggie.

"Really! Bloody hell. He has me up at six-thirty. Thanks. Just what I needed."

He was happy to see her. "Mummy."

Three weeks later, I was taking the laundry up when I heard, "Oh, thank God," from the loo.

I pushed the door open; it was Olivia. The look on her face.

"Kitchen. Now!" I said. "And bring that with you."

I walked in the kitchen. Mack looked at me then saw Olivia. "What is going on?"

Olivia sat at the table. "When did it happen?" I asked her.

"Two weeks ago," she said. Mack saw the test.

"Dad. We were careful. But it, er…" We cottoned on. "I only took it because I was late. Two days."

"Why didn't you talk to us?" Mack asked her.

"Give over, Dad. You two never want to hear it when I do. You'd have a heart attack. Sometimes, it hard talking to you two." Olivia looked at the floor.

451

"Honey, we're sorry," I told her. Mack and I looked at each other.

"So am I," Olivia told us. "I should've told you. I was scared. Don't be mad." Mack hugged her. So did I.

"You will always be our little girl," I told her. "We will never stop worrying about you kids. Ever. But we need to talk. Promise?"

She nodded. She went and had a bath.

"Jesus, Mack," I said. "She was really worried about telling us that."

"She's not wrong," Mack said, passing me a drink. "It's tough hearing that stuff. But we have to listen. We have to."

When she came down, she looked relieved. We knew what was up. The rest of them came in.

"What's going on?" Thaddeus said.

Olivia told them.

"Why didn't you tell us?" Fran said.

"Scared," Olivia said.

Fran folded her arms. "We're family. You're always there for us. Come here." Fran hugged her. "Girls, den. Dad, stick the kettle on. Ice cream and sprinkles. Chop, chop."

"Can we come too?" Leo asked. He looked worried. Olivia nodded. They all piled in the den.

"Olivia, you're our sister," Fran told her. "We're here for you, always." Fran gave her her bowl of ice cream.

"That man. Dad, wrong bloody sprinkles!" she shouted at me. Olivia laughed. I brought the right one in. "Anything else, your highness?" I said.

"No. You may go!" She waved me away, smiling. Everyone laughed. "Please talk to us if something brothers you. Please!"

"OK. I will. I'm lucky to have you all," she said. Leo leaned on her shoulder. "I'm OK, cheeky boy. Promise."

"You haven't called me that in ages," Leo said, smiling.

"So, in future, please talk to us. Maybe we can help," Bella told her. Olivia nodded.

We smiled. "Daddy, we're OK," Rae said to Mack.

Thaddeus looked at Olivia. "I am lucky to have you. You and everyone are the best brothers and sisters ever."

Olivia hugged him and had tears in her eyes.

They spent the evening talking. Then Callum walked in. "Good, you're all here. Come in."

This tall young chap walked in. "This is Jonathan. My friend. Jonathan, my family." He said hi.

"So, you and my boy are dating?" I asked Jonathan, smiling.

"Yes, we are." Jonathan and Callum smiled.

"I'm Michael. This is Mack. Callum's dads," I told him, shaking his hand. Mack looked proud.

"Dad," Callum told Mack, "don't get emotional."

"Please. I'm a tough nut," Mack told him. I looked at him.

"You lying shitbag!" I told him. "You're a bloody wimp! You cried at Oliver's play. You cried at 'Frozen'. Bloody 'Frozen'! You were in the army! Dickhead!"

The kids laughed. Jonathan smiled.

"Stay for dinner?" Thaddeus asked him.

"Thanks, but I have to pick my brother up. You still up for Friday night?" he asked Callum.

"Yes. Fox and hound. Seven?" Callum asked him.

He said yes.

Mack and I looked at each other. "What?" Callum looked confused.

"That's where your dad and I went for our first date. Then every Friday, till we got married," Mack told him.

"Really!" Callum was surprised. I nodded. "It's a good omen."

After Jonathan left, we told him we liked him.

"Go for it," I told him.

"Cheers, Dad."

Rae came in and hugged Callum. "I'm very proud of you, Callum. You're just like Dad," she said, pointing to us. "I'm glad you're my brother. Now, fancy a cuppa?"

They sat for the longest time. I propped myself on the door. "You know, Callum," I told him, "when Rae first saw you, she was really happy. She looked at you and said, 'I love you, Callum. I promise to be a good sister. You're perfect'."

Callum had tears in his eyes. "She promised to always look after you. Like the others," Mack told him. "Your dad and I are very proud of you." That was it. Everyone crying.

"For God's sake," Thaddeus said. "Grow a pair."

453

A few weeks later, the kids laid on a surprise for Olivia.

"What's this?" she said walking in the den.

"It's our way of saying thank-you for being our big sister and being there for us," Thaddeus told her.

There was flowers, a card, a tea and cake. Olivia had tears in her eyes.

"I'm your sister. It's my job."

"We love you very much," Callum told her.

She told them, "I'm very proud to be your sister. I'm glad we have each other. You are very important to me."

Chloe ran to her. "Thank you for being my sister like the others. Can we have tea now. Oh here. For you." It was a picture of them all.

Olivia burst into tears. "I don't deserve you all."

"Yes, you do," Bella told her. "I remember when I came home, I was so scared." She welled up. "You stayed with me and told me that you would never hurt me. You would always be here for me. No tears. Come on, Chloe is right. Tea."

They all had a good time. Then we got a call from Lydia. Joel had had a heart attack. We rushed to the hospital. They were all in bits. Mack went to see him while I sat with Lydia.

"This is my fault," she sobbed. "I'm always giving him a hard time. Michael, I can't lose him."

"You won't. He's had to put up with you for almost thirty years. He's not done yet," I told her, trying to lighten the mood.

Mack sat with Joel. "How you doing?" he asked, quietly.

Joel nodded, with tears in his eyes. "I thought I was a goner. I'll be OK. Time will help. Is Lyddie OK?"

"She will be. You really scared her, and us," Mack told him. Joel started crying.

"Hey, hey," Mack said, taking his hand. "It's gonna be OK. Promise."

Lydia walked in. I nodded to Mack to leave them to it. "Bloody hell, Mike," Mack said.

"I know. I've told Lydia the guys are going to stay with us while he's here. We'll manage. Family first. You know that." Mack agreed.

We all piled home. The mood was sombre. We heard a scream from the den. It was Alfie. He was really crying. Those two were close as anything. I hugged him.

"I can't lose him, Uncle Michael." Then the others started. It finally hit them that this had happened. Lydia came home and sat with them.

"Guys. The doctor said he is going to be fine. It wasn't as bad. But this was a wake-up call for him. For us. Dad will be there for a few days. He's scared. He's not showing it. But he is."

"How are you, Mum?" Jack asked her.

She burst into tears. "I thought I was going to lose him. But I'm not. We both got a second chance. I'm OK. Just. Alfie, come here." Alfie did that. She wrapped her arms around him. "Trust me when I tell you, Dad is getting well. We don't lie."

"I'm scared," he said though the tears.

"I know you are, son. I know you all are. Emily, you OK?" Lydia asked her. She nodded. "Come on, you lot, talk."

"Mum, it scared me to think that Dad won't be around," Jack said.

"It scared us all," Alice said.

Maggie got up and walked away. Lydia followed. "Talk to me, Maggie."

Maggie burst into tears. Lydia hugged her. "The thought of little Joel not having his granddad. He loves him. I can't be without him. But I know he will be OK."

We all sat together. Lydia and I sat next to each other. "I love you, little brother."

"Love you too. Always will, always. Joel is a fighter." Lydia was asleep on my shoulder.

A few days later, Joel came home. Alfie stood at the door.

"Come here, son," Joel told him. Alfie hugged him. The others followed. "It's going to be OK. I'm still here. It's going to change."

The next few months did bring change. We all decided to change how we did things. Joel was glad of the support. Then one night, we had a relapse. We ordered pizza.

"This is good," said Thaddeus. "Had enough of eating cardboard."

Lydia walked in and saw the pizza. "Give me a bloody slice before I kill someone. So good." She sat on the chair next to Oliver. "What?" she said chewing on the pizza.

"So attractive. Joel needs a medal to put up with you."

No one noticed Joel walking in. "You serious right now? Pizza. Gimme me a slice."

"Over my dead body," Lydia told him.

"That can be arranged," Joel told her.

She just looked at him. We all smiled. The kids followed. They all ran to the pizza boxes.

"Bloody hell!" I said. "You lot look like you never seen food before."

"I'm sick of eating like a pissing rabbit," Jack said.

"Language!" Lydia told him.

"You swear like a trooper. You turned the room blue when you had that row on the phone with the lady from BT over the phone bill. I'm surprised she didn't need therapy after that conversation. So don't give me that crap. Crazy old lady!" Jack told her, eating the garlic bread and shaking his head.

"I'm not that bad," Lydia said, taking another slice.

"No, 'course you're not. When you're on one, you're the exorcist on a period," Oliver told her.

We all laughed our heads off. Oliver hugged her. "Love you, Lid-lid."

I looked at Mack, he got up and got the envelope from the draw. "Here. From all of us."

It was a long weekend away, to our favourite place.

"Guys, really!" Joel said.

"Call it an early anniversary present. Plus, the fact that you two need a rest. So, suck it up," Mack told her.

"Thank God. NO kids," Lydia said.

Emily looked at her. "You realise that we are more or less grown up? I'm eighteen in a couple of weeks."

"My baby is grown up," Joel said. "What do you want to do for your birthday?"

"Well," she said. "You know that place I love? That woodland place. Where there's a trail and that lovely café? I want to go there. Then the lakes before dinner. All of us. I don't want to go and get drunk like my mates from uni. Doesn't interest me. Can Sophie come with us?"

They nodded. "Don't worry about a cake, Rae and I are making it for you. Your fave."

Emily was happy.

"Then all of you will be staying here for the night. Family night. Emily is in charge of food and films," I told her.

She smiled.

"The day before," Maggie told her, "all of us girls are having a day out to celebrate. Your choice, Emily."

"Really?" she said.

"Yes, really," Maggie said. "It's on family weekend, anyway. Mm, Dad, can you look after little Joel?"

They said yes. They had a brilliant day. As usual, they came back to ours. Lydia walked into the den. I followed her and noticed she was in tears.

"Hey, what's wrong?" I asked her.

"My baby isn't a baby any more," she said.

We didn't notice Emily behind us. "For God's sake woman," she said with her arms folded.

We looked at her.

"Are you menopausal like Uncle Mack?"

I laughed. Lydia looked at her.

"Listen, madam," she said. "I can't believe you're not little any more."

Emily was about to say something when we heard Mack shout. "Thadd! Fran!"

We walked in to see those two trying to look innocent.

"What did you do?" I asked, smiling.

"Nothing, Dad," Thaddeus said, smiling.

Mack walked in with the soap dispenser stuck to his hands and toilet paper on his slippers. We laughed.

"Really!" he said. "Aren't you two getting a little too old to stick bathroom stuff to me?"

"Well, at least it weren't your arse to the loo seat," Fran said.

Thaddeus and Fran high-fived each other. I couldn't stop laughing.

Mack looked at me. "I want a divorce."

"Tough Shit. Never gonna happen," I said.

Just then, my dad walked in and saw Mack and looked at those two. "Good job, you two."

"I hate you all," Mack said and walked off.

Later that afternoon, Thaddeus and Fran sat with Mack. "Good job, you two. I fall for it every time. I'm an idiot."

"You sad old man," Thaddeus said. Fran laughed.

Mack saw that she had another of his old jumpers on. "Hey, that's mine."

"But I'm a princess, Daddy. I always get my way," she told him.

"You kids will be the death of me. Can I win one argument with you girls?" Mack told Fran.

She looked at him. "Really! Are you that stupid? Like that's going to happen. How does Dad put up with you?"

He was about to say something and thought better of it. Fran smiled.

In the years that followed, the kids got their own lives. Leo and Chloe were still at home. Leo passed his A-levels with flying colours. Especially his Maths. A*. He applied for Cambridge like the others. Another family tradition. Chloe wanted to be a fashion designer. She was rather good.

Then one day, Fran and Olivia came over with their partners Richard and Harrison. They had that look about them.

"OK," I said. "What's going on?"

"Shall we tell them?" Fran said.

"No. I don't think we should tell them they're going to be grandparents," Olivia said.

Mack and I were stunned. They showed us their scans. They were both having twins. Mack walked away.

"Dad!" Fran looked worried.

He then did a stupid dance. "I'm going to be a grandad."

We all had a party to celebrate. Then, there was a knock at the door. Lydia stood next to me. I opened it and we were both stunned.

"Hi, Michael and Lydia. How are you?"